ARRIVAL OF THE RIFTED

C. C. YORK

ISBN: 978-0-578-86401-3

Cover illustration: Lena Yang
Map designer: Jon Stubbington

For my parents for teaching me to love to read, and for my brother for showing me what to read.

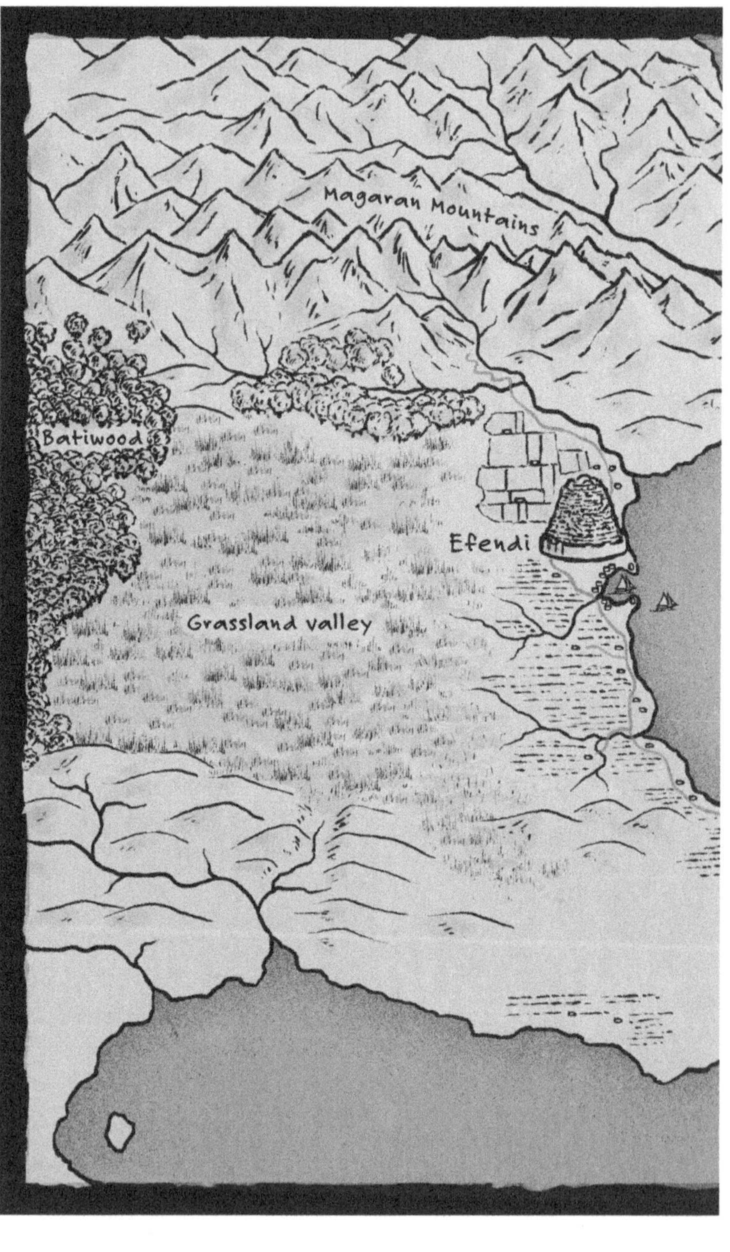
Magaran Mountains
Batiwood
Efendi
Grassland valley

Turkaz Sea
Dvari
N
SAKALID
S
Dvari
Efendi
Bakilar

REED

Reed Wells shifted his handcuffs so they could dig new indentations into his wrists as he rested his temple against the back of the tattered brown seat in front of him. Anyone else would've seen a young man staring listlessly out the window at the flat landscape surrounding I-350, but he frantically fiddled the rough edge of a bandage that had come loose across bloodied knuckles as his mind wheeled.

The attractive blond was a welcome sight when she'd initially boarded the van. Then she opened her mouth. She sat on the opposite side of Reed, the silver metal door locked tight between them, and chatted animatedly with the armed guards adjacent to her. The word "chat" implies a volley of small talk, but she had barely paused to breathe in between her musings in the last three hours of the ride to Livingston, Texas. Reed knew it was a special sort of hell he'd slipped into when he welcomed the sight of the supermax prison destined to be his final home as it sat squat under a sheet of rain.

At least there it will be quiet at times, he thought.

She glanced sideways at him again, curiosity warring with repulsion, and looked away at his stare. Memories have a way of etching into someone's eyes, and Reed's pale grays were no different. The past leached the life from him, leaving his frame holding a husk of a young man alternating between anger and despondence. And fear. Always fear.

His hollowness spread from him the way joy may radiate from someone else, yet women still found him attractive. Years of working on cars and yards had left his lean shell muscular, and even the scruff of a dark beard worked in his favor more often than not. Most women, though, would not linger on their appreciation while he was dressed head to toe in orange and tied down with chains. The guard filled her in early on the how's and why's he was here, which made Reed wonder again at her role if she willingly rode in a prison transport with a murderer.

Murderer. The same shame stuck inside his gut made his handcuffs heavy, and they clinked together as his hands fell back to his lap. His traitorous mind flit back to a conversation he'd had with Staci not long after they first met.

She chewed her nails to stubs for as long as he could remember. The speckled remains of black polish caught his eye as she brandished her cigarette at him between two fingers. Staci leaned back against the underbelly of their middle school bleachers and looked him over from behind cheap cigarette smoke. *"Don't kill me, but where are you from?"*

It was the single most terrifying question he'd been asked. One he had prepared for but wasn't ready, nonetheless. He stuttered out the answer he and his mother rehearsed, but Staci waved the smoke between them. "No. Where are you *from?* Like your grandparents or ancestors or whatever."

He realized that she questioned his light brown skin tone, a watered-down version of his mother's black skin and a hint at what his father likely looked like. Strangers would later ask him or anyone else of mixed race the same bizarre question, but under the bleachers, his thirteen-year-old self debated if he should run or continue the lie they'd fabricated. Staci just laughed and looped an arm around his tense shoulders, claiming him as part of her tribe and feet. He was pitched on his side, facing away from a crackling fire and towards a dark grassy plain that was definitely not Texas. Jagged mountains too tall to be anywhere in the US silhouetted against clouds of stars, and both a red, crescent moon and a fat, full blue moon shared the sky. *Bokki,* he thought. The curse coming back to him was as startling as the raspy night bird calls in the distance. He shifted slightly to take stock of any other injuries besides a gash across his forehead and a bloody nose but found none. *No time to panic,* he thought as he breathed in small puffs of cold air to get control of his mind. *Think.*

Reed heard them moving around the fire, muttering and clicking, jaws snapping open and shut. He couldn't see the creatures from where he was oriented, but he heard more than one shuffling behind him. He recognized how screwed up his life had become when he preferred the creatures at his back to the one he thought would be waiting.

Fluffy white sock tips shook in the corner of his eye in tune with a man's gagged cries. Reed's stomach dropped. *He didn't just take me. How many others have been dragged into this hell just because I was in the building with them?* He tried to shift to see who else was tied down, but the movement caused the creatures at his back to still. Reed dared not breathe.

The clicking and snapping resumed, and Reed relaxed a fraction. *The other inmates are not your problem. Get out, get a plan, get home. Ropes first.*

He worked at his wrists. The creatures let loose an excited shrill noise, and their jaws snapped in a quick tit-tat-tat around slurping. He froze again, but the slurping continued. That's when the smell hit him. The crackling fire and the sizzle of fat hitting the flames were familiar. The scent, fortunately, was something new, but he knew the smell of burnt hair. Whoever they were roasting sent the prisoner nearest him into a hysterical whisper plea to the Virgin Mary. *Jesus.* Reed moved as fast as he dared, working his wrists while also inching on his side closer to the grass.

The rope at his wrists was tied loose enough that he made good headway with minimal effort. *Either they don't know how to tie a rope or had too many of us to tie up properly.* Reed dealt with guilt before; leaving prisoners to this painful end would be a drop in the well.

Reed shifted his body further from the fire. Still, he only heard the crackle of roasting flesh and slurping behind him.

Little farther.

He shuffled his ankles to loosen their ties. The heat from the fire no longer licked his back when an alarmed hiss came from behind. Reed got a good look at the milky eyes of a rail-thin monster after its pinched claw gouged his arm to flip him over. A spade-shaped head sat atop an elongated white torso with hinged limbs like that of a massive praying mantis. With an alarmed cry, it raised its other white arm to push its claw deep into Reed's belly.

Reed heaved both of his feet as hard as possible in its chest before it could make its mark. It tumbled back to the fire, losing its footing and tipping onto the roasting spit. Reed didn't let his eyes linger on the man from the bus. The stick impaling the guard's body broke apart into the fire, his skin blackening within the flames.

Ear-piercing screams rang through the night. He shoved the rope from his feet and darted into the field, still gagged. The tall wet grass soaked his thighs immediately, and he shook his hands free from the ties. Reed ran blindly for anywhere but here and felt one of them gaining speed behind him. He spotted woods on one side of the field and tried to force his feet to fly, but a sharp pain shot into his back. He fell face-first into the grass a few feet from a fist-sized jagged rock.

The creature pinned him immobile to the ground out of arm's reach of the stone. Reed reached his hand out, thinking thoughts he hadn't dared in over a decade, but the rock lay useless on the ground. The rail-thin creature with bone white arms reared back to claw his head, and in doing so, put it off-kilter enough for Reed to buck it off. He grabbed the stone and rolled, heaving it at the creature. Reed managed to knock it back and heard another fight going on near the fire. He tackled the beast ahead of him, pinning it down in the tall grass.

Blood ran down Reed's face as he rammed the stone into the creature's head.

Over and over and over again.

He saw Staci's profile near the tub and heard her laughing. He hit harder and harder until the face underneath him was a puddle of white flesh and black gore. Staci's singsong voice rang through him, "They're coming."

Another white claw yanked Reed up, feet dangling, just as a big stick hit the creature across the back of its angular head. The beast slumped down to the grass next to its comrade and struggled to get back up. A prisoner Reed hadn't seen before pushed at him to run. He didn't wait to see if Reed would join him as he made a beeline for the woods, stick still clutched in his right hand and his orange jumpsuit covered in black blood.

Reed caught up to him and yanked the gag from his mouth. "Go right, towards that light! Stay out of the woods!"

Rustling from behind. The creature was on its feet and gaining speed. It released a high-pitched scream, a hawk sighting its prey, and Reed moved zigzag in time to miss its outreached claw. He scanned the ground for anything to use as a weapon as he ran when a shot echoed out in the valley.

The sound bounced off the mountains and reverberated the air surrounding them like a sonic boom. Reed knew in his bones that this world had never heard that sound. It did not belong here. The crack was as foreign and unfamiliar here as that creature would have been in a Kroger back home. The steady hum of background noise Reed didn't register until it was gone, stopped. The birds and critters and creatures of this hell paused. And as one giant, beating chest, they breathed deep once more before erupting into a chaotic cry. The sharp chirping of insects and bestial wails grew into a tidal wave of noise that washed over Reed and the valley, and the woods behind him shook as creatures too big to be birds took to the sky.

They know we're here, Reed thought.

Blonde hair whipped past Reed, "Run, you idiot!"

The woman from the prison transport dashed ahead of him, holding a pistol in her right hand and pumping her arms. Two ragged men from the prison ran after her, carrying the older man she'd hugged before their world ended. Reed froze as horses gaining speed appeared behind them.

At least the incoming cavalry rode creatures like horses, but the similarity ended there. Men barreled down the valley atop Clydesdale-sized beasts with rhinoceros-like skin and short jagged horns at the edge of their nose. Swords glinted in the twin moonlight above the valley, and the men cried out while slashing the handful of tall white bone creatures now fleeing to the woods. Reed ran to the scattered people of his world just as two riders broke off, riding hard for him.

Reed pumped his legs, bypassing the others. The older man cried out for his people to leave him, and the blonde pleaded with the old man to push when the first rider broke through. The rider's tunic stretched under the curved sword strapped to his back as he snatched an inmate by the neck, yanking him onto his beast. Several more riders followed behind, grabbing the older man and his escorts. The woman stood still, frantic eyes and mouth agape. Reed made the split-second decision to tackle her just as a beast thundered to them. Its rider reached for her as well, missing by a handspan. The rider shouted a command to the beast, pulling to a stop to circle back around.

Reed hauled her up with him and ran for the woods the lizard part of his brain warned him adamantly against. Laughter rang out in his mind once more, but he pushed it out as he ducked behind a large, gnarled tree at the farthest edge of the dark woods topped with flaming orange leaves. He pushed his back against its pulsing bark and held the shaking woman tight to him with his hand over her mouth. The laughter in his mind morphed into a deep baritone.

The valley echoed orders shouted from the men, but after what felt like years, retreating hooves finally faded away. Reed's heart pounded as the fear he'd known as a boy threatened to drown him again. *One step at a time. Get out, get a plan, get home.*

He watched the woods, his hand still clamped over her mouth, and ignored her warm tears spilling over his fingers. Reed whispered in her ear as quiet as his aching throat allowed, "Do not make a sound until we are out."

He felt eyes on him. Underbrush shuffled. He did not turn to watch what could have followed as he dragged the woman through the tall wet grass, back into the valley under two moons.

ALIK

Alik Iktidar folded the list of missing Efendian girls into a thick square that barely fit in a pocket now. The square felt heavier than it did the day before, and sharp edges from the additional pages cut into her fingers to remind her that she was useless. She focused on the dark mountain range outside her palace window to blot out the dread of receiving more names today.

Her skin crawled from the inky presence still lurking in her mind from the nightmare. Last night's dream was the same as the others; she chased a child through the Silos, but just as she could reach the girl, someone snatched Alik from behind. The click of her bedroom door pulled her back from rehashing all that she didn't know about her missing citizens.

"Another one then, eh?" Shauna said as she shut the bedroom door. She looked far too bright and cheerful in her soft wheat dress and cherry-painted lips. "Do you think it's a vision?"

Alik shook her head at her maid and best friend and crossed her arms over her silk jumper, still clutching the paper square. "I wish I knew. If I'm a soothsayer, you'd think I would at least know the difference between a premonition and a dream."

Alik drank the water Shauna guided to her, relieved that she didn't have to struggle with her Waterwerk this early. The steady stream of clear liquid snaked across the room like an iridescent ribbon pulled by invisible hands.

Alik teased, "Look at you showing off. It's still dark outside, and not even a drop spilled."

"Perfection doesn't need a clock, Princess," Shauna said as they began the dance of dressing as they had for years. Alik glided in as Shauna pulled the mint and gold embroidered silk around her, the fabric tight enough to smooth out her ample curves but not cut off her circulation. Alik watched the sun's rays race across the dark valley beyond her kingdom while Shauna cuffed the bottom of her loose pants. Rolling her shoulders, Alik forced the unease from her dream and the list of names away for the moment.

Shauna huffed a blond strand of hair out of her eyes as she examined her work. "You really should let the tailor have at your wardrobe, Alik, if you continue to refuse heels. This is getting ridiculous."

"The cuff works fine," Alik said as she turned in a small circle in front of the mirror.

At Shauna's deadpan stare, Alik rolled her eyes and continued. "I promise, one day I'll make time and let you and that horrible man with the needles attack every piece in there. Just not in the same week I have to entertain the Dvarians. I can only deal with so much torture."

Shauna said, "Speaking of which...The ship is scheduled to arrive sometime just before moonrise, so you have plenty of time to prepare. Do you want your first meal here?"

Alik settled into the vanity chair and groaned. "Please. I'm facing an onslaught of small chat and tense negotiations in addition to this," She brandished the list of names between them before returning it to her pocket. "A few hours solo is mandatory."

Shauna rested her hand on Alik's shoulder, but a knock at the door interrupted whatever comfort she might try to offer. Alik glared at the well-formed bags under her amber eyes and tried not to think about the heavy volume of trade papers waiting for her or the square of girls she'd failed jabbing her from her dress. She squished her brown cheeks in her hands, inches from the mirror, and squelched fish kisses at Shauna when she returned to ease the worry from her best friend's forehead.

"Alik, we have to hurry. I just got word that the Dvarian emissaries are waiting for you in the Atrium." Shauna said as she began pinning Alik's thick black hair, ignoring her friend's antics and frowning at the frizzy waves that she had yet to subdue.

"So early? That's odd. The emissary usually times his arrival with the feast. Let's just send more wine to their quarters so I can at least have a meal to myself. I have to be with him for all of Hasateen as it is. Surely a meal solo won't be too much of an insult?"

"Yea...Slight problem there." Shauna said around a mouthful of pins, "It's apparently not the same emissary. He sent his apprentice or his nephew; I'm not sure. The messenger was a little flustered."

Alik winced at the sharp poke of a hastily shoved pin. "Why would she be flustered?"

"Eh...your mother might have beat us there?" Shauna cringed at Alik in the mirror.

"Bokki." Alik pinched her cheeks and pressed the berry stain to her lips. "That will have to do."

The pair rushed through her wing but slowed down as soon as they entered the main Palace corridor. Shauna veered off to the servants' hall and gave Alik an empathetic frown before disappearing.

Alik straightened her shoulders as tall as her short frame allowed. Her foot snagged in the wide-legged gossamer pants, but she managed to right herself before tripping in front of a gaggle of snickering courtiers nearby.

Nothing new there, she thought. *You'd think they'd have something better to do than hover around the Atrium. It's as if they're waiting for something to make fun of.* She glanced down at the cuff at her ankle threatening to fall, grateful at least that she didn't have heels on. *Shauna's probably right about the tailor.*

Early morning sunlight splintered into a myriad of colors on the opal floor through glass ceiling panels. The Palace was an onslaught of variations on white, blinding at times in Alik's opinion. According to her tutors, the First Queen kept everything monotone so she would stand out in every room. Alik applauded her long-dead predecessor's vanity when she watched her mother stride through the halls in dramatic jewel-toned saris and silk gowns. Yet, she still loved this room of smattering greens, blues, and gold best.

The Queen was just turning into her private study off the corner of the Atrium but arched a black manicured eyebrow at her daughter's entrance. Queen Firtina's silk pants flowed down her statuesque frame like dark cherry wine from a decanter, and Alik waited for the cutting remark.

"Alik, so nice of you to finally join us," Queen Firtina said through pursed lips.

And there it is, Alik thought.

She brushed down the sides of her outfit before stilling her hands. Alik fought the urge to smooth her hair as well and looked to the group of men waiting. "Please accept my profuse apologies for my tardiness." She walked to the heavyset man in the Dvarian white linen suit, "We are pleased to have you here to mark the end of another successful trade year."

The sun barely poked her head from the sky, but moisture already beaded on his thin upper lip.

He's definitely related to the last emissary then, Alik thought.

Firtina stared at Alik for a few terrible beats, and she panicked for a moment. *What did I do now?* She glanced around to see what she had done wrong, but her mother disappeared into her study without another word to anyone in the Atrium. The tall wood doors banged shut with the flick of Firtina's hand.

Alik hadn't noticed the young man before he stepped from

behind the emissary. A few years older than Alik, he wore the dark leather pants the pirates of Perise loved so much. He even had his shirt unbuttoned to an indecently low point like the Perisiens favored and jangled when he stepped forward, silver necklaces swaying. He was also, undoubtedly, the most attractive man Alik had ever seen in the 19 years she'd been alive.

He held up a ringed fist to his mouth and cleared his throat. "There is no need to apologize, Princess Iktidar. We arrived earlier than expected."

His voice reminded her of the still pool of water in the reflecting pond behind him. *I might actually enjoy poetry if it came from those lips,* she thought. She caught herself as her eyes began to drift over him, and her resolve hardened when she realized he smirked at her. *Focus, Alik.*

"And you are?" Alik asked, forcing herself to keep her eyes on his.

"My name is Agnian. I am the fortunate fool sent here from Dvari to discuss the trade agreement."

Alik flushed at his dangerously enticing smile. The men around Agnian, particularly the one still sweating profusely, shared a look behind his back.

Alik paused, still as stone, and quickly scanned the men with her *Dua.* Her bizarre ability to read auras made up for her horridness at the traditional Dua her countrywomen possessed. The men pulsed with confusion, one with anger. She guided her Dua to the good-looking one, and he radiated disgust. Her practiced smile faltered at the unexpected ferocity.

"Forgive me, I... was expecting your predecessor. You and I will be spending quite a bit of time together then as I'm leading negotiations."

His disgust shifted to an orange tinge of surprise, and Alik managed to restrain an eye roll as her eyes cleared. *Leave it to a Dvarian to be shocked at a female negotiator,* she thought.

"If you'd follow me, we've set up preparations in the garden."

Alik led the way for the group but turned back when only one set of footsteps followed her.

Agnian brushed the tips of his fingers to Alik's elbow, "My companions are weary from our travels. Is it possible to show them to their quarters while you and I proceed alone?"

Alik studiously ignored the flip in her belly and stepped back a few steps. *Act like you've seen a man before, Alik.* She nodded to the silent team of servants waiting in the eaves, and a flurry of movement bustled the emissaries through another corridor.

Alik and Agnian left through the Atrium's massive arched doors to the gardens. A white tent billowed over a long wooden table prepared for ten at the edge of the first terrace. Sea wind snagged at Alik's high braid, and an annoyingly long dark strand slipped out with the pull and danced in her eyes before she could surreptitiously right it. Birds sang in the treetops in the terrace below them, though, and the sweet smell of gardenias permeated the garden.

She braced herself. *Now is when this beautiful man remarks on the heat or the view,* she thought, but to her delight, he let the silence between them settle as they approached the tent. Alik glanced behind her to see his head on a swivel, taking in the steeply tiered gardens that dropped to the waves far below and the vertical gardens growing up the sun-bleached walls. She tipped her head back for a moment to the early morning sun, steadying herself for an arduous week. His boots crunched pea gravel as he gingerly peered over the edge before turning back to her.

"I've never been to Efendi before, Princess. I'll admit, I was a little weary given the stories of chaos and cacophony passed to me by my predecessor," he said.

"They weren't wrong," Alik replied. "Efendi is a ladder of compressed life, bound by a high Perimeter Wall rimmed with fire and bursting with frenzy in every pocket in between. Twenty-eight semi-circular Tiers stack on top of each other to make up this kingdom, and the lowest rung is home to the poorest and weakest

Efendians." She gestured behind her, "The Palace squats at the highest Tier, which apparently makes it look like we all live inside a massive, gilded cake if seen from the valley."

Agnian stopped her. "Wait. You've never been outside the Perimeter Wall?"

"Hardly." Alik snorted. *Real attractive, Alik.* She turned away to get her composure back and continued. "The grassland valley and the Perimeter Wall are all that separates us from the Batiwood and its monsters at the edge of the world. It isn't a place we often picnic."

She peered over the edge of this Tier to the waves below. According to her first tutor, every Tier ended at the seaside bend in the kingdom in order to protect the royal family from scaling invaders. But Alik knew better. *My ancestors likely preferred to see and smell the sea when they walked outside instead of our people.*

Alik replied, "It's certainly a lot to take in, but up here, the chaos feels a bit more orderly." She sidled up a few feet from him and looked down at the verdant rows of orchards and vegetable gardens stacked like stairs down to the tumultuous jade sea frothing far below.

"I took the liberty of having Lemon Salt tea prepared for you. Would you care for some?"

Agnian barked a laugh, "I thought only Dvarians enjoyed that tea. I'm glad to see it's taken hold here as well."

Alik bit her lower lip at how much to say and just tried for honesty. "I actually loathe it but thought you and your countrymen would enjoy a taste of home while you were here."

The Dvarian cracked his first genuine smile, prompting her to scan him with a glance of her Dua. The quick swirl of pleasant periwinkle and marigold surprise wrapped around him took Alik aback for a moment.

"Thank you, that is very thoughtful."

He took the chair to her left rather than any of the other eight chairs, and Alik's best friend Shauna began to pour the tea from the far edge of the terrace several paces away. His knuckles turned white as the steaming water floated through the air into his waiting cup, the deep vee of his shirt pulsing up and down with each breath.

Alik raised her hand to stop the flow. "I'll take it from here, Shauna, thank you."

An uneasy quiet hovered between them while she gave Agnian time to compose himself. She debated the merits of calling out his discomfort to her advantage for the negotiations or continuing this polite dance when he said, "Sorry. It's not often that I come across Dua so close. It took me by surprise."

That's odd, she thought as she sipped her coffee. The bulk of Duawielders, women Goddess-blessed with powers found only in Efendi, lived within her kingdom's walls. Yet, some were positioned in places of power in Dvari and the lesser kingdoms outside Efendi. *An emissary should run into our Duaweilders stationed there all the time.* She made a mental note to ask her brother what his spies knew of the Dvarian court and their mother's vassal tasked with monitoring the Dvarian king. Alik only took on the annual negotiations recently from her mother's advisors. *Perhaps I've overestimated our influence there.*

"I'll try to remember that. We Efendians tend to use it as subconsciously as a Dvarian swims. If it upsets you, I will have my staff ease its use during your stay." She should tell her mother about his bizarre behavior, but for reasons she didn't want to explore, she felt reluctant to reveal this particular man's weakness.

"No need, but thank you," he said. He sipped his tea and watched Alik over the rim. Sun-kissed chestnut hair tipped into his coffee-colored eyes while he drank.

They passed the time with surprisingly easy conversation over sweetened nuts and split pomegranates. Alik knew she should guide the discussion towards their uneasy trade agreement, but she enjoyed swapping stories about their siblings and childhood instead.

"I can't believe your brother convinced you to eat the eel pie! Was it as awful as it sounds?" She laughed after swallowing her fifth *last bite* of a honey almond pastry.

"Worse," Agnian confided, "But that is the way of it with him. He has this enthralling ability to convince anyone of anything. It's probably not saying much about my intelligence that I fell for it, but after your story of the Garfu eggs, I had to tell." He winked at Alik, and she gave a full laugh.

I never expected a Dvarian to be this charming, she thought as he leaned closer to tell her another story. *Any Dvarian I've ever met seems so guarded or pompous, yet this one is funny and self-deprecating.* It was a welcome change from the courtiers doling out ridiculous compliments with dead eyes. She genuinely enjoyed their time and felt lighter because he seemed to as well, despite the earlier reading of disgust from him.

Perhaps this week won't be so terrible, she thought.

Alik idly stirred her coffee and bit her lower lip at the thought of what this man would be like at home laughing with his family. She glanced up to see that he was watching her intently again, but when he caught her eye, he stood up with his cup to face the sea once more. His leather pants accentuated strong legs, and a white linen shirt pulled tightly at corded muscles. Alik let herself imagine for a moment what it would be like to be wrapped up in those limbs.

Get it together, Alik. She cleared her throat, "And what of your parents? Surely your mother had her hands full with two boys intent on out-tricking the other."

He stiffened and didn't say anything for a beat, but when he turned, his enticing smile was back. "She never knew what to do with us. My father is a tradesman of sorts, and she his right hand. The pair often left us to our own devices until we got to a certain age."

Shauna appeared then, face tight with worry. She slipped Alik a note with "27" scrawled hastily on it in familiar writing. The dark maw Alik forgot from her dream flashed in her mind, mouth gaping wide and pitch black. Her cup slipped, and she patted the spill on her pants as she stood.

"Is everything alright?" Agnian asked.

Alik nodded, "I'm sorry. The time slipped from me, and there are several matters I need to attend to before tonight's festivities for the start of Hasateen. My maid, Shauna, will show you to your quarters. I'll see you tonight at the feast."

She paused at the edge of the tent, "Thank you for this morning. And please don't take offense, but this was surprisingly enjoyable."

He laughed at that and gave her an exaggerated bow, "Pleasing you is my top priority, Princess," and winked. Shauna wagged her eyebrows teasingly at Alik from behind his back.

Alik laughed as well. Her heart fluttered, and she had a hard time schooling her grin, despite the note. She turned to leave, but her curiosity refused to abate. She scanned him with a passing glance, hoping to see some sign he felt the same pleasantness and eagerness she did. She walked down the corridor with a practiced indifferent look at the courtiers milling about, but inside she questioned everything they discussed.

The overwhelming emotion he read was maroon, unfettered hatred.

***

Damari waited for her in her study. Her little brother leaned against the wall of glass windows facing the sea, dark hair mussed in a way that made him look every bit of 18.

He asked, "How was the Dvarian emissary this time? Did he try to grab Shauna's derriere again?"

Alik waved him off. "No, fortunately, he sent someone else in his stead. I'll introduce you later as I think the two of you would hit it off dangerously well. Now tell me, how could 27 of our Daughters go missing in a single night?"

Damari told her the numbers his Eyes recorded and how the missing girls were not only from Low Town but up to the Trades now as well. "No one has seen a thing. It's as if they've vanished."

"What does the Canavar Company say? They have their beards in every shady aspect of Efendi, and their numbers have been growing."

"My Eyes are watching them, but they haven't seen anything yet."

Alik chewed on her fingernail while she paced. "Apart from the status level, is there anything different you see?"

"The locations. Before, the disappearances were isolated to the Silos or the docks. Now we have one girl missing from the heavily guarded home of a merchantress and another taken just before moonrise in the middle of the Trades."

Alik's mind whirled. At first, no one thought to tell her about the missing girls. One advisor had the audacity to tell her it was the unfortunate lot of the poor to be susceptible to life's worst crimes. She first heard of it through Shauna and pressed the advisors for all details. Yet they still brushed her off, which is why she sent the Palace's best spy out for news.

"Brother, it's the first night of Hasateen. Efendians will be out later than normal, and we'll begin to see more outsiders by the month's end. If the numbers continue to increase, it will raise the alarm beyond our borders that the Iktidar line cannot offer protection. Have you brought Taavi in?"

"Bring me into what?" Their older brother strolled in and unstrapped his curved blades from his back to set aside. Taavi was the only Iktidar child to share their father's fair features. One would never know it, though, given how grime piled on his short, cropped honey-blond hair. Even his curls still looked rank with sweat.

"You look horrible," Damari said while Alik said, "I'm so glad you're home!"

Taavi ruffled Damari's dark hair and swept Alik into a hug.

She put a hand to her nose. *He smells worse than he looks.*

"Taav, how much do you know of the missing Efendian girls?" Alik asked while he poured himself water from her crystal pitcher.

"Only what Damari relayed in his note early this morning. My men and I just returned from patrol, and one of his Eyes was waiting for me." Taavi winked at Alik.

"Ugh, don't." Damari's Eyes were known by sight to only the three siblings. Alik wasn't even sure how many in total Damari paid, but each woman she'd seen was breathtakingly beautiful. "*The perfect distraction for information to slip,*" he'd once told her.

Damari just laughed.

Alik's brothers both had enough charm to make even the oldest matriarch blush. Taavi, in particular, was a legend among the Horde for his skills in the hunt and border skirmishes. Still, most Efendian women simply knew him as "the Beautiful One." His men once taunted him as "Beauty," but he took it with gusto and now uses it annoyingly often in the third person.

Alik, in her opinion, was infinitely more forgettable by contrast.

She ripped a leaf from one of the potted plants, pacing. *Where would anyone take so many Efendian girls? More importantly, how? They're young into their Dua, but they're not without some protection.*

"What reasons do the Dvarians have to hate us?" She asked.

Damari began to list on his fingers, "Well, for one, we took over their country."

Taavi chimed in, "Uh, we prefer 'liberated their country,' brother."

"By killing off their king." Damari shook his head at Taavi but continued, "We also have a very robust trade requirement of them that, as you know, is a *little* one-sided."

"We are an arrogant lot," Taavi supplied happily.

"And our women have Dua whereas theirs do not?" Damari finished.

"Right, right, right. I know all this, but Dvari has prospered twofold since Mother's war. And they hated their king." Alik recalled the emissaries' odd reaction, how they looked nothing like the predecessor's typical entourage, and how they arrived early without anyone learning of their arrival. "Are there any new reasons we've given them that they could be targeting us through these kidnappings?"

"Not that I'm aware," Taavi said.

Taavi and Alik knew every significant decision their mother made now that Alik finally sat in the advising sessions. News of new boundary pushes or restrictions placed on the kingdom of islands would have reached at least one of the siblings.

Alik continued her slow pace across the opal floor. *Apart from a handful of skirmishes after Mother's war, the kingdom fell under the Efendian bosom with little pushback and was rewarded with peace. Why would they disrupt that years later?*

Alik asked, "Damari, do you have any spies in Dvari?"

He shook his head. "None."

Taavi answered her unasked question. "I doubt Mother has any spies either. The vassal there now insists that any additional Duawielders on the islands cause unnecessary tension. She requires every female Efendian, regardless of power, to report in as soon as they arrive and are tracked until they leave. She explained to the ministers that keeping a low profile helps soothe the Dvarian egos in court."

That could explain why the emissary seemed so surprised at seeing Dua up close, Alik thought.

"See if you can find out if there is growing tension from whomever this new emissary is," Damari said.

Alik felt a little stupid as she confided, "I can try. He's radiating hatred toward me, but he hides it well."

Taavi took his little sister's hand, "We are Efendian, Alik. Everybody hates us."

Alik swatted at him, "I'm serious. This feels, I don't know, different. More personal? Like I've done something to him, and yet you'd never know by listening to our conversations. He's amiable and engaging and---" She trailed off at her brother's smiles and crossed her arms. "What?"

Damari glanced at the windows, nodding his head east as if they could see the Dvarian archipelago. "Alik, think about it like this: Your mother beheaded their king, and your kingdom is the most powerful in all of Sakalid. You are the Efendian heir and the Queen's right hand,"

In theory, Alik thought.

"—so it's likely that every Dvarian you meet will see you as an extension of her before they'll see who you are as a person."

"Deep, brother," Taavi teased. "If you could make that rhyme you could turn it into a song and make every Efendian women's under—"

"Stop," Alik interrupted as Damari laughed.

The tease in Taavi's eye dimmed as he said, "Alik, don't worry about him. You will marry anyone you wish. Who cares what a Dvarian thinks?"

She replied before thinking, "Taav, I'm 19. We had one meal together. Marriage is the furthest thing from my future right now."

She winced. Taavi was already old enough to marry off. Much of their mother's politics revolved around which Elite family would claim his hand. *I will make sure you have a say in this, Alik thought.* She didn't know how, but whatever influence she had over her mother, she'd use to help her brothers out of an arranged marriage that all royal Efendian males faced.

"Anyway," she continued, "I need to focus on finding the missing girls. If I'm around the emissary more, I may figure out why they feel off. I need both of you at tonight's dinner. I think Agnian would hit it off well with you."

"First names then, eh sister? Is he as charming as the last emissary?" Taavi teased.

Alik grimaced, "He's an improvement at least, and fortunately, he doesn't seem as handsy as his predecessor."

"Fortunately" might not be the right word, though I'd rather eat

a Garfu egg again than say that aloud. No need to give these two any more reason to tease me about my love life. She glanced down at her half uncuffed pants now pooling around her flats. *Or lack thereof.*

Damari said, "I'll go to dinner, but it is First Night. I'm not missing the show."

A hidden corridor in the Trades hosted the city's best musical talents most nights and commanded all of Damari's free time. The first week of Hasateen, though, took the dancing and revelry to unparalleled heights. *I could use a night out,* she thought, ignoring the nagging guilt for wanting to dance when girls were still missing. *I am not getting anywhere cooped up in the Palace,* she justified. *Maybe I can see something Damari's Eyes have missed?*

"I'll go with you." Alik said, "We can see if anything seems amiss in the Trades." Alik's Dua readings were at their best when she was physically close to one person, but she could also get vague impressions from a broader perspective.

Taavi immediately flipped to his unofficial Captain Rules status. "No, Alik. If there really are this many girls missing in a single night, we can't risk you being vulnerable."

Alik winked at a grinning Damari who, as usual, was steps ahead of Taavi alongside her. "Even better! It's been ages since the three of us celebrated First Night together. We'll go in disguise after the Dvarian dinner tonight. Bring Ty and some of your men if it makes you feel better."

Ty was Taavi's best friend and equal rival for the nickname "Beauty." He was also the deadliest member of the Horde. Alik spent an entire season pining for him as a kid until he told her he wasn't interested in girls. It worked out for the best, though, because he, Shauna, and the Iktidar trio were inseparable throughout their childhood.

"Shauna will come as well," Alik declared despite Taavi's weak protests. She clapped her hands. "I'll see you both at dinner. And don't grill the emissaries. It's a long shot, but I don't want them to know we're suspicious."

She understood that the new emissaries could be responsible for the kidnappings or at least know something about the disappearances. She just hoped Agnian was uninvolved.

Only one way to find out, she thought.

ELAINE

Elaine Reynolds skidded to a halt. Muffled laughter, as if a conversation occurred behind a closed door, flitted through her mind. The voices she'd heard her entire life before arriving in Efendi months ago came waltzing in again as if they hadn't disappeared six months prior. Wary but relieved, she closed her eyes to better hear.

Nothing.

She kicked at a fat, fire orange flower the size of a tomcat that trailed from a turquoise pot. *I couldn't get the voices to stop chatting in my ear back home. Don't know why I thought I could bring them back any easier,* she thought. An unexpected but familiar chord of loneliness strummed through her.

"Elai!"

Kara's voice, decidedly not in her head, echoed through the corridor. Elaine dashed underneath the maze of floating candles at the main staircase entrance that would cut through each Tier up to the Palace high at the top of the mountain. Before she even rounded the corner, the sound of the gurgling fountain where fathers mended clothes together greeted her. Her new home, a circular cluster of fabric lean-to's, came into view where her two favorite people were waiting for her.

Reiki, one-half of the reed-thin twins that had taken Elaine in as their unofficial little sister, grinned at his scowling twin. "Ready for a nice, easy stroll?"

Kara rolled her eyes with Elaine as they finished loading baskets into the leather ladder. Kara and Reiki hefted it horizontally between them up the hundreds of uneven, steep steps to the Trades. The only perk of being 13 and short meant that Elaine didn't have to help carry the grain.

Kara trudged up the curving alleyway, complaining incessantly about the small pebbles stuck in her sandals and the broken bits of pottery. Elaine hadn't known this world or the twins long, but she still knew them as well as she did the root-ridden path behind her old trailer in South Carolina. Elaine shared a look with Kara's twin brother Reiki. *Just a few hundred more steps and Kara will stop complaining.*

The curved burnt orange and khaki walls opened to sapphire, jade, fuchsia, and plum stone buildings. Kara smiled wider at the rainbow bend, and the happiness the twins shared whenever they arrived spread as easily as the desire to dance to the riotous drumbeats that greeted them.

Everything overwhelmed Elaine when she first arrived in this world from South Carolina, but the riot of colors and sounds in the Trades Tier took sensory overload to new heights. It was the heart of the Efendian kingdom—a breathing monster of purple-hued walls, vats of orange and amber grains, and jade-toned glass. It marched to the discordance of horns, flutes, and drums the Towners played for coins. The air pulsed with smoke, baked bread, and tinny coffee grains the Efendian chewed like tobacco while boiling them in hot nut milk. Colorful fabric stalls clung to either side of the Tier. To walk through untouched was an art because everyone, from Towners to the most powerful Elite, thronged past performers dancing or playing around them.

Kara and Reiki shuffled their grain ladder into their stall, narrowly avoiding a matriarch parading past with her retinue. In any other Tier of the kingdom, the Elite of the Upper Tiers would never rub elbows with someone from Low Town like them. But the status of Dua, the magical abilities of Efendian women that Elaine still gawked at, did not matter here as much as coin did. And coin was the most sought-after power in the Trades.

Elaine liked to crack nuts on the high basket behind them and watch Reiki charm any woman, regardless of rank or age, that came within three feet of him. The neighboring stall owner, Kabushi, paid Elaine in soft lead for her journal if she cracked the golf-ball-sized nuts akin to pecans while he roasted them each day. She grew adept at filling the cloth bags of grain Reiki and Kara sold without spilling too much and was learning the different coins the twins deftly exchanged.

After a while, Kara winked at Elaine, her silent signal to run amok before they packed up for the day. Elaine dashed off the basket and blew a kiss to Kabushi. She had yet to run the entire length of the Trades, so each day, she pushed herself faster to see something she hadn't the day prior. Yesterday she glimpsed a tiny alley filled with floating glass lanterns in a myriad of colors that she wanted to explore. Most shopkeepers smiled when she dashed by; others shouted at her to watch her step or slow down. She jumped over displays of colorful furs skinned from kingalias and under the arms of the Elite examining jewelry floating in the air, snatching bits of conversation as she zigzagged past.

"Another disappearance. Her parents saw nothing."

"Taken—one moment she was behind him, and then she vanished—"

She skidded to a halt at the last tidbit of eavesdropping and slunk behind a stall selling multicolored bees the size of her fist. *I got zero magic and even less coin, but gossip is the next best thing around here. Especially when it's about the missing girls.*

The gossiping women lingered ahead of her, their ruby and gold saris swaying with each brush of another Efendian walking past. Elaine swatted at the smoke from the neighboring stall to better see. The taller matriarch glanced behind her, but like so many Elite, didn't notice the slip of a girl sandwiched between fat bees and a spiraling hunk of glazed meat.

"It's getting worse. It was one thing when it was just a handful of Towner trash disappearing, but this time it took one of ours."

"Hey, get out of here," the beekeeper hissed. She pushed Elaine with a puff of her meager Airwerk. "No one will stop if it looks like I'm only selling to other Towners."

Elaine glared at the woman but stepped back because she knew it was true. By the time she turned, the bustle of the Trades had folded in the wealthy women, and she couldn't see them any longer. A man holding a wooden cage of magenta and orange birds bumped into Elaine, nearly pushing her into a fountain of the water goddess, Sulu.

Her reflection in the water still showed a mess of dishwater blonde hair run feral, straight at its skinny roots and ending in scraggly ringlets perpetually unbound despite Kara's braiding skills. Her cheeks finally seemed full enough, though, to support her large eyes the color of burnt walnuts. She had the Hadishi family to thank for months of steady eating since she arrived in Efendi. Elaine missed few things about her life in the world she left behind; being hungry wasn't one of them.

The air cooled down considerably as she entered the narrow alley of lanterns, and the cacophony of the Trades died down to a low enough hum that she could hear herself think. The lanterns floating in the air filtered the brutal afternoon sun to dabbled pink and blues across the cobblestones, and tendrils of fat, lime leaves spilled down the sides of amber-tinged walls. Elaine ran her fingers over the powdered walls as she explored further down and tried to picture how she'd sketch it later.

Then, as suddenly and unexpectedly as they had before, the voices in her head came back. *Finally!* Grinning ear to ear, she danced a little jig in the narrow alley before she composed herself to listen. *Wait, what'd she say?*

Frustrated at the lack of clarity, she walked deeper into the darkening alley, heart pounding. She strained to hear the conversation just out of earshot, not noticing the lack of people around her. *She squealed, There!*

"---Rutzgar, please hear me. I need—"

The woman's prayer was cut short as Elaine's brain registered a closer, distressed whimper around the bend in the alley.

Kara's warning to stay within eyesight of other people at all times came to mind at the sound. Girls her age disappeared every night. She tapped her fingers at her sides, debating if she should go back to the safety of the crowds or continue down to better hear the voices in her head that she desperately missed.

Elaine was never particularly good at dashing her curiosity, even when she knew in her bones that whatever she would find would not be good. She stopped questioning why she heard voices no one else did around the time she was 10. The voices were a distracting balm to the loneliness she felt even when she still went to school, so Elaine learned to tune in and enjoy the glimpse of a stranger's life. The first time she felt like one of the voices spoke directly to her, she followed it to this magical new world called Sakalid.

What if all the years of being called crazy and a liar were for something else? Surely I'm hearing them for a reason. What if I'm hearing the missing girls? What if they're trying to lead me here? To them?

The voices in her head brought her to a life better than she ever imagined. *The least I could do is help find them.*

A sharp slap echoed off the dimly lit walls, deciding for her. She knew that sound well.

She walked as light as a cicada and peeked around the corner at the next turn. A scrawny girl, no older than she, stood with her head bowed and shoulders curved in. She cowered before a ginger man the size of a boulder. Elaine flattened further into the wall when she realized the man had the letter C tattooed around his eye, and another of Kara's warnings echoed in her mind. *Never, ever get in the way of the Canavar Company gang.* Elaine couldn't hear what he was saying beneath the red beard that engulfed his face. He shoved the girl back in the curtained doorway, and she glimpsed several other men lounging on couches in the room beyond.

A sick dread settled in her belly. *They have to be the ones behind it. Everyone knows they're the worst gang in the kingdom. Maybe I found their lair.*

She inched closer.

Rumors of girls snatched from thin air whispered throughout the lower Tiers, but the Elite did nothing. *Queen Firtina doesn't even do anything*, she thought, creeping closer to hear the damning evidence.

The man's small eye within the C flicked to her, widening in alarm. Elaine bolted back out the alley, past two women dressed in paper-thin short gowns and sad eyes, and into the bustling throng of the Trades before his shout could reach her heels.

She didn't stop running until she saw Kara's stall. She failed miserably to calm her ragged breath and the shake in her hands. Even the hot sunlight and bright turquoise fabric walls couldn't stop a chill from creeping over her. Kabushi saw Elaine first and beckoned her to him.

He crouched down to be on eye level with her. Today, his eye patch was a jaunty teal fabric trimmed with yellow stitches and an emerald green outline of an eye. His patch frightened Elaine when she'd first met him, but her heart rate slowed now at the cheery bright eye.

"What happened, Little One?" He asked.

"Nothing. I just got a little shook up." Elaine didn't want to give anyone reason to stop her solo expeditions in the Trades.

"Nothing is a lot of somethings when you look like you've just seen a Garfu," he said.

Elaine had heard Efendians speak of the bear-sized Garfus

with circular rows of teeth that roamed the valley. They were terrifying creatures that preyed on those unfortunate enough to be on the roads outside the Perimeter Wall at night.

She desperately wanted to see one.

"You can tell me," Kabushi pressed as he handed her a sweetened nut.

She told him about the girl and the bearded man but left out the telltale tattoo. Kabushi's white bushy eyebrows raised at the mention of the lanterns covering the whole alley. He looked over her shoulder at Reiki and Kara chatting with the night stall vendor getting ready to take their place. They both cocked their head in tandem in a way only twins seem to do.

Kabushi simply said to them, "I think our Little Wanderer found the Lantern Pit today."

Kara's mouth parted slightly, and Reiki clenched his teeth, sharpening his jawline.

"I'm sorry, I didn't know I wasn't supposed to be there. I just thought it was pretty and all, and—" Elaine was interrupted by Kara, who hunkered down to be on eye level with Elaine.

"You did nothing wrong, Elai. I didn't realize you could have gone that far; otherwise, I would have warned you away." Kara continued gently, "Come. We're done packing up. You can help lead the way this time." Kara used the meager Dua she was born with to pull the scattered grains into a bag with a wave of her hand.

Firewerkers tossed bobbing orbs of firelight along the staircase now that the sun was slipping to the horizon. An orange-robed woman close to Elaine cradled a softball-sized flame a few inches above her palm.

No matter how many times I see that, it's still cool.

The Firewerker tossed the flame high above their heads, where it will hover until sunrise to light the way. Elaine loved the drop in temperature during this time of day because it brought a respite from the blistering Efendian sun as well as the magical firelights that dotted the kingdom instead of streetlights. When Elaine still went to school, she had an art teacher claim that Venice was the most beautiful city in the world. She couldn't imagine a more beautiful place than Efendi.

The Trades' bright colors had faded into the muted orange browns of Low Town when she finally asked the pair, "What's the Lantern Pit?"

Reiki looked at her over the leather ladder slung between him and Kara. "I know Efendi seems wonderful to you, Elaine, and it is, but this kingdom can be as cruel as it is beautiful sometimes."

Kara, as she was prone to do, cut a more direct path, "Not all boys and girls of Low Town have good parents like we do. Some are orphans; others are sold off by people who should take care of them. Most wind up as semi-slaves in households. Others work in the fields from dawn to moons. The uglier they are, the safer. The prettiest are taken to pleasure houses like the one you saw today to work as no kids should."

Elaine's stomach dropped at the implication. Her parents were a far cry from gems, but she never was in harm like that, even at their worst.

"But there are powerful women here! With magic. Why don't they stop them?" Elaine asked.

The twins passed a look at the word *magic,* and she chided herself silently. *It's called Dua. They don't call it magic here.*

Reiki replied, "There are many kinds of atrocities that you don't see, Elai. The Towner kids always have the worst of it, and if they survive, they often don't have any way of living without going down dark turns of their own when they become adults. The Efendians of the Upper Tiers and the Iktidars never see us beyond the coin we make them, and if we want help, we have to help ourselves."

Kara muttered something like, "Bokki tumbles down Tiers," as another Towner from their cluster caught up to them.

He balanced copper pots on a long stick across his thick shoulders. His eyes lingered on Kara, "Did you hear? Another girl was taken early this morning. This time, from the Upper Tiers. Her friend swore she was next to her and then, whoosh, nothing but air."

"Why hasn't anyone arrested the Canavar Company? Y'all say they're behind everything shady in Efendi." Elaine said, thinking back to the ginger man in the Lantern Pit.

Kara, perpetually looking for the Canavar Company over her shoulder, shushed Elaine, but the neighbor shook his head. "Couldn't be them. Even they can't make kids vanish out of thin air." He glanced around, nearly knocking Reiki with his pots, and whispered, "*I bet it's Rifters.*"

"Oh please," Reiki groaned. "You don't honestly believe that do you?"

Kara stiffened, prompting Elaine to ask, "What's a Rifter?"

The neighbor's eyes grew wide, "Evil women that snatch children for their skins and--"

"Enough. Save the tall tales for a better storyteller," Kara kicked a stone from her sandal, "Filbish pebbles."

They were almost home.

***

Kara and Reiki's mom, Farisha, hulled grain at the reed and wood table in the Hadishi kitchen when they arrived. The twins' home was a smidge larger than a lofted tent, complete with a grimy white cloth draped at the entrance in lieu of a door. The twins and Elaine slept in the loft, and the only time they all gathered inside for any significant length of time was to sleep.

Elaine pushed the dark, swirling thoughts of the Lantern Pit aside. She breathed easier once she walked over the Yapi-stamped dirt floor, the grandmotherly goddess beaming at being the center of the home. Farisha softly hummed as she split grains, the husk peeling off multiple grains at a time as she skimmed her tanned leather hand a few inches over them. Farisha explained once that she felt most at peace when she worked in her element, and since grain came from the ground, her meager Groundwerk was like meditation. The basket vibrated on the floor next to a mismatched chair leg as the grains churned slightly to loosen their husk in tune with her hum.

Kara sat beside her mother wordlessly to assist, though her frantic energy pulled the husks at a quicker, less precise pace. Farisha pursed her lips but said nothing, and Reiki set to work on soup for dinner. The twins chatted idly to soften the quiet, and soon Farisha was laughing with them at their stories of failed pranks and then admonishing them for plotting new schemes.

Elaine used to sit at the yellow-tinged linoleum table in her trailer back in South Carolina and pretend her mother was talking to her while she paced the kitchen. Ma would chat so much on her phone that Elaine once thought it'd be easier if she just duct taped it to her right ear. Ma seemed at ease gossiping and laughing away at jokes Elaine couldn't hear. Her smiles always died off, though, at the gravel crunch of her Da's pickup filtering through the screen door or when she'd catch Elaine's eyes at the kitchen table.

Elaine realized the trio of Hadishi's were looking at her expectantly. "Sorry... What'd you say?"

Farisha wrapped her threadbare beige shawl over her shoulders as she added dried herbs to the bubbling soup at the fire. "I understand you explored a bit today. Do you want to talk about what you saw?"

"No, ma'am. It just took me off guard, is all. I won't go back down that way again," Elaine replied. She tapped her foot under the table and hoped Farisha would leave it at that. Fortunately, the canvas door flapped open to reveal the twins' father, Otum, grin ready.

A chorus of "Bapa's!" and "Ho's!" went up, and he bussed the cheeks of the dark-headed twins before scooping his wife up in his arms. Kara tossed the empty grain husks at the pair, and Reiki feigned disgust while they spun for a kiss. Otum smiled wide for Elaine and tucked a thin iridescent flower behind her ear from his pocket, his limp more pronounced after the kitchen twirl.

"And what did you discover today, Little Wanderer?" he asked, light green eyes twinkling.

Reiki fortunately intervened. "It's almost time. Help me bring the bowls outside."

He passed out small clay bowls, and the hot liquid warmed Elaine's grimy hands. The sight of the two moons, one crescent, and the other fat, still thrilled her even after all these months. Stars glittered between the red and blue moons, and some of the neighbors lit small fires throughout the compact, round courtyard tucked between the lean-to homes. Elaine helped Kara unfold their blanket while the rest of the Hadishi clan chatted idly with the other families sitting on blankets, stools, and steps nearby. An elderly matriarch walked to the lone stool in front of the courtyard fountain, and the small crowd settled. Elaine pulled her knees in tight to her chest, tugging the hand-me-down linen dress the color of day-old oatmeal to her shins.

The ancient matriarch at the front asked above the muted chatter, "What should we tell tonight?"

"Tell us about the fight between Sulu and Ates!" Someone shouted.

"No! The one about Ruzgar and the First Pillar!"

"Yanash, you old goat, she told us that one last night," someone else in the courtyard said. "It's almost harvest. Let's hear something dark. Tell the one about the Edicisi and the lost sun!"

Arguments ensued as they did every night in this cluster of Low Town, but Kanne Da'neen smiled conspiratorially at the young kids gathered closest to her. She raised her bony arms high above her head and mimed an arc with her knobby pointer fingers.

"My children, do you know why our two moons run from each other? A hundred years before our hundredth Queen, we were in a terrible famine. That Queen did not believe in Ruzgar's wrath or warm her feet by Ates' flame. The Goddesses were ignored, and so the husks of the grain were empty, the greens did not blossom, and the waves tossed our nets and boats back to us. Yapi was so betrayed by our indifference that she called forth the Edicisi from the depths of the Batiwood.

"The legendary monster crawled out of the roots of the oldest gnarled tree and formed legs from its branches. It took finger bones from Garfu nests to form its arms and hands and beckoned its Handmaidens with the cry of a Yurutec."

The audience hissed and wiggled their fingers at the wide-eyed children before Kanne Da'neen continued. "The Handmaiden Rifters brought skins from their human prey and sewed a terrible cloak for their master so it could walk in the sunlight like a man."

Rifter, Elaine thought, *that's what the neighbor claimed took the girls.* Chills ran down Elaine's spine at the word, and she imagined hunchback witches waiting in the flickering shadows for her. She nestled her skinny frame securely into Kara's warm side. On the other side of Elaine, Reiki leaned forward to make the pretty Efendian in front of him giggle.

The woman continued, "The Edicisi came for us then. It swept the fields into its gaping mouth and smothered the fire from the top of the Perimeter Wall with the dirt it had gathered. It ate its way up the Tiers, first with Low Town's children and then with the Pillars of the Elite. Up and up, it rose until it reached the Palace gate. At the steps stood a young woman from Low Town. She was a servant sent to deliver gowns to the Palace courtiers. She watched the Edicisi climb to the Fountain Tier and knew she had to act.

"The woman was Sulu's favorite. She was wily and quick-witted, and though she had no real Dua of her own but a meager trickle, she could flow between ranks as nimble as the sea. She quickly put on the most delicate gossamer gown in her package and stood as proud as the finest matriarch in front of the gates.

"The Edicisi came to her then, prepared to sweep her into its mouth when she smiled widely and bowed low. 'My good sir, it's good to see you in such strong health! I was afraid you might not make it on time for my first tale.'

"The Edicisi abruptly stopped and shrunk down to the size of a man. He garbled his question to her, breath rank with the blood of Efendians, 'Who are you?'

'Why, I am the storyteller of my town, the keeper of our tales, and I was sent here for your entertainment, of course.' She sat at the steps and gestured for him to sit with her.

"Intrigued, the Edicisi sat down at her feet. She told him tales of her Towners, of the Goddesses and their fury, the stories brought to her from her pirate lovers. For three full turns, she spun tales for him without food, water, or sleep, and for three full turns, he fell harder and harder in love with her. On the fourth moonrise, he asked for her hand in marriage.

"'Alas, I would love nothing more, but my mother said I may only marry the man that can catch one of our two suns.' She feigned great grief, 'But no one is powerful enough to do that, so I must stay a virgin forever!'

"The Edicisi was, after all, part man." At this, the men in the audience rolled their eyes and groaned in unison. Kanne Da'neen smiled wide at the barb, "so he puffed up his skin-cloaked chest and declared, 'I can catch a sun for you. No one is more powerful than I!'

"He grew and grew until he was taller than the Palace dome. He stepped over his future bride, over the fountains and domed roof of the Palace, and into the Turkaz sea where the smaller sun began to sink. He opened his arms as wide as the sea to scoop the sun, but the skin cloak the Handmaiden Rifters wove was too tight. He shed his cloak, thinking only of his future bride in his bed, when the sun's light hit his skin. He burst into flames, and the sea around his ankles turned to steam.

"Ates was so angered that a devotee to Sulu would use her sun without permission to harm their sister's creation that she scattered the smaller sun into thousands of stars." Kanne Da'Neen tipped her head back. Elaine followed suit to appreciate the multitude of pinpricks sparkling behind trails of smoke from the fires. "The moons split into opposite directions in search of the missing sun so that once a year, they dip below the horizon simultaneously and cloak us in darkness for a full turn. We paint our capstones bright orange to remind the Edicisi of the sun's flames until Hasateen has passed."

The old woman continued, "The Queen awarded the Towner with a fine home in the uppermost Tier and gave her the charge to hunt any Rifters found in the kingdom. It was the Towner that founded our army of Duawielders, but she also showed us that power is more than the Dua we are blessed with."

The audience clapped and thanked Kanne Da'neen before meandering back to their homes. Elaine had every intention of forcing the twins to take her with them to the street party gathering in the alleys beyond their cluster, but the loft was warm and cozy, and her journal was waiting with her hand-drawn map of Efendi. She marked two X's where she heard the voices again and silently willed the voices to return. She drifted off to sleep at some point while sketching the Edicisi creature from Kanne Da'Neen's story. Elaine slept fitfully without the twin's warm body heat as she alternated between dreams of lost suns and floating lanterns.

She ran through the Lantern Pit towards a crying voice when she woke up to screams below.

REED

Reed finally stopped running and learned through aching breaths that her name was Monti. Monti's Texan Pride blowout, which somehow had survived the hellstorm and tornado of getting to this godforsaken land, was finally defeated. Honey blond strands clung to her sweaty throat. Reed assumed Monti would be too tired to talk after being chased by monsters and then armed men riding rhinoceros-like creatures, but he underestimated her. The pair ran on and off for a full day, pushing farther and farther from the gnarled fire-orange tree line behind them, while Monti questioned or berated Reed the entire while.

Her litany of complaints faded while he listened to the wild calls of birds and small critters in the grass valley surrounding them. The sun hovered over the horizon, a steady slinking reminder that he had to make a decision since the mountains were still too far away to reach before nightfall.

Monti's arms and legs splayed out like the body of a crime scene within the tall grass, but it did nothing to drown out her whining.

"I can't breathe," she moaned. "We have to stop. Figure out where we're going."

He rested his back against the warm boulder and vaguely

gestured towards the jagged stone monstrosities off in the distance. His chest still heaved from their brutal run to this point. "We gotta head towards that mountain range."

Monti paused her rant and stood over him. "How in the ever-present hell do you know where we should go? You were just locked up in a supermax in the middle of nowhere Texas." She circled her arms dramatically at the grassy hills and spiked peaks in the distance. "This seem like Texas to you?"

The mountains looked like teeth jutting into the sky, its eye-tooth curving upward to pierce fat pink clouds that tinged purple at the edges.

"Woman, are you going to buck at everything I say?" Reed muttered, eyes on the mountains.

"I'm *sorry*? You were just locked up in prison for murdering your wife. Excuse me if I don't do a trust fall every time you suggest something stupid." She waved her finger in the air between them and spoke before he could, a rapid-fire of words leaving no room for interruption.

She pointed back to the white and gold kingdom, a city of walls at the edge of the ocean that he veered away from over an hour ago. "No. Let's recap because that's always fun. Number one, my Daddy is back that way. Back that way is civilization, and I don't know much about wherever *here* is, but I know that the people that took him were just that. People.

"Number two. Some monsters just tried to *eat* you, and they came from those creepy woods way back there. Have you ever been to West Virginia? Cousins rarely ever improve in the mountains. Let's not go in the opposite direction of where people live to find something worse than what we saw come out of those woods.

"Finally, number three, I don't care what 1950's ranch you came from. My name is Monti Banks and I don't answer to 'woman,' so let's just keep it civil while we journey to the center of hell together. OK?"

She pursed out her lips so the 'OK' sounded more like

"mmm..k". Reed was not proud of many things in his life, but he felt like any man in the same situation would have also considered leaving Mmm'K Monti in the fields to fend herself. *At least the thought would have occurred.*

He stood up and stepped into her personal space, "You like lists then do you, Miss Banks? Mmm...K, here's mine. Number one, while you were hysterically crying these last several hours and tripping over those *ridiculous* shoes, I spotted the roof of a barn and fences in that direction. That's where we're heading so we can rest and move again during daylight, preferably with some food and a game plan.

"Number two, I'm 24 years old, and number three, you wouldn't know what West Virginia looks like because you likely never left Texas. I lived there for a year, and it's beautiful."

Monti's saccharine smile made his teeth grind. "Of course you did."

They glared at each other for a few heartbeats. Monti finally uncrossed her arms and fluttered her hands ahead of her. "Well then lead on, Lewis."

She shifted her pointed shoes in the grass and said under her breath, "Not all of us are as fetching in orange and white."

Reed snorted, and the side of his mouth ticked up. He realized then that he hadn't said more than a handful of words to anyone since his trial. He couldn't even remember the last natural smile he had. *It likely was at Staci*, but the thought of her made his chest feel hollow, and the smile died as quickly as it tried to rise.

He cleared his throat. "We shouldn't talk till we scope it out in case the owner of the barn is around. We don't have much daylight left, and we gotta make this work."

Monti mock saluted him.

I should have left her in the woods, he thought.

Reed led the way towards the squat barns in the distance. The sky faded into a dark purple haze, and the fat pink clouds melted into each other to float past the horizon. Reed knew he was taking a considerable risk by coming here, but they had little choice. *I should be used to picking between a bad and worse choice by now.*

His head pounded, and his chest ached. *How did he get us all here?* The feeling of being watched crept over his shoulders again after years of freedom without it, catching him off guard now.

What happened to the others? He waited for the lullaby to start again, dread filling his stomach, and scanned the tall grasses surrounding them. *If he found me in prison in Texas a world away, how long will it take him to find me in his world?*

Reed halted at a rustle to their right. He grabbed Monti's wrist and put his finger to his lips, "Shhh—"

"I wasn't talking," She loud-whispered, yanking her hand back. She ducked down, though, with Reed.

The squat barn was just ahead. A sloped roof capped the three-sided structure, and dark stone stacked to form its broad rectangular base. A few of the giant beasts the soldiers used milled around in the fenced-in field beyond the barn, but he didn't see any riders.

"You still have your gun?" He whispered.

"Yea, and I'm not giving it to—" Reed interrupted Monti.

"I'm not asking for it wo-Miss Banks—" he corrected himself and almost smiled at the fire darting at him from her hazel eyes.

"Just keep it ready. I'm going in first. If anything comes at you without me, fire without question, and then run towards those lights in the distance. Find whatever shelter you can, but don't move during the dark." Reed ducked low and took off for the thatched roof barn before she could reply.

The only sounds beyond his own were the giant beasts snorting in the grass. He crept to the back and, hearing nothing inside, snuck around through the opening that faced the animals. He pushed away memories that threatened to overwhelm him at the smell of the straw. He spotted a trunk tucked near a wooden bench and clay pitcher under a spigot. *Perfect.*

Reed doubled back to wave Monti in just as the sun finished

melting on the horizon. The tip of the red crescent moon drifted up to the left of where the sun disappeared, and her sister blue moon rose at a more rapid pace to the right.

She walked in, the beasts rambling closer to the open wall just behind her. "Won't those things bring predators in?" Monti whispered.

Reed debated how to tell her and settled on, "We're alone, and those things look like rhinos. They're likely tough to eat and dangerous as hell if attacked."

Reed noticed the half-full cup of water next to the spigot when he turned back. *We'll have to be out at dawn then.* The barn was wide and tall enough for several of the beasts to find shelter at once in the front, but he had to duck when he filled the clay pitcher under the spigot to hand to Monti. Reed scanned the mountains and the dark valley through a narrow rectangular window on the back wall while Monti drank her fill. He started rummaging through the trunk in the corner when she poked her head over his shoulder.

Reed was never a vain man, but he was instantly aware that he hadn't showered in a couple of days, and that grime covered the scruff on his face.

"Here," he said as he tossed Monti a beige cloth over his shoulder. He found a small pair of boots and turned to give them to her as well.

Monti stared at him with her brows furrowed. He answered her unasked question, "It looks like whoever mans this barn stays here occasionally. There's a cot over there near the window."

She mercifully didn't say anything else but held the men's khaki overalls up to her. They were far too wide, but she was a tall woman in her own right and likely wouldn't need more than a roll or two at the hem. Reed found a well-worn white shirt with hand-sewn buttons and another pair of khaki-colored pants.

He turned to give her some privacy and watched the moons through the window. He gave Monti a piece of hardtack he found on the windowsill, "Here, it's stale, but it's edible."

She must be exhausted if she's reverted to grunts only, Reed thought.

The four beasts from the field rambled inside the shelter. Reed froze with the hardtack halfway to his mouth, but they stopped a few feet from him. The beasts turned, lined up shoulder to shoulder with each other, and faced their horns out to the open wall and fields outside. The two moons stopped their rise at ten and two. He could barely make out the Tiers of the Palace from here, but it emitted the only other glow around the valley. He brushed the crumbs of his dinner from his face and tried to ignore the growing anxiety threatening to choke him.

Reed tossed Monti a blanket and nodded for her to take the cot. He shook off the sleeves of his prison jumper so that they hung limply at his sides and cupped his dirty hands under the spigot. The cold water spilling over his head and bare chest did nothing to break through the dirt caked in his skin. He wanted a river to dive into and was thinking of where to find one when he heard Monti's sharp inhale.

He whipped around to see torchlight dance over the tops of the sleeping beasts. The pale bald creature holding the torch barely came to Reed's shoulder. Long, fleshy ears bookended its round, wrinkled face, and a hooked nose divided two eyes the size of Reed's fists.

It tsk'd, "It's not too often that I find Efendians stupid enough to seek shelter behind Aygir they do not know."

The creature clicked his tongue, and the Aygir beasts abruptly turned as one. Dust billowed under their feet as they turned to face Reed and Monti from either side of the small creature. The creature's upper torso was similar to a human, but its blue legs tapered down into sharp pincers as if it walked on scissors. It clicked a different sound, and the Aygir lowered their heads, their sharp horns aimed at them, and they readied in a low stance as if prepared to charge. Reed ran his hands over his close-cropped hair and glanced at a frozen Monti, eyes wide.

The creature looked at Monti as he said, "Tell me why I shouldn't feed you to my Aygir and rid Sakalid of you?

Reed hadn't slept since they came here and had barely slept more than a few hours each night since Staci. He didn't hear the creature sneak up on them. He needed real food and real sleep. Monti gripped her gun and pointed at the ground as she inched closer to Reed's side. He weighed his bad and worse options yet again while he stayed her trembling hand.

After an uncomfortable beat, he'd made his decision.

"Peace, Itreni. I am Reed Wells, son of Alisha Welnis. We meant no disrespect but needed to find shelter for the night."

"The singer's boy? Even I've heard of your mother, though it's been an age since any caravan came through these parts. Why don't you come down and rest in my home where it is safe?" The old creature smiled a grin a few inches wider than comfort, and his black pupils narrowed to a pinprick within eyes that dominated his face.

Monti dropped her gun and gaped at Reed. Her eyes shifted from alarmed to outright horror.

He held up placating hands and whispered, "I can explain."

ALIK

Alik's low plunged lavender gown seemed like a fabulous idea in her room but felt obscene sitting across from the aging matriarchs and their partners now. Her face ached at holding an unwavering smile for the last two hours. The fuchsia feathered headdress on the woman seated across from her shook as the woman gossiped with glee about a matriarch a table over.

What I would give to be seated with my brothers, Alik thought for the second time that hour. Damari chatted with an attractive brunette at a polished stone table in the far corner of the room. Taavi stood at the front near Alik, surrounded by a group of laughing men. Queen Firtina draped across her chair like a dangerous, black Magaran cat in her slinky dress on the raised marble dais to Alik's left. To anyone else, her mother appeared as bored as Alik, but Alik knew her mother scanned the courtiers with sharp eyes as she spun her hovering wine glass in the air. Water fell in a thick, suspended veil behind her chair, the Waterwerkers slowly rolling their hands in unison on either side.

Someone told her of Agnian's unease then, Alik thought as she snuck her hundredth glance at him on the opposite side of the room. Fortunately, the music ended then. Alik tipped her head back to the open sky above them.

Thank the goddesses.

Queen Firtina stood and thanked the crowds of courtiers and Dvarians. She said the lines regarding a healthy harvest expected of a leader on First Night with practiced poise before sauntering out with a bottle of wine floating alongside her and an attractive courtier trailing behind. Alik slipped out from the gaggle of matriarchs gathering suspiciously close to her with their sons at the ready. She searched the room again for a particular chiseled jawline.

Hundreds of wings fluttered inside her belly. *Stop being ridiculous. First, he hates you. Second, he's hiding something. The only reason you need to get close to him is to figure out if whatever he's hiding has to do with the missing girls.*

Alik's inner monologue shifted into an argument when she saw him staring at her from across a break in the crowd. He watched her with curiosity and something she couldn't name, like a Kingalia debating if it should pounce, causing her to still. His eyes trailed over her, a slow stroll that had her heart stuttering and stomach tighten. A lithe woman regained his attention with a hand on his arm, breaking the trance he held over Alik. Alik pulled the intricate braid in her hair around her shoulder, fiddling its feathered edge, and walked briskly to him before she could reconsider.

Again she lied to herself. *It's for the girls.*

Alik tried to feign nonchalance at several of the gorgeous house Pillars eyeing him with interest but faltered at their smirks when she approached his back. *I look as ridiculous as the sops standing behind their dates. How can they just stand there while the women flirt shamelessly with him?*

She'd grown up with these Pillars as they were all the strongest, or in Alik's case, the only, daughters of their families. The snickers and cutting eyes were nothing new. Their disdain, though, took a dangerous turn after a couple of Elite families voiced doubt in Alik's ability to take her mother's throne.

She slowed when she reached Agnian. *Do I tap his shoulder? That feels awkward. Maybe I clear my throat? Oh, for Atessake, just—*

She stumbled back at his sudden turn, and his hand wrapped around her waist. Then his other hand gripped held her arm, his face searching hers. Alik let him hold her for a few beats longer than necessary.

"Forgive me, Princess. I'm so sorry," Agnian said, stepping off of Alik's now throbbing toe.

Her neck craned back at his proximity when he righted her, and she smiled as she had the first time she held a boy's hand. *I didn't know a clavicle could be attractive,* she thought. *Get it together, Alik.* She tried to ignore the tanned chest at her face and focused on his full lips. *Eyes, Alik. Focus on the eyes.*

He grinned as he shifted so Alik could join the circle of Efendian women. The two closest to Alik shared a snicker after a stilted pause in conversation among the group. Willowy Aslynn Tinti, arguably the most beautiful Efendian woman after Firtina, reached her arm across Alik to touch Agnian's forearm, effectively boxing Alik out once more. *This was a mistake.* But to her delighted surprise, Agnian walked away from the horrible woman mid-sentence, pulling Alik with him.

He leaned over their linked arms as they walked, "I expected some sort of bow from them at your arrival. They practically kissed the ground when Queen Firtina walked in."

Alik tamped down her embarrassment. "They'd at least acknowledge my rank if my mother were still in the room, but we've known each other long enough that I don't force the issue."

Liar.

Changing the subject, she said in a rush, "It's tradition to have an exceptionally boring First Night dinner in the Palace. I hope it exceeded your expectations?"

"Ah, in that case, yes. The dinner went fabulously well." He grinned a crooked grin at her, and she forgot for a moment that a hundred eyes watched them.

He had changed out of his dirty pirate clothes into clean pirate clothes that clung to his chest. He pulled his shoulder-length dark hair back but left the salt and pepper scruff on his face. Alik never noticed if graying was attractive on anyone else, but somehow it suited him well.

What has life thrown at him to gray his beard so soon? She stepped ahead of him as they reached the stone patio above the garden terrace, rubbing her arms at the slight chill. *With my luck, it was likely kidnapping girls since he's this attractive.*

Agnian said, "I heard this city was good for music and dancing if nothing else, and yet this event was as tame as my babushka's tea."

"Well, you'd need the right guide, but there *are* legendary parties beginning tonight," she replied.

The Mina moon cast azure light over the garden path they meandered, and the salt-kissed wind drifted around them from the ocean thrashing far below. Agnian reached for her arm again, his featherlight touch stopping her as quickly as if he tackled her under the twin moonlight.

"I doubt the parties would be worth the tale if you were not in attendance," he said quietly, though no one was around them. "Would it be inappropriate of me to ask you to be such a guide?"

Alik let out an awkwardly low laugh and nearly fell out of her dress in surprise. *I am so over my head, and I am perfectly fine with that.* She didn't scan him with her Dua, though. *Let me pretend for a moment he is genuine. There is ample time to read him anyway.* She alternated between annoyance and relief when her younger brother took that moment to sneak up behind them.

Damari whispered in his ear, "I'd be honored to show you the dark crevices of Efendi."

Alik laughed at his antics and was happy to see Agnian stumble as awkwardly as her laugh a moment before.

"Agnian Taladier, my brother Damari Iktidar'an. Damari, I see you've thoroughly creeped out our guest in your first introduction. Point to you."

Damari bowed low just as Taavi joined them. Her brothers took the lead to invite Agnian out tonight after their jovial small chat about the horrid dinner. Alik couldn't see her kingdom from the garden terrace, but she heard drumbeats and horns floating up from the Tiers. The music carried over colorful bobbing lights from the boats pulling in the dark harbor to join the parties.

The drums reminded her of the first time she and her brothers snuck out to join the festivities in disguise a few years before. Alik didn't want to dwell on the list of girls left in her room, or the thinly veiled comments about her lack of Dua, or her mother's perpetual displeasure in her. *I just want to go out. I want to dance and drink and laugh with my friends. And I want to pretend that this gorgeous man is flirting with me because he wants to, and not because he wants something from me. What's the harm in one night?*

"Settled then?" Damari nudged Alik back to their conversation before continuing. "Alik, we'll meet you and Shauna by the orchard hearth. She has your clothes, and we'll be down there shortly with Agnian."

"See you soon, Princess." He said, winking at her before strolling away.

Alik forced herself to read him at her brothers' expectant stares. Her stomach sank a little as he trailed a haze of gray determination and green opportunity. *What did you expect?*

Damari and Taavi gave her a moment for her eyes to refocus, and she nodded to them in affirmation, pretending she didn't see their teasing smiles. "We may be able to find something from him tonight."

***

"Goddesses, to walk through this place unnoticed every time would be a blessing," Alik said as she followed Shauna through the servant halls. "No one would whisper when I walked by or wait for me to fail at something else."

"Sometimes it pays to be invisible," Shauna replied.

They wore matching loose beige pants and simple tunics, a stark contrast to the preening courtiers bustling through the Palace for First Night parties. The hallway leading to the Palace steps felt like a teeming mass of glitter and feathers, each gown and headpiece more garish than the last. Alik spit out a sparkling feather that swiped her face, the owner glaring at her for sharing her air. *Almost out.*

She breathed a sigh of relief once they reached the gardens. Alik readjusted the simple cloth mask over her eyes as Shauna passed her a dark blackberry lip stain to reapply before they met everyone else. The quiet rows of orchards blocked out a star-speckled night sky, and the music from the Tiers below felt a world away. Pea gravel crunched under the girls' leather sandals as they walked further from the Palace.

Shauna said, "It's been too long since we've done something fun, Alik."

"Goddesses, tell me about it. You know, though, you don't have to always stay in because of me. You should be out exploring this city every night. I know I would."

"You're my person, Alik. I know I could, but it isn't nearly as much fun without your terrible dancing." Shauna smiled and sprayed her with a push of Waterwerk.

She gasped at the shock of cold water dripping from her face and used her meager Waterwerk to pull from the fountain as well. It fell in a single drop on Shauna's forehead, and they both burst out laughing at the pathetic trickle. By the time the path came to an end, Alik felt more wet than dry, and Shauna had a handful of droplets in her hair.

They nodded to the women guarding either side of the stone archway at the end of the path. Taavi, Agnian, and Taavi's best friend Ty waited for them dressed in servant's attire as well. Alik and Shauna laughed even harder at their faces when Alik's half-soaked dress came into view.

Ty shook his head and smiled, "It's as if we're all 15 again."

"If I remember correctly, if we were 15, we would have snuck into your aunt's tavern and be drunk by now," Taavi said.

Alik smiled as they rehashed a First Night memory, chiming in only when they forgot a funny detail. She rang out her dress as best as she could next to the stone fireplace while they waited for Damari, and bit back a smile when Agnian shifted closer to her.

He asked, "Couldn't you just use Dua to dry yourself faster? You're Queen Firtina's daughter, so you have the ability to control all four Duawerks, right?"

Alik snorted. "Clearly, you haven't been in Efendi before. My handle with fire or air would likely just singe the dress or blow a few strands of my hair back."

He wouldn't be able to see the change in her pupils in the darkness, so she snuck a scan of him at the admission. Orange surprise mixed with a tinge of chartreuse apprehension circled his face as he smiled broadly at her. *At least he's moved on from disgust or hatred for a moment.*

"Where are your companions? Did they not want to join you?" She asked.

His aura flooded with a pale blue shame, startling Alik. "I'm sorry, I didn't mean to imply—"

He cut her off, "No. You didn't say anything wrong. I just didn't tell them where I was going." His crooked smile came back as he leaned in, "I wouldn't mind a night without the politics if you know what I mean."

She watched his aura shift again in the moonlight and blinked to clear her eyes. *He's not lying, but he's certainly not saying something.* It had been a couple years since Alik couldn't understand her readings, and the conflicting man next to her simultaneously confused her and drew her in. *It might be nice to be with someone that I can't read entirely.*

Damari jogged to them. "Ready?" He asked as he reached around the statue of Ates. He pulled a lever hidden behind her carved hair. The low flames hissed in the hearth as a stone door dropped to reveal the hidden stairwell.

The group walked down the steep steps that wound around the public halls of the Palace. The lower they dropped, the louder the Trades' music rang out until they reached an iron door. The guardswoman at the door opened at Taavi's silent nod, and they spilled out into a narrow alley filled with discarded chairs, cracked lanterns, and mismatched tables. Damari looked back at the group with a wicked smile when a stunning woman with beautiful obsidian skin in a white silk dress joined them from the broken chair she waited in.

Alik rolled her eyes. *Always an Eye.*

If the haphazard route, the latecomer, or the onslaught of noise they faced in the main path of the Trades surprised Agnian, he didn't show it. Streams of musicians spun past with Efendians of all ages dancing behind them in a long parade that would wind all the way up to the Palace steps before the night's end. Firewerkers set off sparkled powder in the middle of the path. The ruby and gold embers glittered down on night stalls lining both sides of the path that sold masks, food on sticks, wine, and more potent vices. Alik's party bumped merrily along with the crowd, linked arm in arm, to wade through the deafening noise. Agnian, sandwiched between Alik and Shauna, turned back to Alik several times with an increasingly expanding grin.

If I scan him now, I'll likely just trip. Might as well enjoy this. Alik smiled wide at a Groundwerker pulling delicate flowers from a crack in the Tier wall and nearly bumped into Agnian at his abrupt stop.

Alik couldn't see what he stared at in the throng of people.

"Is everything alright?" She asked, looking over his shoulder.

Shauna stopped ahead of them, a question in her eyes, but before Alik could scan him, he shrugged off the tension in his frame and smiled at her again. "It's just a bit much to take in."

"Too much?" Alik asked, "Because where we're going, it doesn't exactly calm down."

He held his hand out to her, and she placed hers in his warm palm. "Not at all. I just didn't expect to enjoy it this much."

Alik decided she liked this smaller, crooked smile best as she took the lead to rejoin everyone.

Their little parade stopped at a narrow street beyond a fountain of Sulu. Water flowed into the path, and the naked and laughing goddess was carved so that it appeared she splashed the crowds. Waterwerkers altered the colors in the fountains to the warm hues of garnet, marigold, and burnt orange in celebration of Hasateen, and Shauna trailed her fingers in the shimmering water as they passed.

They weaved down the crooked street, laughing. A group of young men dressed in black rags and ghoulish masks raced past them, bumping into Agnian. He looked at their group, startled, and Shauna answered his unasked question.

"It's the First Night of Hasateen, and some people dress up like the Edicisi," she explained. Shauna laughed at his perplexed look and continued, "It's folklore of ours. The Edicisi came on the First Night of Hasateen and ate the fires of Efendi, shrouding us in darkness." She pointed to the orange powder swiped above one of the doorways they passed. "We mark our doors each night this week to show him we remember so he doesn't snatch our daughters and sons while they sleep!"

"Do your holidays all revolve around such ghoulish creatures?" He asked Alik.

Laughing, she replied, "Only the fun ones."

She and Shauna linked arms with Damari's Eye, who introduced herself as Mara. Mara pulled them back from skipping past an unassuming umber-stained door. She blew air from her open palm like a kiss, and a series of curving locks appeared on the door frame. Alik's heart raced when the door swung open to reveal a rainbow-colored hallway throbbing with drumbeats from inside. She felt drunk with giddiness at escaping the Palace for a night and grinned wildly at Agnian as she and Shauna pulled him down the hall. Her brothers jostled each other behind them, arms around each other and already singing.

Alik shouted to Agnian over the din, "You are about to see one of the many reasons why we love our city. Tonight, you'll be an honorary Efendian!" She led him into the fray at the end of the hallway where two scantily clad Firewerkers parted a 10-foot flame so they could enter the thumping room beyond.

Airwerkers twirled spirals of glitter above a crowd that jumped to the beat of horn and drum players onstage at the end of the cavernous room. Waterwerkers flew streams of shimmering almond liquor at the open mouths of the young Efendians, and everyone cheered as more drum players took the stage. Shauna and Mara came back with ale for everyone that frothed over their mismatched wooden mugs, and their group found their own space in the throng to dance together. Alik rolled her eyes when Shauna stepped behind her right shoulder to guard her back, but her best friend just shrugged and hopped to the drumbeat while pouring a steady stream of ale to her own mouth through the air.

Alik glanced at Agnian ahead of her with her Dua to see his reaction to everything but only found shimmering white wonder swirling around him. He laughed with Ty and joined the fray of dancing that would last hours into the night.

The dark ale was a welcome bitterness as she scanned for any abnormalities while they danced. A few plumes of deep blue came and went with drunken fights before guards tossed the aggressors outside, but she didn't see anything ominous. Taavi stationed a few Horde members to patrol the Silos and Low Town tonight, and she relaxed a bit more with each sip.

She scanned Agnian, and sparkling gold merriment swirled with faint mint guilt. She thought back to his statement in the garden about wanting a night without politics, and she brushed off the first tinge of alarm at registering his second emotion. *I know what it's like to feel guilty doing something for yourself.*

She watched her loved ones dance together, unhindered by the burdens she carried. *You have the rest of the week to deal with the trade negotiations, Alik, and the Horde is now patrolling the streets alongside guardswomen. No one else will go missing tonight, and you scanning this crowd will do little for the girls already gone. Tonight is one night in a full year of duties. Everything else can wait.*

She cleared her eyes and waved a Waterwerker over to arc wine into her mouth. Alik spent the next couple of hours dancing circles with her friends and strangers alike.

***

They were drenched in sweat by the time they all looked at the door longingly, and Alik could see through her brothers' linen shirts through the cloth mask plastered to her face. Agnian lifted his shirt's hem to wipe his face, revealing pointed tips of black tattoos that crawled over a flat stomach from beneath his leather pants. Alik, Mara, and Shauna caught each other watching him, and the three dissolved into laughter. Everyone hugged their newfound friends surrounding them goodbye before weaving out of the crowd and back into the crooked alley, still laughing.

Damari and Agnian led the way singing one of the songs from the festivity, badly and loudly. Taavi and Ty twirled Shauna and Mara behind Alik. She clapped in tune with the drumbeats coming from the main road a little way ahead and turned back to see Shauna dancing.

She noticed the man then.

He followed them dressed in a black, ragged cloak that covered his head. *Why does he feel wrong?* Another pulse of alarm shot through her. Her eyes glazed over to read him, and thick black smoke engulfed him. She shouted her warning, and Shauna and Mara jumped in front of Alik with their hands in the air. Shauna's vile of water at her wrist swayed with the abrupt movement.

"What is it, Alik?" Damari asked.

Alik's brothers and friends said little about her readings in front of strangers as it was not public knowledge. Queen Firtina insisted that she play the weak princess with minimal Dua so that her peers would not learn of her other abilities. This worked well enough for Alik most of the time since she was abysmal at the other werks, but in situations like this, she felt helpless.

"I thought I saw someone. A man, dark black cloak around the bend."

Mara said in her steady, quiet voice, "There are a lot of men in dark cloaks out tonight, Princess."

Alik waved her off, but doubt crept in. Agnian withdrew a wicked knife from somewhere in his boot. She scanned him when his eyes were on the path behind them and saw only a flare of red alarm. Ty ran back from the party's entrance, knives in hand as well now, shaking his head.

"I didn't see anyone, Alik, but a few drunk partiers," he said.

They stood still, ignoring the confused looks of a young couple walking around them, but Alik saw nothing else.

"Let's just go. Taavi, don't take the Ates stairwell. Let's take the boats to the top." *I don't want to wind through the crowd this late, and I'll happily play the princess card if it means we can take the boats. I'll deal with the consequences if Mother finds out.*

Taavi nodded his agreement. They walked quickly through the alley, heading for the boats that hovered over the center of the Trades that would glide them above the domed rooftops home. Mara shifted ahead of them at the main road of the Trades. Alik's ears popped at the push of air Mara forced around them to shuffle the crowd out of the way. A few people were clearly annoyed at the disturbance as they scurried past, but most were too drunk and happy to do much but dance out of the way.

Alik breathed a sigh of relief when they all loaded into the waiting ferry cars. The cream and gold cars only accommodated two at a time, so Damari and Mara took the lead, followed by Alik and Shauna. Taavi and Agnian brought the rear. Ty circled back with a few Horde members to patrol the crooked alley once he saw them off.

She described what she saw to Shauna as they waited for the Airwerkers below to lift their ferry car into the air. The Mizi moon cast a scarlet glow over half of the celebrating city, and the other half glowed a faint blue under the smaller Mina moon.

"It's been a long night, Alik, and you've spent every night looking into missing girls. I don't doubt what you saw; I just know that you've been on edge as well."

Alik shrugged as Damari and Mara's car took off. She looked to her left to see what was taking their Airwerker so long to get them off the ground. The woman's aura was the dull yellow of boredom, and Alik read exhaustion and a gray unease off both Agnian and Taavi behind her. She sighed contently as the car began to rise and leaned over her edge to watch the Trades sink below them when the ferry dipped for a moment. A chill of ice-white fear brushed past her just before her eyes cleared.

She jerked up to see what Shauna saw, only to find her friend had vanished.

***

Alik sank in the cushions of the dove white divan hours later with bloodshot eyes and a raw throat from screaming Shauna's name. Her pounding headache subsided to a dull ringing in her ears as she drank, but didn't taste, the warm liquid put into her hands.

"You should have someone look at that," Tryska said, gesturing to Alik's legs.

Alik brushed her hand over the dried blood on her knees but didn't answer the guardswoman. She leapt out of the ferry car when Shauna disappeared and landed on her knees and arms several feet later. Her chest constricted at the panic threatening to consume her again. Panicking caused her Dua to focus and refocus constantly, so she closed her eyes to lessen the headache.

I did this. I caused this. Shauna would not have gone out had I not insisted.

Firtina's study door opened to release a beige-cloaked servant that nodded to Alik to enter. Alik said goodbye to Tryska and shuffled into her mother's lair. Four of Firtina's longest-standing advisors waited near a massive oak table at the center of the circular book-shrouded room. No windows graced her mother's study, so the only light flickered from her orderly rows of firelight orbs hovering above them and the low flame in the hearth. As a child, Alik used to think the books stacked tightly from the floor to the ceiling were waves threatening to crash down on her, and she fought off her childish unease at the sight of them. Firtina, wrapped in a magenta robe, stood like a stone pillar with her back to everyone else in the room. She turned only when her advisors stopped speaking at Alik's arrival.

Alik knew she looked as horrible as she felt when her mother's eyes widened. At a head jerk, the advisors fled the room. Alik never liked those particular sycophants much, but she smiled her thanks to them for gathering this late on Shauna's behalf.

Firtina stood still. Alik knew this game well and was adept at losing it, so she spoke first. "Thank you for gathering your advisors so late. I didn't know what to do when we couldn't find her."

"How many people did you encounter in the Palace before you came to me now?" Firtina asked, picking at her sharp nails.

Alik's mind was unusually soft. Sometimes she could guess where her mother's thoughts were leading, but she was exhausted and emotionally drained at Shauna's disappearance. She shrugged and said a rounded answer, "Ten or so? Excluding the guards and your advisors, so maybe that's closer to twenty-four?"

Firtina stalked to Alik from the opposite side of the table. She snatched a piece of paper and a pen off its polished surface and shoved it across the room at Alik. Alik caught it in the gust of Airwerk her mother used, stepping back at its force.

"You will listen to me, and you will do only as I say for the next several turns. First, write down everyone's name you passed looking like a pathetic Towner. Next, you will rise in a couple of hours looking as marginal as you typically do in your own attire.

You will proceed with the negotiations with the Dvarian emissary as planned, and you will not mention this to anyone else in the Palace, particularly the emissary."

This isn't the time then to mention that Agnian was with us the entire night, Alik thought.

Firtina continued without pause, "Under no circumstances are you to mention tonight again. Am I clear?"

"I will do all that you ask Mother--," at Firtina's raised eyebrow, Alik corrected herself, "--my Queen. May I ask, though, what is the plan to find Shauna?"

Firtina mastered the uncanny ability to move one part of her face without anything else shifting. She blinked several times at her daughter. "The only thing we are doing concerning Shauna is cleaning up the despicable mess you made parading through the Tiers and the Palace like a screaming ghoul."

Other kids may argue with their parents, but Alik learned painfully at a young age that this was unacceptable as an Iktidar. Her hands shook, and her stomach felt like it sunk to the floor. She had never pushed back, let alone confront the terrifying woman in front of her. *It's Shauna, though. There is no option but to find her, whatever the cost.*

Alik took a deep breath. "Surely you cannot mean to ignore this. What about the other missing Daughters?"

Firtina paused. "What about them?" She asked.

"The missing girls, the fact that we have someone, or something, snatching our Daughters from our streets? What about the fact that my best friend wasn't safe when she sat. Right. Next. To. Me?" Alik flinched when the fireorbs flared higher above her, and her mother stepped closer.

"Girls go missing all the time. Most of them run off to Dvari or some other island for a tryst, come back impregnated, and then live out their miserable lives with their miserable Sub Tier kids at our generosity. We have significantly bigger work to focus on than the plight of a handful of wayward teens. Perimeter Patrol spotted a brood of Yurutec in the fields earlier. The guards killed a Garfu trying to ram our southern gate, and the Magarans have stopped their patrol of our western skies. A Perisien ship was spotted off the isle of---"

"One hundred and two," Alik dared to interrupt. "A hundred and two girls are missing before Shauna disappeared last night, and Goddesses know how many more were captured with her."

Firtina had few tells, but Alik knew the number surprised her when she looked down.

Alik pressed on, "And how do we hide that number? Shauna wasn't some Towner anymore. The daughter of a merchantress went missing the night before last in the Trades before moonrise. The court will begin to ask questions, and—"

"Enough." Firtina hissed through her teeth. Her right hand raised towards Alik, shaking. The glass orbs above them threatened to shatter from the growing flames inside, and Alik backed to the far wall with her hands above her head. She opened her eyes again when the glass did not break. Her mother's fist clenched at her side, and the fires in the orbs ahead dipped low again.

Firtina broke the tense silence. "I'll handle it the same way I handle *everything* in this Goddess-forsaken kingdom." She turned her back to Alik, pouring a glass of wine from a bottle at the far end with a flick of her wrist.

I have pushed her further than ever before, but I need her to say the words. "Does that mean you'll help me find Shauna?"

"I said I would deal with the missing girls," Firtina replied as the wine bottle slammed back down on the table. "My advisors will bring me up to speed on the others." Firtina dismissed her by pushing the doors open behind her with a flick of the wrist.

Alik didn't move. Tears threatened to overwhelm her lashes, and her hands still shook at her sides. *This is my best friend. And the advisors haven't done a thing about the other missing girls.*

She took a deep breath, speaking again before she lost her nerve. "I want to be in those meetings. I've been tracking this as well. I've even had some dreams about the girls missing in the Silos and--"

"And look what good that's done," Firtina said. Alik took several steps back as Firtina stalked towards her. Her Airwerk shoved Alik back in pace with each annunciation of her words.

"You've been following this, yet it's only escalated. You predicted this through your soothsaying, yet more have gone missing. You were seated next to an opportunity to stop it and did nothing, even for a person you claim is your best friend. I can't imagine what you'd provide further."

Alik cried out at the final hard push of air her mother shoved at her, her back slamming against the door jamb. The guard pulled her to stand as the doors crashed close behind them. Alik's chest constricted, and her rising panic threatened to overwhelm her senses.

She's right. I am no closer to finding out who is behind this than I was months ago when I first heard of the missing girls. I haven't helped any of them. Alik walked through the wide white stone hallways, noticing but not seeing anyone else. *But did I really look? They are someone's best friend too. Someone's daughter, someone's sister.* Tears fell down her cheeks as she turned into her study. *I kept their names on a list, and I made a few inquiries, but did I do everything I could? I waited for Taavi to send out the Horde. I sat back while Damari's Eyes looked into this. And I assumed that would be enough. That I could go dancing and drink and have fun with my loved ones while these girls disappeared. I am done relying on my mother. On my brothers. And no one, not even Firtina Iktidar, will keep me from finding her.*

She whispered, "I will find you, Shauna. I will find all you."

ELAINE

Reiki and Kara, still dressed from romping through the streets, waited in the courtyard when Elaine and their parents rushed outside. Farisha whispered a prayer of thanks when she saw her children, and they each hugged their parents and Elaine. Fire flashed to life above Elaine's head so the cluster of neighbors could see the young woman sobbing by the fountain.

The cluster of lean-tos circled a wide fountain of Sulu, and stretched linen hung haphazardly between homes to provide communal shade during the heat of the day. The lean-tos supported each other like a circle of cards, and one could borrow spices by reaching a hand out the side if you were particularly long-limbed. The tight quarters never bothered Elaine much before, but she felt increasingly claustrophobic as Reiki whispered what he had learned.

Reiki looked around them and whispered, "She was out with a friend from around the bend for Hasateen. They were walking through the Trades, but the crowds were so thick they couldn't get to the main steps to get home, so they decided to cut down through the Silos instead."

At this, Farisha glanced at her husband, and he wrapped her

closer to him, blocking Elaine's view.

"Were you with them?" She asked her children. Elaine shifted around the Hadishis so she could see Reiki and Kara.

"No, Maman, we were just coming back another way when we heard her cry out. Anyway, they were walking through the Silos when they thought a pack of animals was following them."

Farisha interrupted, skepticism in her voice, "In the middle of the Silos?"

"Yes, Maman. She said it sounded crazy, but that's what she heard. Barks and bird calls echoed all around the grain silos, and they couldn't tell which direction they were coming from, so she and her friend started running. She couldn't hear footsteps or see anyone, but she insists something gave chase. They held each other's hands and were almost to the end, but then her friend's hand was yanked away from her. She turned back to grab her, but her friend was gone."

"Did she see anyone then?"

Reiki rubbed his hand on the back of his neck and glanced back at the sobbing girl. "She said she saw a tall man, twice as tall as any Efendian, in a black cloak that covered his face."

The girl grabbed a woman's wrist closest to her, interrupting Reiki. "Edicisi! It was the Edicisi!" She screamed at the crowd, tears and snot running down her face. Several women consoling her raised their hands to their foreheads, palm facing out at her cry. They muttered a prayer to the air Goddess, Ruzgar, for protection.

Chills ran the length of Elaine's wiry body, and she stumbled at the sudden dizziness threatening to take her down to the cobblestones. Reiki grabbed her arm to steady her, but Elaine had an overwhelming urge to flee. Her chest felt too tight for her breath beating to get in, and she wondered if this is what a panic attack felt like. The girl's sobs echoed around the cluster. Elaine flinched at another scream about the Edicisi.

Farisha tugged her family towards their home. "Reiki, take Elai inside. They'll gather a search party, but you two need to eat something and sit for a moment if you intend to go with them."

The Hadishis sat Elaine at the kitchen table and took their respective seats around her. Everyone else acted like they couldn't hear the cries wafting through the flimsy door, but each one hit Elaine's brain like a hammer. Otum brought her a cup of water, and Kara folded her arms across her chest on the kitchen counter a step away to give her dad her stool. Elaine fumbled with a hole in the rattan stool she slumped on without looking at the eight eyes watching her intently now.

"Tell me what you feel like," Farisha said as she ran her cool, calloused hands on Elaine's face.

She huffed. "Little hot. I don't know what happened, but maybe it was the crowd? I just felt a little tight, you know? Like clausterish?" Elaine wrangled her mind into order. "I think I just need to lie down."

Otum nodded his head as Reiki stood to carry Elaine up the loft.

"I can walk. I'm not a baby." Elaine said, immediately regretting the sharp retort. "I'm sorry, Reiki. I don't know why I snapped. It wasn't kind of me." *What is wrong with me?* She thought as she fought off tears. *I am going crazy.*

"Elai, how old are you?" Kara asked randomly from her kitchen counter perch.

"13."

"Do you have your monthly flows yet?" Elaine's eyes widened at Farisha's question. Flame engulfed her cheeks at the thought of discussing her period in front of the Hadishi men.

Kara laughed and shucked a leftover grain husk at Reiki. "Go with Bapa to see what they're doing for a search party."

Farisha interjected with a pointed look at Kara, "Otum, I need you with us tonight. Let the twins go in your stead."

He tried to argue, but Kara cut to the point. "You cannot work all day in the fields and then wander all night in the Silos on your legs. You'll do more harm than good, Bapa, and Maman needs you here. Reiki and I will not go off on our own tonight."

Kara and her mother looked at each other when the fabric door flapped at their exit, but Kara merely repeated Farisha's question to Elaine.

"Agh! No. I haven't. Is that what this is? I get hot when my period is about to happen?"

Farisha ignored Elaine's question with her own. "Did you feel dizzy a moment ago?" The mother and daughter passed a look between them at her nod.

"What?" Elaine snapped, again almost overcome with tears at her reaction. "Sorry."

Farisha waved her off. "We don't need to talk about your life before my children found you." Elaine flinched at the fear threatening to consume her at the memory, but Farisha wrapped her cool hands over Elaine's fists. "No child, we don't need to address that now. But we should talk about what happens to Efendian girls around your age."

Efendian girls? Kara's face told Elaine nothing, but Farisha's weathered eyes made her feel like her past was written down her nose at that moment.

"When a young Efendian woman is about to manifest-"

Kara laughed at the look of disgust on Elaine's face and interrupted her mother. "Let me, Maman. Let's not forget how you brought me flowers to the Trades on the day my Dua came. I thought I would die of embarrassment."

Farisha huffed and waved her daughter on.

Kara continued, "All Efendian women begin to show their talents around the same time they start their monthly courses. It usually takes a year for your Dua to settle, but within this time you'll know if you can work air, water, fire, or the ground, or a combination of them. In the beginning, though, you can get dizzy, get chills, or suddenly get hot. Some people faint the first few times they use their power. You're quick to get mad and then quick to cry, and you feel out of breath. Sometimes it only takes a couple of days after those symptoms appear for your Dua to begin to--," She dramatically lowered her voice to mock her mother, "*manifest.* Other times, it could take a few weeks."

Elaine stopped going to school regularly around her 10th birthday. Her parents said she was ill and needed to homeschool on account of the voices in her head. She was excited at first, thinking that her mother would spend more time with her. Elaine quickly realized it just meant reading a lot of textbooks she could barely fumble through while sitting alone in the kitchen.

I may not be the sharpest tack, but even I know where I'm from.

She mulled over her problem in her head and tried to find the best way to ask the next question. "You say this happens to Efendian girls...." Elaine diligently tore at the reed edges of her stool again. "What about girls not from Efendi? This happens to them too?"

"No. I imagine they have other telltale signs of their monthly courses, but only Efendian women have Dua," Farisha answered.

"So...how would someone find out if it's Dua or just a regular ol' period?" Elaine asked.

Kara said, "Usually girls spend some time with the matriarch of our cluster, Kanne Da'neen. She helps guide you through what the different werks feel like and can help you through those first infuriating weeks when you want to call your Dua but can't."

Farisha smiled and ran her hands down Elaine's tangled hair. "Maybe it's worth some time with her, just in case you aren't aware of your full bloodline."

Elaine tried not to think of her parents too much. *They never thought of me when I lived underfoot; I can't imagine how few thoughts they give now that I'm gone. It only seems fair.* But she thought back to her mother's cold green eyes and her daddy's murky black that never matched her own dark brown peepers. She always assumed they were terrible parents because they were simply terrible parents---the way some people were just short---but she let herself think a hope of something that hadn't ever occurred to her.

What if they weren't my real parents? What if I'm really from here? Maybe the voices I've been hearing are a sign that I'm about to get some magic of my own.

The prospect of having her own Dua and a place here in Efendi trilled through her bones. She grinned widely despite the headache splitting her brain apart, and her mind swam with possibilities.

"I think I'd like that," she answered. Farisha nodded and said she'd arrange a meeting the next day while Kara hopped down to join the search party gathering outside in the courtyard.

Elaine grinned her way to the loft ladder, excited to imagine all the magic she'd soon wield. She imagined all the ways she'd finally be able to protect herself and girls like her with Dua when she thought of another question. "Do the voices go away when your Dua hits?"

The Hadishi women paused.

Farisha shook her head and spoke low, "We don't hear any voices, child. Are you hearing anyone speak now?"

Elaine looked at the two quizzically. *Technically, I don't hear anyone right now.* Kara shook her head behind her mother, giving Elaine another nudge at a lie. "No, ma'am. Just thought I heard someone mention it in the Trades."

She turned and crawled up the loft ladder, wondering once more why the voices called only to her.

***

The next morning Elaine peeked over the loft's edge to hear Reiki's update from the search. He looked exhausted as he leaning over his cup of dark tea, whispering.

"Nothing. We split into groups of five and walked every inch of the Silos. No one saw anything, and there was nothing left behind."

Kara picked her head up off Otum's shoulder. "Girls went missing from almost all of the clusters, though. Twenty-three

Towners were taken last night."

Farisha stifled a cry and muttered a prayer to Yapi. "I don't care if it is Hasateen," She said. "Neither of you is to go out past dark unless you are with a very large search party, and even then, no splitting off into groups smaller than four. Understood?"

Elaine thought the most telling sign of exhaustion was the fact that they simply nodded instead of arguing. Kara talked about the street festivals and dance parties of Hasateen ever since Elaine first arrived months ago. Elaine shuffled around noisier than necessary, and the family stopped whispering.

"Morning, Elai!" Otum said merrily. He put on his weathered reed hat and winced a little when he bent down to kiss his kids goodbye. Farisha and Kara shared another wordless look, and Reiki traded places with Elaine to sleep in the loft.

"Elai, I'm going to take you to Kanne Da'neen this morning for a couple hours. She's expecting us in the courtyard soon, but I need you to help me grab the grain bags first. Walk with me?" Kara asked.

The two took a skinny path behind the clusters, but Elaine frowned when Kara walked past the grain bags stored against the Perimeter Wall. The shadow of the massive umber stone wall cast her friend in gray light, but even this far down, Elaine felt the heat radiating from the fires hovering at the top of the wall. No guardswomen patrolled near their cluster or the next several clusters, but Reiki once pointed out how they changed guards to keep the fires burning high.

Kara stopped near an abandoned fire pit below a rudimentary carving of Ates in the Perimeter Wall. Kara was as tall as Reiki but with wild, short curls that she shuffled in agitation now. She knelt down, eye level with Elaine, and looked at her with a frankness that Elaine usually appreciated but was now a touch wary of.

"Kanne Da'neen is a good woman, kind and caring. But she is as superstitious as a lot of older Towners, so you have to be smart. When Reiki and I found you," Elaine studied her toes and tried to quell the panic rising when Kara put her hand on her shoulder. "No, Elai, it's ok. When we found you, do you remember what I told you?"

Elaine shuffled a pebble with her sandal and fiddled at a cuticle on her thumb. She remembered the dark shack and the sticky blood drying on her face. "You told me that I was safe and that I hit my head really bad."

"That's right. That's why you don't remember how you came here, and you need to keep not remembering when you're with Kanne Da'neen. Reiki and I made up some history for you so that our neighbors won't ask questions, but I don't know how long that will last. However, it's less important where you are from and more important that you never mention *how* you came here."

Elaine opened her mouth to fabricate a lie despite the memories flooding through her brain, but Kara shook her head.

"I love Reiki, but he's an idiot. He believes everyone is good and thinks that all of us should hold hands and sing together, which is why I have to watch his back. My parents are good people. They likely do not believe anything we told them, but they will never push you for the truth either. It's obvious to anyone that you were running from something, and they will always have a safe place for you."

Elaine shucked off a tear that fell out without warning. *I figured I'd eventually have to tell her, but I didn't think it'd be so soon. I don't want the Hadishi's to kick me out.* She began to think of the places she could hide in Efendi if it came to that, but Kara kept speaking.

"I can only protect you so much, Elai. If you want Efendi to be your home, you will have to be tough. Hold on to your story with your teeth, and do not let go no matter how much someone tugs."

"What happens if no Dua comes? What will they ask then?" Elaine asked.

"If no Dua comes, everyone will assume you are Dvarian or

from one of the lesser kingdoms past the Magara. If your *particular* Dua becomes obvious, then we will have a harder battle ahead of us."

Elaine nodded even though she didn't understand what she meant. She desperately wanted to be as magical as the city around her, regardless of how unlikely it was. *It's probably better then that I'll never get magic of my own,* she thought.

Kara took hold of either shoulder. "Follow these rules, and we'll be ok: Don't talk about how you got here. Always forget where you came from. And under no circumstances are you to ever, ever mention hearing voices in your head. Do that, and we'll figure out the rest together."

Elaine wanted to ask what the voices meant but knew she couldn't. So she kept nodding her head, alternating between hope that she'd hear the voices again and prayers that they left her alone once more. Kara studied her a moment longer and then held her hand as they made their way back to their cluster.

***

Kanne Da'Neen was a skinny pile of wrinkles. A sharp stick held together a tangle of white hair piled high on her head, and her liver-spotted hands gripped a rough-hewn stick that served as her cane. She waited for Elaine and Kara on the same rickety stool she told stories from at night in the courtyard. A couple of other matriarchs working from the steps nearby watched Elaine and Kara with interest. They turned away at Kara's hard stare.

"Sit, child. Time hasn't helped my eyesight, and I'd like a good look at you now that you aren't a fuzzy blob." Kanne Da'Neen said and waved Kara off. Kara winked at Elaine and left the cluster in the direction of the Trades.

Kanne Da'Neen ran her hands all over Elaine's face and down her arms, clucking disapprovingly. She examined Elaine like cattle, turning her clockwise and then back. *What does the old goat think she'll find in my ears?*

Kanne Da'Neen had Elaine to pick up a pinch of dirt from between the busted cobblestones under their feet. She made Elaine scoop a handful of water out of the low fountain behind them and later hold in an uncomfortably long breath. Without warning, Kanne Da'Neen snapped the fingers of her gnarled right hand, and a flame the size of a baseball appeared in her palm. Elaine leaned back at its abruptness and then inched forward to peer at the hovering flame in her hand.

"So cool! I haven't seen that up close. How does it work?" Elaine asked.

Kanne Da'Neen narrowed her eyes at Elaine but ignored the question. "If your Dua comes, it will come as naturally as the dirt between your toes, the water cupped in your hand, the breath in your body, and the heat from your blood," she said. "You do not think about walking or swallowing until it becomes restricted. Your mind is restricting your Dua, so your body is fighting it."

Elaine interrupted, "I'm sorry, ma'am, but what if I don't have any Dua?"

"Then you are not an Efendian and you can choose to remain here as an immigrant or go back to wherever you came from to live on, unblessed. But tell me this, are you sleeping well?"

Elaine shrugged, unsure what answer was correct.

"You are hot to the touch and breathing hard," she accused as she leaned into Elaine's personal space.

Well, it is 99 degrees here at sunrise and I'm being boxed in by an old woman and a bunch of onlookers. Elaine folded her arms. "Lots of people get hot."

"We Efendians grow up with the Dua of our mothers and aunts surrounding us. It's not natural for an Efendian girl to encounter Dua at your age for the first time, so perhaps you are not one of us. Time will tell. I am old, and the stairs to the Trades are long. If I'm to waste my time with an angry immigrant, I can at least use you to help me up the Fhazik steps so I can see something other than these prying eyes." She tilted her head, and the women moseying around the fountain blushed.

"Come. You are tall enough to be a decent walking stick at the least, and in return, I'll answer any question you have about Dua."

Elaine's annoyance quickly shifted into excitement. *Kara gets prickly whenever I ask about her Dua, and Farisha talks in riddles about hers. I might finally learn something useful with this one.* The pair walked through the neighboring clusters to the main staircase that would lead to the Trades.

Round clusters of lean-tos, similar to the Hadishi's, make up Low Town. Each community is sandwiched between the next Tier and each other. Elaine and Kanne Da'Neen wound a haphazard path over trash, meager vegetable beds, and kids running underfoot. Elaine thought back to when she first arrived and was given her first impromptu tour of Efendi. Any Efendian woman wanting to buy property in a Tier above the one they were born in had to gather recommendation letters from potential neighbors, as well as perform a test of Dua to show that they belonged. Men were automatically lumped into their matriarch's status, unable to deviate independently. Money could buy or bypass both requirements, but in Efendi, money and Dua went hand in hand.

Elaine and Kanne Da'Neen stopped at the broad base of the main staircase. Kanne Da'Neen grumbled something that sounded like an Efendian cussword before taking Elaine's shoulder to begin the trudge.

Staircases scattered throughout the kingdom were broken up by Tiers, which Elaine likened to plateaus of increasing status the higher one climbed. The homes that clung to the walls of the mountain under Efendi became more stable, more elaborate, and grander with each Tier until they ended at the Fountain Tier below the glittering domed Palace.

Elaine and Kanne Da'Neen stopped for a break at a Tier just below the Trades. Elaine ignored the pointed stares at her dingy beige clothes. "But what I don't get is how you pull fire from your blood?" Elaine asked after Kanne Da'Neen explained that she felt flush and loose-limbed whenever she called her Dua to her.

The old crone laughed and opened her weathered palm to Elaine. She nodded to the thin, silver rings around the first knuckle of her thumb and middle finger. Elaine could see a small, flat stone on the inside of one ring.

"Flint."

The matriarch snapped again closer to Elaine's face before continuing. "The second ring scrapes against the stone to produce a tiny spark. Our Dua does the rest." She closed her palm, smothering the flame. "All Duawielders keep their element close. Waterwerkers wear jewelry with vials of water just in case they aren't near a water source. The fountains are pretty, but they're everywhere because most middle-class Efendians work in water."

"And air?" Elaine asked.

"Do you see a lack of air anywhere?" Kanne Da'Neen waved her arms around her with an amused look on her face, and Elaine laughed with her.

"Some Groundwerkers will carry dirt in their pockets if they leave Efendi, but most of their power is lost while at sea. That's why most never leave for the islands," she continued.

"Why don't men have Dua?"

"Do the men in your kingdom birth children?" Kanne Da'Neen asked with a twinkle in her eye. "Why is it such a leap to think women have special powers when they already create us from a seed?"

Makes sense, Elaine thought, and she wondered if Kanne Da'Neen would let her play with the flint rings.

Kanne Da'Neen stood up from the step she had been resting on and placed a hand on Elaine's shoulder to continue up the last segment of stairs to the Trades. Elaine turned to help her, wondering how Firewerkers didn't get burned and accidentally knocked over a stone cup. Dark red liquid pooled in front of an unremarkable door, and Elaine jumped back to avoid its reach. A deep, familiar laugh chilled her to her bones.

She glanced around to find the owner of the laughter, ignoring whatever Kanne Da'Neen had just asked her, but they were alone. Her heart sped up, and she tried to breathe through her nose to tamp down the panic. She tapped her hand at her side with the increasing urge to flee. *I remember this voice. The others always felt harmless, but this one gives me the creeps.* The laugh came again, as if it heard her thoughts.

Not now. Not now. Not now, she thought.

"Are you alright, child?" Kanne Da'Neen asked.

She didn't understand why it was terrible to hear voices, but Kara always looked after her. *Don't let her think you hear something she's not,* Elaine thought. She ignored the laughter and the odd singsong voice filtering through her mind and focused on Kanne Da'Neen's voice instead.

"Yes, ma'am, just a touch dizzy is all," Elaine gave a weak smile, and the pair continued their climb up the steps. The walls faded from the beige tans of the lower Tiers to a turquoise color indicating the beginning of the Trades. She was watching her feet instead of the path ahead, so she saw the man's wide shadow before his face. Kanne Da'Neen sucked in her breath as the giant man from the Lantern Alley stood before them.

He rubbed his hand over a thick, red beard that ran past his chin and grinned yellowing teeth. "Hello Maman. Taking in another lost soul, eh?"

REED

The Itreni creature warily watched the standoff between Reed and Monti in the barn. "I'll give you a moment, but do not tarry. The tunnels are used by more creatures than me these days."

It turned and clicked out of the barn, leaving Reed to face the wrath of Monti after his admission. She backed away again, this time with the gun barrel aimed at his face.

"I don't care if you are the only person I know that can get me home. I will shoot you in the face if you don't tell me what's going on right now."

He held his hands up. "My name is Reed Wells. My mother and I fled this miserable nightmare of a world twelve years ago and have lived in the US since then. I only want to go back, even if it means prison for life."

"How did we get here?" Monti demanded. "What did you do?"

"I had nothing to do with this. Someone else, someone very powerful, and someone we never want to see is likely behind it."

"How did this person take us then? And why the prison?" She lowered the gun a touch but didn't put it away.

"I have no idea why the whole prison was taken. It's unheard of. There are people called Rifters here that can walk between realms. I've seen one take two people at a time along with themselves, but I didn't think it was possible to do anything on a large scale."

Monti on a mission was surprisingly succinct. She turned but didn't pause her interrogation as Reed shucked off the prison garb in favor of the white shirt he found.

"How do we get home?" She asked.

"The only way to leave is to find another Rifter. They were hunted almost to extinction before I was born. The best chance to find one is in the mountains, but it's a full day's ride from here."

"How are you so sure it wasn't one of the other prisoners trying to get out?"

"Because Rifters are only women, and you were likely the only woman in there during the Rift."

Monti opened for another question, but Reed stepped close to her. He gently took the gun from her hand and slid it into the holster hidden at her back, careful to not startle her. Reed was more than a little satisfied at her sharp inhale and to see her eyes dip to his lips for a millisecond. He mentally shook himself back to the problem at hand. *What is wrong with you? Focus.*

He spoke quietly in case the Itreni hovered nearby. "I promise, I will answer every question you have once we are out of here, but right now, the only chance we have at shelter is with a creature thought too dangerous to live near humans. It's important that you follow my lead and do not speak. It's not safe for both of us to sleep below ground at once, so I'll take the first watch when we get settled."

"Let's get one thing straight if you want me to be at all cooperative," Monti said as she stepped back. "I am getting the *hell* out of this place with my dad, and you are going to help me. I don't care who else comes with us, but that is our only goal. Understood?"

"Yes," Reed said, relieved that this woman who had

complained and harassed him since they arrived was on the same page. He walked to the slim opening between the Aygirs but stilled at her cool hand on his arm.

"And we are going to have an awfully long chat when we're out of here, but answer this first," she said. "What is Sakalid?"

He ignored the feel of her soft hand on his forearm and let himself acknowledge the shit storm of his situation. "You're standing in it. Welcome to Sakalid, realm of magic and misery."

ELAINE

A July sun is slow to sink in South Carolina, but Elaine found her gator just as pockets of the marsh turned dark with twilight. She had tied her DIY dinner of a PB&J and a Coke in a plastic bag to her handlebars and was barreling down the brackish water's edge to the spot she'd deemed most appealing to a gator days before. She didn't see the scutes barely submerged in the dark creek when she unpacked her feast, or when she shucked off her shoes, or even when she dipped her sandy toes in the water. She wasn't sure how long the living fossil had been watching her, but when she did, she knew in her bones that he'd had his black coin eyes on her for a while.

Elaine felt the same way looking at Hvard Canavar.

"Hvard, you look as bearded as usual," Kanne Da'Neen said nonchalantly. However, she stepped in between Elaine and the brutal-looking man towering over her on the steps to the Trades.

He rolled the edge of his coarse beard in between a calloused thumb and a forefinger and let the barb roll off his meaty shoulder. "Why don't you introduce us, Maman?"

"Hvard, this is Elai. Elai, this is my son, Hvard. Now, I'm afraid we were just leaving, so have care."

Her son? The cane Kanne Da'Neen used was more substantial

than the collection of wrinkles and bones that made up Kanne Da'Neen. She rapped it on the stones twice and pulled Elaine down a step.

"I'll walk you down. Wouldn't want anything to happen to you, would we?"

Hvard took the old woman's hand off her shoulder and placed it on his tattooed forearm. Black ink warred with freckles, scars, and strawberry blonde hair in the vague shape of a massive octopus ravishing a boat.

Elaine still fought to quiet the chanting voices flitting between her ears, so she almost didn't hear Hvard's question.

"My Maman is such a kind soul, little Elai. Has she told you of the little boy she took in years before you?"

Elaine shook her head, not meeting his eyes. She watched his meaty hand pin Kanne Da'Neen's frail hand in the crook of his arm. Her flint rings pressed flat and far apart from each other over the Leviathan tattoo.

Kanne Da'Neen stared grimly straight ahead and said nothing.

"There was once a little boy who was born to a powerful house. The woman decided, though, that her home was no place for someone without Dua, so she cast him out to live in the streets," he said.

Elaine glanced at Kanne Da'Neen in question, but he shook his head.

"No. This lovely woman was not the little boy's birth mother. She found him months later, fighting rats for food in the Silos. It took her years to become the second mother to abandon him," Hvard said.

The high sun baked Elaine's scalp. People pressed around them on the stairs like water filtering through a rock crevice, yet Elaine shivered. Her legs itched to run, and Elaine tapped her fingers against her leg in agitation. *I could run, but I don't wanna leave Kanne Da'Neen with this creep, even if she calls him "son."* She stilled her fingers when she saw Hvard watching them tap, brows furrowed.

"Hvard. My house has always been open to you, but not to your cruelty. Yapi has forgiven us for many faults and would welcome you again if you admitted your guilt," Kanne Da'Neen said as she gripped her cane.

He barked a laugh that boomed between the walls of the staircase. A few people gave them a wide birth despite the lack of space. There was nothing merry in his laugh.

"I need Yapi like I need your pathetic flame." He spit on the ground just as a lanky man with matching C tattoos around his eyes approached and whispered something to Hvard.

"I'm afraid I have to leave. Perhaps I will come around soon, Maman, to visit with you and your little one. There is something familiar in this one." His eyes washed over Elaine again before abruptly leaving, and she shivered despite the heat.

Neither said anything on the walk back down. The chanting Elaine had heard was finally quiet, but Kanne Da'Neen would not look at her. Elaine looked around for a way to shatter the palatable silence between them when Kanne Da'Neen finally spoke.

"Hvard had been alone for almost a year when I found him. He barely came to my waist and was as feral as the wild Kingalias in the valley. I thought time would lessen his anger towards his mother, towards Dua in general, but it built on itself as his life unfolded. He hated working in the fields and thought other Towner work was beneath him. He blamed his mother, me, and the women around us for his lack of upward mobility, and he started to lash out in his teens physically. He left the city for Dvari for a few years and later spent another year on a Perisien raider ship. Yapi forgive me, but I was sad when he returned.

"He spent time in the dungeons for stealing, but when a girl from a cluster around the bend accused him of rape, I forbade him from coming home. I didn't see or hear from him for many years until word of the 'Canavar Company Troupe' made its way to Low

Town. He had collected other men like him and formed a popular performing caravan that came around Efendi for a few months each year. I was happy for him."

Elaine prompted her when she stopped speaking, "And then what?"

Kanne Da'Neen stopped the two of them before they entered their cluster. "Something happened. I'm not sure what. He dropped the troupe but not all of the men, and they became simply the Canavar Company. He claims he's a merchant now, but I'd wager my cane that there is nothing legal or moral about what he trades."

Kanne Da'Neen told Elaine they'd meet each morning again for the rest of the week. Elaine was at the Hadishi door when Kanne Da'Neen stopped her.

"I don't believe Hvard will come here again, Elaine, but if he does, stay as far away from him as you can."

Elaine nodded solemnly. *I know a thing or two about keeping away from bad men.*

***

Kara's irritability hit new heights the next few mornings, so Elaine happily stayed out of the way. She harassed Kanne Da'Neen with every question she could think of regarding Dua without asking the one question she desperately needed to be answered. She sat with Otum to mend grain bags by the fountain and helped Reiki in the Trades. She searched for the pockets where she could hear the voices again to no avail. Efendians watched each other warily, and even the Trades felt thick with tension as more reports of disappearances occurred. Elaine kept her romps through the Trades closer to their stall, ignoring her increasing urge to explore. She chewed her nails to stubs as she scanned the crowded Trades for any sign of the Canavar Company men.

Reiki finally caved after several hard hours of whining about taking her out for proper exploring on one particularly slow day in the Trades. It was either the whining or Kara's festering mood that prompted him to take her farther than she'd ever been, all the way down to the Dockside outside the Perimeter Wall. *Maybe I'll hear the girls' voices again down there.*

Elaine's makeshift map in her journal put the Palace squatting at noon, so the Dockside was somewhere around three o'clock in the bend at the very base of the Tiers. It took even longer to walk there because Reiki stopped, or was stopped, by almost every young woman in the Trades. They finally reached the street that would lead them to the Dockside when Reiki leaned against a stall at its edge to talk to another Pillar out of his league.

Elaine tapped her foot anxiously against the stone. *I'm never going to find out if I hear the voices in the Dockside if we stop every two minutes.*

Reiki's laugh grated her, and she snapped, "You about done?"

The attractive brunette laughed like Elaine was adorable. Elaine desperately wished that she had pull with water to dump the cascading fountain nearby over her head. Instead, she settled for glaring mutiny at the pair while she tapped her foot on the steps.

What is wrong with me?

She thought back to one of the last days she'd seen her parents. Elaine was starving, but the only food in the house was moldy bread, a few cans of expired Spaghetti-O's, and shelves of PBR. Ma had waltzed out of the house hours earlier to load up on the back of a motorcycle with a man Elaine hadn't ever seen. Her Da blared a crap sitcom with the same laugh track set to go off every three minutes. Her head ached, she was hungry, and despite the dark sky outside, the trailer was still hot and sticky. She opened the screen door to hunt down a breeze anywhere but there when her dad scowled at her.

"Where the hell do you think you're going?" He slurred.

She was as agitated then as she felt now, which is why she didn't catch herself snapping, "What d'you care?"

She should have run then, but she didn't have anywhere to

run to. Her Da stood up from his recliner and pushed the TV tray away, pills rolling across its laminate surface. She felt the first hit square across her face, but not the second, or third, or the kicks to her ribs. When she came to in a hospital bed, a police officer spoke to her Ma in the corner.

When the officer left, her Ma came to her side and hissed, *"What did you do?"*

She never told Kara or Reiki that the gash on her head was from stitches torn apart. She couldn't walk well those first couple weeks in Efendi, and it was Reiki that waited on her hand and foot with warm broth and water. Reiki and Kara protected her, and their family made her feel safe for the first time in her life.

Water welled in Elaine's eyes as she juggled guilt with irritation again. "I'm sorry, I shouldn't have said that," Elaine mumbled to Reiki when he walked away from the disappointed brunette.

He shrugged and wore the easy smile he slipped on often. "She's one of many Efendian beauties, but there's only one Dockside to explore."

They ran down the widening steps, and Elaine relished the salt-tinged breeze she could finally feel. The Dockside is a mess of rotting wood, rank fish heads, and booze-tinged sweat to some. But according to Reiki, it is also a gateway to green-blue seas, opportunity, and kingdoms without walls.

He chatted animatedly about the goods hauled down from a large boat and sniffed a fistful of coffee beans from an open barrel. He pointed out all the names of the vessels and convinced a bored Airwerker to show Elaine how she could fill one side of the billowing sails to steer the boat ahead of them. It was as bustling as the Trades, but the chaos felt driven by purpose and destination rather than the slow stroll and idle chat of the colorful Tier far above. Throughout it all, Elaine strained for a hint of the voices again, but to her disappointment, she heard nothing.

Elaine sidestepped a man rolling several barrels with a stick, only to run into another standing atop an upturned crate.

Sweat poured down his temples and into his black cloak with ripped edges. "Hear me, men! The time of the Edicisi has come! Forfeit your gambling, your disease, and your worries. Make your offerings and await the Rectification!"

A Waterwerker sitting on the railing of a gleaming jade-toned ship nearby shot a stream of seawater into the man's face. She and several other women laughed at him sputtering on the ground.

"What's a Rectification?" Elaine asked, chomping on the smoked fish Reiki passed her from a Dockside vendor.

He held his fish stick in between his teeth while he wrapped his dark hair into a high bun off his neck. He said around the stick, "It's the same bokki Kanne Da'Neen makes up at night."

He bought her a cold, pink-hued drink that tasted like sugared cranberries and himself a dark, frothy ale from a neighboring vendor. They sat on weathered barrels-turned-tables outside of a rowdy bar before he continued.

"The thing is, Kanne Da'Neen's stories are just stories. Some men, and some women mind you, put their faith and rage into a false god like the Edicisi. Instead of listening to folklore, they hear prophets, and instead of making the best of what they have, they wait for a monster to even the playing field."

"I don't get it. What good does a monster like the Edicisi do for them?"

Reiki leaned back against the stone wall to face the rows of various ships and boats wading in the emerald sea a few paces away. "Legend says that the Edicisi can gain power by eating Dua from Duawielders. He can suck up their talents temporarily by touching them and use the power against them."

He nodded towards the damp-haired man climbing back up to his pulpit. He had a crudely drawn white skull on the back of his cloak, its bone jaw gaping wide. She shivered in the heat.

"That's why, in every story, the Edicisi is always scooping up something in his mouth. He's draining the power from the Efendian Duawielders."

Elaine thought back to the smiling grandmother stamped all over Low Town and the stories Kanne Da'Neen told of the soft-spoken nature goddess. "But if Yapi is so kind and peace-loving, why would she make the Edicisi?"

"Dua is derived from nature, and in nature there is always balance. Our Efendian ancestors had a hard time explaining why only women are blessed with Dua when men are not, so they fabricated this immortal being that drags himself up from the Batiwood every thousand years or so to even out the Tiers. Some believe that the Edicisi is the rightful ruler of this land, and outside these walls, some of the other kingdoms would love to see an Efendi without the advantage of an Ordu of Duawielders...regardless of who replaced our Queen."

"What is 'ordu'?"

"It's the host of Duawielders Firtina commands when she is at war."

That sounds awesome. "Why does Firtina allow the Edicisi to be honored by Hasateen then?" Elaine idly stacked the coins Reiki gave her and tried to figure out which ones bought the tart drink she'd downed.

Reiki laughed and pointed out the two smallest black coins. "I'll answer another hundred of your questions if you fetch me an ale when you get your fizz cup."

She dashed off, and when her hands were sticky with overflowing foam, they toasted.

Reiki continued, "They're not really honoring the Edicisi at Hasateen. It's more of a decoration to go with the spooky feel some of the Hasateen parties favor. Queen Firtina would never allow even that if she thought he was real."

"But that guy thinks he's real?" Elaine asked.

"He wants to believe he's real. The Edicisi of our stories only comes to take his rightful place as ruler when the Efendian Queen is deemed unsuitable by the Goddesses. Queen Firtina's grandmother started the tradition of dressing like the Edicisi during Hasateen as a lark, and it caught on. And yet, you will rarely find anyone openly worshiping the Edicisi."

He raised his glass to gesture to the cloaked man now shouting about deliverance and justice on his crate. "*That* man has a death wish. Queen Firtina is not known for her tolerance of anyone discussing a change in leadership, particularly because there are now several Pillars of powerful houses that could challenge Princess Alik for the throne when Firtina dies."

"So what's with the cups of blood?" Elaine asked, remembering the cup she accidentally knocked over on her first walk with Kanne Da'Neen. She'd seen a few more tucked under eaves since then and thought it was a disgusting way to decorate for a holiday.

Reiki paused with his beer halfway to his mouth. "Where did you see cups?"

"I dunno. Stairs to the Trades, saw another in a cluster around the bend—the one with the garden, you know?"

He shook his head and watched the colorful sails bob in the harbor for a few minutes. Elaine learned a while back that the Hadishis let go of the best information if given enough time. So she waited.

"That's a little different. Dressing like the Edicisi is a joke, but the cups are meant to be an offering to his Handmaiden Rifters."

"The witches that skinned people for his cloak?" Elaine shivered again. "They drink blood, too?" Stories of ghosts and monsters never frightened her much, but witches scared the heck out of her.

"I don't know what a 'witch' is, but the Handmaidens are based on true stories of a dark time in Efendi. Some women had the power to move unseen and shift to new places across the land with only a thought, though they were rare. They were only called Handmaidens in the stories about the Edicisi. The real ones were called Rifters, but they were hunted to extinction a long time ago."

The fizz cup in Elaine's belly suddenly settled about as well as a stone dropped on a pile of chicken eggs. She took a few moments to gather her questions and ignore the chills scampering across her body. "What's the difference between that power and regular Dua?"

"It was unnatural. Duawielders have to use the elements already found in nature—they can't fabricate their werk from nothing." He swigged the ale before continuing.

"See, Rifters only had to use their minds to go anywhere. I'm not even sure I would call what they do 'Dua' really. Because they could travel without restrictions or laws, unknown to anyone, they were dangerous. Some of them became notorious criminals. A particularly crazy Rifter went on a killing spree murdering dozens of Efendians, including children, before being caught and killed.

"After that, the Iktidars declared a kingdom-wide hunt to kill any Rifters found. A few probably escaped to Magara or the islands beyond Efendi, though they were hunted worldwide. Some might have been desperate enough to shelter in the Batiwood, and every decade or so, people claim they've seen a Rifter in the Tiers, and another Hunt begins.

"Are there any left?"

"No. I can't imagine there are any left. It's hard to hide as a Rifter. Nature takes something from everyone, and they began to show physical signs of the toll."

Reiki brought their glasses back to the vendor, and the pair walked across the cracked gray wood pocked with watermarks towards the stairs. Elaine fiddled with the hem of her linen shirt, her heart racing and palms damp with sweat.

"What kind of signs?" Elaine asked, dread and anxiety warring in her belly.

"Well, for one, most of them acted crazy. They talked to themselves, swore they heard voices in their head. Duawielders can get sick if they don't use their talents, and Rifters were no different. The ones trying to hide would not Rift for prolonged periods to avoid detection, so they got sick and weak. The Iktidars learned that if you tied down a Rifter with a chain made from a particular metal, they'd be unable to Rift. After enough time, their minds gave out, and they'd either die from insanity, or their bodies would begin to decay from the inside. That's part of how the cups of blood fit in—apparently drinking it revived them."

Reiki continued, not noticing Elaine's shallow breathing or face paling. "Anyway, avoid people putting those cups out. That is something that could attract the Iktidars' attention, and the last thing you'd want is to find yourself in front of Queen Firtina."

ALIK

Alik lifted the wayward curls that clung to her neck under the sun's oppressive heat. *This is a waste of time,* she thought. She stood from the table, the abrupt movement startling the emissaries and threatening to topple her chair. *It's been three days since Shauna disappeared, three days of trade negotiations I've barely heard, and three days of Agnian skipping every meeting.*

Alik sat in the meetings with Damari's Eyes the previous mornings. They'd turned up little about the missing women and now tracked all of Agnian's movements as well. Despite her brothers' opinions, Alik was convinced he had something to do with it. *Yet they'd found nothing.* She stalked inside from the outdoor terrace, leaving the heavyset emissary calling after her with a question she hadn't heard. She spent most of the morning scanning each emissary, trying to read what lies they were telling her but ended up with only a splitting headache.

I need sleep, she thought. She snuck out each night, scanning the crowds within the Tiers with her Dua, but was no closer to finding Shauna and the others than she was the night Shauna disappeared. Haunting images of a dark mouth gaping wide from her nightmares hung over her like a blade on a feather. *I know the dream means something, but what?* A woman dressed in soft white and walking on silent feet bumped into her, littering the floor with Alik's papers. Alik managed to swallow the curse halfway out of her mouth when she realized who ran into her.

"Forgive me, my Pillar. Please, let me," Mara handed the papers back to Alik and left without another word. Alik opened the note she slipped in and hurried to her study.

A map of the Tiers dominated her study wall now, littered with pins marking the last-known locations of the missing girls. *125,* she thought, *23 more since First Night. All of whom are missing from Tiers above the Trades now.* She touched the pin representing Shauna. *The Elite can't ignore this anymore, yet still, no word from Mother or her advisors on any progress made.* Alik gritted her teeth at the memory of her mother's advisor shutting the door in her face at the council meeting the day before.

She ran a hand over the map, marking the latest missing girl's Dua in a note beside her pin. *Where are you, Shauna?* She rubbed at her eyes, willing them to see something she missed before.

Damari entered without knocking. He looked over the strewn papers and her haggard appearance.

Say something, Alik dared silently.

"Agnian is a dead-end, Alik. Mara confirmed this morning that he spent the last two nights stalking the streets before winding up at the same tavern, alone."

"Stalking?" She asked.

Damari said, "Mara's words. He seems to be looking for something every night, and yet each night, before half night, he's back at The Kech until sunrise."

Why do I know that tavern? Alik thought through her recent conversations with Damari, the advisors' half-hearted updates on the missing girls, and her secret romps through the Tiers as a teenager with Shauna. Her chest constricted at the thought of Shauna's laughing eyes and terrible dancing.

"That's it! I know that tavern. Shauna took us dancing there one night while her mother was still alive. Her mother worked at

The Kech but quit when it became a haunt for the Canavar Company's trolls. Agnian must have ties to them."

Damari looked wary. "I have multiple Eyes within Canavar Company now. It's not them. And Taavi can't put any more men on it. Firtina has specifically forbidden his involvement and has sent them to try to flush out the Magarans."

"What? Why would she do that? It's the middle of Hasateen, and we have a crisis on our hands for Atessake!" Alik threw her hands up in the air, upending a platter of forgotten food from the night before.

"You told her, then?" Taavi asked before the door was even shut. "It's been weeks since the Magarans last met with our patrols. The treaty is clear: They must report each week. Add the fact that there are packs of Yurutecs within sight of our perimeter and—"

"Just keep nodding, Taavi. No objection from her favorite child, isn't that right?" Alik mocked. "The Magarans are constantly pushing back; that's nothing new. Someone is coming in and going out with—" Alik stumbled at whether or not to use the word "dead," and she fought off tears while starting again. "Someone is leaving with our countrywomen. Dozens, potentially, at a time. And if they're not leaving, they're hiding them here, and you're off like it's any other day on patrol."

Taavi's neck flushed red before the color flooded his face. "You're not the only one who loves Shauna, Alik. Damari has been out every night since she disappeared, and he is working on less than five hours of sleep, total. I've had every man at my disposal combing the Tiers and No. One. Has. Seen. Anything."

Alik folded her arms level with Taavi's stomach, glaring up at him. "Girls do not just disappear into thin air, yet *somehow*, that's exactly what happened."

"There are some women who can disappear into thin air," Damari said quietly, diffusing the tension between his two older siblings.

"Oh, right. I can just see Mother's face if I tell her I think it's a *Rifter.* I might as well tell her the Edicisi is here to claim the throne," Alik said.

"They were eradicated decades ago, for one, and I think I would have felt something as powerful a Rift right next to me." Flashes of chasing a girl through the Silos in her dreams came to mind, but she shook her head.

"No. We focus on the evil that's in front of us and not buried in folklore. Damari, I'm going with your Eye tonight to watch Agnian. Taavi, don't start—" Alik held a hand before Taavi.

He tossed his hands in the air on par with his little sister's temper. "Think, Alik. Girls are going missing all over this kingdom. Someone took Shauna while she was next to you. Has it occurred to you that maybe they missed and were aiming for *you?"*

"Of course I have! All the more reason I have to find her! She was out that night because of me." The fountains around her study threatened to overflow, but her brothers, fortunately, said nothing at her flared Dua. She rubbed her hands over her face, eschewing the dark charcoal eye makeup the interloper her mother sent as her maid did that morning.

Taavi asked, "What if they're trying to use Shauna as bait to get to you? Have you considered that? She might not even be alive, Alik."

Every muscle tensed, and it took Alik a few moments not to shove every scrap of Dua she had at him. "Do not say that. She is alive. And I will find her."

"How, Alik?" He asked, arms crossed.

"I don't know. But I know this: I've doubted myself every step of my life, but there is no room for doubt when it comes to finding her and the others. So either help me or get out of my way."

She headed for the door, "I'll meet your Eye in a few hours, Damari." Nodding once, "Taavi."

She stalked out of the room before she could embarrass herself with more tears. She knew she needed sleep, but guilt kept her from even trying. She glared at a woman in a bright yellow sari trilling with laughter at another Pillar in the hall. *I just need a place where there aren't packs of courtiers milling about to think. If word got out that this many Efendian Daughters are missing, no one cares.* The laughter and gossip in the Atrium made Alik want to shatter every window above their heads.

She found herself weaving through the orchards that she and Shauna walked through on First Night. She made her way to the hearth of Ates at the far end. No guards stood at the stone arch leading to the hidden passageway, but that was to be expected, given it was still daylight. She leaned back against its cold stone and breathed a sigh of relief at the thick shade the canopy provided above. She half-closed her eyes when she saw the figure.

The rudimentary offering was tucked away in the corner of the grove in the underbrush. Even from this distance, the shape felt off. Alik didn't need to get closer, though, to know it was an offering to the Edicisi. The reeds tied together and painted black formed a small doll with its arms held out to a T and its head bowed. Dark red liquid filled the cup next to the effigy.

Alik shuddered when she picked it up, and the dark gaping mouth from her dreams flashed before her eyes.

You're ridiculous, Alik. It's just a pile of straw. Damari's suggestion that Rifters could be back echoed in her mind once more. *It's Hasateen. Some child from the Palace is likely playing pranks. But why here? Hardly anyone comes to this end of the orchard any more.* She eyed the dark red liquid again. *That's harder to explain if it's real.*

Only the very desperate openly worshiped the Edicisi and his Handmaidens, and an insult like this within the Palace walls was akin to poking a Garfu in the side. The effigy could be overlooked as a Hasateen prank. She sniffed the cup and shivered again. Blood. *The cup for a Handmaiden Rifter is a death sentence, though.*

At least a dozen people in the Palace knew of this passageway, but Alik couldn't help but remember how they'd taken Agnian here just a few days before. *It still doesn't make any sense why someone would leave an offering here of all places—let alone a Dvarian.*

What if the Dvarians are trying to contact a Rifter? What if they already have? Goddesses, I'm losing my mind if that's where my search has turned.

"Filb it. I've got time." She tugged the lever behind Ates and walked down the stone passageway.

***

Alik intended to wait at the base of the stairwell to confirm that Agnian used it to sneak out of the Palace. Patience had never been a strength of hers, which is how she ended up walking through the Trades again, scanning auras in hopes of finding something. Anything.

"I'd kill for the breeze the Airwerkers push through the Palace right now," Alik muttered to herself as she unstuck the sweaty veil plastered to her face.

She walked past a stall selling honeyed Kingalia meat when she felt eyes on her. Spinning around, she scanned the sea of people bumping around her but found no telling black or gray swirls. She couldn't shake the feeling that someone watched her. Taavi's suggestion that the kidnappers meant to take her came to mind again. *I'll come back with one of Damari's Eyes.*

She aimed for the busy, guarded staircase a few streets past the hidden one she took down. *I could shout, but that would only give the vying houses another reason to push me off the throne.* She is the daughter of the most notorious Pillar in Efendian history. *Mother would rather see me dead in an alley than beg for aid from a merchantress in the Trades.* She tripped over a metal cup at the edge of the Tier and dark red liquid pooled out at her feet, flaring her Dua in alarm involuntarily.

What in the Ates?

Blood iced in her veins when she lifted her eyes to the crowd. A tall figure cloaked in black stood still in the river of people several paces ahead. She couldn't get a good look at his face, but pitch-black mist engulfed the space where he stood.

Alik ducked into the nearest alley. She blinked rapidly to clear her eyes, praying to Ates that a flame was nearby. She was marginally adept at Firewerk and could use it for self-defense if left no other choice. Colorful lanterns floated above the alley like a carpet of rainbow glass. She sprinted down the narrow passage, frantically pushing locked doors on either side to find a hiding place. The path curved, and she suddenly found herself at a dead end. The deep violet-colored lanterns above blocked out most of the sun. Alik yanked the veil off her face to see her attacker better as footsteps thundered from around the bend in the alley.

Bird calls echoed around her, and the same gaping wide mouth from her dreams flashed in Alik's mind. Laughter rang throughout the alley, but it reverberated so much that Alik wondered if she imagined it instead. A firm grip grabbed her from behind, and a hand muffled her scream.

"Shh, Alik, it's me." A whisper of scruff brushed her jawline and the patch of skin below her ear. She stopped struggling at Agnian's voice. "Quickly, through here."

He shoved open the last door, hugging Alik to his chest to conceal her face. She glimpsed several men seated at a couch beneath scantily clad women and bare-chested men through the corner of her eye. Agnian picked up a thick bottle of wine with a broad base, obscuring her view further.

"I'll take thissa one," he slurred, stumbling but never letting Alik stand fully. Someone close to her mumbled a response, and a bag of coins jingled as Agnian tossed it over her shoulder. He swayed, dragging her left and right down a dark hallway lit only by candles. They abled through, his heart thudding wildly under her cheek. Panic pulsed her Dua; her eyes focused and refocused over and over in the dark hallway.

Alik flushed at the naked flesh inside several open doorways as they passed. "Almost there," Agnian breathed in her hair.

Voices up ahead of them, arguing in whispers. "How could you let her slip?"

"I wasn't sure it was her!"

"Do you know what this means? He'll kill us if he finds out we let *her* go when she was right there."

"She has to be here somewhere. There's nowhere else to go."

The men ran towards them. Agnian shoved Alik through the closest open doorway into an empty room. He pushed her on the bed, his heavy muscular body pressing down on hers while his hand tugged up her thigh before she even processed what was happening. She shoved at him with a cry at her lips when he covered her mouth again with his hand. The sharp tang of metal from his rings danced over her tongue, his dangling silver necklace pooled into a cold mound over her chest.

His eyes did not waver from hers when he said, "I need you to trust me, or we are both dead."

She barely finished her nod before he pressed his lips against hers. She'd been kissed by courtiers before, small wet pecks and hard, distracted tongues. This was demanding and something entirely different. Full lips, intense and not nearly enough at the same time, moved on hers, and all thoughts fled. He cradled her head in his palm, pulling her halfway on top of him with her back to the door. Her right leg straddled him, the slit of her lightweight dress shoved wide so that every inch of her touched Agnian.

The door burst open, its thud a crash of glass to Alik's emptied mind. Agnian kept Alik's head to him, facing the opposite wall. He roared out, "What in the Atessake am I paying for? Shut the filbish door!"

Someone muttered before shutting the door. Agnian held Alik still for a moment more and then, without looking at Alik in the eyes, untangled himself and was off the bed, ear pressed against the door. She had yet to move from the bed. *That is what a kiss is supposed to feel like?*

Her mind had yet to come up for air when he hissed, "What are you doing? Let's go!"

Flustered and mortified, she stood and adjusted herself. Agnian glanced at her wide eyes while she fumbled with her veil. A brush of impatient air and his fingers reattached the hooks near her temples. His eyes caught hers for a moment before he said, "Please tell me that wasn't your first kiss."

Alik shoved at him, "No. Not really. At least—Ruzgar bless. Can we get out of here?"

I will beat that smirk off his face, she thought as he stuck his head out the door. After a few more minutes of fumbling through the dark, they came to a guarded doorway. Alik kept focused on the jade tile floor while Agnian exchanged some unintelligible pleasantries. They stepped into the main corridor of the Trades, quickly getting swept into the throng of people unconcerned with the life-altering kiss she just had.

He gripped her hand as they strode through the crowd. *He's heading for the ferry launch*, she thought in a panic. She pulled his hand. "I can't. Not yet."

His eyes searched hers. He nodded once, pulling Alik instead up the stairs above the Trades that ran alongside the floating boats. He stopped a few Tiers below the Palace and spoke Dvarian to a waiter setting up tables at a tiny cafe at the edge of the Tier. Alik's body sank in the wooden chair, and she watched the sun begin its slow descent behind the Magarans as the drumbeats for Hasateen began far below.

They didn't speak until the waiter left them with the food and wine. Their chairs aimed towards each other, lovers to anyone else, but Alik bristled inside for a fight. Anything to keep her mind off that kiss.

Focus, Alik, there is much more at stake.

"What was that place?" She asked.

He looked at her flatly. "The Lantern Pit is notorious throughout lands beyond even Efendi. It's a maze within the

Trades where anything can be purchased with discretion."

She remembered the girl younger than Damari at the edge of a bed they'd passed at the end, eyes dead, holding herself.

"Firtina will never let this stand. There was a girl---"

He snapped, "There are hundreds of girls, and hundreds of boys, too. Open your eyes, Alik. Efendi is the biggest importer of flesh. Most of those women and men were sold as children stolen from their homes in lands beyond your borders. Who do you think sanctions it?"

Alik pushed away the bread that turned to sponge in her throat, shaking her head.

"You're blinded by whatever grudge you carry against my family. Just because your people don't like our involvement in Dvarian affairs doesn't mean we're evil."

Agnian looked like he was going to chew on his own broken teeth. He clenched the fork in his hand as he ground out, "And you are an idiot if you think your *involvement* in my country's affairs is anything short of evil. No wonder you are too blind to see why your Efendian girls are disappearing."

Alik reared back as if slapped; the candles at the edge of the Tier flickered higher. *He does know something.* The scrape of chairs and distant conversations faded. *And that is the only reason why I should not shove him off the Tier with an Airwerk. Or a chair.*

Perhaps sensing her murderous thoughts, Agnian held up his hands placatingly and said, "I'm sorry, that was uncalled for. I rarely keep a level head while discussing Efendi's actions in my kingdom."

He huffed out a breath and ran his hands along his stubble before saying, "I don't think you are your mother. Or grandmother."

No one does. I am as far from the powerful women in my family as one could be, Alik thought, tracing the edges of the soft linen napkin in her lap.

Agnian reached across and grabbed her hand. "No, Alik. That

is a compliment. To be honest, I'd never met an Efendian that I liked until you. You and I want the same thing."

Alik tamped down the traitorous thrill running through her and focused on more important matters. She pulled her hand from his warm palm and reached for her wine. "And what is that?"

"To find who is responsible for your missing girls."

She stilled, the wine glass hovering at her lips. *This is it.* "What do you know about the missing Daughters?"

He pulled a small leather book, curved from its life in a back pocket, from his leather pants. Scrawled names in columns. "One hundred and twenty, yes?"

"One hundred and twenty-three," she allowed.

"I know that the kidnapper is looking for specific abilities," he said. "And since the latest missing girls are more high profile, I believe they are looking for someone in particular who has been hiding. We believe the kidnappings will only stop once they've found whomever they are looking for."

"The men that chased me in the Trades. They felt---off," Alik said, fumbling for how to explain without disclosing her ability to read auras. "Are they the ones kidnapping my countrywomen?"

"I was following one of Canavar's men to find that out until I had to stop and save your life. Why would you come here, of all places anyway, with no protection? Or do you frequent these halls?"

She ignored his questions, focusing instead on his admission. Loyalty to the Iktidar line was never a choice for Alik; straying from its harsh line felt akin to wandering the valley below unarmed and alone. Her role was to make sure Efendians knew the Iktidar family was unwavering in its responsibilities as protectors of the realm. It also meant that the other kingdoms must never glimpse their weaknesses.

What will you do when she dies, Alik? She cast that constant companion aside.

"Why would a Dvarian dig so far into an Efendian matter?

What is in it for you?" She asked, keeping her voice low. *Tell me why you're really here.*

He laughed—a cold, harsh sound lost to the air cooling rapidly with the moonrise. "*That's* your concern? Now I understand how you can be content to sit at the negotiation table while your best friend is still missing."

Alik straightened, anger and embarrassment and incredulity raging across her face again. *I would give anything to find Shauna. Including maiming this man if I must to find out what he knows.*

He continued before she could argue, leaning into her space over the bistro table, "The problem with Efendians is that you never leave your borders. You have no idea what ramifications this has across our world. What it could mean."

What? She quickly scanned him with a glance of Dua, not caring if he noticed how her pupils dilated in and out. Frustrations of orange, flares of red hate, and bright yellow incredulity mixed together, but no lies. "Tell me what it means then, Agnian. What do you know?"

He rubbed his hands over his face; silver rings catching in the candlelight dancing in glass on the Tier edge. Small, black tattoos etched the edges of his fingers, symbols unfamiliar to Alik. He looked at her, gaze unflinching.

"Trade me a truth, Alik. I'll tell you what I know if you answer me honestly." At her wary nod, "Do you think Firtina is doing *anything* about the missing girls?"

The lie was halfway out of her mouth when she shut it. She had no reason to trust this man and every reason to listen to the lessons of obedience and loyalty drilled into her since birth. *But it's Shauna missing. And I've failed the others long enough.* A beat, and a few words shifted her place in this world: "No. I know she is not doing anything to find them."

He nodded grimly. "We believe Firtina is not only doing nothing to find them, but she is the one sanctioning their kidnappings."

That's the most ridiculous thing I've heard since Damari suggested Rifters were involved.

Alik scoffed, "You are a fool then. Firtina is many horrible things, but she would never do anything to make the Iktidar line vulnerable. The Elite will eventually open their eyes. When they realize how many girls are missing under our protection, they will challenge our claim to the throne for the first time in decades." She sipped the wine in her hand, still shaking her head, "No. You are wandering down a path with no destination."

He crossed his arms, leaning back against the wooden chair. "Then tell me: Where does your mother go when she leaves in the middle of the night for days on end? What would make the Magarans stop their patrols of your skies? Surely you must have questioned this yourself."

Alik's mouth gaped. "I knew you were terrible at politics, Agnian, but I didn't realize you were foolish enough to blatantly tell me you had spies in Efendi." She stood from the table, the chair grinding loudly against the stone, "We're done here unless you have something tangible I can use to find my best friend and my people."

He grabbed her, a plea and a command tied together around her wrist. "You can disregard me, but are you willing to forgo a chance to find your friend? Your mother knows something. We know the Canavar Company is behind this, but they could not do this on their own. Someone is helping them, and we believe it is Queen Firtina."

"How do you know the Canavar Company has their hands in this? We have spies in among their ranks, but despite my suspicions, I haven't been able to prove anything."

"It isn't company-wide. My sources believe only a handful of Hvard's most trusted men are behind this, and I doubt a newcomer in the ranks would be privy."

"Who are your sources?" She asked.

"That is none of your concern."

"My concern is for my best friend. For the missing girls. Any information is relevant, particularly if I am to believe your ridiculous claim that my mother is involved."

"It is not my role to get you to believe me. I just need your help."

"What is your role then, Agnian? Because it sure as Ates isn't an emissary. You've missed every negotiation. You're looking for the girls as much as I am. Despite what you've shared tonight, you are still hiding something." Alik scanned him again, and the same red hatred simmered under a swirl of mixed emotions. "And you still hate something about me, though I can't imagine what."

Agnian tossed his napkin to the table, leaning into her face as he said, "I hate your family for murdering my king. I hate your kingdom for blocking our waters and then stealing our ships. I hate your Duawielders for threatening my people even as they *starve.* I can't imagine why you would think I could harbor anything but hate for you when any of those are reasons enough."

He stalked away, leaving Alik alone at the table and a cafe full of patrons gawking. Grateful for the veil covering her face, she fled the café, refusing to let tears even well in her eyes.

"Stealing our ships?" She asked the air. *Threatening his people* "even as they starve?" *Our trade agreement favors Efendians, but we are rebuilding their kingdom, their trades. We protect them from the Perisiens. We are the only reason they still have a king, albeit a new one.* She shook herself as she wound back up the nearest stairwell to the Palace. *I'll deal with that after I find Shauna.*

She scoffed aloud, startling a perched fuchsia nightbird. *And he knows nothing of Firtina. There is nothing she wants bad enough that she would jeopardize her standing above the rest of the Elite. And what good would it do to allow someone to kidnap Efendian girls?* Alik worried the fabric hem at her hip, her thoughts zig-zagging as she strode up the fireorb lit stairs. *I should have pushed him more. The Canavar Company is no surprise. I just have to find a way to prove it is them. If what Agnian says is true, the maze of vices could hide that many women. But why haven't our Eyes seen anything then?*

She felt the spray from the Palace fountains when she heard a man singing a lullaby, deja-vu knocking her mind askew for a moment. *Where have I heard that before?* Unease crept over her shoulders as she spun to see the disembodied voice. A guardswoman called out to her, but she saw no one else.

Voices suddenly began to chant in her mind over the haunting melody. Her Dua overtook her body, blacking out her vision. She couldn't see her hands but knew she cradled her head in them while her mind split open. The trickling fountain, the guardswoman's voice, the distant clatter of Aygir hoofbeats ceased. All noise surrounding her halted simultaneously for a moment before rushing back in a vacuum.

When her vision cleared, the cobblestones at the Palace gate indented her knees. She stood, wiping the blood from her nose on the back of her hand, and told the hovering guardswomen to call her brothers to her study. *What was that?*

She struggled to get to her study, staying a hand at any guardswoman that tried to help. Her senses were still raw, her Dua sparking. It was as if her entire body screamed at her to focus, to pay attention. *What am I missing? Something just happened, as if everything will be marked before and after.* And she had no choice but to find out what it was.

REED

Reed didn't have time to explain his intentions to Monti. Most Itreni lived alone, notoriously jealous of each other, and convinced that they lived in exile outside the Perimeter Wall because of their brethren. *I need this Itreni to live alone,* he thought as they followed him from the Aygir fields.

The creature swayed ahead of them, its pincer legs poking shallow holes in the dirt like a pockmarked trail. The Itreni opened the grass-covered, round portal camouflaged in the ground just beyond the stables. As it focused on the doorway to its home, Reed scanned the ground for a weapon. The Aygir at his back ruled out striking the creature in the field, but he remembered stories of how well these creatures fought underground. It was one of the few reasons they could survive out here when Garfu and other monsters roamed the valley, and Yurutec tunneled below.

Monti followed Reed the frayed rope ladder into the bowels of the ground. Veins of blue light snaked around the tunnel, lighting their way, and in the dim light, he made out a series of crude iron doors, mismatched in size, on either side of the tunnel. The way was tall enough that Reed did not have to stoop, but he had to walk sideways at more than one narrow point. His nose grazed the Yinka bugs that produced the blue light along the dirt walls. The back of Reed's shirt tugged down in Monti's grip as they walked, and just as he wondered if they should have taken their chances above ground, the Itreni stopped at an intricately carved iron door. The creature's chest heaved in and out, as if it were excited, as it slipped a crooked piece of root into a hole like a key.

"Where do the other doors go?" Reed asked.

"Places. I wouldn't wander, though," the Itreni muttered as he pushed open the door. "Not all doors are mine anymore."

It led them into a low roofed room where hair-thin roots from the grasses above dangled from the ceiling. The Itreni muttered to itself as it tapped the walls to wake the Yinka bugs, their agitation flaring blue veins of light within the dirt walls. The small hairs on Reed's neck stood at attention when the light did not reach the dark hallway that jutted off the main room. The base of a tree trunk was the only piece of furniture in the center of the room, and a flat stone boulder served as its seating. The Itreni swayed to a nook carved into the wall like a makeshift shelf and began to slice carrots with a wickedly sharp dagger pulled from the ragged vest it wore.

"What can I do to repay you for shelter and food for the night?" Reed asked as he and Monti sat at the tree stump table. "When I was a boy, I worked with an Itreni and his Aygir that traveled with our caravan. Perhaps I can help you with yours in the morning?"

The head of an Itreni rests on only one socket pivot, similar to owls. Though Reed remembered this, it was still disconcerting to see the creature turn its head almost entirely around while chopping carrots. Even more so as it smiled wide, causing the corners of its mouth to disappear around its round head. Reed held Monti's thigh in place when she jerked back, though it took everything for Reed to not run for the door as well. He remembered the stories about the Itreni creatures before they wore Efendian clothes and trained the Aygir for the Horde. They fled the woods as the Batiwood encroached, but their bloodlust took years to control.

It answered Reed quietly, "No need. It's been an age since we've had Efendians as company."

"We?" Reed asked, slowly dipping his hand to Monti's back to unclip her gun. He chose this seat so his back would be to the door and face the Itreni and the hallway beyond. He did not miss the fact that the Itreni paused its chopping before continuing.

"A phrase. It's been an age since my Aygir and I have hosted an Efendian."

Dirt rained down from the ceiling as movement scattered across the roof, startling both Reed and Monti.

The Itreni hissed, "Hush!"

Reed pulled her closer so that his right hand palmed the pistol in her holster. The Itreni crept to the iron door a few feet away from Reed, dagger in its hand.

It put an oversized ear to the iron and whispered after a few moments, "Yurutec. They're still above ground. They won't bother us if we are quiet."

Something shifted in the darkness in the hallway off of the main room. Reed yanked the gun from Monti's holster as she bolted for the wall to get out of the way. Reed held the pistol at eye level of the Itreni and demanded quietly, "Who else is with you?"

The creature snorted. "A metal stick? It doesn't even have a sharp edge."

The Itreni kicked its scissor-like legs into the dirt wall next to the door, sinking its pincer points into the wall as it ran up and across the ceiling. It flipped over Reed's head, landing at his back, and yanked Monti into its arms. Its dagger cut a thin red line into her neck, and she stopped struggling.

It yanked her head back by the hair, roaming its eyes over her. It hissed to her, "You have no vials, no flint, which means you are an Airwerker or a Groundwerker. Which is it?"

"I have no idea what you're talking about!" Monti shouted.

The Itreni's knobby free hand covered her mouth. "Be quiet, or they'll come."

"She's not Efendian," Reed whispered, as black nails, filed to sharp points, gripped Monti's cheek tighter than before. He didn't have a clear shot, so he held his hands up submissively with the gun loose in his fingers.

"She's...from a village on the other side of Magara. We were on our way to Efendi for Hasateen but got derailed by a Garfu attack near the river. Please. We mean you no harm; we're just trying to get to the Perimeter Wall."

"How unfortunate for you," it whispered. "If she were Efendian, she might have been able to fight back. No one will miss a couple of villagers, and it's been so long since I've tasted meat." It opened its mouth wide at her neck, jaw clicking as it unhinged.

Monti heaved her body back into the creature, knocking it against the wall. She dug her thumb into the Itreni's eye and reached for the wrist holding its dagger. She flipped the Itreni's arm up and out as she spun and kicked it hard in its side, the blade hitting the ground with a thud.

Something launched itself from the dark hallway. The second Itreni ran up and over the dirt wall like a spider, landing on top of Reed, and embedded one of its pincher legs into Reed's left forearm. It pinned him down with its other knee on top of his chest, and Reed screamed out in pain. The creature covered his mouth with his clawed hand, its wide mouth hissing like a snake. Monti stumbled back on the ground, the first Itreni stalking towards her with its remaining good eye.

Nausea rolled over Reed from the sharp pain in his arm, but he grazed cold metal with his free hand. He reached, finally hooking his finger on the gun's trigger guard, and palmed the pistol. He fired three rapid shots that echoed tenfold in the compact room, hitting both creatures in quick succession.

The Itreni's hot blood sprayed over Reed's face and into his mouth before slumping off him. He wiped his eyes, gagging and spitting out the creature's blood as Monti scrambled over the dead

Itrenis. She ripped her pants and swiftly bound the gash from the Itreni's leg with the fabric.

A flurry of movement across the roof interrupted whatever she opened her mouth to say. Reed hauled himself up to sitting, spinning at the pain in his forearm. “Bokki. They’re coming. Get back to—"

She frantically whispered, "What is, Reed? What is coming?"

His mind reeled as he said more to himself than her, "They heard the gunshots."

Reed shoved Monti to a corner between the table and the wall as movement scrambled past in the underground tunnel beyond the iron door. He pressed his body in front of her, wincing at the pain as he cradled his injured arm.

Reed gave her the gun and whispered, "Yurutec are the mantis-like creatures you first found me with."

At her widened eyes, he murmured, "No sounds until they pass."

Slow, steady guttural clicking, like that of a fishing reel as something large takes the bait off a pole, sounded outside the iron door. Reed felt Monti's breath come in faster and faster against his back, her nails digging into his sides. He grabbed her hand in his right, unable to discern who shook harder. *They could just pass. Take the tunnels,* he silently pleaded. *Keep moving; there is nothing here you want.*

Beyond the door, the guttural clicking stopped, replaced by heavy, labored breathing. Quick footsteps scurried in the tunnel on either side of the iron door. A shrill scratch broke through the pounding in Reed's ears, like a claw dragging down an iron slab.

Dirt rained down to the right of the iron door—the compact wall pulsed outwards in spots in the vague shape of a giant claw, pressing in. Dirt fell from the roof into Reed's hair and hands, and something frantically dug at the wall behind them. *We’re surrounded.*

Reed thought of his mother then.

She sat on a grassy knoll with her soft brown curls tickling his face. Her knee poked out of an apricot-colored dress and pressed next to his scrawny shivering leg.

Her melodic voice washed over him. "Did you know that the hard-brown encasement over this is called a seed coat?" She held the apple seed out to him in her delicate hand. He took it, teeth chattering, and leaned back into the strong base of the tree behind him and against his mother's side.

"This big tree was once wrapped tightly in its seed coat as well." Her arms were warm from the hour they'd sat under the 90-degree Texan sun so he could bring his body temperature back up. "The coat shields against the wind and protects the tiny life inside."

Her low voice soothed him, coached him to hold it in, to bind the roots threatening to break free.

Reed shut the digging out, ignored the guttural clicks coming from all sides, and blocked out Monti's muffled cry at the back of his neck. He gripped the dirt falling into his hands and pictured his mother's face.

He squeezed his eyes shut and whispered, "Hold. Hold. Hold". He recited the litany over and over again, not caring what gods were paying attention so long as they heard his plea. "Hold. Hold. Hold."

He felt dizzy. His mother's face faltered in his mind as blackness crept in. The last thing he remembered before passing out was the iron smell of blood and the image of a wide, dark mouth in the trees opening before him.

***

They always started the same.

It's a typical domestic scene of mundane suburban life. Sometimes it's yard work, fetching the mail, or washing his car. In the way that dreams do, Reed always felt a little bewildered when he first found himself holding the watering hose, but then he settled into the comfort of a routine.

Reed's neighbors walked by on the sidewalk, smiling faces and sweaty children on bikes. The humming would start innocently enough. Sometimes it was the neighbor's kid drawing chalk flowers in the driveway next to him. Other times, Reed realized it was he who started the chords as he shuffled mail. Then the feeling of wrongness would seep in like spilled ink bleeding onto the edge of a clean paper. His dream state waking up, realizing this is not real. His neighbors would sing in chorus, sometimes chant, but always, the androgynous voice would sing the lullaby loudest. Staci, arms wet to the elbows, whispered, "They're coming for you."

Reed woke up to Monti shaking him.

"OhThankChrist," Monti breathed. "You're awake."

In the faint light, Reed realized that Monti dragged the dead Itreni bodies to a far corner of the room at some point. He jerked upright as everything rushed back to him, dizziness threatening to overwhelm the fight or flight reaction hammering in his bones.

He said in a rush, "The Yurutec. Where are they? What happened?"

Monti lightly tapped the walls with her fingers as she walked to the makeshift kitchen. The blue lights flared brighter, and Reed shuddered at the dark stains on both of their clothes and the floor steps away from him. She grabbed some bread from a nook in the wall and brought over a few carrots.

She sank next to him, pulling her knees to her chest and eating her half of the meager provisions. "I don't know. One minute those things were barreling down the walls, and it felt like they were just about to break through. Then all of a sudden, the walls held. They beat on the walls and the iron door for several minutes before finally leaving."

“Which, funny enough,” she continued, “could be the most terrifying moment of my life aside from the time I was sucked into a vortex and into this hell.” Monti huffed a mirthless laugh even as she swiped at fresh tears. “Oh wait, that was only yesterday."

She covered her face with shaking hands, and Reed awkwardly

patted her back, lost as to what to do to stop her crying. She said in a rush, "I thought you were dying and that I'd be left down here alone and I didn't know what to do, or what would happen if I opened--" she broke down in sobs before she could finish.

He ran a hand over her hair and tried to think of something to tell her so she wouldn't be so scared. *There's nothing to tell. She should be terrified every moment she's in this hell. We have to get the fuck out of here.*

Monti pulled back when her sobs subsided. She wiped her face on the cleanest part of her shirt and turned fully to Reed, eyes bloodshot but unblinking. "I need goals, Reed. Give me specific things to focus on, and I won't lose it on you."

He nodded at her resolve. "We can't stay down here. It was moonrise when we came here. How long do you think I've been out?"

"Well, their bodies got stiff a couple of hours ago. I don't know if their chemical makeup is anything like ours, but if so, I'd guess 5 hours or so."

Reed huffed out a laugh, "I didn't expect that answer."

She shrugged, "I watch a lot of SVU."

"And the self-defense moves?" He asked.

"My dad is the warden of your prison. Self-defense lessons took priority over piano lessons for my sisters and me."

He ignored the other questions volleying through his mind. "Do you remember the kingdom you saw in the distance before we came down here?" He continued at her nod, "An Aygir is the best weapon we have while we're outside of that Perimeter Wall. They're too tough to eat, so the Garfu leave them alone, and the Yurutec usually fear them. They're also the fastest way for us to travel out here. We likely have another day and night ahead of us before we can get to the Magaran mountains, so we'll need to take one. That's our first goal."

Even as a tear spilled over her cheek, Monti nodded, and something about her resolve struck Reed's core. *She's here because of me. I don't care what it takes; I am getting this woman out of this hell.* He cupped her face in her hands, willing his false bravado to be assuring and his touch something she could lean on.

He spoke more confidently than he felt. "There we'll find my mother's friend. She was a Rifter, and I know she'll help me again. Get an Aygir, get to the Rifter, get the hell out of here."

She moved out of his hands and back into her personal space. "You forgot one. Get an Aygir, get the Rifter, *get my dad*, and then get the hell out of here."

Reed before the Rift would have just left Monti. The likelihood of finding his mother's friend after all these years was hard enough; finding her father within Efendi after the Horde picked him up was a joke. A familiar pain blotted out the pain in his arm. *I've failed enough women in my life; I am not leaving her in this place. If I tell her that her dad is likely already dead, she might lose it.*

So he lied, telling himself that getting her home would be a salve against losing her dad. "Right. Of course. But those riders probably took him to the dungeons. We'll need a Rifter to get him out."

She nodded and helped him up. He gathered a few more root vegetables from the kitchen and stuffed them into a satchel he found in the bedroom. Monti brought him pieces of cloth that she had ripped up and put them on top of their food.

"For your arm," she said. She looked to the door and blew out a deep breath as if preparing herself for what lay outside.

Reed stopped her before she opened the door, cupping the side of her face again so that she looked at him fully. Her wide eyes were puffy, dirt marred her fair features, and blood caked one side of her shoulder-length, honey blonde hair. She bit her full, chapped lips as her eyes welled up again.

He stalled her tears by saying, "Goals, Monti. Say them to me."

She nodded quickly, forcing quick breaths through her nose

and out her mouth. "Get an Aygir, get a Rifter, get my dad, get the hell out of here."

"Good. No sounds, even above ground if it's still dark outside. Stay close, and if we run into trouble, head as fast as you can to the kingdom by the sea. And whatever you do, don't go to the red woods across the valley. I'll try to distract anything that comes for us to buy you time."

She bobbed her head again and quirked a smile. "Who would have thought I'd be safest with a murderer?"

He huffed a laugh. "I feel the same way about the warden's daughter." He grabbed her hand. "Let's go."

He opened the iron door, wincing at the groan from its hinges, and they stepped into the dark tunnel.

ELAINE

Elaine practiced the elements with Kanne Da'Neen under the scorching sun, which amounted to nothing more than getting her hand caked in dirt or cupping palmfuls of water. She'd been nauseous for a full day and night and was tired of the knowing smile Farisha gave her whenever she complained. Reiki's conversation about Rifters stuck to the insides of her ribcage, hovering on her shoulders, and made her jumpy. She bit back the unkindness she wanted to spew at the smirks and stares from the cluster's bored matriarchs hovering nearby and brushed the sweat-slicked hair off of her face.

Elaine said to Kanne Da'Neen, "I gotta get out of here."

The old crone just spat on the ground and waved her off. Elaine sprinted for freedom up the nearest staircase, ignoring the headache that was trying its best to break her skull apart.

She walked the edge of an upper Tier, tight roping the stone wall with her arms out on either side of her, debating what to do if the voices came back. *I've only heard them twice since arriving here, so I just need to avoid those two places. Easy. I don't want to go back to the Lantern Pit anyway, and there's no reason to go back to that Cluster in Low Town where I first heard something.*

She kicked at a pebble, arguing with herself. *But what about the girls? If they're the ones calling you, you can't just abandon them. Or the voices could be Rifters. Apart from the creepy one, none of the voices seem to talk directly to me. I don't think they see me, but maybe they can hear me now that I'm in Sakalid?*

A merchantress of this Tier stared at Elaine as if an ant marched across her rice crispy treat. This Tier was several levels up from Low Town and around the bend, and though no rules expressly forbade her from exploring it, her plain, oatmeal-colored clothes told everyone that she did not belong here. She glared right back, agitation overwhelming self-preservation, and ducked behind stone townhomes to trapeze through their gardens.

Her mother once took a fleeting interest in gardening. She brought white and purple petunias in black plastic buckets from the hardware store in town and spent an afternoon digging up the dirt around the base of their trailer. She asked Elaine to help her, and Elaine could still conjure up the feel of soil and hair-thin roots between her fingers. It was early spring in Beaufort, so the sun was a welcome warmth on their backs and a promise of ocean swims in weeks to come. Da was out of town for a few days at a job site several hours away.

She and her mother spent the following few afternoons watering and waiting for the patch of petunias to turn into Eden, and Elaine felt a kinship building. She took her bike to the small library in town and checked out all the books on gardening she could. She studied flowers at night so that when she and Ma walked into town for more gardening tools, she could point out her discoveries along the way. But her Ma was Ma, and the more Elaine tried, the less interested her mother became in flowers or her. Elaine watered the petunias diligently that spring, but her mother never brought home more flowers. Elaine cried when they died, though she'd never let her mother see.

Elaine kicked at a white and purple coneflower at the memory, knocking her off balance and onto her bottom. She brushed off the dirt from her backside, wincing at the pain. *There's no mistaking* how *I got here*, she thought. *It sure sounds an awful lot like Rifting, but I don't know how that could've happened. There is no way Ma had Rifting magic. She would've left a hundred times over.* She walked along the edge again. *It doesn't make any sense. I can't be a Rifter. Maybe it was a Rifter talking to me that lead me here. Like a trap? Can they do that?*

She thought back to the night she left her world for the world of Sakalid. At the time, she was too shocked to question why one particular voice seemed to speak directly to her when all the others were snippets of conversations not meant for her. *Come*, the voice said. Something else dawned on her. *That couldn't have been a Rifter. That was a man's voice. The same one that occasionally sang a lullaby or gave that creepy laugh.* She stopped mid-step. *What if I'm hearing the Edicisi?* She shivered at the thought of the dark-shrouded monster from Kanne Da'Neen's stories.

Two women began speaking, and her heart leapt before she realized the conversation came from one of the balconies above her and not in her head. *Get it together, Elaine.*

"I heard another four Pillars were kidnapped last night above the Trades."

"No! Is that true? If we aren't safe near our homes, how are we supposed to keep our children protected?"

"Exactly. What is the point of us appeasing an Iktidar queen if she cannot control kidnappers within our walls?"

"Can you imagine what it will be like when Queen Firtina dies, and we're left with Princess Alik?"

"Goddesses, no. It will be terrible," the first voice paused. Elaine felt like the politics of Efendi were as far away as her trailer, but gossip helped her forget her own troubles, so she stood still as an oak under the shade of the balcony above.

The voice continued, "If you promise to tell no one who you heard it from, I'll let you in on a secret...Danisha has been purchasing all of the rights to the mines south of Magaran. I don't know how they've come into so much money, but she's established herself in the court faster than anyone has in years. I heard from someone that her daughter Tenida is adept at all but the fire element and would be a direct competitor to Alik Iktidar."

"But no one even knows who they are? I won't believe it until I see it."

"True, but Tenida is well-liked even if her mother is not. Well-liked enough to one day catch the eye of Taavi."

"Goddesses know we need to branch off the Iktidar line. I feel for the poor girl, but we'd be better off if Firtina were the last Iktidar Daughter. I heard there was a Yurutec attack in the stables two nights ago. It's as if the Batiwood is at our Wall."

The voices trailed off as the women walked inside. Elaine meandered under the balconies while formulating a plan to get to the top of the Perimeter Wall one night so she could watch for these Yurutec. And perhaps see where people could enter and exit the walled kingdom. *Just in case.*

Vines of flowers spilled over the tops of the balconies in thick ropes, and she had to sidestep several unnecessary waterfalls the Elite favored so much. She almost missed the harsh, low voices above her over the cascading water, but she had become adept at listening to conversations not meant for her over the years. She stepped from the protective shade of the balcony to hear better and snuggled herself into a bush fat with hibiscus-like flowers to stay hidden should anyone peer over.

"I don't have the money yet. But I will by the end of Hasateen," a man pleaded.

A second voice, graveled and deep, responded. "And why should I believe that? You've been gambling away in my Pit for weeks now without payment. It's time."

Where have I heard his voice before?

"I don't have access to my wife's coin now, but I can get it at the end of the week when she's gone and then--"

The man was interrupted by the sharp slash of something metal dragged against stone.

"Hvard, please. A few days!"

Elaine froze at the name. She didn't dare breathe or poke her head out, but she knew this was the same giant, bearded man that even his own mother feared.

"I'm not an unreasonable man, Rellyan. You have four daughters, yes?"

"What? Uh, yes. One is just entering the season, and the other three are twelve, fourteen, and sixteen. I'm begging you, please, they need their father."

"You like gambling, so I'll give you one last gamble. If you do not have the money by the end of this week, I'll come for your youngest. If you do have the money, you and your family can go free. Or, if you give me your daughter now, I'll let you keep your coin and even pay you double what you owe."

"Have you lost your mind? I'm not giving you Ada! I'll go to the Iktidars before I see your slave trade hovering at my door."

"Ah, Ada is her name then? I bet she's pretty. She likes the sticky buns at the cafe around the corner, right?"

"How--"

"Yes. Pretty blue eyes. What is her werk?"

"Get out of my---"

A sharp intake, a gurgle, and then a slop were all Elaine's mind processed in the time it took for Hvard to slit the man's throat and toss him over the balcony to her feet. He landed in a puddle with a thwack, blood splattering Elaine's calves.

She stifled a cry with her hand over her mouth, but not fast enough. Hvard peered over the edge.

She bolted. Not caring where she ran, she dashed over the tidy rows of cut gardens and through waterfalls and under balconies until she came, breathless, to a dead end. The stone house had a matching stone wall separating it from its neighbors, so she shimmied along the thin-lipped edge of the wall and the edge of the Tier. Several heavy footsteps ran down the steps on the other side. *They'll see me if they come past the Tier's edge. I'll be trapped.*

A deep baritone of laughter flit through her ears, the same that made her skin crawl and felt different than any of the other voices. She knew she was the only one who could hear the voice ask above a low indiscernible chant, *Where are you? They're coming for you.*

She glanced down, trying to block out the voice and guessing the distance below. *The tops of the Trades stalls are a good three Tiers down. If I jump, I'll be at least one stairwell ahead of them.* Every muscle in her body tensed in alert. She should have feared the fall, but it was as if every cell in her body willed her to jump to the roofs below.

She leapt, or rather fell more than anything, onto the hard, gold tiles of the house below, skinning her knees. Men shouted orders above her. She didn't pause long enough to look over her shoulder before she started slip-running over the tiles. She ignored the ominous laughter echoing in her mind.

She thought frantically, *Next Tier, next Tier. A couple more jumps and then through the arches. I'll lose them in the Trades around the bend.*

She balanced across a thin arch connecting the two sides of the lower Tier, Efendians shouting in alarm below at her precarious path. She reached the opposite side of the Tier, preparing to jump again, but her footing slipped. She careened face forward over the edge, her eyes on the gold tiles out of reach. She squeezed every muscle in her body just before her face hit the cobblestones.

It felt as if she was pulled through a straw, suctioned in over and over like paper folding into a tiny square, the air squeezed from her lungs. And then, *pop!*

When she opened her eyes, she was on the next golden rooftop, and not a puddle on the ground like the man she saw a few minutes before. She didn't take time to register the how's and just squeezed again, eyes tight. When she opened, she was in the middle of her favorite alley in the Trades. The plant-filled passage sold exotic trees of every color imaginable, and their heady flowers blocked her from the shoppers at the mouth of the alley.

She landed on one knee, lunge forward, heart racing. For the first time in weeks, she felt free of a weight she hadn't realized she was hoisting. *Ohmygod, ohmygod, ohmygod! That just happened!* Her mind didn't know what else to do other than spurt a crazed laugh as confusion, bewilderment, anxiety, and joy pummeled her simultaneously. She looked up; Hvard's men nowhere in sight. She wasn't sure if Hvard recognized her from the balcony, but she was giddy with relief despite what happened.

I just Rifted.

Her body practically vibrated with the urge to run. She took off through the maze of flowering trees and sweet-smelling fruits hanging low over the alley entrance. The throng of the Trades was less thick here, which allowed her more space to dart in between shoppers and merchants at a faster and faster pace. She raced to the other side of the bend. She should have gone home or to Kara and Reiki's stall, but she was filled to the eyes with adrenaline.

She dashed down the wide street of the western Trades, seeing but not registering the colorful art and rugs at this bend. When she finally ran to the brink of exhaustion, she stopped to sit down at the edge of the Trades Tier behind a ruby red stall selling exotic purple furs.

Elaine had few things she missed from back home, but one thing she wished she had was her salvaged Caboodle organizer. The top was pasty pink, the bottom hatch a pale mint, and the Caboodle logo was illegible on its grimy white plastic fastener. She loved opening the tray and unfolding its innards when she was alone, little rocks and dried flowers organized in tiny plastic compartments. Elaine sometimes felt like her mind was like that Caboodle. Put an unwanted thought or a bad memory in a little compartment and fold over the trays to deal with later. She wiped at the man's blood on her calves with a chunk of turquoise moss from the crack in the Tier, trying and failing to not think about the thick squelch of flesh hitting cobblestones. Elaine threw up her breakfast into the overlooked patch of weeds behind the stall.

She forced the memory of the dead man to a small, left corner compartment and focused instead on the sudden, unexpected gift of magic at her disposal.

Or curse. Reiki said they hunt Rifters, and their neighbor thought that Rifters were the ones taking the girls. She needed to find more information out about Rifters, but how? She looked at herself. *I don't look any different. There's no reason anyone needs to know.*

But jeez Louise, I want to do that again! She never kissed a boy, but sometimes when she explored the Trades alone she pretended a boyfriend walked with her. Elaine imagined that a good first kiss might be like that Rift. *Knock your socks off scary, but so good you want to do it again.*

She felt a lightness in her limbs and let herself be happy while her mind raced. *Magic. I have magic! Oh my god, does this mean I was adopted? What if this means my real parents are here? What if it's my real family I'm hearing?* The derision from her mother and the abuse from her father over the last few years made a lot more sense to her if they were not her biological parents. *My real parents wouldn't hurt me. I have freaking MAGIC. I gotta do that again.*

She thought back to her map in her journal. *Where can I go where no one will see me?* There was one place she knew she could practice with plenty of cover. The Hadishis' explicitly forbade the twins and Elaine to go to the Silos since the girl from the next Cluster disappeared from there, but she could Rift if there was trouble and there was plenty of sun left in the day. *Even Hvard and his gang couldn't catch me if I Rift.*

Elaine wound her way down to the Silos where Efendians stored all their grain. The giant vats were almost as tall as a Tier and provided plenty of cover the deeper she walked. She practiced a few Rifts from behind one massive stone cylinder to the next, telling herself it was fine so long as no one saw her.

She had no idea that each Rift reverberated past the Perimeter Wall, far across the valley, and deep into the Batiwood where something listened with rapt attention, waiting. Smiling.

ALIK

Alik's father took her sailing to a barrier island a few hours into the Turkaz Sea when she was a child. She basked in the attention afforded to a lone child accustomed to sharing her father with siblings and responsibilities as the two of them leapt in and out of the waves crashing over the glass pebble beach. His joy outside of the Palace was infectious, and his blunt blonde beard dripped water with each dip he took. The day, in Alik's eight-year-old estimation, was shaping up to be the best in her life until her final swim that afternoon.

Waves stacked on top of each other as the sun settled on the horizon. Her father's eyes glittered with adrenaline as he skimmed the cresting waves bare-chested, the sky red and gold behind him. The crush of water on the pebbles drowned out his booming laugh, and Alik imagined herself the world's greatest Waterwerker helping guide him over the waves. He told her to wait on the beach, but she wanted to show him how strong she had become. She waded out into the water and braced herself before what was growing to be the queen of all waves.

Her head tilted back and back as the water built upon itself, its crest curving to block out the setting sun. The seconds it took for the wave to build could have been years for all the fears Alik felt in that moment before the water consumed her.

She felt the same heart-pounding anxiety now, waiting for something ancient and much bigger than she to overtake her as she listened to the fire crackle in her study.

She couldn't name her fear, but she knew without a doubt that forces beyond her control were set in motion. She sank deeper into the worn leather chair and crossed her legs, now clad in loose gossamer pants that pooled around her comfortingly.

Damari rushed in without knocking. "What happened, Alik? One of the guardswomen said you passed out at the gate, and when you didn't meet up with my Eye, I thought something happened to you too."

He wore soft, dark linen pants, his hair mussed, and she felt a pang of guilt for waking him when she knew he needed sleep. Alik asked, "Is she still gone?"

He didn't ask who. "Yea, she slipped out sometime yesterday and hasn't been seen since. If this trek is anything like the others, she'll be gone another day."

Alik nodded. "Good. Can you get me in her study without being seen?"

Damari stilled. "That is a death wish, Alik. What are you looking for?"

She watched her little brother standing before the fire, debating on how much to tell him. *He is the most vulnerable if someone catches us, but he's the only one apart from Taavi I trust with this. And Taavi would never help me sneak into Firtina's study alone.*

"Mother keeps a series of journals under lock and key in a hidden panel under her desk. I stumbled across them once when we were little. I was hiding from Shauna, and I crawled under her desk while she was in the Atrium. The panel was open."

That was the first time Firtina struck Alik. She could still hear her mother's footsteps around the desk, her incredulous face at the chubby kid hovering at her feet with bent knees. Alik didn't know that what she did was wrong, and she cried out when her mother yanked her out with an Airwerk and suspended her high in the study. Firtina slapped her hard across the face just as her father came into the room. Alik brushed off the memory of his arms around her and focused on the task at hand.

She continued. "I think she knows where the girls are, Damari."

Damari had a face with no tells. If he were surprised or emboldened by her admission, she would never know. He nodded once, marked something on a paper at Alik's desk, and walked out the door. "We have to go now if we're to go at all. Follow me."

He handed the note to a beautiful woman polishing the opal floor outside Alik's study. She slipped off without a word, and he hastened Alik down an empty servant's hall to the right. Damari stopped outside an unremarkable portrait, an Iktidar branch long forgotten, and poked a gold key into the man's mouth after a glance around. A click, a creak, and they slipped into another hall with no light. She held onto his hand and, after a few moments, felt him push against the wall.

Alik looked for a flame to push into the empty glass orbs to light the dark study they stepped into, but her head still pounded from whatever occurred earlier. She swore as she stumbled over a chair.

"Alik..." Damari rarely rushed her. He knew how atrocious she was at wielding elements even under the best circumstances, but they didn't need to discuss how quick this needed to be.

"Well, do *you* see a flame anywhere? I don't have my rings," she hissed.

A rock cracked before a sputtering spark flared to life in Damari's hands. He simply said, "Torch."

Alik groaned again at the ridiculousness of her situation. *I'm expected to wield all elements, so I can't even carry the simplest of devices to help me lest another Pillar see me.* She waved the flame to the glass orbs lining the wall. "They'll have to stay there. I don't have the energy for air."

She strode to the wide table at the back wall and pushed against the panel under her mother's desk. Damari fiddled with the lock with a set of blunt tools pulled from another pocket, and Alik held her breath as the panel swung open. *Nothing.*

"Bokki," Alik swore. "She moved them."

Damari nodded, "Split up, hands against the wall. Tell me if you feel any drafts."

Alik ran her hands along the wall, frustration feeding her anxiety. Voices brushed beyond the study door, and she froze just as she felt a small trickle of air under her palm. The voices moved on, so she ran her palms along her find.

She found the hair-thin gap in between the stone wall and the hearth of Ates. Damari looked up at the click echoing through the room. Alik pushed open a trick door hidden behind the cold fireplace and entered a small antechamber, dark beyond the flicker of the orb above her head. Damari met her in an instant, torch lit, and together they scanned the walls.

Alik's steps faltered at what they found. *What in the Ates is this?*

Papers, maps, and rudimentary drawings meticulously lined the walls in neat rows despite the cobwebs dangling between corners. Firtina's handwriting scratched over notes pinned on top of the papers, and multiple stacks of books lined the floor. A huge world map of Sakalid lined the back wall with red flags dotting its landscape. Damari traced the curve of Efendian land and walked to the far side where the wastelands of Bakilar began.

He read aloud as his finger traced the map marked by flags. "What is a 'Ley Line'?'"

Alik shook her head. She was reading a note beside one of the many renderings of the Edicisi. *None of this makes any sense.*

Her mother abhorred local superstitions and blamed a lack of education for why the poorest sometimes worshiped the Edicisi. Yet, the entire room appeared to be dedicated to a study of the Edicisi and his Handmaidens. The idea of her tall, imposing mother huddled in here pouring over fantastical stories was disconcerting.

Damari held the torch high, and its firelight danced over a row of slim books lined in red leather partially hidden by the molding at the top of the ceiling. Alik pulled the farthest volume to the right with the meager Airwerk the Goddesses blessed her with, the journal falling more than floating to her outstretched hand.

"We can't stay in here, Alik, but I think I know where this leads. Bring it with us." Damari heaved against the back wall. It swung open on oiled hinges to reveal a rocky corridor darker than even the room they were in now.

Mischief danced in his amber eyes in the firelight. "How long has it been since you've seen Elder Spider?"

Alik laughed despite the headache and the trouble she was bathing in. "The library catacombs?" She nodded at his smile. "Lead on then."

The head elderman was ancient even when they were kids. Her skin prickled with goosebumps at the memory of his bones and joints popping behind her while she studied. The library, accessible only to the Elite families of Efendi with explicit permission, was the ultimate punishment for royal children. Alik suffered a few hours there throughout her studies, but Damari spent the better half of his childhood cooped up in the belly of the mountain.

Darkness shrouded them despite the flame Damari held over the steps beyond them. Alik lightly brushed the cold stone walls that wound down as they walked the spiraling stairs. Her fingers paused over a decompression in the wall before her mind caught up. She grabbed Damari's hand and held the torch over the carving of "HB and FI" entwined above the symbol of forever. The dark maw from her dream flashed in her mind.

Damari made a noncommittal grunt and proceeded on, leaving Alik no choice but to follow. *Why would anyone carve their initials here of all places?* They kept moving, and the stairs soon leveled out.

Alik whispered, "I don't know how you can stand being here. It still creeps me out."

"It wasn't so bad once I realized the catacombs touched nearly everywhere in Efendi. And once I grew to not fear the dark." Damari winked at her just as he extinguished the torch before a doorway.

Alik yelped despite her age and attached herself to Damari as her eyes adjusted to the half-light beyond the threshold. The catacombs spiraling through the mountain were dedicated space to dead Efendian Elite as well as books. The lack of light and frigid air helped preserve both equally well. Their doorway led them to a sarcophagus of a long-dead consort, his coffin eerily lit by the blue half-light the Yinka bug produced. The faint blue light snaked through the walls like blue veins, light enough to see a few feet ahead but dark enough to still be terrified of what lay beyond.

Her Dua flared with her panic, doubling the pain in her head, but it helped quiet the 'what if's' waltzing through her mind. *Damari was such a scrawny boy until he hit puberty. The idea of him exploring down here alone, without Dua, is terrifying.* Alik prayed again to Ates that she'd only have girls.

A shuffle, then a curse. Someone muttered to themselves just out of eyesight. Alik's heart rammed against her chest as she shoved the red leather journal in her pocket.

Damari's shout shook a few years off Alik's life. "Ho, Josef! Looking good!"

Papers flew in the air before an old man shuffled into their light. "Ruzgar bless! Where did you come from, child? You scared the life from me." He peered behind Damari as if this was a regular exchange. "How many times have I told you, this is not a place to bring your---"

The man's voice gave a comically high squeak, "Ah! My Pillar. I'm so sorry. I did not recognize you. Usually, it's only Damari and his particular *friends* that come down here."

Alik glanced at her brother but gave no indication that this was news to her. "No need for an apology Elderman..."

"Josef," Damari supplied.

"Elderman Josef. It's lovely to meet you. Damari and I were just---" Alik was wretched at subterfuge, so she just let her thoughts trail off, knowing that her brother would run with whatever lie he'd already concocted.

He never let Alik down. "We're snooping for stories to share with the Dvarian embassy about Hasateen. Do you have anything on the Edicisi and his Handmaidens that's not made for children? Something rather ghoulish would be ideal so they never want to come back." Damari grinned in a way that could either be sincere or a joke.

More Rifters, brother? Alik hadn't had a chance to tell Damari about the men that chased her. *Men, not crones sipping cups of blood.* The second cup of blood in the Trades came back to her mind, but the Elderman's response distracted her.

"Huh. That's a new one. Do you remember the summer we spent looking over Magaran texts?"

At Damari's nod, Alik asked herself, *What else do I not know about my brother?*

The elderman grinned. "There's an author that spent most of his life living in the mountains that wrote such a book on the Edicisi's Handmaidens. Let's go hunting!"

The old man lumbered ahead of them at a surprising pace. Damari called after him, "How is it a Magaran would know so much about an Efendian tale?"

Josef paused and glanced between the two of them. His pale skin practically glowed blue when he stood still between two coffins. Damari rolled his eyes, "Trust me; she's with us. You've no fear of recourse for simply telling us facts."

"Forgive me, My Pillar. It's just that your mother once frequented these halls. It wasn't until... later... that we realized why she wanted so much information on the kingdoms surrounding Efendi."

For her campaigns. Alik's mother stood out in a bloodline of powerful Duawielders even at a young age. But she made her name by conquering the lands closest to Efendi on behalf of Alik's grandmother. *For their protection.* Alik once swallowed those lessons without question. But ever since Agnian's tirade, she began to question much in her life.

Alik stalled for a little time on how to respond. "Does she ever come down still?"

"No. Not in several years. We bring her any texts she requests."

Alik noticed the slight lilt in his speech and guessed that he came from one of the lesser islands surrounding Efendi; Islands likely razed from her mother and grandmother's invasions. "We're only looking for stories, not information for another siege."

The bearded elderman nodded and rubbed a hand over his substantial belly protruding beneath a beige cloth robe. "Some believe that when the first Rifter Hunt began, several women gifted with the Rift fled for protection beyond the Perimeter Wall. Some fled for the islands, a few braved the Batiwood knowing that our Horde would not follow, and yet at least two fled to the Magaran mountain range and lands beyond. The author of *Magaran Folkore* gives the most detailed account of Rifters we've seen, which leads me to conclude that he had firsthand accounts."

"I thought the Magaran tribe despised any form of Dua? Why would they allow Rifters in?" Alik asked. She thought back to the images of bloody battles between their winged fighters and the Efendian army from her studies. The Magaran people proved to be the only significant neighbor Efendi could not overtake, so an uneasy truce between the mountain tribe and her kingdom formed before Alik was born. They were supposed to patrol the skies of land beyond Efendian walls, and in return, the Duawielding army would leave them alone. However, the Horde hadn't heard from their scouts in weeks.

Agnian's words came to mind, *"What would make the Magarans stop their patrols of your skies?"*

Josef responded to Alik, "Well, the Magarans certainly hate most Duawielders, but what is the primary principle of Dua?"

Alik responded automatically, "Dua is a temporary gift from nature meant to be borrowed with humility, not taken with greed."

Josef nodded and continued, "Rifters do not take from nature, according to this author. They do not rely on the elements surrounding them, and as such, are believed to be blessed by Ruzgar. From his accounts, we believe there was at least one woman with the ability to Rift among them."

"And I suppose the Edicsi is waltzing through the Magarans as well, according to this author?" Alik jested.

Josef winced slightly, looking almost apologetic. "Something like that. The author includes a tale of the Edicisi more vulgar in nature. It describes him as the offspring of a demon and a Goddess coupling. Some of the images are rather graphic."

"That should do the trick wonderfully!" Damari exclaimed happily.

The trio passed through several halls of books broken up with altars to dead Efendians and then crossed what felt like a mausoleum interspersed with a few stacks of books. Shadows flicked beneath the blue-veined light along the edges. Alik swore she saw another stick figure of the Edicisi in a corner, but she was afraid to be left alone if she stopped. The only living person they passed was a Waterwerker pulling water droplets from the walls. Finally, they came to the center of the mountain where the library's main entrance and catacomb resided.

The narrow walls opened to a cavernous dome littered with stairs and offshoots that eventually led to more dead and more books. Alik swallowed her dread at the sight of the long tables and orb lights under the massive statue of the four Goddesses.

The Goddesses stood two stories tall, their outstretched palms and arms held up the eight primary staircases that led to each of the levels above. Few patrons visited the library of dead and books at any time, let alone during Hasateen festivities, so the only movement came from the handful of workers and elderman moving sure-footed throughout. No one is sure which came first---the books or the dead---but it felt every bit the tomb to Alik.

"The text is beyond the next stairwell. I'll have an acolyte with younger legs bring it down for you. Is there anything else you wish, My Pillar?" Josef bowed to Alik but smiled genuinely at Damari.

"Are property ownership records held here?" Alik asked.

Josef replied, "Yes. Ruzgar's left stairwell and to the right. Is there something you're looking for in particular? I could help you pull records."

Alik worried a cuticle before answering. "Hvard Canavar's assets. Or assets held under his Canavar Company."

Damari looked questioningly at her but turned to Josef. "Thank you, Elderman. I'll walk with you."

They walked together, speaking low, up the main staircase that wound up several stories. Alik confirmed no one was around her before opening her mother's slim volume in her lap. She pulled an orb closer to her and the familiar scrawl danced under the flickering light. Sketches crammed the pages, and questions and reference notes lined the margins. Alik's fingers danced over the notes, reading but not understanding the half-thoughts and maps scrawled on its pages.

Trio of power- Edicisi, Rifter and ???? Who is the third?

Gatekeeper, door. Watchers?

How did the Ley Lines form?

She jumped at the thump of a dusty tomb landing on the stone table. The acolyte mumbled an apology, and Alik waved her off while stashing the notebook away. *I'll have to read it later when I'm alone.*

She slipped her mother's journal into her pocket and flipped through the ancient tomb in case anyone watched her. The book started with fables of winged Magarans fighting creatures beyond their mountain range and interactions with the Goddesses. It later picked up stories of Rifters, but the women were not bent over and haggard as every other text depicted.

She flushed at a detailed drawing of a Goddess and a Demon entangled on an altar. The next page depicted a chiseled, shirtless man with demon horns and the black cloak of the Edicisi. Any image of the Edicisi she had seen before showed him cloaked, so she never saw his face. But this depiction gave the reader the impression that the demon spawn was beautiful. Any other time, she would want to dive into any story about him, but her mind drifted elsewhere as her fingers skimmed the tiny text.

Over the last seven years, she learned painfully and slowly to trust her instincts when reading other people's auras. She once tried to categorize the colors and feelings she read in order to study auras, but they kept adjusting or changing. Now Alik thought less about what each color meant and more about what each felt like to her. She assumed the soothsaying aspect of her Dua would eventually click as well, but she felt as confused about her recurring dream as she did the first plume of an aura at 12.

In every dream, I finally find someone I've searched for, but I still run out of time. That could mean Shauna, but why not show me her in my dream instead of someone else? So who is the girl I am running after? Is she to be kidnapped? And who grabs me? I can't tell if it's a warning to find the girl before time runs out or if the dream is warning me away from finding her in the first place. She assumed Shauna's disappearance made her jumpy, but now that she thought about it, she felt watched the whole dream. *And perhaps that bleeds over into my waking hours, but I felt watched before I saw the cloaked man on First Night, and again in the Trades before those men chased me. Perhaps I'm being watched because I am closer to finding out who, or what, is responsible for the girls? And the men that chased me said,* "he will kill us if he finds out we let her go when she was right there." *Who is "he"?*

She tapped her toe on the ground, recalling the shift earlier.

Every nerve ending in her body pulsed tonight with her Dua, and she banged her head on the open book. *Think, Alik. Your Dua is trying to tell you something, but you are too weak or blind or incompetent to see what that is. Think.* As she drummed her fingers on the pages, a drawing snagged her attention.

She read aloud, "Bakilaran Altar Gift." *That's bizarre.* The rendering under her fingers depicted a stone doorway, laden with chains, and a Rifter accepting interlocking chain links from a bowed couple in servant garb.

Damari's laugh echoed with Josef as they came down the steps.

She asked the elderman, "Why would Magaran folklore reference Bakilar?" Alik thought back to the map on her mother's wall, the sand wasteland of Bakilar stretching far across the Turkaz Sea from Efendi at almost the opposite corner of the world.

Josef paled slightly, urging Alik to scan him on instinct. He fumbled over his first few words, "I, uh, I believe the Magarans...once hailed from Bakilar centuries ago. Scholars once thought it hosted kin of theirs when it wasn't a desert."

She remembered her mother's handwritten scrawl in one corner of the map.

"Are there references to something called 'Ley Lines' as well?" Alik asked.

His brows furrowed. "I'm not sure. Only a handful of texts regarding the Handmaidens mention the term 'Ley Lines' and in sparse words only, so I doubt it very seriously. If you'll excuse me," Josef bowed quickly and limped off out of their eyesight.

"That was odd," Damari said at his retreating back.

"Indeed," saild Alik. "Why would someone renowned for their knowledge fear a fable?" She shook her head to clear the Dua. "Canavar first." The pair divvied up the papers and spread out at the table; the Magaran Folklore set aside.

Damari asked, "What am I looking for, Alik?"

"Maps. Deeds to land in Canavar Company's name or

Hvard's within Efendi's Perimeter Wall. Particularly in the Dockside and anything that looks like the core of the Trades."

He nodded, and they worked side by side in silence apart from the shuffling of papers. Alik shivered at the frigid air. Almost every acolyte and elderman left but Josef and another when Damari's whispers broke her concentration.

"It looks like the Canavar Company began purchasing assets in the Lower Tiers about seven years ago. Small, dilapidated buildings mostly. Then about a year ago, they came into enough money to buy significant blocks of the Trades to use as gambling halls and pleasure houses. There are a handful of arrest warrants for stealing. Nothing we couldn't already guess, though. I didn't find anything showing they held interest in the Dockside---no slips, no boats, no trading documentation."

Alik began to speak when he mentioned almost casually, "I did see several grain silos under Hvard's name."

Her skin prickled. The map of the missing girls in her study had pins scattered up and down the Tiers, but some of the earliest pins clustered around the Silos.

Damari interjected before she could voice her question. "Ty and his men have combed the Silos, though. They haven't found anything amiss."

She asked, "Theoretically, if you wanted cargo to *remain* hidden, where would you go?"

"Truly hidden? The Magaran mountain range may not be within Efendi's walls, but our Horde or Perimeter Patrols would eventually spot someone on the road or fields if they were coming back and forth with ample cargo. The Magaran scouts would have to be on your side as well if you were to remain there, and they hate all land dwellers."

He leaned back in his chair, flicking a stray lock of hair from his eyes, and crossed his arms. He chewed on the corner of his lower lip while he worked through the options, and Alik remembered studying next to him as a mischievous child. She smiled despite the anxiety growing in her belly, but she didn't interrupt him.

He continued, "One of the islands off Dvari would be the best option if you could get to and from the Dockside unnoticed. But again, Taavi doubled the patrol before even Shauna disappeared. A lightweight boat stationed upriver could work, but you'd have to go past our patrols, past the Aygir fields, and the guarded farms to get there. The same would be true if they shipped off as far as the sand seas of Bakilar." Damari paused.

"Say it." Alik wanted him to voice the one place he had yet to mention so she wasn't crazy.

"The Batiwood. You'd still have to get past the Perimeter Patrol and through the valley, but there are few farms and hardly any people between Efendi and the woods. Our patrols do not go there, and the Magarans refuse to fly over. You'd just have to navigate bloodthirsty Yurutec and Garfu, as well as Goddess-knows what other creatures lurk in the bowels of the woods."

"And the Dua of the missing girls would be diminished there," Alik said.

Damari nodded. "Yes. But the Perimeter Patrol would spot anyone coming or going. And some of the missing are as old as you and Shauna, well into their defense study. They would put up a fight. How, then, could they be taken without even a hint of a struggle?"

Alik shook her head. "I don't know, but I know Hvard Canavar is involved. He has to be."

Damari said, "A Rifter would make sense, Alik."

"Nothing about any of this makes sense." Alik's mind spun, and she palmed the red leather journal of her mother's in her pocket. She wasn't sure why she wanted to keep Agnian's theory to herself about Firtina, but she didn't mention it regardless. "I need to get back. Tell your Eyes to comb through Hvard's assets in the middle of the Trades, and report immediately when any of his men go to the Silos."

ELAINE

Turns out, Rifting is exhausting.

After her handful of Rifts in the Silos, Elaine came back to the Hadishi home and slept harder than she ever had before. When she woke up, though, she could barely sit still with the need to do it again. Grateful that she had the excuse to work with Kanne Da'Neen, she spent the next few days practicing in the Silos. Each night she'd sleep like she was hibernating, only to wake up with an even stronger desire to Rift again. She feigned illness to avoid Kanne Da'Neen again and set off for the Silos as the sun rose.

Almost as soon as she arrived, she knew there were too many Groundwerkers loading grain for her to practice. She kicked at a pile of discarded husks, debating where to go instead. *I could just not Rift today.* The thought made her feel like a trapped rabbit.

She pictured a mid Tier where Kara took her once before. *That could work.*

The residents of the mid Tiers had proud homes with permanent walls and small, tidy gardens in front that just poked above the Perimeter Wall. The houses were pastel; light periwinkle windows cut through daisy yellow walls, and next door, lavender trim encased mint green doors. The colors were not as bold as the Trades or as natural as Low Town, but it was a sight more welcome than the upper Tiers. Elaine never understood the allure of the Elite Tiers' stark white stone walls, but even here, she felt like the color was leached out the higher you scaled in Efendi.

The real allure, though, is that most Efendians of this rank worked elsewhere, and so it was as empty as one could hope mid-morning. Elaine ignored the eeriness of her echoing footfalls off the pastel walls as she ran around the bend, checking to make sure the path ahead was clear.

Creepiness aside, Elaine relished the ability to Rift without being seen. She likened Rifting to squeezing in between a tight doorway; she could feel the edges compress against her cheek and chest and thought it helped if she held her breath during the process. Initially, Elaine could only Rift a handful of feet in front of her, but this morning she figured out how to Rift to a place around the bend that she couldn't see.

It's a lot like my bike back home, she thought. Summers tended to mush together in her memory, but there was one that stood out above the rest. Their tin-colored trailer backed up to another man's mobile home separated only by thick wild rhododendrons and sparse crabgrass. She knew she wasn't allowed over there, but Elaine often traded common sense for curiosity, and she'd seen the neighbor leave that morning. She plucked her way through the rhododendrons to explore but came across a rusted red handlebar before she got out.

The bike was ancient. It somehow survived the summer storms and god-knows-what else, and she felt a kinship with the forgotten treasure. She wrestled it from the underbrush, filled its tires at a gas station using some hard-found quarters, and spent the next two weeks mustering up the courage to teach herself how to ride it. When she finally sailed steadily for the first time, she felt like she was flying. She spent the next two years on it, and it became as much a part of her as her walking legs.

Rifting, she figured, *is a lot like that bike.* Once she trusted herself enough to figure it out on her own, Rifting became as natural to her as tooling around the marsh on two wheels.

Elaine ran ahead, breathless, to check out the next turn around the bend. The mid-Tier houses didn't bend with the curve like some of the other Tier homes, so she ran past sharp angles and edges that jutted out to block her next move. Spying no one, she ran back to her predetermined starting position, steadied herself, and drew the lavender home with a taffy pink door in her mind before Rifting. It was the longest jump she'd successfully done, and Elaine had to bend over to quell the dizziness that overtook her.

That's when she spotted the boy standing at the taffy pink door.

He was somewhere between a boy and a man but young enough that Elaine noticed his details. He had thick, chestnut-colored hair streaked by bits of copper from the sun and an almost feminine mouth that parted in surprise. Elaine wasn't as good as Reiki or Kara at pinpointing status based on looks alone, but he looked cleaner than she, so she assumed he belonged at least in the mid Tiers. *Likely at this house,* she thought. *The house that he just walked out of right as you leapt through thin air in front of him, you idiot.*

"Wait!" He shouted as he ran down the pretty pathway and through the fence gate to her.

Elaine ran faster than she had ever run before around the bend. She thought of the chaos of the Trades and the nooks and crannies she had explored in the short time she'd been in Efendi. She pictured the heat of Kabushi's grill and the shift of the grains in her hand as she bagged grain for Reiki and Kara's customers. It would be the most significant Rift so far, but she felt like she had no other choice. She thought of Kara's voice calling out to merchantresses and the way she always knew what to do.

Take me to Kara, Elaine thought as she closed her eyes tight.

It felt like two giant, invisible palms flattened her. She needed air desperately but couldn't find space in her lungs to inhale. Just as she thought she would never make it out, she landed hard on her butt at the back of Reiki and Kara's stall.

Through the wave of dizziness, Elaine registered two things. The first was Kara's eyes comically wide on her and her mouth unhinged. The second was the bulk of Hvard Canavar's frame standing just opposite of Kara on the other side of the table.

Hvard leaned over the table, his meaty finger pointing inches from Reiki's face. Hvard's face was ashen, and he scratched at a few scabs Elaine hadn't noticed before on his neck. Kabushi must have said something because, in the moment Elaine Rifted, Hvard turned towards his stall and not Elaine. Kabushi's bushy white eyebrows shot to the top of his forehead at her entrance.

Kara suddenly flipped over the ladder holding every grain they'd brought to sell. Small pellets of yellow, gold and brown flew like confetti in the air, and merchantresses and passersby alike were bombarded by the hard flecks of grain. An immediate uproar ensued. Hvard's small black eyes focused first on Kara, then the upturned ladder, but instead of turning to the increasingly confused and angry crowd covered in grain, his eyes caught Elaine's.

Kabushi kicked his grill. Flaming nuts and red-hot charcoal spilled out at Hvard's feet, forcing him to jump back with a shout. Kara shoved Elaine behind their back curtain, her shoulders slamming against the stone of the Trades Tier. She could barely stand but forced herself to pull upright and ignore the waves of nausea threatening to overtake her.

Elaine heard Reiki cry out, "What in the ever-present Ates flame just happened?"

Kara, never faltering, "Did you *see* that bird? That was the size of two grain sacks!"

The turquoise curtain draped Elaine's face, and she dared not breathe. She heard Kabushi's baritone voice, "That was a Sisleman Sahin! I've never seen one of those on this side of the Magaran. Are you both alright?"

Kara and Kabushi spoke animatedly over each other, fabricating what would have had to be the most terrifying bird in increasingly detailed depictions.

"It was right here!"

"And then it landed over here and flew off-"

Hvard's voice cut through Kara's lie. "Where is she?"

Without pause, Kara replied, "How do you know it was a female Sahin?"

Kabushi chimed in, "That's impressive, Hvard. I had no idea you were a bird watcher and-"

Hvard shouted, "Enough! The two of you--- Stop. Talking. You know exactly who I'm talking about, and it's not some filbish bird! Where *is* she?"

Elaine slid down behind the curtain to the neighboring stalls. She slipped out a few stalls down and walked back on as steady feet as possible to Hvard's broad back.

"What happened here? Are you guys OK?" She asked, studiously ignoring Hvard and devoting her whole attention on the mess before her.

Hvard snatched Elaine painfully by the arm, hauling her up to her tiptoes. Reiki, Kara, and Kabushi shouted their alarm simultaneously. But suddenly, the crowd behind them began to stir in commotion. Panicked shoppers pushed each other to get out of the Trades as shopkeepers hastily packed up their stalls. Kabushi left to find out what happened, leaving the rest of them in an awkward pause.

Thank you, sweet baby Jesus for distractions, Elaine thought. She wiggled hard enough to rip her oversized shift out of Hvard's grasp and darted behind Kara and Reiki.

Kabushi returned with a Towner Elaine recognized from a nearby cluster. Visibly shaken, he said, "Pack up, Kara, you should get home quickly. Everyone is saying Rifters are among us again and are the ones that have been taking our Daughters."

Hvard stiffened, and Kara nudged Elaine while the man continued talking. Elaine didn't need to be told twice. She slipped out again, not daring to Rift, and ran as fast as she could to their home.

ALIK

❖

Alik sent a note to Agnian the following morning asking him to join her in the gardens. She needed to know more about his role and what wider ramifications the kidnappings could cause beyond Efendi's borders. He referenced "we," which she assumed meant Dvari, but now she wasn't so sure.

She pulled her thick braid over her shoulder and ran a finger over her stained burgundy lips. She spent the final remaining hours of the night alternating between studying her mother's journal and mulling over all the pieces of information she'd learned. The extra effort in her appearance just made her look less dead.

She could care less. Mind-numb and bone-tired, she felt every second she wasted meant one less second to find Shauna. *Agnian can hate me while we work together; I need every piece of information he has.*

Agnian waited at the far bench, boots propped so that his toes pointed off the terraced cliff towards the sun. The water's spray occasionally spits on this lowest terrace, and the waves crashing against the rocks below them drowned out any chance of someone overhearing their conversation. He didn't stand when she came into view, instead only briefly glancing at her before returning his eyes to the Turkaz Sea ahead of them.

This will go well, she thought as she sat next to him. She opted to ignore the awkward rant he left her with last night. *There's nothing I can do about his grudges against my family and me, but I can find Shauna and the others.*

The morning sun warmed the stone bench, and she leaned back, wishing its rays would bake the unease from her skin. She debated how to begin and settled with, "I went through my mother's private study after you left."

She peeked an eye open. His full attention was on her now, so she continued. "Nothing referenced where the missing girls are or gave any hints as to who she would be in contact with regarding their kidnapping."

"I'm not saying that you're wrong," Alik said as he opened his mouth to object. "I just need to know how you came to believe she's involved so I can narrow my search. You said the Canavar Company is involved. I need to know what you've found and who the 'we' is you referenced."

He punted her questions and asked instead, "If she is not involved, who do you think is responsible?"

She couldn't voice the theories in her mind just yet, not even to her brothers. She certainly wasn't about to lay her suspicions on the table with a stranger hiding his own secrets, so she hedged. "I'm thinking that I'm losing my mind and that if I said my theory aloud, it would be crazy enough to lock me away forever."

She glanced sideways at Agnian. He watched her intently before turning his gaze back to the jewel-toned sea. He raked a hand over his salt & pepper stubble and down the back of his deeply tanned neck.

"I hated Dvari when I first came home around seventeen." Alik turned to him at the unexpected turn of conversation. He cleared his throat and continued, "I had just come back after spending my youth abroad, and I loathed the water city. I felt like it was a maze of canals, rope bridges, and ladders and that they were all part of an entangled lure meant to trap me. My father insisted that it was time to return home and learn the family trade, but all I wanted was to go back to what I felt was my homeland."

Alik cocked her head, "Where did you spend your youth?"

He quirked a smile that made her heart flip, and she chided herself for being a ninny. "I grew up on a barren land that has little appeal to most people, but I felt safe in its vast seas of sand."

Alik's mouth gaped at the thought of the expansive fields of red sand dunes from her studies. "You grew up in *Bakilar*?"

Alik thought of the sad little village sandwiched between the sea and the sand that served as the lone outpost for the entire wasteland. She'd never met anyone from Bakilar. The land was on the opposite side of the world from Efendi, a couple months' journey from Dvari, with leagues of sea plagued by the pirates of Perise in between. Her mother sent the most loathsome emissaries there only---ones that had slighted her significantly enough to be punished but not enough to kill or imprison. It was as dull of a place as Alik could imagine.

Agnian laughed at her astonishment and leaned down to toss a pebble over the terraced edge ahead of them. "Yes. I know it doesn't sound as lovely as this, but there is beauty in the undulating umber sand. When I was old enough, though, I spent most of my time on a Perisien ship."

Alik straightened, alarm bells clanging wildly in her head. *The Perisiens would be the most logical buyer of Efendian women if someone is selling them. Their slave trade between their ships is notorious.* She schooled her features and tried to calm the questions pounding through her mouth. "Oh?"

He laughed harder at that. "You have the most obvious tells, Princess." He lightly traced the space between her eyebrows and the bridge of her nose, "Here," and then his fingertips brushed the edges of her eyes, "and here."

She stilled at his surprising touch, alarm bells of an entirely pitch different ringing. Fortunately, he spoke before she needed to.

"I know it would be ill-advised for me to mention that to you.

I am not Perisien, though, as much as I loved them and wanted to be for a time."

Alik sputtered, "But they're *pirates."*

He shrugged, and it made him look like a guilty child that unabashedly felt no guilt. "They're seafarers making a living the only way they know how. Some are as terrible as the tales. I never saw the *Adanuse,* nor did I meet her Lord, but I sailed on a ship crewed with mostly good men. A little terrifying looking, but good nonetheless."

The *Adanuse* is notorious. It is a ship at a scale Alik scarcely believed, and it serves as the floating city for the warmongering pirates. According to their sources, the Perisiens had few rules of law, except loyalty and tithe to its Pirate Lord. No one outside of a Perisien knew what the Pirate Lord looked like--- no names, no history. It was as fabulously terrifying to listen to those stories as a child as it was the tales of the Edicisi.

It wasn't until Alik grew up and was privy to the treaties and woes of the lesser kingdoms that she came to understand that the Lord was a real, living evil. The looting and murdering aside, the most atrocious stories came of their slave trade. Once Dvari came under Firtina's rule, the Perisien threat on Dvarian ships sharply declined. Dvari once served as just a physical buffer between the pirates and Efendi, bearing the brunt of the worst attacks. Now, Dvarian ships armed with Efendian Duawielders served as protection against those same attacks. She recalled his tirade from the night before, how he claimed Efendians stole his country's ships. *Do they not realize we're helping them?*

Agnian leaned in conspiratorially, "The thing about pirates is that they gossip more than anyone." He shifted back, nodding to the boats bobbing out to sea before continuing, "I was mending a sail when our quartermaster came on board from a small island port not far from Bakilar. I overheard him telling the Captain that a man deep in his cups on the docks claimed to be Queen Firtina's lover. He swore that he found a way to make her the most powerful ruler any world had ever seen, and he a living god. But that it would require a blood sacrifice. He was paying heavy coin for information on ships selling a Rifter."

Alik thought back to the cups of blood in the Trades and at the Ates stairwell. They were ridiculous offerings to the Handmaidens, but the idea of Rifters resurfacing in Sakalid paled in comparison to what else Alik believed could be true with each word out of his mouth.

“What happened to the man in the docks that claimed this?”

Agnian snorted and cast another pebble out to sea. "That’s just it. We don’t know. My quartermaster went back at my Captain’s command to find him again, but he disappeared. Even the bartender that served them has never been seen since.”

“So that’s why you’re here? You think that some lover of my mother has come back to make her more powerful than she already is?” Alik stood up, pacing. “I don’t get it. Despise her all you want, but there’s no arguing that she already is the most powerful ruler this world has ever seen. Who could offer her more power?”

She stilled as she said those words.

“I didn’t say *this* world. Neither did he. He said he could make her the most powerful ruler *any* world had ever seen. Not just this one.”

Alik put her face in her hands. *Bokki. I’m trusting a man that has lost his mind.* She continued to pace, thinking back to her mother’s hidden room. *But perhaps we’re all losing our minds.*

“OK. Let’s set that aside for a moment and focus. Your Captain sent you here to find this man from the docks that claimed to be her lover wanting a ‘blood sacrifice’ that required Rifters, right? Do you think he was part of Canavar’s Company?”

I can’t imagine her slumming with anyone from more than a Tier below the Palace, but we may begin discussing crazier things than that.

Agnian avoided her eyes, prompting her to scan him. *Pale green reluctance.* She crossed her arms. “Tell me what you are not saying.”

“There are some things I absolutely cannot tell you. But it was not my Captain that sent me here. There are others. Others that---"

Shouts of alarm and running footsteps from the guardswomen above cut him off. He stood before she could push him further. "There must be news. Let's go."

REED

Reed could have wept with joy when they emerged from the tunnel and into the watery light of sunrise. He warily approached the milling Aygir while he answered Monti's question about how he worked with the beasts.

"My mother and I spent some time with a traveling caravan--gypsies of sorts. A half-breed Itreni was part of the crew for a time, and I helped him perform tricks for Efendians as we made our way up the Tiers of their kingdom."

He had his eye on his Aygir. She was a female, a touch broader than the rest but shorter as well. She looked old enough to have seen several battles, and the scars on her silver flanks confirmed that she'd taken a few wounds over the years. He slowly walked to her side and bowed low as his friend taught him decades before. The wind ruffled Reed's stolen shirt, but he held his position.

The beast took her time before she opened her mouth to him. The blood and gristle still wedged in her teeth told him that she'd already eaten. The Aygir were among the fastest creatures in Efendi, battle-trained, and bloodthirsty themselves. His friend Tilli told him stories of how they'd often turn on their riders for meals if they were kept out of battle too long. Tilli had been full of bokki, but Reed still hesitated before putting his hand in her bloodied mouth.

Fortunately, she didn't eat his hand. Instead, she bowed low for him to loop the leather reign across her thick neck before hopping on. Reed's jump up was not graceful with his injured arm, but he was at least on top now. He pulled Monti up ahead of him, clicking two short bursts that prompted the Aygir to start a quick pace towards the fence. He squeezed his thighs together to give Monti more stability and held the reign in his good hand wrapped around her waist.

Monti fired off questions about this realm, the kingdom, the valley, and the mountains in the distance ahead of him when Reed interrupted her.

"Monti, we got a long ride ahead of us, and you haven't slept in two days. Sleep while you can. I'll answer everything in a couple of hours."

He slowed the Aygir to a trot and aimed for the ice-blue river in the distance that would snake its way north to the dark mountains at the horizon. Within a few minutes, he felt Monti slump against him, and he allowed himself to think about the events of the last 48 hours.

He and his mother were on the run for as long as he could remember. His earliest memories were of hiding in the squalor of Low Town with his mother, Alisha, always peering over her shoulder. Her eyes consistently tight with worry, and her dark hair hidden beneath a threadbare wrap. Reed never met his father, but his mother explained that they were hiding from this faceless man even at an early age. At some point, Alisha got word that his father had fled the kingdom of Efendi and its continent for lands across the Turkaz Sea. She wasn't sure where he went, but she said she felt safer in the expanse of Efendi so long as they never stayed in one place too long. She joined the Canavar Company Caravan shortly afterward as a singer.

The Canavar Company men were hardly a step in the right direction, but Reed and Alisha had their own iron wagon, and some of the men were tolerable. It's where he met Tilli, where he learned stories of his land and its brutal inhabitants, and where he spent the formative years of his childhood. His mother always spoke in whispers, though, when they traveled through the Tiers, making discrete inquiries of the powerful man she once fled. *I don't know how my father did it, but somehow he's figured out a way to drag me back here.*

But Reed knew why, which is why he aimed the Aygir far from the glittering kingdom behind him.

Monti stirred a little while later while the sun was still over the sea in the distance. She must have felt better because she instantly started complaining about her smell, the pain of sitting on the broad back of the Aygir, and the way Reed smelled. Whatever begrudging alliance they'd forged below ground grew thin as she complained.

I can't take another minute of her complaints, he thought. The tumultuous river that ate through the valley devolved into a slow current at this section, and Reed gave no warning before he clicked the Aygir to dive headfirst into the ice-cold water that rose above their knees. He pushed Monti off the Aygir, smiling when she thrashed like a cat doused in the water. He dove in, keeping the Aygir between them, to use the beast as a shield from her wrath and laughed.

She splashed at him, glaring mutiny as she proclaimed, "You son of a one-legged whore. You could have at least warned me before you tossed me over like a heap of potatoes."

However, she ducked under and shot back up through the sparkling water, laughing, and Reed momentarily forgot how to blink. He rubbed his calloused hands over his face. Swimming away, Reed focused instead on scrubbing the dried blood off his body. He winced as he washed the wound in his forearm, and when the refreshing water took a turn for frigid, they dragged themselves back into the grass.

The sea of green and gold grass swayed with a slight breeze coming off the mountains, but the sun's heat penetrated even his wet clothes. The Batiwood loomed far off to the west, and the kingdom of Efendi was a small, golden toy cake behind them. Reed stomped his feet to bring the blood back to his stiff legs.

Reed loved this Aygir. Monti opened her mouth, likely to complain more, just as the beast rambled back from the water, holding a large, mangled fish. The Aygir took that moment to shake off all the excess water, showering Monti. The fish, gored open by the Aygir's sharp teeth and curved horn, landed with a thick plop on her shoe.

Reed fell back in the grass, laughing as hard as he'd laughed in years at her fish gut shoe. "Your face is worth whatever tantrum I'll have to endure."

To his surprise, Monti tipped her head back, laughing as well. She had a deep belly laugh, one used often and without reservation. Grinning, Monti tilted her chin towards the sun and shook her hair like a wet dog. She bellowed something between a yell and a war cry at the sky, and Reed stopped laughing. The fear of facing his father took up most of his thoughts, and the chaos of landing here, fighting the Itreni, and hiding from the Yurutec took up the rest. But now that they put distance between themselves and the Batiwood and the kingdom, he realized with a start that Monti was breathtakingly beautiful.

She motioned to the grasses that reached her knees. "Is this patch of grass safe to take a break, or will dragons come barreling over that mountain there?"

Reed smiled, "Nah, the dragons won't fly during the day." He laughed at her incredulous stare and relented, "That's a joke. There are no dragons in this world."

"That's not even remotely funny," Monti said as she wrung out her hair. "Now turn around; I gotta get down to my skivvies so my clothes can dry."

The sun almost reached the mountain peak now, and the loudest sounds were the fish bones crunching beneath the Aygir's teeth. Reed stripped off his shirt and pants and dropped to the soft grass to dry as well. He heard Monti do the same behind him as he rested back on his good side, rewrapping his injury with the cloth she swiped from the Itreni's home for him. He ripped up some grass seed and handed the golden stalks to Monti without fully turning to her.

"Eat this. It tastes like the wafer crackers in church, but it'll tide you over."

The sun's kiss warmed his pebbled skin, and Reed just closed his eyes when Monti said, "Alright now. Tell me everything."

He groaned. Reed turned to Monti and caught her golden-green eyes through the stalks watching him like a tiger on the hunt. She flipped over to her belly and faced him with her head on crossed forearms. The ends of her hair dried into soft golden waves, and she swatted a strand off as it slipped over her eyes. Reed tried to think of anything terrible and came up with a myriad of options quickly.

"Don't 'ughhh' me. I've been chock-full of patience. Start with this, are we really in another world? Is it like a planet or another dimension?"

Reed thought back to how his mother explained it to him years ago. "Imagine this: you're in a library with aisles and aisles of books stacked together. They're pressed in tight from floor to ceiling. The characters and worlds within every book exist on their own without any knowledge that there's another story smashed alongside it, bound by another cover. Our world is like that. It's just behind the next cover."

"So if we hop covers, we could be in Hogwarts?" Monti looked hopeful.

"Jesus. No. I'm just trying to give you a visual."

"So, how does it work?"

"Do I look like Carl Sagan? If I knew that, we would be out of here. That's why we have to find a Rifter if we want to get home."

"Who is Carl Sagan?" Monti asked.

"Nevermind."

She kept firing without pause. "But you know where one is? A Rifter?"

Reed explained how his mother's best friend fled to the Magaran mountain range with another Rifter like her. He watched her brows furrow as he said, "The Magarans took them in when the Efendians renewed the hunt of their kind years ago."

Monti interrupted, "Wait. So Rifters are witches?"

"No. Efendian folklore and ignorance turned them into something like witches. Efendians think they eat human flesh and snatch unruly kids from their beds, but in reality, they're no different than other Duawielders."

"Dua whatters?" Monti was back to munching grass seed while drying her dismantled gun on the hem of her shirt. Reed was simultaneously relieved and disappointed that her damp shirt was back on.

"Women in this realm have power. Like magic power that revolves around soil, fire, air, and water or a combination of a few. The most powerful are the wealthiest, and the women with very little power are in a caste barely above, sometimes subpar, of the Aygir."

Monti paused her drying, "Every single woman has power?"

Reed stood up to stretch his arms over his shaking head and clarified, "Efendian women are the only ones with any sort of Dua---magic-- in this world. It's why they're the most powerful." He tilted his head to the distant Tiers stacked near the sea behind them. "This valley is part of the Kingdom of Efendi, but there are other human lands beyond it. The women from the surrounding villages and kingdoms do not have Dua."

He bent down to pick up his shirt and saw Monti's eyes linger over his torso before dropping down to the gun again. He bit back a surprised smile and asked, "What did you do for a living back home?"

She replied quickly, "Marketing. How many other kingdoms are there?"

"Dvari is the next largest kingdom, though when we left this realm, the Iktidar Queen was launching an assault to take it over as well. It's an archipelago a couple of weeks by sea, made up of hundreds of small islands." He nodded to the peaks ahead of them. "The Magarans live in those mountains. They're a race of creatures that look like a cross between a falcon and a human. They're hostile to everyone outside their race, but they hid Rifters when no one else would. There are minor villages and farming communities scattered on the other side of the mountains that are a mixed bag of humans and creatures that would make the Itreni look normal. They live together under the protection of the Iktidar rule, though they are little better than serfs."

Reed blew out a breath and ripped the grain from the stalks surrounding him as he continued. "Let's see...On the far side of Dvari, there is a sand wasteland called Bakilar that may or may not still have villagers, and there's a race of pirates that sail the seas in between everyone that call themselves Perisiens."

Monti looked to the orange-red tree line across the valley. "And that? Are the woods part of the Efendian kingdom?"

"No. That's the Batiwood, and no one, other than the realm's foulest creatures, goes there willingly. It's said to be cursed. It destroys the land under its roots slowly over time, turning it to sand. It's a lot closer than I remember to the gates of Efendi, and the Efendian race has been working for years to figure out a way to stop its encroachment."

Monti arched an eyebrow. "You guys have magic. You mean to tell me they haven't figured out a way to stop some trees from growing?"

"First, there's no 'you guys.' Only Efendian women have magic, no men. Second, the Efendian Queen is the most powerful Duawielder in over a century. There are few things she'd ever need to fear, and yet, even she wouldn't ride through those woods."

He tilted his head to the Aygir. "Come on. We're significantly safer with an Aygir that's taken to us, but we still can't be in the middle of the valley after dark. I'll answer as much as I can while we're moving." Reed gathered up a handful more stalks and walked to the beast's side before he realized Monti hadn't moved.

"First, tell me this. What were you and your mother running from that you had to go to another world to get away?" Monti asked with arms crossed.

Reed thought back to the wide, gaping, dark mouth from his nightmares. "I never met him, but my dad was apparently a ruthless man, very powerful, and didn't take kindly to my mom running away with me. My mom believed that whatever we faced a world away would be better than him finding us."

He looked down at the grass and tried to shrug off the nagging guilt creeping into his belly. *Monti is capable of keeping her wits together, but she doesn't need to know everything.*

Reed expected to see pity or at least her eyes softening when Monti didn't respond. Instead, she looked at him with sharp eyes and a raised eyebrow that all but screamed, "Bullshit."

ALIK

Optimism always found Alik. She believed the missing girls, Shauna in particular, waited for her to find them, scared but unharmed. When she and Agnian approached the gathering crowd back in the Palace, she expected good news; to be relieved.

"They Rifted a whole building."

"There must be dozens of them!"

Chills spread over Alik in waves. *Rifters.* She gathered a meager puff of an Airwerk and shoved her way to the front of the crowd to get context for the snippets of conversation that provided little information. Courtiers, advisors, and servants took a few steps back, opening a path. She managed to gain control over her labored breathing by the time she reached the rail-thin advisor flinching from questions in the open circle before the gathering crowd.

A strong, commanding voice carried over the crowd, speaking before Alik could. "What is the meaning of this?"

Queen Firtina had a way of walking. Sure-footed, heeled steps preceded her in an announcement to any room. The crowd's blanket of mixed conversations settled when she strode to Alik's side. She still wore her traveling clothes, though most in the crowd would never know it. The long camel-colored cloak tapered to hit her heeled boot within a hair's width of touching the floor; her cropped riding pants and cream gossamer blouse would have been speckled with grime if it had been anyone else riding outside the Perimeter Wall. An off-white turban littered with strands of Magaran gold covered her black hair, though Alik knew if she removed the turban, her hair would cascade down to perfection. The only color on Firtina was the deep burgundy lip stain she favored.

Firtina looked once to Alik, her cat eyes glittering, as the advisor whispered in her ear.

The Queen's voice carried with ease as she pulled her riding gloves off one finger at a time. "I've searched for our missing Daughters for months, looking for a culprit outside our walls that wish us harm. It appears that our kidnapper was not foreign, but one of our own."

A few gasps cried out, a woman in the front dramatically clutched her jade necklace while her friends soothed her. Alik restrained an eye roll. *No one in this Palace was too distraught to stop attending Hasateen parties. No one had been looking frantically for these girls like I have. And definitely, not my mother.*

Agnian stood crossed armed adjacent to her, face tight as Firtina continued.

"Patrols have picked up a small group of people completely foreign to our kingdom and of the kingdoms surrounding us. They were Rifted, along with dozens of others now presumed dead."

Firtina raised her palm at the shocked reaction of the crowd for silence. Alik's mind raced. *That was the shift I felt. It was a Rift.* She was too young to understand the last Rifter Hunt, but she remembered her nursemaid boarding up the windows in the nursery. Years later, she read about the panic-stricken patrols with torches.

"You are the first to know this information."

Not likely, Alik thought. *At least half the Trades know by now if Rifters were indeed spotted.*

Firtina continued, "I'm issuing a decree that will be sent to every level of Tiers. We have Rifters among us, hunting us. They've primarily attacked at night, so I'm implementing a curfew. The remaining nights of Hasateen are hereby canceled until we capture these demons and bring our Daughters home. We will arrange for Horde patrols in every Tier, beginning at the Fountain Tier, and work our way down. Anyone caught harboring a Rifter will be hung and--"

Courtiers do stupid things.

A woman once insisted that her pallu be lined with matches to show off her control over flame. Someone in her staff happened to be a Waterwerker, so she survived. Another Airwerker believed she could fly if she leapt off a tall enough balcony. No one in her entourage was adept at putting her back together. Yet, the dumbest thing Alik ever witnessed a courtier do to date was interrupt her mother. *And in front of a crowd, no less.*

"What good is the Horde against Rifter demons?"

A wide swath opened up before the speaker, courtiers tripping over themselves to gain distance from the insane young woman with arms crossed and blonde hair so pale it was almost white.

Alik placed her name. *Tenida Grynic.* She'd seen her several times at court dinners, usually trailing after Taavi with the usual herd of women. *She appeared to be of sound mind the few times we spoke.*

Firtina's smile crept across her face like a black Magaran cat stalks her prey. Alik's skin itched with the agonizing pause while the rest of the group volleyed eyes between the two women. Tenida, to her credit, didn't break the silence first.

Firtina replied, "We have the same Tuzaga chains that worked so well to contain Rifters of my predecessors. I would imagine we could reconfigure the chains to form muzzles as well."

The courtier ignored the threat. "My family has recently discovered a vein of Tuzaga in one of our mines southwest of the

Magaran. We will furnish the kingdom with any new chains required for free, and my staff and I will volunteer for patrol duty if you grant me one humble request."

Firtina replied, "And what *humble* request do you have?"

Here we go, Alik thought. *Will it be more land? She's bold enough she might just ask for Taavi's hand in marriage here and now.*

"Most of our miners live in Low Town, and several have missing Daughters of their own. I merely ask that the patrol my advisors and I are assigned to begin in Low Town first and work our way up to meet you."

The advisor whispered something to Firtina too faint for Alik to pick up. She nodded and simply said, "Done. My advisor will reach out to your mother to work through the details. Patrol begins at moonrise."

Firtina turned, dismissing everyone else in the hall. Alik quickly scanned Tenida while dozens of conversations bounced off the polished opal floor. Tenida darted past Agnian and the now curious courtiers milling around her, her aura radiating pale yellow worry. Agnian trailed after Tenida with plumes of confusion and disbelief pouring off him, distracting Alik.

Alik had more pressing matters at hand, though. She was the last to enter her mother's study and joined Taavi and Damari at the offset stone table. Advisors spoke animatedly over each other, quickly detailing the decree that would soon spread throughout the Tiers. Firtina pulled a glass decanter to her and poured an amber liquor while she paced and listed orders.

"What do you know of Tenida?" Alik asked Taavi quietly. He spent some time with her before Hasateen, though now that Alik thought about it, Tenida had been absent since at least First Night.

"Not much," Taavi replied. "Her mother is a woman named Danisha Grynic, and she and Tenida came here from a minor village beyond Dvari when Tenida was first gaining her powers for training. No father, no siblings. Her mother is a mining matriarch; they struck an agreement with the Magaran tribes to mine in places we never were granted access."

Alik fiddled with the embroidered edging of her pallu as she mulled over the news. "How long has she been at court?"

Damari chimed in, "Not long. Someone mentioned that her family was new money and that they came here with little more than their mining equipment."

She never heard of a foreigner gaining access to the mountain range without extensive backing by the Iktidars. *Perhaps they came from a place less hostile to the Magarans than Efendi.* Alik mulled this over while mentally flipping through the rural villages and minor kingdoms in the archipelago.

"What of these foreigners?" Alik asked. "Where are they now?"

"I don't know. This is the first I've heard of any foreigners myself." Taavi looked at Alik. She didn't need to say how abnormal it was for their mother to know something a Horde patrol found before Taavi did.

Damari said, "I'll see what my Eyes can find out. They should be in the dungeon by now. But, Alik, there's something I need to--".

Firtina's voice stifled their conversation as she asked everyone but the siblings to leave. The three remained close together, a wall of shoulders facing the Queen. Firtina did not speak, but the heat from the fire orbs flared above them in pulses while the last advisor filtered out.

Firtina said without preamble, "The three of you are worthless. Your ineptitude has put me in a position foreign to any of my ancestors." She stalked behind her desk, her heeled boots setting a steady pace like a war drum.

"Taavi, you are the general of my Horde, and in the space of a few weeks, creatures from the Batiwood have attacked our borders. The Magarans flat out *stopped* responding to our missives, and now a population the size of half a cluster dumped themselves in the valley. Yet, I find you here, meandering around the Palace, while you had your second oversee the massive disturbance reported in the valley..."

"I didn't---" Firtina held a hand up, and Taavi immediately stopped speaking. Taavi was the most loyal son Alik could imagine. *He placates every wish of hers yet never lives up to the increasing standard she demands.*

Alik grit her teeth as her mother continued. "....and you are the only one that has had frequent interaction with *that woman*, and yet again, no one mentioned that her family had control over a new vein of Tuzaga."

"And you," Firtina pointed a fingernail shaped to a sharp claw at Damari, "Not only did I allow you to live, but I allowed your place in my Palace. As a bastard born, you should remember that the only reason I initially did so was at Talik's request. I could rarely tell your father no, so you can imagine how difficult it was to swallow my pride and allow his offspring from a mistress to live amongst our children. Your ability to discover information allowed you to live even after his death. Yet you failed to provide a hint of who *that* woman was and failed to give any mention of lost foreigners claiming they're from *another goddess-damned world.* Take care to remember that your father is no longer here to beg for your life."

Her brothers stiffened at Firtina's unspoken threat. As children, Firtina often singled Damari out to remind him of his half-brother status. Damari proved himself invaluable, though, so she only brought out the reminder on occasion now. She had yet to threaten to kill him until now.

Alik's fists dug half-moons into her palms as she recalled the bright-eyed Damari as a boy left in the darkness of the library catacombs. She refused to look down this time from her mother's stare. Sweat poured down her temple at the heat of the arching flames surrounding them.

Firtina said to her, "And you. Everything I do, I do because I have no Pillar to rely on. Your ineptitude at Dua has forced me to take unthinkable measures to keep an Iktidar on the throne, but I thought I'd at least gain something useful with your soothsaying abilities. Yet a *Goddess-forsaken Rifter* is here, and you blissfully slept through her dumping a dozen people within our borders from another world. I've given you time. I've covered for you. And. I'm. Done."

Alik opened her mouth to speak, but her jaw snapped back at the gust of Airwerk her mother fired. The tang of blood pooled in her mouth, and she held her aching jaw as her mother paced ahead of them.

"I've been too easy on the three of you. My mother would have had my hands mounted above the throne if I showed even a fraction of your ineptitude. So, we'll try something new. I need this Rifter, alive, and I need her found by the week's end. The Hunt about to begin should have been a distraction until that *idiot* girl volunteered Low Town first. Therefore, Taavi, you are assigned to her patrol. Keep her distracted; she cannot find the Rifter first.

"Damari, find several women to charge as Rifters. I don't care who they are or why you chose them. They need to be "discovered" soon before the Tiers erupt in chaos.

"Alik, you will find the Rifter and bring her to me. Should you fail, I will separate the three of you to the corners of this world. Damari, useless as he is, will be sent to live the remainder of his days in Bakilar. Taavi, you will be demoted to a foot soldier and married off to whoever is desperate enough to have you then. And Alik, you will marry the Dvarian prince to solidify our hold and spend the rest of your days on their planks. There is word of an uprising, and believe it or not, I'm disinclined to slaughter another line of Dvarians just to keep the peace."

The three siblings stood agape, trying to process the threats their mother casually ticked off on her manicured nails. No Iktidar daughter ever faced an arranged marriage, let alone one outside of Efendian Tiers. The men of the Iktidar line always borne that brunt, and Alik thought to only protect her brothers from it. She never imagined she'd need protection from it herself. *I should have known better. All the lessons on strengthening my Dua stopped last year. I thought the lessons ended because she wanted me in the council meetings instead. But she stopped seeing me as the one to take her place long before this. Otherwise, she never would send me away.*

Her mother continued as if she hadn't just given Alik a life sentence. "You have only a turn or two before this city upends itself." She flipped open a book at her desk, dismissing them as easily as she did the courtiers in the hall.

Alik's mind still spun around the rumor that Rifters reemerged in Efendi, but all the signs pointed to this unlikely truth: *Rifters are here. It explains how the girls disappeared without any indication of a struggle.* She shut out the threat of an arranged marriage, recalling instead her childhood stories of disfigured women vanishing and appearing in the blink of an eye. Alik's heart flipped as she thought back to something else her mother said.

The flame in the hearth behind Alik flicked in tune with her quick pulse, and she fisted her hands at her sides to still their shake. Taavi and Damari stepped away from the heat, glancing at each other and Alik. Taavi's hand went to his sword.

"*This* Rifter, my Queen?" Alik asked.

Firtina looked up from her book. "What?"

"You said you need 'this Rifter,' and yet you alluded to a group of Rifters in the hall moments ago. Who is this Rifter? What do you know about her? And how did you learn of her?"

Firtina stepped forward, and it took all of Alik's willpower not to back up.

Alik said in a rush, her hands ahead of her, placating. "You need me to find this Rifter. I need to know any information you have in order to find her." Alik did not ask why her mother thought Alik, of all people, could track this woman. *Shauna may be running out of time, and if this Rifter brings me to her faster, so be it. I don't care about the mechanics of how I can find her, only that we do.*

"One would think that I'd be used to spoon-feeding you

everything you need by now," Firtina said. "You are looking for a girl barely into her powers. She will be 12, maybe 13. Start with the Towners first, and when you find her, bring her to me alive."

Alik did not turn to leave. Instead, she said, "For months, I've heard singing, like a lullaby, and chanting in my dreams. And the overwhelming feeling I have when I wake is that someone, or something, is coming, and we are out of time."

Alik paced ahead of her brothers, too focused on her thoughts to see Firtina still.

"Someone is taking our Daughters. Shauna vanished without a single one of us seeing her kidnapper. My Dua went haywire the other night while you were off to Goddess-knows-where, and I'd imagine that is when the Rift occurred. And if you are telling us that *one* Rifter brought this many people from another *world*, she is more powerful and more dangerous than any in our history."

Alik recalled her mother's hidden room and the hundreds of notes on the Edicisi tucked inside. And then she said the theory that had danced in the background of her subconscious since she saw her mother's hidden room. "Do you think she brought Edicisi back?"

"What did you say?"

Alik braced herself but did not repeat her question in the lengthy silence hovering in the room. She expected laughter, rage even.

Not curiosity.

"What makes you think it's the Edicisi?" Firtina finally asked, her quiet question hammering Alik's heart in her bones harder than if she had lashed out.

Taavi stepped closer to Alik, and Damari's hand slipped in hers. *They likely think I've completely lost it,* Alik thought. *But I need to know what I'm up against so I can bring Shauna and the girls home. And if what I believe is true, I will need Firtina on my side.*

Firtina stalked around her desk, the slow clip of heel gaining momentum until she towered over Alik's short frame. Alik had no idea how she would get Shauna and the others out if the monster from their folklore kept them hostage, but she'd find a way. *This Rifter knows where Shauna is, Alik, focus on that.*

"Taavi, Damari, you are dismissed," Firtina answered.

Her brothers paused momentarily, but Alik nodded to both. She turned to face her mother as the door shut again, unable to meet her blue ice eyes.

Firtina circled Alik and asked, "Would you like the Edicisi to come? Hmm? Wipe out our powers and bring us on equal footing for once?

"What would you do then, my weak Pillar? Read me and tell me I'm angry? See that I'm disgusted with the one worthless female I managed to produce before my body could bear no more?"

Alik shook her head, "What? No, my Queen. I would never. I don't know what's harder to believe---that the Edicsi is real or that you actually believe he's real as well."

Legends claimed that the Edicisi monster came when an unfit ruler sat on the Efendian throne. *Is she trying to stop the Rifter from bringing him? Or is he already here, and she's preparing for battle?*

Firtina said, "I believe that there are powers far greater than even my own. I believe that we've only begun to tap into our potential and that worlds are waiting for those smart enough, bold enough, to take them."

Alik glanced at the wall that hid the maps and notes in her mother's secret room and the stacks of books surrounding them now. She recalled her father's nickname for Firtina, *The Bloody Scholar.* He once joked she spent as much time studying in the Catacombs as she did hacking people apart. Alik did not remember Firtina ever laughing at that.

The engraving behind Firtina's secret room flashed in her mind. *The initials certainly don't belong to my father.* "Who is H.B?"

Firtina's step faltered behind Alik, the fire orbs sputtering. She pinched Alik's cheeks with her forefinger and her thumb, wrenching Alik's face painfully to her own. "What did you say?"

This is the first time she's physically touched me in years. Alik wasn't sure why that thought shot through all the rest spinning in her mind. She also wasn't sure why the initials felt so important or why she suddenly felt the need to press this question most of all. "H.B and F.I. You are F.I aren't you, so who was H.B?"

Firtina shoved Alik's face away, the force knocking Alik down to her hands and knees.

A thick band of air wrapped around her waist and lifted Alik into the air. Alik's hands scrabbled at the second band of Airwerk tightening over her throat as her mother said, " I want you out of Efendi. You are stripped of your title as Pillar and Iktidar and no longer an heir to the throne." With each Airwerk, Alik twisted and tumbled in the air, gasping for breath. "You should have never been my daughter in the first place, and my mother's soul will rest easier knowing the Iktidar line is without your taint. I will find this Rifter myself."

The study doors banged open to the Atrium, revealing several gawking courtiers as Alik flew through several feet in the air. She landed with a thud on the opal floors, the pain ricocheting through her bones. The breath was knocked from her, stunning her for a few painful moments while black dots marred her vision. She curled into the fetal position when air finally hit her lungs again.

Alik willed herself to stand despite the confusion and the pain and the mortification, but she remained curled up on the floor, voices murmuring around her. Her eyes blurred with tears as her brothers herded the handful of courtiers out of the Atrium. Agnian came to her side first.

He lifted her off the ground, scooping her as if she was a child. She buried her face against the soft linen shirt stretched tight across his hard chest, unable to look anyone in the eye. She squeezed her eyes shut and breathed in his scent of the sea and new leather as he carried her down the hall in the direction of the guest quarters.

What just happened? She banished me because I asked about the initials? She would have helped me if I didn't press that. She panicked more with each racing thought. *I can't do this on my own. If the Edicisi is real, I need her to get Shauna and the others. Oh Goddesses, Shauna, please be alive.*

The thought of Shauna in the clutches of a demon pulled her from the well of sadness she wallowed in. She lifted her head enough to meet Agnian's eyes. "I think I can walk now."

Agnian nodded, "I know you can."

He cradled her tighter, though, around her knees and waist as he continued down the white stone corridor, thankfully devoid of anyone else. He carried her into a room where sunlight filtered through delicate linen curtains and a soft cream blanket adorned the neatly made bed. He gingerly sat Alik down in a leather chair near a cold fireplace and pulled the curtains aside to reveal a wide window seat that overlooked the Magaran mountains in the distance. Agnian stacked the books strewn across the seat into a neat pile on the floor. He moved the pillows and blanket from the bed to the window.

Alik tracked him, finding strange comfort in his efficient movements and the way his shirt pulled across his forearms as he rearranged the room. Neither spoke. He was a stranger to her, and yet she felt safe in the silence of this small, cozy room far away from the Atrium and the tall doors closed off to her.

Agnian scooped her once more in his arms, dragging her mind back from the morose path it gravitated towards. He placed her among the pillows at the window seat, and slipped off her shoes. He walked to the bathroom after draping her with a soft linen blanket, leaving her alone. Focusing on his small, regular movements helped Alik from drowning in her thoughts.

Agnian returned with the glass bowl of water and a white cloth. Kneeling next to her, he raised the damp cloth raised close to her face, and at her nod, cleaned her bloodied temple and lip. His face hovered a few inches from her own, and she focused on his chiseled jaw as it tightened each time she winced with his featherlight passes.

Alik swallowed, breaking the peaceful silence. Her words ushered in the reality of her situation. "I have to find a particular Rifter before my mother does."

At his cocked head, she poured out everything that occurred moments before with her mother. "I don't know what she wants to do with this Rifter or if the Edicisi is real and already here. I don't even know what I will do once I find Shauna. My whole focus has been to find her, not what will happen once I face her kidnapper. The Canavar Company has to be working for the Edicisi, so Shauna and the others must be with him. What if he's eaten her as the legends claim?" She felt like her breath did not fill her chest with each ragged pull.

"And I have no home now. I am exiled. She expects me to leave. Immediately. But I can't go without finding Shauna and the others. I'd rather be dead at the Edicisi's hand than leave her. I don't care if I am worthless, and I do this alone. I will not leave her to that fate."

Agnian stopped dabbing at the blood on her face and turned her to face him directly. He held her face in his hands and said, "Breathe, Alik. You are not alone. And you are more capable than you know. We'll find her together, and when we get her and the others away from this monster you believe is real, I will make sure you have a home in Dvari."

"Why would you help me even after we find the missing girls?" Alik looked down, recalling their conversation from the café, though it felt a lifetime ago now. "I thought you hated me?"

"I should never have lashed out like that, and for that, I am sorry. I hate a lot of things about your family and your country; nothing will ever change that. But I don't hate you."

Not exactly the heart-pounding words I would have liked from this man, but I suppose that's an improvement.

Alik gave a mirthless laugh. "It seems I am bound for Dvari no matter what. Before she exiled me, my mother threatened to marry me off as a bride to the prince of Dvari like beads to be traded and strung into a pretty but useless necklace. I didn't think there could be a worse fate than an arranged marriage to a stranger, but as it turns out, I was wrong."

Agnian stilled. He did not meet her eye as he asked, "Which prince?"

"What do you mean? I thought there was only one?"

He walked away, setting the bowl and now pink-hued cloth on a side table. He spoke over his shoulder, "There's only one that matters, but there are two princes of Dvari. They look similar but are two completely different souls."

He sank in the cushions across from her on the window seat, resetting her blanketed feet in his lap. Sunlight danced over the salt and pepper stubble along his jaw as he leaned back against the window.

Alik leaned her temple against the cool glass. "It doesn't matter anyway. All that matters is that I find a way to Shauna and the others. The life I thought I'd live has been taken from me regardless of which prince I'm given to or if I'm simply thrown out of the gates."

Agnian absently rolled his thumbs over the arch of her foot, and she bit back a sigh at the comfort of his touch. She imagined Shauna and the other girls huddled together somewhere, terrified, and shame washed over her. She dropped her feet from his hands and stood.

She said, "There's no time to waste. I need your help."

ELAINE

Elaine ran through the fabric tent door of the Hadishi's home and stopped suddenly at the sight of Farisha at the kitchen table.

"Elai! You scared me. Is everything OK?" She asked.

Elaine's mind raced, each thought tumbling into the next. *Well, I'm a Rifter that's about to be hunted by everyone in Efendi, including the kingdom's most terrifying gang leader. The only scrap of hope is that I might have my real family somewhere in this world, but I have no idea how to find them. My skin is crawling, and I feel like if I don't Rift right now, I'll jump out a window. And I'm beginning to think the creepy laugh in my head is the Edicisi calling me to him. Ohmygod am I going to want to drink blood soon?*

She swallowed all the troubling thoughts and put a hand to Farisha's back. "I'm...good. Everything is good. You good?"

Farisha tilted her head and watched Elaine with narrowed eyes but didn't press. "OK...Kanne Da'Neen has been looking for you, Little One. Would you like to see her?"

Elaine wanted nothing more than to bury herself under the ragged blanket in the loft above them, but she needed to formulate a plan. She had no idea where she could hide in Efendi but figured Kanne Da'Neen was the most knowledgeable woman in the Low Tiers.

If anyone can help, she might.

She fought past tears at the thought of being alone, but she had to hide somewhere if a Rifter Hunt began. She worked through how to broach the subject as she walked to her small tent at the Cluster's edge. Kanne Da'Neen stirred something in a cracked clay pot over her fire, muttering to herself.

Kanne Da'Neen said without turning, "It's about time you showed back up. Have you found your Dua yet, child, or are you still cowering beneath the covers?"

"Just plain me still. Did you hear the news?" Elaine said as she hopped up on top of the table and worried a cuticle at her thumbnail.

Kanne Da'Neen swatted her cane into Elaine's knees and pointed the stick to the low stool instead. "What news now?"

Wincing, Elaine hopped down. "They're saying there are Rifters again, and they're ones kidnapping the girls around here and--"

The old crone interrupted, clearly not as surprised as Elaine expected, "...which means the patrols will start soon. I remember the drill."

"You were alive during the last Rifter Hunt? But you seem so young..." Elaine trailed off. She felt hot and wafted a hand in front of her face that did absolutely nothing.

The woman grunted something between a "Harumph" and a snort, so Elaine continued.

"What was that like? Did they find Rifters?"

Kanne Da'Neen paused before finally taking turning to the slip of a girl sitting in her kitchen. "It was terrifying. Everyone thought that they were seeing Rifters, but the patrols never came through the Low Tiers. The Towners began to patrol our own streets at night with torches, and when that Iktidar queen announced a reward for Rifters, neighbors turned on neighbors. By the end of the first week, over ten women were 'captured.'"

To Elaine's disgust, Kanne Da'Neen spat on the floor at the

word 'captured' before continuing without pause. "None of us could capture a Rifter. Or if they did, the Iktidars didn't hang them like they did those poor girls."

Elaine stopped rocking back and forth on the rickety stool and wiped the sweat from her brow. She jiggled her foot on the hard-packed floor, trying not to think about torchlit hunts. "So, there were no Rifters after all?"

"Oh no, I'd imagine there were a few among us then, but most Rifters found their way out of the kingdom and to the Magarans or lands beyond decades before." Kanne Da'Neen tossed Elaine some grain to shuffle through, and she began the laborious task of husking the grains with the heel of her palm.

I could find another Rifter. They'd help me. But what if they are as terrible as the stories? I don't want to skin anyone. And I definitely can't drink blood.

"How do you know where some went?" Elaine asked as she smashed the grains beneath her palms. Her mind raced with ideas to slip out of the Perimeter Wall and find a Rifter.

"Because I am ancient and know all." Kanne Da'Neen said before sighing at Elaine's dubious face. She kept talking over a slow stir at the pot.

"I knew one once. In the next Cluster. She was a young seamstress that was part of an immigrant community that came over from a rescued slave ship taken back from the Perisiens. Shy, but beautiful. She confided in me once when she felt like her Cluster was beginning to suspect something was off about her. She lived a quiet life, alone, and would have found her way here had things not taken a turn."

Elaine stopped grinding the grains. "They caught her?"

"No. Before the Rifter Hunt, she caught Hvard's eye. He pursued her relentlessly, but she would have nothing to do with him. She came to me one night and told me he forced himself on her. That was when I told him he was no longer welcome in my home."

Elaine's already sick stomach turned. She pushed the meager husks she'd pulled and said to Kanne Da'Neen's back, "That's awful."

"It was the worst night of my life." She shrugged, her bony shoulder piercing the air under her ear. "What could I do?"

They both stopped talking for a few moments; the only sounds the crackling fire and folks gathering outside.

Elaine finally asked, "What happened to the seamstress?"

"She told me once that her people came from the land of sand called Bakilar. Everything I heard about Bakilar sounded like she had found a much better home here," she grimaced. "Miserable way to live. Anyway, she said that she was leaving to find her way back there. I never saw her again after that night, but perhaps Hvard saved her life."

"What? How did Hvard save her life if he raped her and made her leave?"

"The Rifter Hunt began the following week. I don't know if anyone else knew for sure what she was, but if they even suspected it, they would have turned her in. No one wanted to defy that Iktidar queen."

Kanne Da'Neen looked beyond Elaine out to the courtyard, where several people rushed past. She said to herself more than Elaine, "Queen Firtina is even more terrible than her mother. We have a dark time ahead of us if she sanctions a Rifter Hunt."

***

Elaine left Kanne Da'Neen and headed back to the Hadishi home, too busy thinking about the desert called Bakilar on the other side of the world to notice the people gathered in the Cluster. The amber sun sunk below the top of the wall, casting deep shadows over Low Town. She felt the eyes of the other matriarchs of the Cluster on her, and they whispered to each other as she passed.

Elaine heard a man's laughter and a singsong voice. *The Edicisi. Does he know I can hear him?* She stopped walking, waiting to see if he would speak to her directly again. She was so focused on the voices in her head and trying not to cry that she didn't hear the commotion inside the Hadishi home until she heard a sharp cry from inside.

She rushed through the grimy flap. Reiki held Otum's arms, and Kara bent over him on the table. Kara's blood-soaked arms wrapped a bandage over the mangled mess of his right leg. Farisha ground foul-smelling herbs together at the counter.

"Elai, thank Yapi, you're home. Don't go outside tonight, child. Fear makes people do terrible things." Farisha nodded to the basket of linens at the edge of the table. "Now start ripping bandages. We need long, thick ones."

"What happened?"

Otum winced as he spoke, "Walking home. Two men in black cloaks pulled me into an alley. I told them I didn't have anything, but they didn't say anything at all. Why couldn't they have clubbed the bad leg?" His attempt at a laugh turned into a hiss as Farisha patted the poultice over his leg.

Reiki held his arms so he wouldn't shift and picked up where his dad left off. "He said they had a C tattooed around their eyes." He was talking to Elaine but watching Kara, who would not meet his gaze. "No one knows why the Canavar Company would have targeted him."

Silent tears spilled down Kara's face. She looked ashen, and her hands shook as she wrapped the bandages tighter. All thoughts of the voices in her head vanished as Elaine realized what this meant.

I did this. I brought this to them.

She sunk to the floor and ripped bandages, each harder to rip than the last with her shaking hands. The four of them finally finished the bloody task after what felt like hours, and Farisha gave Otum a liquid to help him sleep before slipping out to clean more bandages. Reiki made up his parents' pallet in the corner and lifted his father gingerly down to it. Kara caught Elaine's eyes before slipping outside and walked beyond their Cluster. Elaine followed close behind.

A low horn sounded as the moons rose, and they looked up at the sound of a group of people running past in the Tier above them. Kara whispered, "There will be chaos in Efendi, Elaine, while they look for these Rifters."

"Kara, I---" Elaine started.

"I know. I know you're sorry. I know how you got here, and I know what happened today. I know what you are. I've always known." She wouldn't make eye contact with Elaine. "Someone saw you. That's why he came today to the stall. Someone must have told him." Kara whispered more to herself than Elaine. She didn't sound accusatory, just flat.

Elaine glanced around them, seeing only grain bags and discarded broken tools. She whispered, "I accidentally Rifted in front of someone today. I was running from him when I came into your tent. I'm so sorry; I was so stupid."

Elaine thought she was tough. She had been through hell with her parents several times over and gained some satisfaction that she rarely cried in front of them. She cried now, though, folding over herself.

"I'm so sorry. I never meant to bring this to you. I didn't know."

"Shhh. It's OK. I'll make it OK." Kara held Elaine, and Elaine felt worse that she was the one doing the comforting. Elaine never had a brother or sister, but she knew in her bones that there was no better big sister than Kara.

"I have to leave. There's this place called Baki-something that I can go to. Kanne Da'Neen told me."

Kara pushed Elaine out at an arm's length to look in her face but didn't release her. "*You told Kanne Da'Neen?* Don't you know she adopted Hvard?"

Elaine shook her head, "I didn't tell her anything!"

"But you think she knows?"

"No. I don't know...Maybe? I don't think she would tell anyone, though. She told me today that she knew a Rifter once, and she kept her secret."

"Back up. Tell me everything. First, who was this person you Rifted in front of?"

Elaine told her about how she accidentally Rifted when running away from Hvard, how she taught herself to Rift, about that morning in the upper Tiers when she ran into the guy outside the lavender house. She told her verbatim what Kanne Da'Neen said that afternoon. The smoke from the Cluster fires blocked out the stars above, and the wall loomed overhead behind them. She felt suffocated and fought off an increasing urge to run.

Kara stopped her. "She said that this woman had family in Bakilar? You know what this means, right?"

Elaine hadn't quite processed everything. She felt like this morning was years ago, and she just kept slipping into more trouble. She knew she had to leave, but she just found Efendi. *I love this place, its people, and its magic.* She felt safe for the first time, loved even for the first time, with the Hadishis. She thought back to Otum lying on the table and Farisha's bone-weary face. Her chest ached. *I have to get as far away from them as possible before I bring more trouble to them.*

Kara knelt; her long wiry body bent over to look Elaine directly in the face. "Elaine, this means you could have family in Bakilar."

It was the first glimmer of good Elaine had felt since this morning. She never intended to go back home to her parents when she first fell into this place, especially when she found a home with the Hadishis. She had no idea what Bakilar was or how to get there, but she found a pinprick of light at the end of a crooked, suffocating tunnel.

The two girls sat on an old stone bench against the wall, not speaking. Elaine should have been hatching a plan, but she couldn't help the overriding thought above all else.

They were not my parents. I have a mother somewhere.

She glanced over to see Kara staring off, worry etched over her face, chewing on her thumbnail. Elaine asked, "How do I get to Bakilar?"

Kara looked at the ground instead of her eyes, "I'll get you there. I think I know a way."

Reed

Monti asked rapid-fire questions about the Iktidars, the Tiers, and what he knew of Rifters as they trotted further along the icy blue river. A day ago, Reed would have thought this was torture, but he found that he liked Monti's quick, acerbic wit and her self-deprecating jokes. By the time their conversation evolved past an interrogation, their path had morphed into a dusty road. She told him some of her college stories and hilarious conquests between jokes about being raised by a prison warden and a Sunday School teacher.

She tilted her head back, and for a brief moment, rested it on Reed's peck as she sighed, "I don't know how it happened. I never thought I'd want to return to Texas after I graduated from A&M a couple of years ago, but New York feels like it's swallowing me whole. I love the people, the energy, everything. But to be honest, I don't love who I'm turning into, if that makes sense. I thought New York would feel like the beginning of my future, but now it just feels like a dead end."

Reed's mind flitted back to a tiny brunette named Maddy as it always did when someone talked about plans. He ignored the constriction in his chest and distracted himself by prompting Monti to talk more. "Is it someone or something that's making you think you have to leave New York altogether?"

"Bit of both, I suppose. I met someone I thought was a dream. Gorgeous, *obviously*--" Monti leaned back and dramatically winked at Reed before turning back to the road, "---charming, disgustingly wealthy, and fabulously interesting. He gave me this once-in-a-lifetime opportunity to work for him. Something I couldn't pass up. But the more I worked with him, the more things felt off. I came back to Texas for one final project that involved my dad's prison. That's why I happened to be there when all hell broke loose."

"Marketing?" Reed asked, wondering what she was working on in New York that brought her to a Texan supermax.

She nodded emphatically. "Yep. Prison reform...marketing. Er, marketing for policies involving prison reform. You know, philanthropic stuff."

Monti spoke before he could ask another question. "So how did you and your mother survive when you first got to our world?"

Reed flashed back to the smiling woman, white teeth and a beige hat covering her auburn hair. That was the first time he'd ever seen a cowboy hat, and he still felt welcomed whenever he saw one even years later.

"There's a network around the world that helps immigrants from Sakalid. It's not extensive, but they're incredibly loyal to each other. Our Rifter took us to one of the *colonias* outside of McCallen initially, and her contact met us there."

Monti's face dropped, and he knew she saw one of the border towns where hundreds of undocumented immigrants from Mexico and Central America set up simple wooden homes and haphazard shacks on the outskirts of Texas.

"We stayed with a family paid by that network for the first few nights. They gave us food and water, and their sons showed me my first soccer ball. A few days later, an Efendian that had crossed years before picked us up. We stayed with her for a few weeks while she forged social security cards for us. She helped my mom learn the basics of life as an illegal and got her a job cleaning houses with her. I enrolled in middle school after watching American TV for hours on end in her apartment."

"Jesus, that must have been hard. Is that how you learned English?"

"Ha, not quite. Our Rifter explained that local linguistics instantly passes through to everyone Rifted based on the Ley Line they used. It's why you'd be able to understand Efendian now. I learned Spanish before I ever knew English, so we blended in among the border towns. People assumed my mother was Afro-Mexicano because of her dark skin."

"Where is your mother now?"

"Dead."

Monti said the only thing anyone ever said when you talked about death, "I'm so sorry."

Reed spoke to break the awkward silence that always followed conversations about the dead. "She was happy for a time there. It felt like hope. Like we could finally stop running and just make a home together."

Monti chewed on her lip before gesturing to the rolling fields of grass around them. "Monsters aside, wouldn't it be better for you to stay here? Going back means you'll go to prison. Why not just hide from your dad here instead of going home?"

Reed huffed a laugh. "First, there is no *home* for me anywhere. I came to Texas as an illegal, undocumented immigrant who was too black to hang out with the white kids, too white to fit in with the black kids, and not Hispanic enough to fit in with any Mexican kids. I was a wide-eyed foster kid that never got any of the jokes and failed every test. Staci was the only home I ever had, and I---"

He stopped speaking to swallow the lump gagging his throat. Toxic as she was, Staci was the wild and beautiful America he glimpsed when he first arrived and his first friend. She flouted stereotypes, opting instead to hate everyone equally while she smoked stolen packs of cigarettes and dyed her hair pale pink. Staci sang lines from Langston Hughes while plucking a guitar and fucked like she was leaving town the next morning. Most importantly, she never pressed Reed on his past so long as he never pressed why she sometimes came to school with a busted lip or a black eye. They were either wrapped around each other or at each other's throats, and they clung to each other like the scrubby hackberry in the desert when their nightmares chased sleep away.

He cleared his throat, refusing to look at Monti's searching eyes. "Anyway. I never knew my dad, but my mother gave her life to get me away from here. I don't care where I go so long as it's not in this world."

They were quiet for a time. The Magarans grew more imposing the closer they got, but a sea of grass still surrounded Monti and Reed now. Reed cantered the Aygir and listened to the wind rustle the gold-green stalks. Now that he was not running, he acknowledged that the grassland surrounding him reminded him of his mother more than anywhere else. He could almost hear her deep laugh and hushed songs in the wind.

Monti's voice broke him out of his memories. "What do you think this queen of yours will do to my dad?"

Reed shook his head. "It's hard to hide a building that comes out of nowhere. She'll assume they came with a Rifter and are hiding her somehow."

He grimaced. His mother relented one night and told him how her Rifter friend escaped during a Rifter Hunt. Neighbors sold out neighbors they disliked, torches marched past windows, and frenzied crowds cheered as the Iktidar cronies executed women and girls. Another hunt would be underway if they thought a Rifter was among the Tiers again. As if Reed needed any further proof to get as far away from Efendians as possible.

He debated on how much truth to give Monti. He imagined the panic he would've had if it was his mother captured. "We'll get to your dad. The Queen will want he and the others alive to get as much information as possible."

Reed expected Monti to say aloud whatever thoughts she had when it came to her dad, particularly since he was locked up in prison in another world. But she never did. *It's not my place to press.*

Instead, she gestured to the caravan heading their way and asked, "Who are all these people?"

The jewel-tone carriages cast diamond-shaped azure, emerald, and gold reflections on either side of the valley. Faint music ran over the patches of wildflowers and bounced back from green-gold grassy knolls loitering in between. Someone was singing, loudly, if they could pick it up at this distance, and Reed felt a familiar pang of loss.

"Performers, more than likely. It's got to be close to Hasateen, or the Efendian harvest, and there will be celebrations at the end of it requiring dancers, musicians, actors, and such."

"Will you recognize any of them?"

"Doubt it. We only spent a handful of years with our troupe before its leader threatened to sell our whereabouts to my father. Most of our troupe were thieves or sellswords, and almost all of them were pricks."

Reed thought back to the brutal-looking troupe leader, ignoring his desire to break something between his fingers. Pebbles scattered beneath the Aygir's feet. *I am no longer the boy hiding behind his mother.* He forced himself to relax.

"The man that threatened to sell us out to my father was named Hvard Canavar. It wouldn't surprise me if he traded the life of a wandering actor for more lucrative thug work within the walls of Efendi."

Despite the bitter memories, he felt a nostalgic tinge watching the troupe come into view. He loved sitting on top of the lead wagon with his little legs swinging over the side. His mother would usually be alongside him, singing a new song she wanted to try for the next show. If he wasn't on top during the treks between shows, he was usually hovering around Tilli. Tilli was the halfbreed Itreni in the troupe, and Reed the youngest boy. Reed loved demonstrating the Aygir tricks Tilli taught him to wealthy Efendian boys, and Tilli loved the coin he brought in.

For a moment, Reed allowed himself to imagine the life he could have had if his father didn't haunt them. *I could have watched my mother grow old, perhaps find love and protection, and we could have roamed the kingdom under the hot sun as we pleased. I might have picked up the guitar even without Staci's help, and*—he stopped. Even in his daydreams, his worlds collided, and every could-have involved a sacrifice. He felt adrift, unable to anchor on the foundation of a home or memory without pain.

He shifted off the road to give the caravan more room. A handful of young men lounging on the rooftops and back porches of the wagons gleefully shouted praise at Monti. Her version of lying low was to wave back jovially while laughing and dramatically bowing over the Aygir. Reed spit out some of the hair getting in his mouth at another enthusiastic head toss and ground his teeth. Staci hadn't been beautiful in the way Monti was, but she had a dangerous charisma that caught most men's attention. And she always flaunted it even after they were married.

He pushed the Aygir harder at the memory of her smirk and held onto Monti a little tighter than necessary. The last of the troupe wagons passed them, and Reed shifted back onto the road. He was thinking of Staci dancing in their bar when Monti twisted back to Reed.

"Jealous, much there, Lewis? Lemme guess... Wife murdered in lover's quarrel. What, did she sleep with your neighbor?" She widened her eyes comically, "Don't tell me you caught her!"

Reed should have expected the barb with a tongue as sharp as Monti's, but it still caught him off guard. He let his hand drop down to their sides and glanced briefly at Monti before training his eyes on the mountain ahead. "Something like that." he said.

Her face dropped, and the ride the next hour was awkwardly quiet. Reed would have relished the long-denied silence, but he realized he enjoyed their traded insults and banter. It had been a long time since he just talked with a woman that made him laugh. Reed shifted the Aygir towards the narrow path again that led through trees and swatted at leaves and branches that swiped him back as they passed.

I should have just laughed it off, he thought. *I could have made a joke about her talking too much and moved on.* He huffed, and her hair shifted to reveal the slope of her neck. He bit back a groan. *Since when am I turned on by a neck? Get it together, Reed. What would Staci say? This woman is only with you because you are literally the last man from Earth that can help her. It doesn't matter if it's awkward or if we say another word to each other the rest of the time we're in this hellish realm.*

The Aygir shied and sidestepped further away from the stream that suddenly frothed to their right. The water swirled around itself in a small whirlpool and splashed up the bank. Reed slowed his breath again and pushed any thoughts of Staci or Monti out of his head. The water calmed as he did, but the beast nipped at the air in agitation.

The Magaran range was close enough now that the sun was barely visible over her jagged ridgeline even though true moonrise was still an hour away.

Reed cleared his throat as he weaved the Aygir through the thick trees. He hopped down and helped Monti climb off as well before letting the beast meander into the stream. Monti watched him while he shook off the pain in his legs from the ride. *She knows you're a murderer, Reed. What did you expect?*

He tried to calm her nerves. "We'll be safe here tonight. These trees are a lot older than the Batiwood, and the worst monsters don't venture this close to the Magaran mountains. Anything else that would be a threat will stay away from the Aygir."

She looked uneasy in a way Reed hadn't seen since the Itreni caught them in his loft. He walked a few steps closer, "Monti, I know you know about my past. But I promise, you have nothing to fear from me. I am not going to hurt you, and I won't let anything else in this world hurt you either."

He instantly felt stupid at the bemused purse of her lips, so he tried to fix it by completely ignoring the new level of awkwardness he brought into their night.

"I'm gonna get firewood. You can wash up in the stream, but the temperature drops quickly up here, so I wouldn't go for a swim. Just shout if you need me and keep close to the Aygir until I get back."

He made it a few steps when Monti called out, "We could name her 'I'm with dipshit'?"

He turned, "Eh?"

Monti walked closer and tilted her head towards the beast, aggressively bobbing for fish. "She needs a name."

Reed rolled his eyes at her barb. "You can do better than that," and he turned to the task at hand. She followed him a step behind while he gathered sticks off the forest floor.

"No, I mean...Ah hell, Reed. I'm trying to say *I'm* the dipshit. I shouldn't have joked about your wife like that back there. I don't know you at all, and you helped me this entire time without really needing to since I don't add much value to our expedition...and I've been trying to put the two and two together of jailbird Reed and you and it just doesn't match up. What I'm trying to say is I don't know why you killed your wife--"

She waved him off when he tried to interrupt, "No. I don't need to know why. All I'm trying to say is that you seem like a good man. And apart from my dad, a few of the guards that are more like uncles, and that *really* good looking lawyer in the lobby," Reed laughed and she smiled as she pressed on. "I'm glad that, out of everyone in that prison, I got stuck with you."

Reed ran a hand over the scruff on his face and smiled despite himself. "Thank you."

He laughed at the physical strain on her face of trying not to ask something. He waved her on with a stick, "Go on. Ask."

"Why *are* you helping me get Dad anyway? I mean, I

appreciate it, don't get me wrong. But you didn't have to haul me with you."

Reed chewed over how much he should tell her when her mouth ran off rambling again as she picked up sticks alongside him.

"I mean, if it's sex... ehhhh. You seem nice and all, but I really don't know you. Not that I'm saying it could never happen, just not like *right* now. You're probably good-looking under all that... Scruff. That's where I was going. Anyway, it's been a really long time since I slept with someone that wasn't my boyfriend, or ex, I suppose by now, but..."

She was snapping twigs into quarters and tossing them back on the ground without really looking at them or Reed as her monologue shot out of her mouth.

"Besides, *even* if you were to rescue my dad and me and bring us back to our world, I still think you need to put in some serious time and effort before… I'm not like a prude or anything, but I've got standards... and,"

Reed cut her off, "Oh my god, Monti. Stop talking. No. I'm not doing this because I'm trying to sleep with you." He took the sticks from her hand before she could snap all of them into matches. "I feel guilty."

"What?"

He ran a hand over his shaved head. "I'm the reason we were all brought here."

"How do you figure?"

Reed walked ahead under the tree canopy and picked up more sticks for the fire. He glimpsed the first stars and the rising moons through the jagged edges of leaves and debated how to start.

"I've had these nightmares my entire life where I hear a song my mother said was playing the night she met my father. If I described the dreams to you, they'd sound innocent enough, but they terrified me. But something changed in the last year, and people around me started to say phrases and doing things out of my dreams."

"Like deja vu?" Monti asked, glancing around them at the darkening trees.

He arranged the sticks in the clearing near the Aygir, his thoughts on the mailman.

"More than that. The first day I realized it was happening again, I was standing in the yard watering flowers Staci and I planted at the new house. I had the nightmare a few hours before, and it sounds ridiculous, but it's just someone singing a lullaby in my ear. The thing is—I know in those dreams that if I turn towards the voice, something terrible will happen."

Monti held out her hands over the smoke filtering through the sticks, and Reed blew the embers to a toasty fire. He could still feel the genderless voice tickling his ear, inching closer to him. He relished the heat of the flames against the chill spiraling down his spine.

"Anyway, that morning, the mailman walked by. And this is going to sound absolutely crazy—"

Monti cocked her eyebrow, "Crazier than being sucked into a vortex and dropped in a new realm?"

He laughed, "Fair. The mailman came by singing the same song that was always in the nightmares."

Reed would never be able to forget that song.

Take me down to the river
The river that's wide and blue
Take me down to its water banks
So I may swim with you

He shuddered and continued, "Then the mailman just waved at me, chatting small like normal, like my heart hadn't just dropped out of my chest. And for the next several weeks, I kept running into strangers humming the same tune. I started to ask around, googled the song, the whole thing, but no one ever knew where they'd heard it. Most never even realized they were singing and looked at me like I was crazy. Staci thought I was paranoid and brushed it off as my imagination. She was with me a few times when the singing started, and she swore she never heard them sing. The only person who ever heard it when I did was my mother."

He rifled through the bag on the Aygir's saddle and sat back down with the grain stalks, shoulders brushing Monti's, and continued.

"Then bad things happened. I woke up to a few dead squirrels in our front yard, then a few days later, a hawk beat its bloody head through the glass in our kitchen window. All the grass, the trees, and the flowers died overnight in every yard except ours. The kindest man you'd ever know got arrested for beating his wife to death two doors down. He later killed himself, and his note said he didn't even remember picking up the hammer."

Monti interjected, "What'd Staci say then?"

The Aygir settled behind them like a cow made of steel, and Monti leaned back against her belly. Reed tensed, half expecting it to bite her, but he realized that Monti had a way of charming everyone around her. The Aygir was not immune.

He tossed a broken stick into the fire, looking away from her. "We had just brought Madeline home from the hospital. I wanted to move, but she refused. We saved for months for the down payment, and she didn't want to move with an infant."

"I didn't know you had a kid," she said.

Monti looked at him in a way he didn't want to examine. He tamped down the emotions threatening to overwhelm him as the fire spit higher into the air. Monti jumped up from the blaze and patted out the embers scattered on her pant legs.

Reed brushed down a stray ember from her sleeve, "You alright?"

The Aygir jerked up, gnashing her teeth at something in the dark beyond them. Reed dropped, shoveling dirt onto the fire, and then stood still in the swirls of smoke and moonlight, straining to hear whatever spooked the beast. He heard nothing but the wind rustling through leaves and water trickling past in the creek alongside their camp. He turned to mime a warning shush to

Monti to ward off another loud-whisper when he saw it.

The winged figure perched on a branch a few feet from Monti's head. Black wings tucked behind a sculpted chest and curved up into pointed daggers behind crossed arms. It had the head and upper torso of a man, but feathers that appeared soft enough to touch covered its crouched legs. Sharp talons gripped the tree branch when it shifted further into the moonlight.

Monti turned at Reed's stare and fired the final bullets in her gun without hesitation. The shots echoed through the trees alongside the beast's roar as he dove to tackle Monti to the ground.

The Aygir barreled in, kicking its hindquarters, and knocked the winged man off Monti while almost trampling her as well. Reed scrambled to Monti and tugged her deeper into the trees, running blindly away from the Aygir's screams, now mixing with low growls and grunts.

The wind beat down on his neck before his brain registered their presence. Three more winged men landed on the ground just ahead of them, blocking their path. Monti split left through the trees but was swooped into a fourth's arms and held upside down while she kicked at its face.

Reed's stomach dropped to the ground. He leapt up to catch Monti's arm, begging for the wind to lift him higher, but the sudden gust of wind just knocked the beast and Monti further away from his outstretched hand. They tumbled over each other in the air and hit a tree.

The three creatures left on the ground looked at Reed with renewed interest. Before he could do anything other than panic, they tackled him and then raised him high in the air. He was suspended in the night sky by two of the beasts while the third led. Reed's eyes watered in the wind as they sped faster under the two moons.

Reed reached for anything to hold onto, thinking thoughts he knew would kill him faster than these creatures, and the pair gripping his shoulders bucked wildly at another guest of wind. The leader ahead of them turned back to Reed. The last thing he remembered was the sharp talon kicking him in the face before everything went black.

ALIK

Alik silently thanked the Goddesses again that Agnian offered his room as a meeting place for her brothers. *Servants are likely packing my things at this very moment, and if I walk out this hall, there will be a hundred eyes waiting to see my disgraced exit from the Palace steps.* She winced at the ice at her lip, still fat from the altercation with her mother that morning. The sting bit through the fantastical theories ricocheting through her mind, each more unbelievable than the last, until one solidified among the rest.

"I don't understand," Taavi said as he paced in front of Agnian's window. "You believe that the Edicisi, the monster that we shared stories about as kids, is real? Even if he is real, even if he has Shauna and the others, there is no guarantee this Rifter will lead you to him. And even if you do find him, you have no way to fight him. He's more powerful than any Duawielder. He can drain their powers, and I love you, but you do not have Dua to spare. Let Mother find him. Go with Agnian to Dvari until this is over and she has calmed down."

"That's what you expect me to do? Flee so that someone else can find my best friend? Firtina has no interest in helping Shauna and the others."

Taavi tossed his hands in the air, "What are you talking about? She knows a Rifter is taking the girls, and now, so does everyone else in this kingdom. She has no other option but to find them."

"She has no obligation to find them *alive,"* Alik corrected, and at her nod, Agnian explained his theory about Firtina's involvement and the man searching for Rifters from Perisien pirates.

"This is absurd, Alik. Less than a week ago you thought Agnian was responsible, and now you want to believe that some delusional drunk is Mother's former lover hellbent on blood sacrifices?" Taavi said.

Damari waited motionless next to Alik, listening, but likely not hearing, Taavi speak. He asked, "Why are the initials important, Alik?"

She thought about their trek to the library catacombs and the thick initials her fingers brushed in the darkness. She opened her mouth, closed it, and after a beat tried again.

"How many lovers has our mother taken that you are aware of?" Alik asked, ignoring Taavi's grimace.

Damari replied with a halfhearted shrug, "Countless. She swaps out her companions like she does her jewels. Which is why if she is 'F.I,' I don't understand why the 'H.B' is important."

Alik asked, "What did that room feel like to you, Damari?"

He quieted for a moment before responding. "It wasn't a room. It was a shrine."

"An obsession," she nodded. "And hidden behind the secret shrine room was another secret door, and that's where she, and whomever H.B is, carved their initials together. She took someone back there she never wanted anyone else seeing. H.B must be the same man Agnian said required a blood sacrifice and a Rifter."

Taavi rubbed his hands over his face and sat. "Fine. Let's assume everything you've said is correct. How does this tie back to the Edicisi and you not getting killed by him?"

"I think Firtina and this man are trying to bring the Edicisi here."

The only noise for a few moments in the room came from the fire-orange birds roosting outside Agnian's window.

"No one," Taavi said, "especially the Efendian Queen that will be usurped and likely eaten by the Edicisi, would willingly bring him here."

Alik took a deep breath, saying aloud something else she never imagined saying. "I don't think she means to confront the Edicisi. I think Firtina intends to use him."

"For what?" Agnian asked.

"I don't know. Firtina is the most powerful Duawielder in history. Perhaps that's not enough? Perhaps she can gain something from him? I have no idea. But understanding her motive is not as important as finding this Rifter and forcing her to bring us to Shauna and the others. Even if that means we face the Edicisi. And we have to find her before the Horde, the search parties, or Firtina does. Though I don't know---"

Damari interrupted, "I think I saw her."

"Who?"

"The Rifter Firtina is hunting," he replied.

Alik's mouth dropped open, "And you're just now mentioning this? Let's go!"

Damari scowled at Alik. "You don't understand. It can't be her."

Taavi, unexpectedly assuming the role of the calm one, said, "Walk us through this, Damari. Where did you see her, what does she look like? Everything."

"It's not her. She can't be behind the kidnappings, and she couldn't be responsible for Rifting a group of people. She's a kid--"

Alik snapped, "Exactly as Firtina said. She is the one we're after. Don't you get it? If we don't find her, we will not find Shauna and the other girls."

"If you are right and the Edicisi is behind this," Damari said, "you are walking to your death. And I will not help you to your grave."

Taavi added, “Let Firtina fight him or control him. You don’t stand a chance.”

Alik wanted to smash each window in the room and hurl every jagged shard at the wall above her brothers’ heads.

Instead, fists clenched, she ground out, “I am sick of everyone telling me all the things I cannot do, of being told to look the other way, to flee. Or to let someone else handle my problems. My Dua is little more than a puff of air and a speck of sand. There are fountains here more powerful than my Waterwerk, and girls 12-years old have shown better control over flame than I do. But that doesn’t make me incapable. I am the daughter of Firtina Iktidar, heir to the Efendian throne and Pillar of the Iktidar line. I will find Shauna. I will find the other Daughters. And I will bring them all home.”

She took a moment to breathe before she stepped closer to Damari. “Now you can help me get them back, or you can stay here and hide. But either way, you *will* tell me where you found the Rifter.”

Damari dropped his hands to his sides. After a heavy pause, he said, "She is 10 or 11 at most. Small, maybe here," He raised his hand to his chest. "She is fair-skinned, long tangled blonde hair half out of a braid. Towner clothes. I saw her in the Solmus Tier this morning just before I came to you."

Taavi asked, "What were you doing in the Solmus?"

But Alik didn’t hear his question. She knew this girl. The final piece shifted in place.

A knock at the door silenced the three of them. Agnian motioned for Taavi after answering it.

Taavi said, "I have to go. My messenger still can't find Ty, and he doesn't know where Mother is keeping the foreigners. They're preparing for another patrol, and I am supposed to lead Tenida through Low Town soon. I'll see what I can find out from her." He turned to Damari, hand still on the doorknob. "Damari, can you put an Eye on Ty and the foreigners? Mother should have put them under guard, and it doesn't make sense that Ty or his men are still not here."

Damari nodded and moved to follow him out.

Alik, rooted in place, said, "Taavi, keep Tenida away from The Silos."

Her brothers and Agnian looked at her, perplexed.

"Every dream I've had is chasing a little girl through the Silos at night. I've seen this child's back a hundred times. Damari, Agnian, and I will find her there tonight."

ELAINE

Kara wasn't home when Elaine woke up after a night of panicked dreams. She still felt Hvard's beady eyes on her even a day later, and she watched the Cluster for his ginger beard. Reiki interrupted her thoughts.

"Anything you want to tell me, Elai?"

She looked at him fully as he loaded the grain ladder. His olive-green eyes were a match to Kara's, but where hers were hard and mischievous most of the time, his were always kind. Elaine wanted to tell him. *I know he'd never tell anyone this secret, but I don't want to see his face when he knows I'm the reason his dad likely won't walk again.* So she slipped on the blank face adults often bought and shrugged, "No?"

He gave her a long look but simply tugged a ratty tendril of her hair before hoisting the smaller ladder of grain over his head. Elaine went back inside the Hadishi home and took up a post next to Otum since Farisha took his place in the fields. She watched the strip of sunlight from the doorway travel over Yapi's face on the floor, praying to gods of two completely different worlds that he'd get better.

The chanting in her head rumbled through in waves, sometimes so loud she couldn't drown them out, and other times quiet enough that she couldn't make out any words. *None of this makes sense. Why do I hear only that chant now? Why haven't I heard any others if I could hear them in Efendi before?* Sweat had covered Elaine by the time the sunlight had passed entirely over Yapi, but she wouldn't dampen the fire in the hearth while Otum still shivered.

Farisha and Reiki eventually came home to prepare dinner, but Kara was still gone. Elaine couldn't watch Farisha brush Otum's sparse hair back while singing to him anymore, so she told Reiki she was going for a walk. Elaine wandered, shaking, her mind lost in a sea of questions and sat by a broken fountain of Sulu behind the adjacent Cluster. Kara found her just as Elaine felt she might throw up if she didn't Rift soon.

"There you are! I've been looking all over for you. We have to leave. Now."

"What? Why what happened?"

Kara clipped a fast pace ahead of her, bypassing their Cluster.

Elaine ran up and tugged her elbow, "Where are we going?"

She shrugged her off and kept walking. "I found a way. I'm getting you to Bakilar."

Elaine stopped, shocked. She felt like her mind was tumbling down a steep hill of questions. "Now? I don't have anything with me. I didn't think it would be so soon. I'm not ready. I have to say goodbye!"

Kara turned to her, face hard. "There is no time. The patrols start tonight. Reiki and my parents will understand."

"But—"

"No but's, Elai! It's now or never. I stole a cloak for you; they'll have everything else." She turned and continued their brutal pace.

Elaine's heart raced. She fought back the tears at the thought of not seeing Otum smile, or hugging Farisha one last time, or thanking Reiki. "W-who will have everything? Are you not coming with me?"

Kara stopped again; her jaw clenched tight before speaking. "Do you think this is easy? Do you know what situation you've put us in that I have to fix?"

Elaine had seen Kara snappish before but never felt her anger directed at her. Tears welled up, and Elaine shook her head quickly back and forth. "I'm sorry. I—"

The horns echoed through the Tiers, signaling the beginning of curfew. Kara glanced around them and pulled Elaine to a skinny path behind the lean-to homes. "There is no time. The patrols will likely come around our bend tonight. It's now or never."

Elaine nodded, not noticing how Kara did not meet her eyes. Kara set a brisk pace. The path dumped out to a much wider space after they passed the final Towner home. Elaine dimly registered the entrance to the Silos as the voices in her head pounded louder and louder. Over the steady chant, she heard his voice, the voice she felt in her bones belonged to the Edicisi, ring out, *Come.*

The sparse fire orbs hovered high above the Silos, dimmed to just a flicker with no attendants. Large, stone vats almost half as tall as the Perimeter Wall stood in pairs along either side of their path. The constant background noise of Low Town faded enough here that her footsteps in the path helped drown out the chanting in her head. Elaine took Kara's hand. When they passed under a fire orb, she realized tears were running down Kara's cheeks.

Elaine squeezed her calloused hand. "It's OK, Kara. I'm going to my family. I'm not scared. It'll all be OK soon. And I'll figure out how to write you or come visit you with my parents."

Kara stifled a sob, letting go of her hand to swipe her tears. "I can't—"

A shrill whistle interrupted her in the darkness ahead of them. The girls stopped, and Elaine grit her teeth against the need to run. A bird call answered behind them. *The girl from the cluster said they heard animal noises in the Silos before her friend disappeared.*

She whispered, "Kara, we gotta get out of here. Now." She spun frantically around at the footsteps behind them.

Kara, though, stood still.

Two men appeared in the pool of light, each wearing a long

black cloak and dull black boots. Elaine tugged at Kara, pulling her as she screamed, "Run!"

Yet Kara did not budge. Instead, she gripped Elaine's wrist as a man's laughter ricocheted off the Silos surrounding them. Hvard Canavar stepped into the pool of light.

"I always knew you were a smart one," he said to Kara. Another man looped a thin, dark metal chain around Elaine before she even realized he stood behind her.

Chills ran down Elaine's arms and legs, and the chain felt heavier than it did a moment before. *This isn't happening. This is a mistake. Or part of some plan Kara has that will wind up capturing Hvard Canavar so that I don't have to leave right away.*

Elaine faced Hvard, ready to make a run for it at Kara's signal, but she glanced at the girl that saved her months ago and realized no chains looped her. She asked, "Kara?"

Kara just cried harder.

The Hadishis had been a giant raft in a dark sea, Kara, her anchor. Elaine couldn't get enough air in her lungs, and with each struggle, the chain pinned her arms tighter to her sides.

"Kara? Please." She didn't want to beg, but she would. "I'm so sorry. I never wanted your family hurt. I will go away. I'll get to my family in Bakilar. Please. Help me."

The men around her laughed, Hvard leaning into her face. "She told you you've got family in Bakilar, did she? And you believed her?"

Elaine thought of the taffy pink door and the bewildered older boy. She held her breath once more, closed her eyes, and...nothing. She tried to Rift to the next set of Silos, to Kara, to anywhere. But nothing happened.

Tears marred Kara's dark charcoal-lined eyes, and they were the only things that belied a face otherwise devoid of emotion. A cloaked man reeking of booze bound Elaine's legs with another chain and stuffed a cloth in her mouth before Elaine could scream more than, "Please!"

Elaine frantically kicked and wiggled, but to no avail. She sobbed into the scratchy cloth threatening to choke her.

Kara finally met her eyes and said softly, "I'm sorry. I didn't have a choice," before she melted back into the shadows without another word.

Elaine thought she knew what helplessness felt like. She felt it when her parents left her for days alone with empty cabinets, when they screamed at each other, when they hit each other. She felt it the night her Ma took so many pills that she couldn't speak. And she felt helpless the night her Da put her in the hospital. But when Elaine couldn't move her arms to swipe her tears, she felt the floor shift under her, and she could not breathe.

She spiraled into a panic, past the denial of Kara hurting her, past the fear of what will happen. She felt smaller than she ever had before, small enough to fit in a locked compartment in the darkest part of her mind.

Then a voice, one she'd never heard before, whispered to her, "Lock it away."

Elaine focused on that phrase, repeating it over and over in her head. She rocked herself back and forth, pushing Kara's betrayal far down into a locked section of her mind. She pushed the faces of the laughing men down into another cranny and shoved the fear of what will happen into a space she could address later. *Lock it away.*

Hvard turned sharply at something in the shadows beyond her and ordered one of his men to check it out. Another man lifted Elaine over his shoulder and into a grain cart just beyond the pool of light. He took off his cloak, his scabs glistening along the side of his face under the dim light. He wrapped it over her, light as a gossamer veil. She strained to hear the voice that calmed her, but only a familiar one echoed in her mind once more.

"Come."

ALIK

Alik pinned a light opaque veil over her nose and mouth. The ends of it skimmed the unremarkable servant garb Damari sent, and she slid her flint rings over her fingers. Mara strapped on a slim dagger in a holster wrapped on her thigh, hidden once she tied her wide-legged dhoti. A thin, black chain wrapped around Mara's waist. Alik had no idea where she and Damari obtained the Tuzaga chain, but her mind volleyed too many questions and fears and hopes to ask. The sun outside her east window began to melt into the jade sea.

"It's time," Mara said.

She led the way through the garden terraces to the hidden stairwell behind the hearth of Ates. Alik thought back to the carefree time she and Shauna walked through this orchard on First Night, never realizing how much things would change in a matter of hours. *We are so close, Shauna. Stay alive. We are coming now.* She didn't dwell on the possibility that Shauna could be dead. Or how terrifying the Edicisi would be if they found him. She kept her mantra up, willing every positive thought to go to her best friend. *Stay alive, Shauna. Stay alive.*

She and Mara circled down the stairwell to the alley in the Trades. Damari and Agnian waited for them at the bottom near the same broken chair Mara waited in on First Night. *So much change in just a few nights*, she thought. *Soon, this will no longer be my home.*

Even as the low horn of the curfew reverberated through the Tiers, the main path of the Trades emptied; its usual throng a distant memory. Stragglers shuffled quickly into stairwells that would lead to their homes and hideouts at its mournful bale.

Shadows bounced off the covered market stalls, and wheeled carts shrouded in chains gave Alik the impression they were not alone. Yet no patrol had reached this central Tier.

Damari and Mara took turns leading through a labyrinth of stairs that wound around the Trades and down to the mid and Sub Tiers, Agnian only a step behind Alik. Aygir hoofbeats echoed in unison from above, where they patrolled the Upper Tiers. When they finally reached the bottom, the only sounds came from the fabric Towner roofs snapping in the wind. *The Hordesmen will be on foot in Low Town,* Alik thought. *There's no way the broad Aygirs can wind through this web of Clusters.*

The fire-rimmed Perimeter Wall usually comforted Alik, a massive stone barrier between her and the beasts roaming the fields beyond. Down here, the wall felt suffocating. It blocked out one moon's light, and dark shadows cast over Low Town. The only light came from a few meager fires spaced out, so they walked in a checkerboard of darkness and light. She tripped over a small, crude effigy of the Edicisi near a broken fountainhead, and Alik shuddered despite herself.

"We must hurry," she said, trying to calm the frantic pulse of her Dua.

The four rushed through the Clusters, ignoring the eyes that peered out from behind the shanty lean-to's surrounding them. Finally, the back entrance of the Silos appeared around the bend.

Alik scanned the surroundings, holding onto Damari's shoulder, as her eyesight blurred. Before she cleared her eyes, she spotted a shadow of smoke gray behind one of the silos. Heart pounding, Alik said to the group, "Mara, you and Agnian walk the opposite path. Damari and I will take this one."

Damari and Alik slipped into the black shadows of the Silos adjacent to the Perimeter Wall. The thick vats clustered together in rows of two; the only light drifted from the fire orbs in the wide center path. Alik could no longer see Mara or Agnian in the darkness.

Damari stilled, and Alik heard it a moment later. A creak of a wheel, the crush of gravel, and affirmation that she was right. *I may not know what my dreams tell me most of the time, but I am learning to trust myself.* She nodded once to Damari, and they crouched low to peer between two vats into the clearing ahead.

Two men blinked into the light. That's the only way Alik could describe it. No one was there one moment, and then the next, they stood in the center of the meager light. By the way Damari stiffened, she knew he saw the same thing. The men pushed their dark cloaks from their heads to reveal black ink curved around their eyes.

Hvard Canavar stepped into view, and Alik nearly laughed.

Thank you, Ates, this makes so much more sense. I genuinely believed the Edicisi and his Handwaidens waited for us here. She grinned ear to ear, gripping a bewildered-looking Damari. *Thank you Sulu, thank you Ruzgar and Yapi. I have never been so happy to see that ugly thug and his men.* She didn't know how the cloaks hid the men in plain sight or muffled all their sounds, but it was far less daunting to confront these men than a monster.

The stories from the girls that got away make sense. Hearing voices, seeing no one, the number of girls missing. It was a man I saw in the Trades that chased me. Alik felt foolish for her fantastical theories of the Edicisi; she blamed the creepy effigies. *This makes more sense. This we can kill.* She was almost giddy.

Her relief evaporated as the trio of men separated into the recess of shadows. One brutal-looking man stepped into the darkness mere steps from Damari and Alik, hunkering low. Alik stilled, not daring to breathe, and then she heard footsteps on the center gravel path.

A girl sobbed, "I can't," and the man closest to them whistled, loud and shrill. Alik held onto Damari as two girls came into view, a bird call calling out far to their left.

The older girl was tall and lean, a riot of black curls cut high on her head and dark coal makeup streaked down her angular face. She held a little girl's wrist, and Alik understood why Damari didn't believe this girl could Rift multiple people at once. Alik only saw her back in the dreams, never her aura. It took a moment's glance of her Dua to realize that this Rifter was as much a victim as Shauna and the others.

The man Alik crouched behind and another from across the path stepped out into the light.

The little girl screamed, "Run!" and the most painful thing Alik ever witnessed occurred. The older girl held her in place, eyes on the men. *She's giving her to them!*

Hvard's booming laugh echoed around them before he walked into the light ahead of the pair. Alik put both hands on the sides of Damari's face and forced him to look at her, not the scene playing out in front of them.

She whispered as low as she could, "They will take this girl where they have taken all the others. I'm going with them." She put a hand over his protesting mouth, and his eyes surged with anger and fear. "Shhh! I need you to listen. It's the cloaks. Not the Edicisi."

He whispered, "No kidding. But why would Firtina want this Rifter in particular?"

"How would I know? I clearly don't know a lot of things," she whispered. "But men, not that Rifter, took Shauna somewhere. I can't go back to the Palace; I'm supposed to be in exile already. You, Mara, and Agnian follow us and rescue the Rifter. Hide her in one of your haunts; you're the best person for that. Tell Firtina she—I don't know, is in the Magarans or something. Lie. Then send Taavi and the Horde."

Damari shifted on the gravel, grabbing her by the arms. "That's the worst plan I've---" Alik shrugged him off and put her hand back over his mouth. One of the men peered at the shadows they hunkered in and slowly walked towards them. As he reached their shadows, Alik shoved Damari behind the vat and stumbled into the light.

"What's this? A pretty one, eh?" The lanky man scratched oozing welts that covered his neck and chin under the flickering light. "Hvard, lemme have her. We've got all we need, and I could use a bit a fun."

Alik prayed to each Goddess that Mara or Agnian would not step out. She took several steps back like she was going to run, and another man roughly grabbed her by the arms. Hvard stood ahead of them. The scrape of a match fractured the otherwise silence while he lit a short pipe.

"Not much Dua in that one if she's not trying for a fight. We've got the one we need. I can't have her telling anyone about this, so do what you want with her."

Alik hadn't expected that. She quickly snapped her flint rings, drawing flame to her palm, and pushed a ball of fire to the man behind her. His pants caught, and he abruptly fell back with a shout and stifled the flames with his hands. The second man pinned her palms flat down at her sides while Hvard watched her struggle. He took a puff. Sweet smoke wafted through the still, cool air underneath her veil, and Alik dared not look to either side in case the men followed her eyes to her brother and friends.

Hvard nodded once, and a rough bandage shoved into her mouth before a man hefted over his shoulder and shoved Alik into the waiting cart.

REED

The Magaran mountain range snags the sky with jagged white tipped teeth. It looks like one sheer vertical stretch into the sky, a stone wall separating Efendians from everything else from a distance. Reed thought, though, as he came to suspended over the range, that it was less like a wall of stone and more a sea of stone waves. Dark valleys of undulating burgundy and gold trees sandwiched in between the crests far below.

Efendians never saw beyond the first monolith that greeted the dead-end dirt road from Efendi Reed now flew over. The Canavar Company Troupe once spent a week pit stopping at farmhouses and Aygir training facilities with little coin to show for it. Hvard had aimed the caravan at Magara, unfazed by legends of its winged creatures and encouraged by the lack of competition. Reed had been giddy with excitement as he sat on the roof of the first wagon, his mother next to him worrying her cuticle.

"Do you think one will let me touch their wing, Maman?"

Alisha hissed and turned him fully to her by his chin. "Heed me, child. Do not get close to them. You are to stay next to me the entire time. No tricks with Tilli today. If I have to sing, you are to stay in the caravan, do you understand me? Hvard has lost his mind coming here."

Alisha adjusted her bone-white dagger beneath the slit of her dress and whispered a prayer to Ruzgar. Their wagon bumped over holes and pockmarks of the road. Reed's mind whirled at the possibility of seeing a Magaran up close by the time the caravan finally snaked into a half-moon at its entrance.

Usually, the announcement of a caravan is met with eagerness, or at a minimum, curiosity. But as the troupe waited at the end of the road, no one came. The mountain base was one vertical wall, with the first crevice high in the sky above. Reed assumed that there would be an entrance of sort, guarded by the fearsome winged creatures. Or perhaps they would defend a ridgeline above like the Perimeter Patrol of Efendi. Yet the troupe saw no one.

Hvard stood in the center of the half-moon awaiting an audience, but none came. He shouted for the troupe to set up, to run through practices, and the troupe did so with reluctance. They spent the remainder of the sunlight practicing routines in front of each other that they could have done in their sleep. Yet still, no one came.

Finally, when both Mizi and Mina were high in the dark sky, the creatures came. The fires outside the iron caravans bounced off the stone wall and flickered with shadows high above them. Reed curled against his mother in the caravan, her low sung songs vibrating against his ribcage when she abruptly sat up.

They landed with a soft thud like rain pellets hitting glass. The first three Magarans stood taller than even Hvard, the claw tips of their wings a few feet higher. They stood, unspeaking, with swords hung loosely in each hand and malice rolling off them in waves.

Reed recalled the nervous way Hvard began his entertainment pitch, an unnatural hint of fear lining his deep vocal cords. When they still said nothing, Hvard beckoned Alisha to them. Reed watched his mother sing through the open slit of their curtained caravan window. She started with a tune he'd heard a hundred times before, but then the creatures moved in silence to enclose the caravan in between them.

Alisha stopped mid-song and switched to a language he'd never heard. Her melody turned from carefree to haunting, her voice modulating from a jaunty tune to a sung chant that ran chills up his bones for the duration of the song. She stopped abruptly, the final high note echoing off the stone wall ahead of her. For a moment, no one said a word. The air strung tight between them. Suddenly the creatures shot into the air and back into dark pockets out of eyesight, startling everyone. Agitated dust from their launch danced around the tallest three Magarans that remained on the ground in the firelight.

Reed jumped back from the window, but not before seeing the final three nod once to his mother before launching up into the mountain.

Back in Texas, Reed only unpacked his memories of Efendi in small doses as if just the thought of his former life would drag him back to this hell. He assumed Magara would be a stone fortress with pockets of caves to huddle in at night. And so, it was with little surprise that Reed was taken aback at the series of roped bridges and wooden structures he was thrust upon when his captors dropped him unceremoniously from several feet in the air. He landed hard on gnarled wooden planks and found himself in what felt like an elaborate village of treehouses that stretched throughout the valley before him in a series of bridges, terraces, and thatched roofs.

A group of winged male Magarans stood behind a stocky, pale female. Instead of feathered legs like the males, her smooth legs were heavily muscular like an Olympian. Strong thighs stood hip-distance apart under a leather dress crisscrossed with small blades. Her hair was shaved down to the scalp, and she wore an ivory bone beaded headpiece that crested thin, white, membranous wings. She was beautiful in a brutal way. Angular cheekbones, marred with lines, supported tawny eyebrows that arched over hard golden eyes like that of a hawk. She said something in a language Reed couldn't understand, and his abductors knelt before her before they too spoke in the foreign language.

She looked sharply to Reed at whatever was said and walked barefoot to him with her arms still crossed across her chest.

"What are you doing in my trees?" She spoke, clipping out words he could understand through a thick accent.

Reed ran his hands over his face, his calloused palm coming away dirtier than before and a little bloody. "Please. I know that there were Rifters among you once. Someone, or something, took my friends and me from our world, and we just want to go back. We mean you no harm, and we will take nothing that is not given to us. All we ask is for some shelter and the guidance of a Rifter."

"You speak in pluralities. Do you mean there are more of you than just this?" She gestured behind her without turning.

The wall of Magaran males shifted to show Monti, gagged and bound, in the fetal position against the trunk of a tree, and Reed's heart plummeted to the ground several hundred feet below them. Blood trickled from her scalp, and a violet bruise blossomed under her eye. He could scarcely see her chest rising and falling, but she looked at him with panicked eyes. He didn't even realize he had moved until the blade of a sword etched across his neck, and a Magaran male stood between Reed and their leader.

"What did you do to her?" Reed asked low. The leaves in the trees whistled in the wind and the leader turned abruptly to the swaying branches before narrowing her eyes at him again.

The leader said, "No harm will come to your female if you speak truths. Tell me, who told you Rifters were among us?"

An old crone shuffled down from steps to their right while the leader spoke. When she lifted her face, her pale yellow irises were faint enough that they almost blended in with the whites of her eyes. Her wings hung low behind her, dragging the ground like a white train. The leader dipped her head once, and the elder Magaran sat at a bench brought out from somewhere behind him.

Reed had no reason to trust these creatures like he had little reason to trust anyone else. He only remembered his mother's fears of them and the malice they radiated years ago. The leader began a slow circle around him. "Tell me, Efendian. Who sent you here for a Rifter?"

"I am not an Efendian. At least not anymore. I want nothing to do with their people, let alone their world. My name is Reed Wells. I just want to go home." He tried to slow the panic in his chest at being circled like prey.

The crone croaked out one syllable, and the leader nodded. "Truth. Good, you are not as stupid as you appear, then." She came to a stop before him, hands resting on the blades strapped low on her chest. "You did not answer my question. Few among us know that we have housed Rifters before, and even fewer land-dwellers have ever stood among our treetops. Answer carefully as it doesn't look like you will fare well if we decide to toss you over the edge."

Reed thought back to the night of his 12th birthday, a few days after their visit to the Magaran base. His mother had hovered around him the entire day, not letting him out of her sight for even a few moments. That night she tucked him into Tilli's wagon between two Aygir beasts. She kissed him goodnight, and he dozed happily off as she spoke low to Tilli. Tilli woke him in the middle of the night, his wide dark eyes shimmering in the twin moonlight filtering through the curtains.

"Come with me, boy. I'm to take you to your mother. No words, no sounds."

Reed had never seen Tilli without a smile, and so he nodded and followed the creature outside, where a sleek Aygir waited for them beyond the caravan fires. They made little noise as they slipped into the fields or even as Tilli urged the beast to a full sprint. Reed, wide awake at the prospect of being in the valley alone at night, scanned continuously for Yurutecs or Garfus. After some time, they came to a rock outcropping shining bright under the red and blue moons like a violet island in a dark sea of grass.

Two cloaked figures stepped out, holding hands. Reed's

mother dropped her hood and hugged Tilli while the other woman looked Reed up and down warily. She had a puckered, red scar across her neck that he had a hard time looking away from.

His mother released Tilli after a few moments, and he cuffed Reed behind the ear. *"Take care of your mother, boy. We are only blessed with one."*

Before Reed could respond, Tilli hooked a pincher behind the Aygir's head and galloped back the way they came. Reed's mother was smiling in the way she only did when she was nervous, rare for the performer. She took Reed by the hand, and her friend took his other before she said with a half-hearted smile, "We're *going on an adventure."*

At her nod, his world slipped away.

Reed shook his head at the memory and met the Magaran's hard stare straight on. "My mother was Alisha Wellis. She was friends with a Rifter that once took pity on us and gave us the best chance at escape when I was a child. I lived in another realm called Earth for the last twelve years with no intention of ever returning. However, a group of us were Rifted from our world into here a couple of nights ago. She and I have been on the run ever since. We just want to go home."

"Even if Rifting realms wasn't absolutely forbidden without permission, it is almost impossible for anyone but the strongest Rifter to do so. Why would anyone take the risk of Bakilar's wrath for a few land dwellers? What is the name of your Rifter?"

Bakilar's wrath? He wondered how the desert village could ever be in a place of authority, but his mind spun around the possibility of something else she'd said. No one ever spoke of Rifters so plainly, and it never occurred to him that one would be forbidden to return them to his world. He looked again to Monti on the ground behind him and tried to slow his rising panic.

"My mother never told me her name. She said it was too dangerous for everyone involved. But she had a scar across her neck that looked fresh and wrapped her throat almost ear to ear. Even twelve years wouldn't erase that scar."

A guard behind the leader stiffened at his description of the Rifter. *Clearly, at least some of them can understand what I'm saying.* Only the leader kept her eyes on Reed.

Monti stirred, breaking the silence.

Reed held his hands out to them, "I have no more secrets. I'll tell you anything you want to know but let me check on her. Her head is bleeding badly."

The leader tapped her foot on the wooden planks. The red crescent moon hovered almost level with the full blue moon, separated by jagged mountain peaks. The leader's bones in her beaded headdress shook with each tap, and Reed thought he'd go mad if she didn't say something.

Finally, she stopped tapping. She clipped something Reed didn't understand to the guards behind her. Without warning, a guard scooped Monti into his arms and threw her over the terrace's edge to the valley far below.

Reed reached. Any broken promise to his mother, the warnings drilled into him for the last twelve years, fell with Monti. She was worth his secrets and was better than his lies, and Reed swore he'd get her home. *I am not failing another.* He shoved his hands out and held his breath at the top of his lungs while he frantically pushed the air around them to the retreating form almost out of eyesight below.

The air surrounding the group whooshed out, snatching all the leaves and small branches off the limbs surrounding them at this height. Reed felt dizzy with power, a thrum in his veins like a chord struck in a cavern. He felt Monti catch, the same way he would have if he had held out a giant net and pulled her to him. Every eye was on him as he lifted her floating form from the edge of the terrace to him, and she shook with shock in his arms.

He ignored the stares and murmurs and knelt with Monti on the ground. He took her head in his palms, brushing her hair back to search for more injuries. He ripped his linen shirt and held it with one hand to her temple, and cupped her head with the other. He repeated so only she could hear, perhaps more to himself than anyone, "I have you. I have you. I have you."

All but the leader and the crone now knelt before him when he looked up.

The female merely nodded once, "It is as I thought. Come Edicisi; there is much to discuss. She will be well taken care of. I just needed proof."

Reed

The Magarans ushered Reed and Monti down a set of stairs to a large open-air room supported by a massive tree on the far end. Reed set Monti on a low table, and several female Magarans waiting with bandages, water, and herbs of some form fussed over her. Reed wasn't sure if he should murder every one of the Magarans walking with him or hug them. The secret he'd held onto his whole life, the one that his mother felt forced to flee worlds for, was out. More so, the leader appeared to expect it.

The leader walked alongside Reed and nodded her head to a door beyond them. "Bathe, Efendian. She will be safe, and you will attract beasts we'd rather let pass with your smell. She will be here eating when you finish, and then someone will attend to that wound on your arm. We will discuss what needs to happen next."

He walked in a daze to the small room with a large, round, wooden bathtub steaming in the chilled night air. A female attendant left a stack of linens and a towel with him, and he sank quickly under the water. He scrubbed with the herb satchel left on its edge, wincing at new cuts it discovered.

Reed felt adrift in his skin. *Maman made me swear to never tell another soul about the curse in my veins. It's why she lived in fear and squalor in Low Town, why she put up with the men in the Canavar*

Company Troupe, and why she fled to another world. What happens now? I want no part of Efendi. He splashed his face with the water, begging answers to come. *Will my father sense that I used that power? Maman believed doing so would lead him to us even a world away. Fuck. Fuck. Fuck. I have to get us home.* The water was murky with dirt when he dressed in the beige linen clothes left out for him.

His reflection in the dingy water was one he'd hardly recognized. He ran a hand over his shaved head, brushed the scruff that had bearded on his face, and walked out to the domed room on bare feet.

Monti sat at a table under a thick blanket, propped up against the base of the massive tree that supported the main room. Her hair had become a mangled mess of gold gone airborne, and her bright green eyes tracked Reed as he walked to her. She cupped a wooden mug of something steaming between her hands, and a clean bandage haphazardly gripped her head. The leader walked away from a group of Magarans on the opposite wall at Reed's entrance. She took the stool across from him as he sunk next to Monti.

"I have questions---" she began, bristling at the hand Reed held up as he turned to face Monti directly.

"Are you OK?" He asked. His thigh pressed tight to hers so he could be as close to her as the prickly woman would allow.

She arched an eyebrow at him. "I will never be OK, Reed. But I might feel better if I can pitch that woman off a balcony as well."

Reed laughed, relieved. He didn't doubt her for a moment, and he felt an unexpected sense of pride that she was likely plotting someone's death rather than falling apart. He smiled, unable to restrain the quick touch he stole to her jawline as an attendant changed the bandage on his other arm.

The leader just smirked at Monti before continuing, "My name is Uci. I am the Oonder of Magara, and I have as many ridiculous titles as your queen, but they're a waste of time. We've been looking for you ever since the first power began leaking from the Batiwood. Tell me. Do you have the Katapak?"

An uncomfortable pause hovered in the room, a bubble on the verge of a sticky pop. "The what?" Reed asked, mind blank.

Uci's smile flattened. She opened her mouth but closed it again before trying once more. "The Katapak. Of the prophecy. As the Edicisi, you are the only one that can carry the stone and rid us of the Others once and for all."

Reed had every eye in the room on him but could think of nothing better than a shrug in response. "I have no idea what you're talking about. But if we can just talk to your Rifter, it would only take a moment to go home. I remember that clearly. I want nothing to do with whatever prophecy you've deluded yourself into believing."

Monti's head cocked at an angle he likened to battle prep. "Steady there, pumpkin. We're not going anywhere without my dad. That was the agreement. That is the only reason I didn't shoot you in the farmhouse. I don't care if you did just save me from a deadly fall; I will kill you if you try to go home without both of us."

"We don't even know where he is," Reed said and then abruptly changed course at Monti's face. "What I'm saying is that we will find him, obviously. But it does no good without a Rifter. We find the Rifter, then she takes us to your dad, and then we go back home."

Monti set the cup down to better cross her arms. "Why should I believe you? You told me verbatim that men of this world didn't have magic, yet you just did something that looks a hell of a lot like magic. And why does she keep calling you 'Edicisi'? What does that even mean?"

Reed clenched his fists on the table. "It means I'm cursed. A monster. That's what you want to hear? It's the reason my dad hunted us years ago across worlds. It's what ruined my life. It's what killed my mother. It's the reason my wife is dead and why I had to give up my daughter." He swallowed the lump in his throat,

"I want nothing to do with this world. I don't care what happens to it so long as I'm off of it. And no one, not even you, will stop me from leaving."

Monti had a wind-up face. It was a tell Reed discovered within the first day of knowing her and signaled the deep inhale she used to launch a verbal assault. A blade cut her off midway though as it whistled between their faces, sinking deep in the tree behind them.

Uci spoke low, her fists clenching on another blade hilt on the table before them. "My people have been stationed in this mountain range for hundreds of years. Waiting. Watching, to ensure that the Others do not consume our world. Your resurrection signifies that they are on the brink of breaking through. Our scouts have gone missing over the Batiwood, and its creatures are creeping into our mountains. And now they have one of our most powerful Rifters."

She slipped the blade into a pocket on her vest and stood. "We leave at dawn to bring them all home ourselves. I'm done waiting on orders; you'll leave in the morning. I will not jeopardize the fate of them or this world because you are too ignorant or too selfish or too stupid to realize your role in our prophecy."

"Say what you want about me," Reed said, leaning back. "I just need us to get home. I am not a tool in your prophecy, and this world is better off without me."

She shook her head in disgust and gripped her face in her hands for a brief moment before turning back to Reed, fingers curled as if she intended to strangle him. "You are a boy playing at a man. You are not going home, you fool. You are being sent to Bakilar to learn how to control your powers so that when the war comes, you are ready."

Monti raised her hand. "Back up. War? Can someone explain to me what this prophecy is, seeing as it's trying to keep me in this hellhole as well?" She jerked her head at Reed. "And what in the hell is he?"

The Magaran at Uci's shoulder was one of the scouts that captured him and Monti. His wing tips flared over bare skin that matched his hickory feathers as he spoke. "The Edicisi is prophecy-bound to be the most powerful Duawielder in our realm and the only one strong enough to permanently fight off what is coming with the assistance of two others prophesied. The Rifter and the Reader. He and the Reader only come in dire times of need to protect us from the *Others.* World eaters. Demons, hovering on the skin of our world seeking a chance to come in."

Reed said, "I don't even know how to do any of this. I've never even heard of the *Others.*"

Uci snapped, "That's because you ran. You've been running your whole life, and because of that, we will be months behind in preparation. You are wholly unprepared for what must be done. We have yet to find the Reader, so we cannot close the portals indefinitely, but he or she must be living if you are here." She turned to the group of Magarans waiting behind her. "The best hope we have is to kill whoever is opening the gates from within the Batiwood and bring our Rifter home. Risindi, send word to Bakilar that this boy-man will arrive soon and to prepare for the worst. Tell them he does not have the Katapak, so they must hasten the search."

"Wait, please!" Monti leaned across to grip Uci's arm despite the anger pulsing from the Magaran. "My father was captured by Efendian guards. I can't go to Baki-wherever. I have to go to him. He and I have no part in this, and I have to get him home. I will go alone on foot if I have to."

Good to see she has no problem leaving me here with the monsters, Reed thought.

Uci yanked her arm free, interrupting Reed's thoughts. "You said you were Rifted a few nights ago. Did you see the Rifter that brought you here?"

Reed shook his head. "No, but she took an entire building with her. Most died in the Rift or its aftermath, but at least five of us survived. Efendian Hordesmen took three others fleeing with us. One would have stood out. He wore an outfit of all orange that looked nothing like what an Efendian would wear."

One of the guards leaned over to Uci and said something in their native language. "Two nights ago, one of our scouts spotted several men bound and gagged in a wagon. He noted it because they headed towards the Batiwood and not Efendi. They did not return. One wore something similar to what you've described."

Monti slapped her hands on the table, throwing the blanket off her. "Then that's where I need to go."

"Land Dweller, if you go to the Batiwood, you will die. I've sent my best warriors there, and they've not returned." She turned to leave with Monti at her heels.

"Then let me go with you. I will fight. I can't leave my dad."

"You are a liability, and you will get my kin killed. I'm sorry to be the one to tell you this, but your father is likely already dead if the Horde took him." She nodded towards Reed, "Even he, as dumb as he is, knows that. You are not my prisoner. You can choose if you want to go with this worthless man to Bakilar or be dropped at the gates of Efendi. But know this---they do not treat women without Dua well. The best life you can hope for there is on your back. It's your choice."

Uci stalked out of the room with the bulk of the Magarans. The round room felt significantly more cavernous as Monti stifled a sob back.

Only the Magaran named Risindi, Reed, and Monti remained in the room. Reed clenched his jaw at Monti's proud back, racked with tears, as she stood apart from them.

Something is waiting in the Batiwood, and it's tied to my father. Uci's words were true. Reed was wholly unprepared to face what he had been running from his whole life. If he couldn't get back to Texas, the speck of a village a sea apart from the Batiwood was the next best thing.

Monti swiped at her face. When she turned, she shed no more tears, though she didn't look at Reed. She asked Risindi, "You're the one taking me to Efendi or this Bakilar place, right?" At his nod, she continued, "No need to take me the whole way to Efendi. I just need to be dropped off where you found us."

The Magaran scout watched her for a moment silently and then nodded his head once. "If you are to go to the Batiwood, you'll need this." He slipped out a heavy dagger the size of her forearm and tightened the leather sheath from his waist around hers to slip the blade back in. "You need to leave now if you want to do this. Uci will not be as lenient if you jeopardize her plans."

She nodded, perhaps more to herself than him. Some of the blood from her temple seeped through the white bandage, a pink dot wreaking havoc to Reed's plans of fleeing. "Thank you."

Risindi said, "You remind me of Ceren. She is the Rifter Uci spoke of that is missing. She could have stayed behind to let us seek out this power source from the woods on our own, but she threatened to Rift us all to the Efendian Palace if we tried to leave her. She will like you, and she would skin me alive if she knew I kept you away from someone you loved."

Reed's heart sped up. He was sure no healthy 24-year old died of heart failure, but today was testing that theory. "Monti, please. You don't understand. You cannot go there. It is an evil unlike anything our world could describe."

Monti held her hands up in question. "How do you know, Reed? I can't read between your lines when all of them are half-truths. What are you not saying?"

He held his hands in supplication between them, close enough to see the specks of gold fire in her eyes. "I can't explain it, Monti. I don't know myself, but I *feel* it. The voices, the despair, my nightmares. It's hovered over everything I touch for two worlds. It's coming from the woods. Please don't do this. I'll find another way; just give me time."

She closed the gap between them, full lips pressed against his cheekbone. His brain split apart as to whether to pull her to him or stay still to let her choose what happened next. The decision made before ever asked as she said, "Sometimes we don't get time to be brave. Sometimes we have to do life scared shitless."

She squeezed his hand as she turned, maroon nails ragged and plastered with mud. "Thank you for keeping me alive this far, but I can take it from here."

Risindi and Monti walked out of the room to the empty terrace above. Reed wavered while his mind shot out every bad possibility of what to do.

He ran up the stairs behind them. The sun would rise soon, but Monti was cloaked in darkness when he got to the uppermost platform. She looked once back to him before Risindi cradled her in his thick arms and shot into the sky without a sound.

ELAINE

Elaine didn't know if her nausea came from the thin metal wrapped tightly around her, the swaying of the cart, or the fear of what would come next as they bumped through the underground tunnel. Her eyes adjusted to the darkness not long after the men removed the hood over her head, but she had no idea if hours or days had passed. Time felt stagnant underground when she couldn't see anything in front of her face, and she focused only on keeping her panic at bay.

The hidden tunnel beneath the Silos felt smooth at first, but enough holes, roots, and rocks littered this section that Hvard's men often had to stop the cart. The lone lantern at the head of the cart swayed over Elaine and the woman next to her before illuminating a gnarled mess of roots blocking the dark path. The men hacked at the roots, the silver gleam of an ax flashing in the firelight.

"Filbish roots. How in Ates did you get past this without cuttin' it off?"

"I already said. It weren't there before."

"Or you took us the wrong way you idiot."

"Oh now I'm the---"

Elaine's temple bumped against the wooden cart as she lay curled on her side. The pounding in her head and emotions threatening to drown her preoccupied all thoughts, but one broke through as the older girl shifted closer to her. *She should get out now while they're not paying attention.*

It didn't occur to Elaine to do the same herself. Now that she stopped struggling, the thin, dark chain across her arms and chest slipped with each movement, but it felt as if a thick oak tree pinned her down to the cart.

A cool hand grabbed her own as a whisper cracked through.

"Did you hear me? I need you to hold on a little longer. My friends are coming for you."

She could just make out the shape of the older girl in the dim light. Elaine looked dubiously at the pitch-black tunnel around her and whispered, "I think you've hit your head. No one is coming for either of us down here."

The voice in the dark whispered back. "You will get you out of here. Do you think you can Rift if we get the chain off you?"

She shrugged, though in the throes of nausea, she forgot the stranger couldn't see her and that no one was supposed to know she was a Rifter. *Guess the gig is up. Doesn't matter, though.* Elaine felt like she'd never Rift again now that the chain had settled over her.

"We'll see. I need you to stay with my friends. Do not Rift without them; they will protect you." The lantern swayed, jostled by one of the men pulling a shovel out from the driver's seat. Elaine glimpsed olive skin, jet black hair spilling in waves, and wide, caramel eyes. She was lying on her side as well, tied up with rope. At some point, she lost the veil that covered her face when they first shoved her in with Elaine.

Elaine nodded to the frayed rope the girl loosened. "You could leave now. You should."

Elaine's eyes welled at the thought of being alone in this black tunnel with Hvard's men, though she didn't know how she could cry anymore.

The girl scooted closer. "It's OK. It's going to be OK."

That's exactly what she said. Elaine's chest constricted at the memory of Kara. The way she stood there while they carted her off like a sack of grain.

One of the men stopped hacking. "Did you hear that?"

Everyone stopped speaking. Elaine held her breath, afraid the men heard their conversation, but then she heard the scratching. The tunnel amplified all sounds, and in the darkness, she would not be able to know what scratched along the walls until it was on top of them. *Whatever that is, it's coming faster.*

Digging, faint clicking, nails on a dirt floor.

The girl grabbed her hand painfully tight, a tremor attached to her palm. Elaine twisted to see ahead of them but could only see the men standing stone still in the lamp light, watching the funnel of black ahead of them.

Hvard's men tossed down the shovel and scrambled into the cart. One crawled over them to the back edge of the cart, holding a dagger in one hand and his cloak in the other. He laid down next to them, the other girl pressing herself as close to Elaine as possible at his proximity.

He said low, "Hush luv, you'll want me close in a minute." He opened the cloak wide and draped the three of them under it like a blanket.

The light cloth was deceptively heavy, their breaths pushing and pulling small puffs of air into threads that reeked of cheap tobacco and sweat. The cloak sucked into Elaine's mouth as the two next to her frantically pulled air into and out of their lungs. *They know what's coming.*

Elaine tried to see beyond them as the other man extinguished the lantern, but the man sharing his cloak whispered, "No moving. The cloaks can only hide so much from them."

The clicking and digging came closer. Something scaled the walls of the tunnel. A white glow appeared at the front of the cart, and Elaine shook when something heavy joined them in the cart. *Yurutecs.*

She'd heard stories of Yurtuecs from the Clusters, but they sounded so improbable that Elaine assumed they were made up. The thin cloak did not hide the hooked claw, the spade-shaped head, or the elongated torso as the Batiwood creature passed over them. Spindle legs, jointed at multiple points like a spider, gripped either side of the cart. It looked like a praying mantis, but only if a mantis stood taller than a man. The creature's stark white skin glowed in the dark, illuminating massive pinchers protruding from its mouth. Another Yurutec crawled the opposite wall. They clicked a guttural noise rumbling deep within their throats as the cart shifted back and forth. The second Yurutec joined on top of the cart, rocking it back and forth, testing it.

Warm liquid trickled down to Elaine's knees, and she didn't know if it was the girl or the man next to her that pissed themselves. The Yurutecs jabbed their front turned claws, hitting the inside of the cart to Elaine's immediate left and another near her feet, clicking and stabbing at the cart. The girl whimpered, gripping Elaine's hand tight as a third Yurutec appeared on the ceiling of the tunnel, kicking one of the others in the head as it passed. The injured Yurutec launched at the newcomer, and all three creatures tumbled in the tunnel past the cart. Their glow inched further and further away, a light disappearing down a tube.

Ear piercing screams echoed through the tunnel in the darkness a few minutes later. Hvard's men, the stranger, and Elaine laid there, quietly panting while the danger either passed or returned to them. The wrongness of the cloak felt heavier and heavier over Elaine's small frame as if it pressed itself to every inch of her body.

After enough time in silence, the man next to them took the cloak off, a lid lifting off a stifling trunk. She breathed deeply, finally, and heard the girl whisper a prayer to each goddess. A match struck, the catch of the pitch in the lantern, and the men carved a path for the cart without another word to each other.

The older girl didn't say anything else to Elaine but never let go of her hand. The cart continued its slow rumble down the tunnel, and adrenaline and fear warred with exhaustion, the latter finally overruling all else. Elaine jolted awake when the cart stopped moving. She still couldn't see anything beyond the lantern's pool of light, but the air tasted different. Less stagnant.

One of Hvard's men stood on top of the cart, lantern held high, and the light flickered over an indention in the shape of a circle in the ceiling. He grunted, and as he pushed up, dirt rained down on his head. The top opened like a portal to the night sky. Clusters of dust poured light into the hole, and Elaine blinked several times before she recognized the dust as stars.

She didn't realize how much she missed Efendi's stars until that moment. A pang broke through the container buried in the recesses of her mind as she realized she would not see the Trades again. She grit her teeth. *Lock it away. You'll figure this out too.*

One of the men used an ax handle to pull down a rope ladder while the other released one bound hand from each captive. Head spinning, Elaine climbed up behind the first man with one hand and an elbow. She heaved her body over the lip in the ground, rolling over in the tall grass.

The city of Efendi rose high above the fields like a squat, gilded cake. The domed roofs of the Palace glittered under the two moons even from this distance. Elaine tracked the hair-thin line of fire at the top of the Perimeter Wall, guessing where the Hadishi house lay against its imposing base.

That doesn't matter now. It's not like I'll--

Elaine cried out as one of the men kicked her ribs.

"Get up. We're suppose' to feed 'ya. No good to him if you're dead."

The dark-haired woman scrambled to her knees in between them and demanded, "Who? Who wants us? Where are you taking us?"

The taller of the men backhanded her to the ground near Elaine's feet. "Not so strong now that you've been under the cloak are ya? The only thing that fire of yours will do is getcha eaten. Nice, tasty snack. I wonda' if he'd notice a different taste if I had a go at you first?"

"Enough." The older man pushed him aside. "Give them the bread."

The horrible one snickered, a wheezy exhale somewhere between a cough and a leer, and yanked a canteen from a pocket. His black pants slung low on his hips, held up only by a crude rope belt over his gaunt frame. He scratched at an oozing scab at his neck and tossed the women a hunk of bread found in another pocket.

Hunger outweighed disgust, and Elaine gnawed a hunk off with one hand and gave the rest to her friend. *Not friend. I don't even know her,* she reminded herself.

The men bickered about the first watch as the sun started to rise behind Efendi, a warm beacon of light fanning quickly over the jade and gold grass surrounding them in every direction. Elaine faced the Magaran mountains, watching the sun crawl over their jagged peaks. The early rays had yet to touch the Batiwood, the woods Efendians spoke of only at night, in the far west. The orange-red horizon formed a veritable wall of *other* that no one ventured to, and everyone avoided its proximity. After months of living in this new world, Elaine only knew that the Aygir refused to walk through those gnarled trees, and the Yurutec and Garfu creatures called it home. The line of encroaching trees at the far edge of the valley might as well have been the edge of the world to Efendians.

"Sleep while you can, lovelies. We move in a couple hours." The older man shuffled a few feet from them, hefted the window to the tunnel closed, and sat with his back to them while he lit a pipe.

His discarded cloak lay several feet away, but the wheezy one used his own cloak like a pillow, snoring within moments. Elaine curled on her side, dizzy with nausea, and the girl mirrored her in the tall grass.

"I'm Alik," she whispered.

I don't need to know your name. You'll be gone like everyone else that comes around me. She closed her eyes, ignoring the waiting caramel eyes on her. *I don't know why I thought this world would be any different.*

"I know you're tired, but you must be ready. My brother saw you on the Solmas Tier, and I've been looking for you for months without realizing it."

Elaine opened her eyes at the admission, her body tensing with the need to flee. The chain at her waist tightened.

"I've never met a Rifter. When did you come into your--"

Elaine tracked the movement at the same time the girl stopped speaking, stifling all conversations Elaine didn't want to have. The grass swayed above the portal. She tried to sit up, but Alik held her to the ground. Her bound forearms leaned into Elaine's mouth as she shook her head silently. The chains around Elaine squeezed with each struggle against Alik, but Elaine did not stop trying to get away as the portal to the underground tunnel pulsed up. Something below struggled to get out.

Elaine, wide-eyed and shaking, muffled for Alik to get the cloak, but Alik did not take her eyes from the portal in the ground.

The older man turned as the door swung back to the ground with a thunk. "What the—"

Both men lifted off the ground, grasping at their necks as they kicked their legs. The thing that emerged was not a Yurutec, but almost as haunting. Black gore streaked her dark hair, and her midnight eyes sparkled while she raised her fists in the air. Terrifyingly beautiful, Elaine now understood the difference between the Dua she'd been around in Low Town and the power radiating from this one. *She's Efendi's Monica Rambeau*, she thought in awe. The men gagged and gasped against the Airwerk the older girl shoved down their throats with a satisfied smile.

A sword broke through the opening, followed by hands tattooed with black markings and fingers stacked with silver rings.

He brushed gore off the sides of his leather pants and close-cropped beard when he emerged fully. His eyes skimmed Elaine, but lingered over Alik as he nodded once. He leaned back into the hole, helping a third stranger through it before closing the lid with a thunk. The final arrival withdrew a dagger from his waist, eyes on Elaine.

She managed to wiggle from under Alik, away from the boy she recognized from the pastel Tier. *Alik said her brother saw me.* Anger rolled off him in waves as he stepped closer, but before she could question anything else, he slit the thin chain cutting off her circulation.

Alik said, "Mara, stop. I need one of them alive."

To Elaine's surprise, the warrior immediately dropped them. "Do you have a preference, Princess?"

Elaine's head whipped back to the girl in the grass, covered in dirt. A dried stalk stuck out of her mangled hair. *That's a princess?*

Alik glanced between the two kidnappers for less than a heartbeat before motioning to the older man watching her with wide, pleading eyes. The warrior, Mara, barely acknowledged the choice as she clinched her fist in the direction of the wheezing one. She held a deep breath at the top of her lungs. When she breathed out with a sigh, Hvard's man lay dead in the grass.

Alik held her bound hands out to the man cleaning off his sword, and rubbed her wrists after the ties fell. Next to Elaine, Mara sank down, legs splayed in the grass with her head bowed. She drank from a leather skin pulled from the dead man with an Airwerk, offering it to Elaine when she finished.

Alik stood over the older man on the ground, "What is your name?"

"Handen. I'm so sorry, Princess Alik. We had no idea who you were. If we did, we never would have--"

Alik's soft eyes took a hard turn as she hissed, "You wouldn't have what? Kidnapped me like you have dozens of other women? Children like this one? How many have you taken?"

Handen looked to the ground. "I tried not to count. I'm just followin' orders."

"Who's? Hvard's?"

He nodded but said, "His. Yea, but he follows the Dark One's commands."

Alik stilled, and Elaine's bones chilled at the laughter ringing out in her head. Elaine whispered, "The Edicisi."

Alik whipped her head to Elaine, her brows furrowed. But she turned back to Hvard's man, " Keep talking."

He shook his head, lip quivering. "I can't."

Mara flicked her wrist, picking Handen up in an Airwerk like a rag doll several feet into the air. She slammed him back down, hard, into the ground before he even had time to scream.

The warrior looked a little woozy as she shrugged. "It's effective."

Alik nodded to her and turned back to the man curled up on the ground. "I have grown up with terror, and I can assure you, no one is feared more than Firtina Iktidar. Start at the beginning. Who is this Dark One, where are we going, where are the girls you've kidnapped? Everything, or I promise, I will keep you alive and deliver you to my mother as a Cez."

Elaine only saw the "Cez" once. When she first went out on her own from the Trades, she followed streams of people to the uppermost Tier. The crowd wound its way to the widest plaza where a man screamed, suspended in the air, with ribbons of skin hanging from him like a macabre maypole. It was the first and only time she'd seen the Queen. She stood underneath him, picking her nails with a bloody dagger as streams of blood fell around her as if she held an invisible umbrella. Elaine threw up on the steps before running back to Kara. "*The Cez,*" Kara explained, "*is an example.*"

Handen cried out and held his head in his hands. Tufts of white hair poked through wrinkled, grime-laden fingers.

"I'm dead either way." He shook his head. "Hvard said it'd be the best paying job of our life. It was supposed to be my last. We took strays--girls no one cared about at first---and then he got specific. Needed someone with this Dua, one with this Dua, ones well into their powers, others not yet in full control. Sometimes he had specific names, other times just a description. It ranged. We were to take them through a secret tunnel to the Batiwood where he's waiting."

Alik's hands clenched at her sides. "Go on," she said.

"We don't know his name. I don't think even Hvard got it, so we started calling him the Dark One at first because of his cloak. He's got an underground prison. That's where he keeps them. Their Dua is weakest the further down you go and he only comes above ground for the 'ritual' with a prisoner."

Kanne Da'Neen's stories of the Edicisi crawling from the roots of a Batiwood flashed in Elaine's mind as Alik pressed, "What does he do with them?"

Handen stopped speaking for a few moments while Alik flicked her flint rings back and forth, a tiny spark in a dirty palm. He whispered as if afraid someone would overhear him, "One of the company followed him one time. Too stupid for his own teeth. He didn't like the splits and wanted to see what Hvard was selling us for. He said—" Handen stopped speaking and fisted his shaking hands before continuing. "He said that he takes them one at a time to the surface. He's got a table there. Tools. He said he carves them. Chunks at a time."

Elaine's stomach roiled. She wished for the first time that the voices in her head would drown out whatever came next.

Tears fell down Alik's plump cheeks, and Handen watched her with pleading red eyes. "He's eating them, Princess. Bits at a time."

Alik doubled over with an anguished cry, clutching her chest as she fell to her knees. Mara whispered a prayer to Ruzgar, hands over her mouth in horror while the bearded man with her vomited in the grass. The boy from the pastel Tier rubbed a hand over Alik's back, his other hand shaking. Every part of Elaine willed her to run as far away from this as possible as she held herself with shaking hands. *Even home is better than this. This is who has been calling to me. A monster brought me here while he has eaten kids like me.*

Handen said through tears of his own. "It started as a job, but now, none of us can get out. Hvard says he knows us all by name."

"Why does he do it?" The bearded man next to Mara asked, wiping his mouth.

Handen shook his head. "He's looking for someone. He's evil." He jerked his head towards the black cloak in the grass. "Evil like these cloaks. He gave them to us one day when he got more specific with his requests. They ain't right, and they're doing something to all of us. It's like the more you wear it, the more you need it. Even Hvard. I feel like it's eating my soul, but the others don't seem to notice."

Alik demanded, "Shauna Tyid. Was she one he called for by name?"

He shook his head. "I'm sorry. I don't know. We divvied up lists. I was put on this one for a while now." He nodded to Elaine. "I've been with Hvard the longest. I was supposed to find the Rifter, but he found her first. I swear---if I'd been alone and knew she was this young, I wouldn't have ever turned her over."

Alik watched him with flat eyes. "Good to see you have a moral floor. At what age is it appropriate to give girls to a monster? 13?"

He cried harder, snot running down his upper lip. "I'm sorry. I'm so sorry. I didn't know what it was for, and then it was too late."

"You will not live to see this month's end, Handen. But if you help me, you will have the chance to redeem yourself in front of the Goddesses before I kill you." Alik said.

He nodded, slowly at first and then more emphatically. "What do you need?"

***

Elaine tracked the sun's rays shift across the valley as Alik, Agnian, and Damari grilled Handen on details and layouts of the prison.

After hasty introductions, they promptly left Elaine out of the discussion. She listened though.

I can't believe Alik is going in there knowing what is waiting in the woods. She's gotta be as powerful as the Queen if she thinks she can take the Edicisi on. But didn't Reiki say she had hardly any Dua? Elaine shuddered. *This princess is insane.*

Elaine walked to Mara's at the edge of their makeshift camp. Her hands spiraled in the air as the paper she scrawled on moments before floated on the horizon, a mere glimmer now.

"What are you doing?" Elaine asked.

"Sending word to friends. If we're to go in the woods, we'll need help."

Elaine turned back to the fire-orange tree line in the distance. She whispered to Mara, "I can hear voices."

"Now?" Mara asked, scanning the woods behind them.

She shook her head, "No. Like in the Trades. I heard girls' voices sometimes when no one else did. I think they've been calling me for help this entire time, and I did nothing."

Elaine looked at Mara's ramrod straight frame, her lean muscles, and determined face. She rushed to head off Mara's anger or disgust as the others walked up to her side. "But I could go with you. I can help," Elaine said.

Damari pointed to Elaine, "Absolutely not. Besides, if what my sister believes to be true, a Rifter could be the weapon this monster needs the most."

Mara, to Elaine's surprise, gently squeezed her shoulder. "He's right. We need to get you somewhere safe."

Damari ignored the argument Elaine tried to take up and said, "Alik, please reconsider. You have to have Firtina if he's the Edicisi."

"And what if she wanted the Edicisi here to begin with?" Alik asked.

Elaine laughed at that, but everyone else listened as if she was serious. *Ohmygod, she's serious.*

"She. Is. Firtina. Iktidar," Damari said. "If she wants the Edicisi, she will find a way to get him. Running through the Batiwood on your own doesn't keep her from him; it just gets you killed." He grabbed her shoulders. "Wait for her. If it is Edicisi, you have no way of protecting yourself, let alone the others."

Elaine watched Alik pace, wondering what it would feel like to be brave enough to fight this world's most horrific legend willingly. Mara, with crossed arms and an unfazed look on her face, did not try to convince Alik the two of them should not go. *They would never have left me to Hvard.*

Kara was once her idol, the funny, bold, confident big sister she desperately wanted to be like since Kara helped her stand that first day in Low Town. *But she was so angry and so bitter. All the time. And so afraid. She said she had to give me to Hvard.* She watched Alik and Mara hash out a plan. *But then you've got these girls. They could wait for the scariest Duawielder in history, but instead, they're gonna go face the Edicisi alone. All to help other girls they probably don't know but know they need help.* Elaine's realization cut through the fog of pain since Kara left her with Hvard.

I will never be like Kara.

I will not run from this too.

She took a deep breath, readying herself. "I want to go with you."

The response was instant and simultaneous between the others arguing around her, "No."

Alik spoke as if Elaine hadn't just made a life-altering proclamation. "We'll do this: Mara and I have a few hours' heads start on the Horde. Damari, go back. Get Firtina and the Horde, and we will stick with my plan to sneak in with Handen. That will at least buy me time to get Shauna and the others out before Firtina gets to this Dark One, but it will put Firtina in place as a back-up if things go horribly wrong."

Damari rubbed his face in his hands but nodded. He asked Mara, "Which Eye did you send the letter to?"

She didn't look at him when she answered. "I sent the letter for Taavi as you requested. This one is not for an Eye, but a friend. A friend who may be able to deliver faster aid than even Firtina."

Damari's brows furrowed, but Mara interrupted whatever he was about to ask. "We need to go, Alik. Agnian and Damari, leave now for Efendi. Stay on guard; some Garfus have been spotted during daylight. The Horde will meet us at the Batiwood. I'll keep Alik safe in the meantime."

"Wait for them, Alik. Just a little more time," Agnian said.

She tossed her hands up. "We've wasted enough time arguing! Handen said he picks someone new each moonrise. I'll not let another girl be tortured while we wait."

"Then I go with you," Agnian said as he slipped his sword into a sheath on his back.

Alik growled her frustration. "We've been over this. Handen said that they beat all male prisoners before taking them to a separate cell far away from the girls. You'd be no help, and if you fought back, you'd jeopardize us before we can get Shauna. You can't hide in the woods safely for the time it will take for the Horde to reach us. And most importantly, I'm not taking a little girl to that place or back to Efendi. She can barely Rift more than two feet right now after that chain of Tuzaga."

Elaine sputtered, "I can go more than two feet." *Maybe.* She shook her head. "I still want to go with you."

All four simultaneously said, "No," before ignoring her again.

Elaine threw her hands in the air. *Of course, I'd land in an entirely new world and still get ignored.*

Alik put her hand to Agnian's chest. "Just make Elaine disappear. Take her to Dvari with you. Get her as far away from the woods and Efendi. I don't know what the Edicisi wants, but I sure as Ates am not bringing a Rifter on a dinner plate, and I don't want her near my mother."

Elaine raised her hand, "I'm right here. You could ask me."

They just kept arguing. Agnian turned to Damari, "You're

fine with her going alone?"

Damari hovered by Elaine's side, watching the pair argue. He crossed his arms and said, "Absolutely not. But the only way I see either of us accompanying them is if we wear the cloak, and Handen believes the Dark One monitors the cloaks." He dropped his arms and continued, "Alik is stronger than you give her credit, and Mara is the most powerful Airwerker outside of Ordu ranks. I don't like it any more than you do, but I believe we'd put them in more danger by going."

Mara nodded to Damari and said, "Come, Princess. We have to go."

"You heard Handen. Dua is practically useless if you are in those cages. Why not send the kid back with Mara?" Agnian said, half pleading and clearly grasping at straws given the way Mara stared at him.

"I knew how to kill long before I came into my Dua, Agnian. You should take her to the Magarans. They will protect her."

Agnian's eyes widened at Mara, but she kneeled to Elaine's eye level. "Be smart little one. Efendi is not safe for you like the Batiwood is not safe for any of us."

"We can send her with you to Dvari when this is all over," Alik said. "The Magarans might be safest for her, but not for anyone else. They haven't answered any of our missives in weeks. If you have to go there, do not linger and don't tell them you are working alongside an Iktidar."

"I have never been on the Iktidar side, Alik, but I'm always on yours. I'll figure out what to do with her and follow the Horde's trail back to you."

Agnian picked up the meager bag of provisions they'd divvied up and stalked towards the Magaran mountains. Damari hugged Alik tight before pulling Elaine with him to follow. Elaine glanced over her shoulder, watching the princess and the warrior walking towards the Batiwood across the valley.

Reed

Reed scoured his hands in the pale blue river that would eventually snake its way to the Turkaz Sea. There was no blood on them, but he felt death caked on his palms regardless for the second time in his life. He ran the rough river rock not yet smoothed with time over his knuckles and tried to block out what he did moments before, his mind alternating between his first murder and what he assumed was his second. The sound of water forced that memory to the surface.

The water turned on upstairs as he cleared the plates. He and Staci fought enough for one night, and they silently agreed that he'd remain downstairs to tidy while she put their daughter to bed. He wiped off the linoleum counter, thinking of another path in his argument to convince her to move. The same despair that followed him all his life now crouched in the flower bed they planted when they first arrived, a shadow of darkness blotting out sunlight on anything he touched. It perched on their bed at night and waited in the dark crevices between their clothes on bent wire hangers. His curse followed him everywhere, and he knew it was time to move again.

Staci was adamant that he was losing his mind. She called him a psychopath, told him to leave if he was that scared of shadows and mocked him when he told her about the cashier singing the same haunting lullaby to him that morning. Perhaps he was losing his mind, but Maddy was his priority now. Reed needed to get her away from this place before he finally found them, a sinkhole at the ready to suck them into the pit of darkness he ran from.

Reed knew he could show Staci his powers to force her to believe him, but his mother ardently believed that any use of Dua would be a beacon to his father. He couldn't do that, not with Madeline in his life now.

Maddy, the world changer the size of a football. Even now, he had a hard time believing she was his, and though he knew she was sturdier than glass, he was so nervous that he'd accidentally break her. He never appreciated how hard it was to hold a baby. Is he holding her too tight? Not tight enough? The nurses at the hospital laughed at his panicked face when they put her in his arms the first time.

He never wanted to be a dad this young, but he would figure out how to be the best parent he could be now that she was here. He didn't realize that there was a 7.2lb, 19-inch hole the shape of a little girl in his life until that day. That day changed everything. Every paranoia he'd been ignoring became a real threat, and it was his responsibility to keep her safe above all else. He knew in his bones that his father was coming. It was time to move again.

He felt better when he touched Maddy. Sometimes he'd wake up in the middle of the night to just put a hand to her swaddled belly to make sure she was OK. Small hills of breath that barely filled his palm became the most soothing balm to his frantic heartbeat. He folded the dish towel and figured he'd sweep after he just checked on them. He was at the base of the stairs when he heard Staci singing.

Take me down to the river
The river that's wide and blue
Take me down to its water banks
So I may swim with you

He flew. Two, three stairs at a time. The bathroom was a quick turn at the right up top. He glimpsed beyond the two-inch molding of chipped white paint that encased the open doorway, and his heart stopped. Staci's back was to him, the bathwater running over the lip of the tub in fat rivulets to the floor and pooling around her bare knees. Staci sang the song this time, and Maddy giggled in Staci's hands, kicking her chubby legs through the water. Reed leapt over them, jabbing his palm into the faucet handle to turn the water off.

"Look at me, Staci." Reed reached over to grab Maddy, but Staci blocked him with a shoulder.

Staci looked over her shoulder at him with a maniacal glint, otherworldly in her muddy green eyes, and smiled small. "They're coming. He's waiting."

The voice reverberated in his brain, and he felt someone reach for him as the voice in his mind said, *"There you are."*

The paisley wallpapered walls surrounding them pulsed in towards Reed as the bathroom lights flickered. On, off, on, off. Something was reaching. Maddy wailed, and Reed turned just as Staci pushed her under the water to the bottom of the tub.

He shoved. With air, with the water, with the floorboard, his hands. The air sucked out of the room like a vacuum. Every drop of water pushed against the far left wall so that only a wailing, naked baby laid in the tub. Laughter rang out in between his ears.

He had to step over Staci's body for the towel.

The blood from her head ran down blank eyes; her neck unnaturally bent against the wall below the towel rack. Maddy's cries shook him out of his stupor. He picked up his shivering baby with the towel, its bottom edge dotted red with her mother's life, and he ran out of the destroyed bathroom.

The pulsing walls stopped, the lights back on, as he sank to the floor in the hallway opposite the bathroom door. He rocked Maddy, quieting now that she nestled in the towel against his chest. He shushed her the way YouTube taught him weeks before when they first brought her home. Reed stared at his dead wife's legs lying on the floor in front of him while he made his decision.

He held Maddy with one hand and called the cops with the other.

Reed splashed the icy river water over his face to wash away his tears. The Magaran he'd convinced to take him to the valley floor to retrieve his things was a still pile of wings and legs in the grass several hundred feet behind him. He didn't have time to check if he was still alive, but his body's unnatural stillness was uncannily similar to that horrible night in Texas.

I hate this fucking place. Everything I touch dies, Reed thought. He stood up from his knees and wiped his face with the edge of his borrowed shirt. *They'll be looking for me soon.*

He didn't know how well the Magaran scouts could see through the tall valley grass, but the bright pink cloudless sky would at least be easy to spot them coming. He looped the bag he'd lifted from the Magarans over his chest, forced down the bread and fruit he'd found inside, and started running in the direction his body screamed for him to run away from.

The Batiwood was an orange-red line in the distance ahead; leaves like fire formed a blanket under which the sun's rays could barely penetrate. The trees' gnarled trunks were indiscernible from this distance, their dark bases a charcoal smudge on the horizon. Their fire orange leaves would never leach their color, and the trunks twisted and bent a little more each year. It looked enchanting, but their roots drank a wrongness that seeped through the forest floor and scattered from their branches.

He continuously scanned for signs of movement, a blonde head in a break of grass, southern-tinged curses at the heat. Monti had at least an hour's lead on him, but more if she got the Aygir. *The Aygir may not have let her on its back,* Reed reasoned, *and Monti is too stubborn to convince it to obey.* He flipped between anger at her for forcing him to hunt her down, fear of what could happen to her, and nausea at the thought of what he would have to do if she reached the woods. *Why couldn't she just trust me and leave this place? There is no guarantee her dad is even alive, and it's far more likely she'll get killed before she even reaches him.*

The thought of his own dad curdled his stomach. Reed's father had always been a faceless threat, someone to run from, someone trying to hurt him. He didn't know how or why, but he felt in his bones that it was his father lurking in the Batiwood. *There are too many coincidences. The Magarans claim their scouts went missing over the Batiwood, and then one of their Rifters goes missing right as we're all dragged here from our world. He has to be behind this. If not, who else?* Every step he took towards the Batiwood felt harder than the last. Reed felt his father's eyes on him like a bird perched on his shoulder. He assumed nothing would ever bring him back to this place, never imagined facing his father. The idea that he walked voluntarily to where he thought his father waited would have been unimaginable a few days ago. Before Monti.

I won't fail someone else in my life.

The chanting and voices had stopped at least. Reed held his palm parallel to the ground and gingerly tested his Dua, pulling the dirt up like a magnet to iron filings. Testing, uncoiling the abilities he'd ignored his entire life.

His mother taught him how to hold his Dua in, to work through the nausea and aches that came from never using it. The slight drop of power he'd used to save Monti still rang through him. He felt stronger than he ever had before, like he stood taller and broader than even a few hours ago. His mother never said if his powers would be intuitive or not, but they felt as natural as breathing once he allowed it.

Reed had to slow hours later as stalks of gold-green grass swatted at his perspiring face. It was thick, impossible in a few places to traverse without a machete or scythe the closer he got to the Batiwood. He watched the ground for breaks where other creatures carved a path hunting each other. *Where are you, Monti?*

He begrudgingly admired her no retreat attitude when it came to finding her father and hated the way she thundered forward with little information and no room for fear. *Why couldn't she just wait? I would have come around.* Reed kicked at a stubborn stalk. *That's a lie. I would have convinced her Bakilar was the best option. We could still go there if I convince her that her father isn't in the Batiwood, and there is no reason I can't catch her before she gets in the woods.*

His heart sped up as the sun began to set, a sinking feeling in tune with its steady descent. The valley was dangerous any time of day this far out from the Efendian guards, but it became a hotbed for creatures of the woods at night. The swaying grass looked like fire under the descending sun, and he spun again in each direction, looking for a sign of Monti. He couldn't see the gilded Tiers of the city from here; he was adrift at sea. Reed hugged the Magaran side of the valley the entire way here and prayed to the Goddesses for the first time in over a decade when the Batiwood stood just ahead. *Please don't let Monti reach the Batiwood.*

Sharp cries rooted him to the ground. The Magaran mountains lobbed the cries back to the valley's center and to the trees, echoing over the valley. *Something is coming.* Thundering hooves ran towards him, a beast pushing its way through the thick stalks. Reed frantically scanned the grasses to see it as he held his hands out ahead of him.

He almost fell to his knees in relief when the Aygir, and not a Batiwood creature, pushed through the grass. The same squat female he stole from the Itreni barely slowed her pace as she circled him with spit spun to foam in her mouth and her eyes frantic. Reed didn't have time to do the appropriate dance of calming the beast. He just held firm onto her armored flank and pulled himself up, hoping she didn't attack him. The cries continued in the distance; shouts of alarm mixed with a high-pitched screech that belonged to no human. The Aygir took off in that direction, the wind battering Reed's face to the point where he could do little but hunker low and trust.

His eyes had yet to adjust to the onslaught of wind when he saw them. The matted black fur of a Garfu partially blocked out a sway of blond hair, and chills broke over his entire body. Monti, a man, and a little girl fought against the monstrous creature mere steps from the Batiwood. The Garfu slashed at them with its six-fingered claws, massive bone curved at the tips meant for digging. He couldn't see its head from this angle, but he imagined the fear gripping Monti as she stared straight on at the fleshy pink-red receptors that opened wide like a skinned starfish around circular rows of sharp teeth. The Aygir reared back, kicking at the creature twice the size of a bear. It spun to Reed, rage and spit bellowing through its outstretched receptors.

He tugged at the ground, trusting that his instincts would know how to use the power filling his bones. Piles of dirt, rocks, and roots crested high above the beast like a wave, blotting out the slim curve of the sun over the trees. He aimed.

And it did absolutely nothing. The beast shook off the dirt as if he'd just taken a bath.

It screamed, though, receptors flaring wide like fingered red hands, as a blade stuck in its side. The dagger the Magaran had given Monti remained lodged in the creature's flank despite Monti's tug. The man spun around her to hack at the Garfu's neck. Blood spewed from its wound, arcing over their heads, and landed next to the kid hunkered down behind them.

Reed frantically looked around while the Aygir reared up for another kick. He pictured all of the boulders perched at the base of the mountains behind him. Reed pulled, launching jagged boulders in an arc over his shoulder and into the Garfu. The creature did not move again.

Reed slumped off the Aygir, dizzy with exertion. Monti ignored him for the little girl, but the man with her came to Reed's side. He approached warily, eyes wide in disbelief. He didn't touch Reed but held his sword at the ready and stood between the women and him.

"Glad to see you grew a pair, Reed!" Monti happily said as she hugged the kid close to her. "And now I'm less pissed at that Aygir for running off in the middle of trouble. Seems she thought you'd be helpful here."

The man turned sharply to them and back to Reed, confusion and incredulity slapped across his face. Monti joked as if there wasn't a massive alien beast lying in a pool of blood to her side.

"Turns out having a bit of magic is pretty damn handy, huh? Think you can do that without throwing up in there?" She gestured to the woods with her demolished hair speckled with black fur and blood.

Reed smiled despite himself, "I'll try."

He turned to the young man still gaping at him, "I'm Reed. I see that you've already met that hellion named Monti."

The man released a breath he'd been holding, seemingly deciding something. "I'm grateful to you both. My name is Agnian. My friend, Elaine. We were on the way to Magara when we ran into the Garfu nest. This woman, Monti? She came running out screaming like a Hordesman, dagger overhead, and took a chunk of its hindquarter out when it attacked us." He gestured at Reed's hands. "Does that mean you are who I think you are?"

Reed opened to reply, Monti quick to answer for him. "Oh Curse-ed One? Man about Magic? The Edicisi? Yep, that'd be him." She smiled wide at him, mischief dancing above her brows and daring him to lie his way out of this one.

Reed chose to ignore Agnian's shocked face and sank down to the scrawny girl, also taken aback. "You OK?"

She clenched her shaking fists and looked him straight on. "Nope. Always wanted to see a Garfu, but not that close." She was slight of build, bird bones in the shape of a girl, with wide, brown eyes. She tilted her head at him. "You don't look like the Edicisi from the stories."

"I hope not. I don't know what stories you heard, but if

they're anything like the ones I heard as a kid, I can assure you, I'm not like them. For one, I'd rather not wear skin-cloaks. And equally as important, I don't eat people."

"Can you talk to other people's minds?"

Confused, Reed shook his head. "I don't think so?"

That seemed to put the little girl's mind at ease because she smiled. He stood back up as she said, "You don't sound like an Efendian or anyone else from around here. Where you from?"

Reed replied, "We're from a place very, very far from here. One that I doubt you've ever heard of. I've got some food if you're hungry?"

She crossed her arms, hip out, and said, "Texas? It's been a while since I went to school in South Carolina, but I'm pretty sure I remember a map and an accent."

Reed stumbled back, mind spinning at the implication. *If a Rifter pulled the prison, how many others did she yank into this hell?* He eyed her Efendian clothes as Agnian walked to her side, putting his hand on her shoulder.

He stood behind her, brows furrowed, and asked Reed, "Can you not tell one of your own?"

Reed shook his head, confusion warring with too many questions to answer properly.

Agnian looked between Reed and the girl. "She's a Rifter."

Elaine tensed. Reed caught Monti's eyes over her shoulder, eyebrow cocked. He glanced at the Batiwood fanned out behind Monti, the first row now visible. Reed expected to see disappointment and rage on Monti's face when he answered, but his mouth betrayed him by saying, "We are heading into the woods. I could use your help."

ALIK

Alik's plan to slip in unnoticed and rescue Shauna fell apart within minutes of passing through the first row of Batiwood branches. Mara blocked Alik as a group of Canavar men, armed with swords and spiked mace stopped them. Each wore the same black cloak on their back, though the hoods did not cover their heads yet.

"Is that you, Handen?" A man asked Alik's guide.

"Aye," Handen replied, walking towards the men.

Alik palmed the manacles in her pocket, wondering if they would feel as wrong as the cloaks. *"We take the girls from the underground path with these cuffs,"* Handen explained earlier when he gave Alik and Mara a set of manacles carved from Batiwood branches. *"It restrains their Dua until we can get back underground where the woods do the work for us. If we run into anyone else, either kill them or put these on and trust me. But know that your Dua will weaken under the Batiwood branches, even above ground."*

It took every minute of pleading and convincing for Mara to agree to play prisoner rather than fight, so they compromised. Mara could kill any group less than six, but anymore, they played prisoner. The sixth man forced Mara's hand to slip inside her set of manacles.

Alik snapped her set of restraints behind her back, expecting to feel something. *Nothing,* she thought, though Mara sharply inhaled as her manacles clicked. Alik released her held breath when Handen declined the men's help to walk them inside the prison.

The trees grew closer together the further they walked into the woods as if the trees herded them in one direction. The forest floor appeared to writhe like snakes, the roots twisting and turning over each other. Yet when Alik focused, the roots remained still. Head spinning, she forced herself to walk in a straight line, though Mara stumbled enough that Alik had to walk alongside her to keep her upright. *Is this the woods or the manacles?* Something darted behind the trees to Alik's right, ceasing all questions in her mind. Handen stilled. She remembered his warning from the valley.

"No speaking once we're in the Batiwood. The cloaks can hide us from the creatures, but not from the Dark One. I wouldn't put this on unless there's no other choice."

Alik strained to see what Handen watched but saw only the still, fire-orange leaves on the branches. After a few moments in silence, he motioned them on, moving at a faster pace. Even her dimmed Dua flared on and off in alarm as if each step further brought a warning. Every part of her willed her to run, to get as far from the Batiwood as she could.

Alik's nerve broke when they arrived at the arched doorway leading to the prison. Each panicked inhale sucked in the veil over her nose, and tears began to blur her vision. She didn't trust herself to speak; instead, she just nodded at Handen to proceed when he paused at the door.

You are almost to Shauna. Get to her first. Deal with everything else afterward.

Crude hallways, carved from the crevices of the domed room they entered, led to darkness. An elaborate staircase hewn from gnarled roots connected the center of the room to a round opening in the ceiling. Firelight danced off enormous Batiwood trees that blotted out the moonlight far above them. And dominating the middle of the room was a cage of Batiwood branches and still forms.

Alik did not hear what Handen told the other guards as they removed her manacles. She could only search the group of girls in the cage when a guard pushed her inside as well. Tears streamed down her face at the sight of them, some as young as twelve, lying limply in the center. A few had enough strength to pull Alik and Mara to sit, but Alik brushed them off, frantically picking up each listless face, looking for laughing green eyes and a smattering of freckles across an angular nose.

She cried out as Shauna's face tilted up towards hers, her eyes barely opened. "Alik?"

"Shauna!" Alik gripped the shade of the woman she once knew, thanking every Goddess for keeping her alive.

The color had leached from her skin, and her slim frame felt gaunt underneath Alik's hold. She struggled to sit upright, and though she did not speak, she squeezed Alik's hand. Alik tried to get to Shauna to say anything, but her best friend fell back asleep clutching her hand. Alik leaned back against the bars and shifted Shauna to sleep with her head in her lap. Mara slid down next to them, and as the guards walked laps around their cage, she took Alik's other hand in her own.

Alik whispered to the pair, "Hold on a little longer. Help will be here soon."

She dared not close her eyes under the flickering torchlight. Instead, she coached herself silently as she waited for the Dark One.

Breathe, Alik. You have Shauna. Now just stay alive.

***

After the first few hours in the cage, Alik's relief and determination faded back into panic, the wait gnawing at her resolve and imagination running amok at what was to come as she gripped Shauna's hand in hers.

If anyone recognized Alik under her veil in the dim light, they either did not care or felt too sick to speak. Alik felt the draining effects of the Batiwood on her meager Dua as soon as she walked into the tunnel beneath their roots, but her Dua completely shut off within the cage bars. She tried again, holding her hand towards the torches beyond the cage. Nothing. Mara slowly shook her head at Alik's silent question; her Dua was still worthless here as well.

Alik worried a shredded cuticle as she glanced again at Shauna's limp form. The air felt thick, and apart from a tossed bag of water, the guards did not speak or provide anything else since their arrival. Across the cage, an older girl closer to 18 jerked her head once at Mara's body slumped against Alik's.

"It's not just the amount of time down here," she said. "The cages shut off everyone's Dua, but it seems to hit the strongest Duawielders the most. You must be about as weak as me then, right?"

Alik huffed a laugh, nodding. *I never thought I'd be grateful for my drop of Dua.*

She scanned the guards again, sure that her ability to read auras would weaken. Yet ice white fear plumed above their heads. Firtina's mocking tone broke through her racing mind. *"What will you do now, my weak Pillar? Read me?"*

She's right, Alik thought. *What good does that do? Why would the Goddesses want this Dua to survive in the Batiwood and not any of the others?*

Alik recounted the forty-two girls captured and whispered to Mara, "Handen thought The Dark One sacrificed one girl a night. The others could be in another cage."

Mara's low voice responded, slow as if she struggled now to speak. "Or he's killing far more each night."

Chills crawled over Alik again. The waiting, not seeing her captor, was terrifying. She pushed out the frantic "what-if's" volleying in her mind. *Word has reached Taavi and Mother. I just need a little more time.*

Dirt fell from the ceiling's oculus, followed by quick footsteps, interrupting Alik's increasingly dark thoughts. The tip of a black robe appeared at the top of the stairs. Someone stepped down, their heeled boots tapping a frantic rhythm on the wooden steps in their haste. The black hood obscured the face and arms, but not the mutterings emerging from a man's voice within.

He sang, childlike, a mismatch of words as he curved around the stairs. Alik reared back when he reached the cage. *That is the Edicisi?*

The Dark One was a man in his middle age, tall and gaunt with matte gray eyes that roved over the girls. Oozing sores, wet with blood, covered his face, and bulbous red cysts hung limply across his neck and jawline. He gripped the wooden bars with hands scarred as if someone once peeled his skin off in neat lines. *Cez,* Alik thought. The peeling was her mother's favorite torture, so her mind volleyed a hundred theories at once.

He pushed back his hood, revealing more sores across a mostly bald head. Wisps of pale blonde hair skimmed his ears and stuck inside the hood as he counted aloud, pointing a yellowed nail at each woman in turn. He wiggled his fingers at them, laughing a high-pitched gleeful sound that echoed back to them in waves. Fear overrode the girls' stupor, and they backed against the furthest wall to get away from him.

"Hasateen is almost here; Mizi and Mina will soon be hiding. They said he is coming, and soon, we'll be gifted. But first, we must harvest."

The Dark One ran his hand along the cage as he made a lap around its perimeter. Revulsion blanketed Alik as he smacked his glistening lips and ran a tongue over the wooden bar mere steps from her. He cocked his head suddenly, shushing the quiet guards, though Alik couldn't hear anyone speaking.

"Yes, yes," He said, turning up to the open sky above. "Coming."

The Dark One spun around, and the Canavar Company

guards pressed against the wall, putting as much space between them and the man stalking up the stairs to the woods. Before he reached the top, he leaned over to the guards below and said, "Bring the one in the yellow. We think she'll do nicely while we wait."

A fair-skinned man, lank white hair and sores of his own, opened the gate to Alik's far left. The girls gripped each other, muttering prayers. When he grabbed an older girl in a filthy yellow dress, the group cried out as one, trying to pull her back. He struck the girl closest to him while the other guards shoved blunt sticks at the others through the bars. The first guard pulled her up the stairs, grunting with effort as she screamed and thrashed. Shauna stirred, and though she only whispered Alik's name once hours ago when Alik found her, she renewed her grip on her hand now.

Screams shot down from Oculus above, and Alik strained to hear what Shauna whispered over the cries of the girls surrounding them.

"You need to see Alik. *See.*"

Alik shook her head, "Shh, Shauna. It's OK. I see him now. I won't let him hurt you. Taavi and Firtina are coming, and we will get you home."

Shauna listlessly tilted her head from side to side. "No. Not him. The Other. The Other. Your dreams. *Please*. You must *See*." She tapped a shaking finger below Alik's eye.

Alik felt her blood pool to her extremities and back to her heart. Her Dua flared, blurring her eyes in panic. She distantly heard another shout from above, an order, and the guards entering the cell again.

Suddenly, the guards pulled Shauna from her arms.

Alik ripped the veil from her face, screaming, "I am Alik Iktidar! I am Alik Iktidar, daughter of Queen Firtina and Heir to the Efendian Throne! Take me!"

ELAINE

Elaine walked under the first line of fire-orange tree branches, not caring to rehash the argument behind her. Damari split off from her and Agnian hours ago to ensure the Horde and Queen Firtina received word to rescue Alik. She shuddered at the thought of running through the valley alone with the sun sinking fast. Elaine tucked the Garfu attack securely in the Caboodle of her mind, confident that she would never open that particular memory.

Agnian relayed what they knew, or thought they knew, about the Dark One to Reed and Monti after the Garfu attack. He insisted that they continue to Magara, but Elaine liked Reed's plan best.

"...but if she comes with us, she can Rift Alik, Monti's dad, and all the others out," Reed argued.

Yesterday, Elaine could not stay in Efendi because of her ability to Rift. That same ability might now be the only way she could still call Efendi home one day.

When I help Alik save the others, they'll call off the Rifter hunt, and she will help me find my family in Bakilar. I could bring my parents to Efendi if I find them. It all made perfect sense, which is why she saw no other option but to go into the woods.

She tried to ignore the creeping unease the further she walked on the fallen leaves. The path looked like a carpet of fire among the dark tree trunks, and the soft ground absorbed the sounds of her steps. No birds or critters filled the branches with sound, and the still air reeked of sweet decay, turning her stomach. Elaine thought about Alik and Mara walking towards the Batiwood that morning, forcing her feet to keep moving. *They didn't run from this.*

She heard Agnian behind her first. "Wait, no! *Absolutely* not. I am taking you to the Magarans. You cannot go in there."

Elaine pivoted around, pointing. "Your friends are in there. Alik is in there. Do you honestly think you can get all the way to *that* mountain range and back before she is *eaten*?"

"Eaten?" Monti squeaked.

Monti and Reed walked under the canopy of fire orange leaves a few paces behind them. The leaves dimmed the further they walked in from the setting sun, and Reed kept glancing behind him every few feet.

Monti looked to Agnian when no one answered her. "What does she mean, 'eaten'?"

Reed's face paled as Agnian relayed the rest of the grisly details that Hvard's man, Handen, told them.

"Oh *hell* no," Monti said as she pulled everyone to a stop. "We're not taking a little girl inside the lair of a cannibalistic serial killer. Elaine, wait with the scary rhino-horse thing. Reed and I will go in on our own,"

Reed watched Elaine warily. "How do you do it?"

"What, Rift?"

She shrugged at his nod. "I don't know. I just kinda think about where I want to go and then hold my breath."

He looked dubious, so she kept talking. "I know it sounds ridiculous. But it's not hard in small jumps."

"Who brought you to Efendi then?" Reed asked. "Are there more Rifters back home?"

She started walking again, figuring they'd follow while she talked. *They'll have less to argue against if we're halfway in the woods, and Handen said all paths lead to the clearing.* Soon only shattered moonlight lit the way ahead. Agnian lit a torch from his satchel and walked ahead of them while Elaine talked.

"Never saw one if there are, so I'm pretty sure I did it myself," Elaine said. She told them the story she swore she'd never tell anyone else. "My trailer is a good twenty minutes from town on foot, but I can shave that down to ten if I cut through some woods. There's a big tree there I call Bertha that I like to sit at because I feel like she's mine and the voices are clearest there."

"Voices like a man singing? Or chanting?" Reed asked.

Her jaw dropped, "You hear him too?"

Reed nodded his head. "It's a man singing a lullaby. *Take me down to the river* and all. I've heard it for years off and on, and again just before someone dragged us here."

"That sounds like the same creepy one I heard. But I thought it might have been you. The Edicisi. Calling me, telling me to come here."

"No," Reed said, shaking his head. "I think it's someone worse."

Elaine huffed a laugh. "OK, you're not as bad as I imagined, but what could be worse than the Edicisi?"

"I think it's my dad. He figured out a way to communicate across worlds, and he's hunted me for years, tracking me somehow. We believe he kidnapped a Rifter and forced her to bring me here. But I don't understand why he reached out to you."

Relief and hope brushed some of the unease off Elaine. *Another Rifter? She could know my mother.* She was also relieved that someone after all these years finally heard the same voices she did.

"If it's your dad, he gives me the creeps. I never minded the other voices. I miss them. Do you still hear the others?"

He shook his head, "I've only ever heard his voice."

OK then, I'm back to being the only one hearing things. I need to talk to this other Rifter.

Reed looked around them, whispering as if just speaking about the voices would conjure them. "What happened when you hopped worlds?"

Elaine nudged a shriveled leaf on the ground, its bright color as vibrant as the living leaves above. "I was at my Big Bertha tree. The other voices never talk to me directly; they're usually muffled. But at Big Bertha, I could hear better. Like they were on the other line of a telephone. That night, it was storming. I thought a hurricane was coming through."

Monti interjected, "So you ran to the woods in the middle of a storm?"

"It was better than what I left behind," Elaine said, her mouth a flat line that welcomed no discussion of what prompted her to run, barefoot, that night of all nights.

She recalled the way her fingers scraped against its thick grooves as she stepped over roots more akin to tentacles than tree bits. Sheets of rain pelted through the humid fog of a summer night and doused her skin. She felt pulled towards the tree in a way she hadn't ever before and closed her eyes. The siren pealing in the wind heralded a hurricane as Spanish moss whipped all around her. Warm mud squelched in between her toes.

"When I got to Bertha, the voices sounded like they were at the end of a hallway. I felt like I could chase them, like they were just around her trunk. And then I heard him say, clear as day, 'Come.' And I knew that voice spoke directly to me."

Her heart pounded with each step around the base of the tree. Darkness threatened the edges of her vision as she fought to fill her lungs.

"Anyway, I followed his voice, and I landed here." Elaine couldn't remember the Rift itself, but she woke up in a heap behind a storage pile in Low Town.

Reed paced as he asked, "Do you think you could go back?"

"Never going to. There's nothing there for me anymore."

"But could you Rift somewhere else? Somewhere other than here?" Reed gestured to the still woods surrounding them. He whispered despite the absence of background noise.

Elaine looked to the massive, gnarled tree yards ahead of them, basking in moonlight caught in a gap of trees. *I can do this.* She pictured the wide claw marks etched in its trunk. Closing her eyes, she Rifted.

Dizzy, she slumped down at its base, covered in sweat. She was weaker than she had ever been after a Rift. *Is this from the chain they had around me or the woods?* The wrongness of the trees surrounding her felt palatable as the others ran up to her.

"She won't be able to Rift everyone out like this," Reed said, shaking his head. "She can barely Rift herself." He rubbed his hands over his face and turned to Agnian. "Take her to Magara. Monti, you and I can meet her there after we get your dad."

There is no way I'm going to the Magarans. I'll never get to Bakilar if I do. Helping Alik is my best shot. Elaine dodged Agnian's outreached hand as she said, "Maybe I can't, but you could."

Everyone waited for her to clarify. She thought back to the conversation she'd had with Reiki in the Dockside and held her hand out for Reed's. Her chest constricted; *did Reiki know what Kara planned?* She locked that thought away as Reed took her hand.

"I've been listening to stories about the Edicisi. If you are who you say you are, you can take powers from other Duawielders if you are touching them. I might not be able to Rift everyone out, but maybe you could."

Reed looked unconvinced, so she pressed on. "Try it. If it doesn't work, I'll go with Agnian to the Magarans. But if it does, we can get in and out before the Dark One knows we're even there."

He studied her for a few moments before nodding. Elaine walked him through everything she'd learned about Rifting. They both stood awkwardly after several attempts in the same place, her palms clammy within his tight grip. Monti chewed on a thumbnail near the torch in the ground, watching them and scanning the still woods surrounding them.

"Any luck?" Agnian whispered as he walked back from the dark path ahead.

Everyone shook their heads. Reed asked, "Did you find the place Hvard's man described?"

Agnian traced a map with a stick in the dirt. "The signs stop here, just as he said. The oldest trees are in the center of the wood, with newer ones fanned out in close proximity, so it does feel like all directions lead to the same path." Firelight danced over tense brows, and he crossed his arms, revealing more tattoos tucked under his once-white shirt. "Slight problem, though. Hvard Canavar is several hundred feet ahead of us, down the same path."

He said the last to Elaine, but Reed stiffened as if struck. He craned his neck like he could see the semi-circle of trees drawn in the dirt and pulled Elaine up quickly. "Let's try again."

He immediately loosened his grip at Elaine's wince. His eyes, kind gray at first, were now stone marbles in his face. She wondered which world did such horrible things to him to cage such anger. Reed closed his eyes, and chills swayed her body. Her torso tugged towards him even as she remained standing straight. Elaine squeezed her eyes shut at the nausea, but when she opened them, they were standing face to face with a shocked Hvard Canavar in the belly of the woods.

Hvard dropped his torch to the ground just as Reed dropped Elaine's hand. He grabbed Hvard's neck, and Elaine fell to the ground, weak in the knees. He punched before Hvard could speak, their fight in the darkness echoing in the quiet trees.

Elaine whistled, a trick she'd been immensely proud of the summer her lips cooperated for the first time and hoped it would be loud enough to trace back to Agnian. She shuffled back while the men punched and tackled each other. *Click, click, click.*

She jumped at the guttural sounds that clicked somewhere in the woods behind them. The men stilled just as Agnian and Monti ran into view.

Hvard leapt to his feet and fumbled with the black cloak that fell in the skirmish, but Agnian lunged, grabbing it from him before he could use it. Reed held his hands out, fingers splayed wide, and the scattered leaves from the ground whooshed past Elaine as he yanked Hvard up with an Airwerk. Hvard hovered in the air, clutching his throat and eyes wide in disbelief as he kicked to no avail. The guttural clicks came closer; bone-white flashed under Monti's torchlight as the veins in Reed's neck pulsed.

Elaine watched Jurassic Park once from a thick oak branch that stood at the edge of her town's drive-in. There's a point in the movie when raptors circle their prey, calling out to each other. Her body willed her to Rift, to run, anything to get away from that sound now.

Three Yurutec crept into view behind Hvard; another two shoved at each other to Elaine's left. Monti grabbed Elaine, pulling her close, and Agnian whipped his sword from its scabbard on his back.

Monti brandished her torch towards the creatures, shouting, "Bigger priorities, Reed!"

He dropped Hvard. Reed reached his hand towards her fire, pulling a spark to his waiting palm. The spark in his hand grew to the size of a kickball, and he pitched the flame at the creature closest to him and Hvard. Elaine flinched at its inhumane wails as flames licked up its ten-foot spine.

Agnian hacked an arm off one near Elaine and Monti, and Reed picked the rest of it up with a gust of airwerk, snapping its neck midair, even as he strangled another with a thick Batiwood root. The final two Yurutec scattered, clicking frantically in the distance.

Reed fell to his knees, vomiting in the dirt. Elaine didn't have time to be relieved before chanting pounded her brain.

She clutched her head as Reed asked, "You hear that too?"

Monti helped Reed stand as Hvard dropped to his knees, hands held in supplication. "You are the Edicisi! The stories are true! I don't know what I've done to offend, oh mighty Edicisi, but..."

Reed stepped towards Hvard, voice gravelly with rage, "Alisha Wellnis."

Whomever Alisha was, Hvard knew. His wiry eyebrows shot to his hairline as the color drained from his face. Reed took another step in his direction, and Hvard said in a rush, "The....the moons are up. If you are taking this path to get to the stone altar, the Dark One will be waiting. There's another entrance. A hallway off the cages camouflaged in the woods. I could take you there, and you can kill the imposter."

Monti held Reed's arm back when he pulled another spark of flame to his palm. She demanded, "Who? Who is this Dark One?"

Hvard shook his head, red beard trembling. "I don't know his name. He's insane. He talks to himself and to the woods across from the altar. I don't know how long he's been living here, but it's leaching the life from him. The only time he's at full strength is when he eats them. The girls. The Duawielders. It gives him power that varies with the strength of the girls, but never for very long. Take the girls; you take his power."

"Why would we believe you?" Elaine asked.

Hvard anxiously watched the darkness surrounding them. "I can't get away from him now that I've worn the cloak. I tried to lose it, to burn it, or to rip it to shreds, but it always comes back. I did it for the coin, but now I'd give all of it back and more to get away from this place."

Reed clenched and unclenched his fists by his side. Elaine said to him, "Reed, you Rifted to Hvard. That means we can Rift everyone out together."

Hvard nodded emphatically. "The Dark One had a Rifter once. He used her to open a portal to another realm, like a doorway, and pulled a massive stone building to our world."

Reed's eyes flicked to Monti before landing on Hvard's black eyes, "That's how we got here. How did he do it?"

"I don't know, but it was the night he sacrificed almost twenty girls in one night. He was at his strongest."

Monti stepped to Reed's side. "Reed, he's trying to manufacture power. If the stories are true, you are power. If this Dark One did it, you can as well."

"Let's try it," Reed took Elaine's hand.

"Wait!" Hvard shrank at Reed's glare, hands up. "The last Rifter couldn't Rift again after that for days. I'm not sure if she can even now."

Elaine watched the shadows from the flickering torch dance across Reed's grim face. Agnian debated aloud where they could Rift the prisoners, but Reed's eyes locked on Monti.

Hvard whispered to Elaine in between worried glances at Reed. "How did you get away?"

"I have friends in high places. Friends that don't like men that kidnap kids and break old men's legs."

Hvard dropped his stare to the ground as Monti turned her attention away from Agnian. "Does he have any others from that stone building?" At Hvard's nod, she turned to Reed. "Get everyone out. I just want my dad. We can wait for Elaine's strength to build back up after we're safe, and then we can all go home."

Reed didn't respond for several minutes. His jaw ticked as he looked over the charred remains of the Yurutec to the darkness beyond. He turned to Hvard, pointing between himself and the gang leader. "This is not done. But lead us there, and I will reconsider killing you slowly."

Hvard nodded, wincing at Reed's shove forward, and the group walked towards the center of the Batiwood in silence. The further they walked, the clearer the faint chanting became in Elaine's mind. *Let us in. Let us in.*

ALIK

Mara's nails gouged Alik's arm as the guards dragged Alik out of the cell. Mara stumbled but managed to punch one of the guards on his way out before two men began kicking her repeatedly. Alik's last glimpse before she reached the oculus at the top of the stairs was Mara in the fetal position, hands over her bloodied face.

Alik could not fill her chest with air as she crested the final step. She squeezed her fists tight at her sides, focusing on the pain of her nails sinking into her palms instead of what could happen next.

Think, Alik. Stay Alive. Handen said the woods did the work for them if we're underground. She lifted her hand a fraction towards the flame closest to her, sighing in relief as the flame flicked towards her.

The Batiwood trees grew in a semicircle at a slight elevation above them, their gnarled roots forming holes and small caves surrounding the altar that reached as high as her chest. Several small fires surrounded the semicircle, elongating the shadows from the pits and Batiwood branches above. Two fires burned along either side of a massive stone altar table in the center.

She cried out at its dark red stain. A mangled body, shrouded in yellow, heaped on top of the altar.

"He eats them Princess. Bits and pieces at a time," Handen said a lifetime ago.

Alik threw up. Shaking, she wiped her mouth and forced herself to take stock of the rest of her surroundings. The trees across from the stone altar table arched toward each other, the negative space between them forming a doorway of darkness, black against the flickering light in the woods. The Dark One stood before it, pacing. Muttering. He stilled at Alik's stare, his head slowly tilting unnaturally to his right shoulder as he studied her. She thought of Shauna and Mara below. *Buy them some time. Help is coming.*

Taking a deep breath, she forced herself to meet his eyes. "I am Alik Iktidar, Pillar of the Iktidar line and daughter of---"

"I know who your mother is; I've heard her titles plenty," He said. "My question is, what are *you* doing here at my gate?" He twitched and began muttering as if he hadn't just asked a question.

Alik stumbled a little over his wording. She felt Shauna's grip on her arm, Shauna's whispered plea to *see.* She thought back to her dreams, the wide, gaping mouth at the end of all of them. She ignored the man speaking in riddles to her or himself. She focused her eyes instead on the dark space behind the man, her Dua slow to focus initially, and she fell backward at what cleared before her like fog lifting from glass.

"It is a gate," she whispered.

Scrolls of words in a language she couldn't read spun in gold at the edges of an open doorway, and they shifted to form new words and symbols with every second. The space beyond the entrance showed writhing bodies, massive forms coalescing together in arms, legs, claws, and teeth. Only one object remained still, a small eyeball in the center, blood-red with a milk-white pupil. The Eye watched her watching it.

Chanting, indiscernible but growing louder, echoed in her mind. The cold ground bit into Alik's knees as she hit the ground, all effort focused on blocking the invasive voices out.

The Dark One shuffled to Alik while she clutched her head. He crouched down low, his eyes roving over her face, and she stumbled back. Her shoulders hit the stained stone altar, causing her Dua to flare in alarm again. Through blurry tears, she watched in horror as he brought a fleshy piece of bloodied meat to his mouth. He stood taller than before within moments of swallowing it, the sores less apparent. Even his voice felt different, as if it bounced off the marrow in her bones instead of skittering across her skin.

"Let us see what the yellow girl can do," he said.

He pulled a gust of air to them, a whirlwind of leaves and dirt, suspending Alik several feet into the air, and she gasped anew. *The Edicisi! He is the Edicisi!* She tried to take cover beneath the stone altar, her hands slipping in dark pools of blood, but he wrapped her in an Airwerk, yanking her out. She scrabbled at the tightening band at her ankle, searching the ground for anything to use as a weapon. *Goddesses help me, please!*

The chanting quieted as he spoke, "Why would my Pillar send you here?"

"My Pillar" is a title like any other, one that Alik heard servants call her hundreds of times and to her mother hundreds of times more. It sounded reverent coming from his mouth, a caress, and it churned Alik's stomach as much her realization did. *He is real.*

You need time, she thought. *Buy some time. Anything to keep him talking.*

She said, "She sent me here for the girls you've taken. For the Efendians you've stolen. Edicisi or not, my mother will turn you to ribbons."

He laughed, bloodied gristle slipping from his teeth, and he swiped the back of his hand across his lips. He released the band of Airwerk on Alik's ankle but used another to suspend her in the air across from him, arms pinned at her sides. "Will she now? How well do you know your mother, Alik? Did she tell you what we discovered together as children?"

Alik's brief bravado deflated as she fumbled the pieces together in her mind at the implication. She bluffed. "I would know anything important, and I can't imagine she would deign to discuss a shared interest with a child grown mad in the woods."

"My name is Hayalet Birinci. I was the baker's boy in the Palace, first your mother's best friend, later her confidant and always her soulmate. I am still her greatest supporter. When she comes, she will tell you herself." He grunted as he pulled the bloodied mass under a torn yellow dress towards the dark gate with another gust of Airwerk.

The "F.I & H.B" in her mother's hidden shrine of the Edicisi flashed behind her eyes. *When she comes? She is helping him! Is this who she visits each time she disappears? Did she know this entire time that he took Shauna?* Alik flipped through the racing questions in her mind, growing angrier with each one. She struggled in his band of Airwerk, her fingers straining towards the fires.

His steps faltered, and Alik dropped a few inches in the air before he held her up again with a shaking hand and a meager push of Airwerk. *He's weakening,* she realized. *How is that possible if he's the Edicisi? Is it the Batiwood?*

She heard a faint whistle in the woods behind her that filled her with hope and renewed her resolve. Hayalet talked to the darkness between trees, and when Alik focused on the darkness he addressed, the Eye still watched her.

Alik said the first thing that came to mind to keep him distracted from the sounds in the woods. "My father was the only man my mother ever loved."

He took the bait. He slung the dead teen's body into the dark gate, and Alik quickly cleared her Dua to look away from the gnashing of teeth and frenzied eating in the air beyond.

Hayalet's arms shook as he struggled to keep her aloft with his Airwerk. He snarled, "Your Father was only the stepping stone your mother needed to appease your bitch of a grandmother. I am the foundation she walks on, the altar she will use to rule this world and the worlds beyond." He was panting, sweat beading at sores growing more prominent as she watched him in horror.

Alik said, "Then I pity you. You are as much a fool as anyone that loved her. She will use you and discard you as she has done everyone else in her life."

"Firtina and I have a love beyond worlds. We set off on this quest together decades ago. And---" He doubled over, clutching his stomach.

Alik fell to the ground and scrambled back to the edge of the clearing. "I expected more from the Edicisi. Tell me, does it pain you that our blood builds Dua for generations but can only give you a few moments of power?" She nodded to the gate, "Even that Eye must see that you are pathetic." Alik said, proud that her words did not shake out of her mouth even with the Eye on her in the distance. She couldn't see the outline of the Eye unless she focused, but she still felt its keen interest as it tracked her now.

"You----*you see the eye*??" Hayalet spun, gaunt, and hunched over once more. He ran to her, pulling her upright by the shoulders, his repugnant face inches from her own. "*You* are the Reader? You are the one he's been hunting." He looked past Alik but did not release her. "Did she know and not tell me?"

"As I said before, you have been forgotten." Alik felt pity for a millisecond on the man. She knew what it was like to be a moth to her mother's flame, ignored and entranced simultaneously.

He thrust Alik back, shaking as he paced. "I did all of this for *her*! I opened the gate! I sacrificed my flesh. It was my plan! Mine to grant her immortality. Mine forever. Worlds together. I--"

He stilled, turning back to the gate. Alik couldn't hear what stopped his tirade, but he smiled and dropped to his knees before the gate. She focused her Dua on the dark space to see what was happening.

Hundreds of wrists beyond the gate slit open to fill a metal, spiked chalice. She watched in horror as the cup passed through the gate, hot liquid steaming in the cool air. Blood ran down Hayalet's chin and neck as he drained it. When the cup fell empty, Hayalet stood tall, with no sores of lesions, and walked down the stairs to below. Dua still flaring, she watched shadows of inhumane limbs twitch from his retreating shadow.

Shauna! She pushed herself up and ran on shaking legs to the stairs when a voice from within the gate spoke. *"Reader. Come here. Let us show you what you can become."*

Her feet led her to the gate, the horror she distantly remembered a wisp of a memory. She knew she needed to be somewhere else, but she couldn't remember where. She leaned in, searching, inches from the gate to see herself. Powerful, strong, and just. The true Queen, an heir worthy. She gazed in, mesmerized.

"Step in, let us help you. We have powers a thousand times greater than any witnessed to grant."

Alik heard the whoosh before she felt the slice of an arrow as it skimmed past her cheek. Her fingers came away with a trickle of blood, and she watched a drop of her blood fly through the gate. The pain shook her out of the illusion, and she scrambled backward, away from the laughter within the gate.

"Get away from that!" A woman shouted. Alik turned back as Tenida, the pale courtier stupid enough to interrupt her mother, stepped through the trees side-by-side with a pack of Magaran scouts. A Magaran female with a shaved head and a beaded headdress lowered her bow.

Tenida ran past Alik and pointed to the space between the trees."You-- you see something? Who were you talking to?" Her frantic eyes searched Alik's face.

Alik blinked out of her shock, nodding. "It looks like a gate, a gate with hundreds of bodies inside and an Eye."

Tenida fell steps back, hand to her chest, and said something in a language Alik didn't understand. The Magarans approached, bows at the ready aimed at the gate. *How long have I been standing here? Shauna!*

The small female with the bow looked to Tenida, "She claims she is the Reader?"

Alik snapped. "I don't even know what that means. I just know there is an *eye* watching *you* in that space and that we have to save my friends below from the Edicisi. Let's deal with titles later."

She turned for the oculus, but the Magaran grabbed Alik's arm. Cries rang out from below, the smell of roasting wood filtering up. Alik drew a small flame to her to burn the Magaran's viselike grip off her, but Tenida stifled it with a raised palm and a gust of air. Alik had no time to analyze how Tenida was involved with the Magarans or find out what else she missed about this courtier. *I have to get Shauna out!*

They ignored her pleas as the female Magaran demanded, "Did you see the Edicisi?"

Alik yanked her arm from the Magaran's grip. "He is below! He's eaten kidnapped Efendian girls for months, hidden in the Batiwood, but his powers are weak." Her finger shook as she pointed at the gate, "They gave him something. Blood. From a cup, a moment ago. We have to go now--"

The Magarans spoke rapidly to each other, Tenida shaking her head in confusion. Tenida said, "That was not the Edicisi. We captured the true Edicisi last night, but he escaped. We need the three of you, the Reader, the Rifter, and the Edicisi if we are to close the gate to the Others."

REED

Hvard stopped at the base of a massive Batiwood tree. Its thick roots tangled above ground to form a hole wide enough for even Hvard to walk through standing upright. Reed shook off the feeling of thousands of invisible centipedes marching across his skin as he and the others followed Hvard through. The voices in his head chanted a litany of *He's here. Here. Here.*

Hvard led them through a pitch-black tunnel, wider than it naturally should have been and winding inward in a spiral. A flick of sulfur and Hvard's face glowed as he put the torch to something on the wall. A thin line of fire raced ahead, lighting the tips of doorways holding back creatures from nightmares. Wolves with the body of serpents snapped at them as they passed. Elk antlers protruded from the eyes of a massive bat that clung to wooden bars. Cages lined either side, each more disturbing than the last.

"What are these?" Monti whispered at Reed's back.

Reed shook his head. He ran through stories his mother told him as a boy and of the creatures he overheard the Canavar Company Troupe discuss. He'd never heard of anything like them.

Before he could answer her, human hands gripped the bars in a cell ahead of them. Monti pushed past him and cried out, "Dean!"

Dean, a good-looking man even in a ripped suit and sporting a bloody face, cried out. He hugged her tightly to him when Hvard opened the door.

"Monti! Thank God! How are you here?" He asked just as Monti demanded, "Where's my dad?"

Dean's face fell, and he shifted to block Monti's view from a rumpled lump behind him. Reed knew what was coming, and though he wanted to hold her, he knew he had no place to offer her comfort.

I did this, he thought, as Monti's anguished cry ripped through the cell and tunnel beyond. She fell onto the body of an older man dead by several days. Dean, at her side, offered comfort out of earshot as Reed looked away.

A blond man wearing the Horde's blue colors grabbed Agnian. He held a limp arm, and had a nasty gash across his bruised face. "Agnian! He has Alik. I heard her screaming her own damn name maybe twenty minutes ago."

Agnian withdrew his sword and sprinted for the exit. Reed turned to grab Elaine, but both she and Hvard disappeared. He shouted after Agnian, "He has Elaine!"

Reed ran for the dimly lit entrance at the end of the hallway with the few men from the cells that could fight at his heels. They halted abruptly when the corridor ended in a circular room with a large cage in the center. Efendian girls gripped the bars. Beyond the cage, a staircase spiraled up to a round opening in the dirt ceiling.

He dimly registered Agnian and the others fighting the handful of guards that were waiting for them. Elaine kicked her skinny legs furiously in the air, struggling against Hvard's hand over her mouth to his right.

However, Reed was rooted to the ground; a boy again taught to fear a faceless man. He focused on the cloaked stranger walking down the steps. He never met his father, but there was no mistaking who this was when the man turned to him fully.

They shared the same nose and jawline, the same eye shape, and the same determined brow. Wisps of white hair clung to skin leached of all color, a watered-down version of the skin wrapped around Reed's shaking fists.

Reed's stomach roiled as his father said with an expanding grin, "I've been looking for you for quite some time. Tell me, how is lovely Alisha?"

Reed flashed to the first day they felt him in their new world.

His mother found a job waiting tables; Reed binged American TV. Their new life began to soften like a pair of broken-in shoes. His mother came home to the motel room they paid for by the week, keys not yet tossed to the table, and the neighbor boy walked by the open doorway. He sang the same lullaby that would haunt Reed for the rest of his life. His mother stilled, panic brushing over her face, erasing that fleeting contentment.

Whatever Dua his mother held, she never used in the twelve years they ran from his father, fearing it would somehow bring him back to them. They'd starved, lived in fear, and finally escaped. Reed didn't understand why the song frightened his mother so, but when they ate dinner that night, she explained that his father sang the same song the night they met.

When she and Reed heard it again six months and two moves later, she told him that his father must have found her, and she said that if anything happened to her, he was to call the number she pinned to the motel room door. Reed assumed she was just cautious, but she was gone when he came home from school the next day. He waited an entire week alone before he called the number, and three days after the social worker moved him to a foster care home, the cops found his mother's body on a hiking trail.

The guards tossed black cloaks over themselves, making it appear that Agnian and the others fought air. Reed might as well have been alone in a room with his father though as he stalked towards him from around the cage. The anger coursing through him overrode his fear.

Reed said, "You killed her. She Rifted to another goddamned world to get us away from you, and it still wasn't enough." He opened and closed his fists, feeling the power his curse granted him fizz through every cell of his body. "She killed herself, thinking that would be the only way to sever your tie and It. Did. Nothing."

"And for what?" Reed cried out. The question he had asked himself and his mother for years. "What do you want from me? This??" He raised his arms and pulsed the flames from the surrounding torches high, the room suddenly brighter and the shadows longer.

"This is what you came for? Do you think I'd ever help you? And to do what??"

Hayalet closed the distance to him, stopping at only arm's length. His eyes scanned his son as he spat, "Do you know what irony is, boy? Irony is giving everything you have to become the Edicisi, only for those powers to be leached from you to grow within a seed in a whore's belly.

"I traveled for years across the bridges of Dvari to the sand palaces in Bakilar, hunting for information on the Edicisi. I nearly died within the Magaran mountain range and on Perisien ships filled with murderers for the keys to unlock the greatest secret in Sakalid. And I finally found a way to be the most powerful wielder this world or any others have ever seen. But it all went to *you*."

Reed turned with Hayalet as his father circled him, never wanting to lose track of him. "You can have it. I don't want any of it! I never wanted to be this."

"Oh, I'll have it back, and I'll show this world the true powers of the Edicisi. But first, I had to learn how to take Dua. They told me the only way to get it is to consume. And you know what's funny? I've found I rather like the taste."

Hayalet lunged then, arms wide, and face mottled red with effort as he pulled hundreds of roots from the ground surrounding them. The roots swirled, a cobra at the ready, around Reed and struck, knocking him to the ground. They spiraled around his arms, his legs, and across his chest, lacerating his skin as they tightened. Reed struggled against them, panic overriding any thought as the roots encircled his neck. He thought of Elaine, walking steadily into the Batiwood and of Monti attacking the Garfu. Monti's words came back to him, *"He is trying to manufacture power. You are power."*

I don't know how he created his own Dua, but I am not without power now. Reed imagined the strength of the tornados that had torn across Texas in years past. The breath drained from his lungs as Reed whipped winds around his face and snapped all but the thickest root gripping his ankle with an Airwerk. He steadied his hands on either side of the root at his ankle. Reed's palms sunk into the ground as he shoved the last root off of him, back into the gnarled tree from which it came, with a wave of Groundwerk. He stood, eyes on Hayalet, shaking with rage.

Reed's face flushed with heat as if he were standing in front of a tall fire when he yanked all the flames from the torches surrounding them to his outstretched hand. He formed them into a massive, writhing ball and threw them at his father, dousing him in flame. Hayalet screamed, but it was as if hundreds of inhumane voices shrieked with him.

Hayalet chanted words Reed could barely decipher over the chorus of agonized voices. Before Reed could form another assault, Hayalet threw the flames off of him and at the cage of girls beyond Reed. The Batiwood branches caught, and screams filled the room as Hvard doubled over behind Hayalet. Elaine ran, not to the stairs or the hallway leading out of this hell, but to the cage in flames. She hacked the wood with a sword almost as big as she while the girls inside kicked at the opening she created.

Something shifted behind him. Hayalet bent backward almost in two, arms stretched toward the ceiling, and fingers curved in pain. Reed stumbled back at the sight, scrambling for something to use as a weapon. He held his breath and pulled the nearest sword from a dead guard with an Airwerk, aiming it at his father's chest.

The sword flew through the air, a bronze missile glinting in the expanding flames. But before it could make its mark, four sticky pink arms shot out from Hayalet's ribcage, knocking it aside. They wound around each other, skinless chorded muscles with hundreds of fingers, just as two thick skinless legs erupted from his shoulder blades with a squelch. Hayalet's eyes were entirely black when he stood upright again, grotesque arms reaching for Reed.

Hayalet's mouth gaped wide, jaw unhinged almost to his chest, and as he spoke, his voice was a chorus of a hundred pitches: "Your bones will feed them, the marrow giving them the nutrients they require. I will relish the fleshy bits of you and then let them have the others. They seem to prefer women, after all."

Reed crawled backward, arm outstretched and shaking. He sucked the flames back from the Batiwood cage, his strength already dimming from exertion, and encircled the creature that had been his father in a ring of fire. He distantly registered that Elaine pushed the girls up the stairs and into the clearing, Agnian and the others not far behind. *Monti, you'd better be halfway to Efendi now.*

The creature stepped through the flames, Hayalet's skin peeling back. The disgusting arms grew thicker and longer as they reached for the blackened, empty cage. Reed dodged as the creature launched broken branches of the Batiwood cage at him, and he fell back as one skimmed his scalp. He ignored the blood spilling over his ear and frantically searched the fire-engulfed room for a weapon. He pulled a stone boulder from across the room with an Airwerk, panting at its weight, and threw it at the creature.

The effort cost Reed. He staggered back and tried to blink away the black dots that threatened to block out his vision. Reed tried to draw flames to him with a shaking arm but could barely get a flicker. Distantly, he recalled how Agnian said Dua was less powerful underground in the Batiwood. Flames licked the base of the staircase just beyond the creature.

Just get above ground, he thought. The thing that was once his father pushed the boulder off of its torso with glistening pink arms.

Reed was dizzy with exhaustion, blackness threatening to overwhelm him. He tried to push an Airwerk to shove the creature back down, but it barely shifted the whisps of pale hair that still clung to his father's scalp. The creature cackled a gleeful hacking sound. It wiped its bloody lip with the back of a skinless hand studded with mismatched fingers. His father's mouth opened to say something more, but froze mid gape. His neck tilted unnaturally to the right as it listened to something Reed could not hear.

Reed didn't linger. He ran for the steps, jumping as high as he could over the bottom steps that were sinking in the flames.

The creature gave chase with a howl, and the staircase shook against its weight. Skinless arms reached. Reed scrambled to the top and had just gotten his arm through the opening as a dozen fingers wrapped tightly around his ankle.

ALIK

----N*eed the three of you, the Reader, the Rifter, and the Edicisi if we are to close the gate to the Others."*

As Tenida spoke, Mara, Shauna, and the other girls emerged from the oculus, coughing at the smoke billowing through. To Alik's dismay, the Rifter followed them, with Agnian and Ty steps behind. Alik cried out in relief, though, gripping a haggard-looking Ty in a hug and then embracing her friends. Agnian tugged her away as she gripped Elaine, telling her to get out of here.

"No time, Alik! We have to leave now. They're fighting downstairs!"

Mara, hoarse but no longer stumbling, shouted to the girls, "Let's move! Follow me."

The Magarans blocked them, bows at the ready. "Our lost Rifter is not among you." The leader nodded in Alik's direction, "If she is the Reader, then a Rifter must be here, and no one is leaving until you bring us the Rifter."

"Get out of our--"

Elaine shrugged off Agnian and Alik's outreached grip, cutting off Alik's protestations. "I am a Rifter. Let them go!"

Alik stepped in front of Elaine, "She is not going with you

unless you guarantee her protection."

"Protection from whom? The last time I checked, your family was leading a Rifter hunt," Tenida said with derision.

"No time!" Mara said, pulling at Tenida and the kidnapped girls to the edge of the woods.

A man a few years older than Alik scrambled through the oculus, the right side of his close-cropped hair covered in blood. She didn't recognize him, but he screamed at them to run, panic across his bloodied face as a creature crawled through. Alik's heart faltered, horror-stricken at what emerged among screams from the girls around her.

Hayalet was still part of the creature, but his body looked like a doll's in comparison. It crawled on skinless, wet limbs that protruded from his body. Its feet squelched against the ground as it stalked towards the scrambling man, and its thick, muscular legs grew longer, raising Hayalet high in the air.

The Magarans and Tenida shouted orders to fight, but several girls were still too weak to do anything but fall to their knees as the creature reared back. The bloodstained stranger stood before the monster, his arms out to his sides, and pulled a tornado of wind to him. Alik's hair whipped forward at his pull, and she had to grip a stone to stand against the battering winds. Through the swirling leaves and dirt, she watched the monstrosity of Hayalet hover in the stranger's Airwerk. *The Edicisi!*

Alik scrambled back to the edge of the clearing, shocked. *This is the real Edicisi that Tenida said got away.* Her mind reeled as it tried to reconcile the monster of her people's stories with the young man before her. Steps away, the monster that she'd feared as a child battled a monster worse than any she could have imagined.

The Hayalet creature pulled a Batiwood from its roots, screaming as if a hundred voices bellowed alongside it. It heaved the massive tree at the Edicisi, who batted it away with a gust of Airwerk. The Edicsi shook with the effort to pull two large rocks above his outstretched hands with an Airwerk, but the Hayalet creature smacked the boulders away as if they were pebbles. Alik dove behind one of the boulders to watch the monsters battle each other, silently praying to every Goddess that help would come soon. *We need Firtina Iktidar.* Agnian tried to crawl to her from where he took cover beneath the altar, but Alik shook her head for him to stay while the battle raged between them. She searched for Shauna, Ty, or Elaine, but she couldn't see them from where she hid.

To Alik's right, a blonde woman emerged from the woods, hacking at the smoke billowing up from the oculus and swirling around the fight scene. Her bloodshot eyes widened at the creature fighting the Edicsi.

The Edicisi turned away from the fight at the woman's entrance. He looked panic-stricken at her arrival, shaking his head, but the Hayalet creature boomed a laugh of malicious glee. A sticky, pink arm shot across the clearing and snatched the woman around the waist. The creature held her suspended between it and the Edicisi, and the Edicisi dropped the boulder he held aloft.

What are you doing? Alik thought. *Fight!*

The Hayalet creature put a bloody limb to the dark space between trees behind it, and by the gasps around her, Alik knew the gate was now visible to everyone. The woman in the creature's glistening meaty hand cried out, lashing out uselessly at the claws of fingers gripping her as it pushed her within inches of the gate. Alik's stomach roiled at the grasping limbs and gnashing teeth beyond.

The woman's pleading cry mangled with fear as she shouted, "Reed!"

The Edicisi dropped to his knees, and Alik helplessly watched as he said. "Stop! You can have me. Just let her go!"

No, no, no, no. Alik shook her head, frantically praying to the Goddesses for a quick death to one, or both, of the demons in front of her. *Someone will have to kill the Edicisi or the Hayalet creature before the creature tries to take his Dua too. No one can have that much power, let alone a demon.*

Hayalet hesitated, its limbs jerking as if they fought against his will. He finally dropped the woman to the ground but held onto her arm so she could not flee. He opened his jaw wide to speak as a petite figure darted between his legs. *Elaine!*

Alik moved, rushing forward just as little Elaine sliced the thick corded muscle holding the woman. It wasn't enough to sever the creature's limb, but the hundreds of fingers gripping her arm straightened in pain, giving the woman just enough time to drop and roll out of reach.

Alik took stock of the cowering Efendian girls around her and the tense Magarans at the edge of the woods. *I have been waiting for the Horde or my mother to save us. And yet this little girl, with a sword as big as her, took matters into her own hands.* Alik stepped out from behind the boulder and tugged at her meager Dua.

She shot a small flame at the creature's face as she screamed to her countrywomen, "Push it through the gate!"

The Hayalet creature turned to Alik as arrows flew from the Magarans. He swatted them away, but Mara, Shauna, Tenida, and the others let loose a volley of varying power alongside Alik. Agnian and Ty ran forward, hacking at its limbs and dodging its outraged swings. Water loosened the ground below it, and wind pushed the monster back, back, back as fire blanketed its eyes. The creature released a gargled, wretched scream, raging at the wave of soil threatening to tip it backward as the Edicisi joined their fight with renewed strength. Roots from the ground shot up to bind its skinless limbs, boulders smashed its face, and the creature teetered within a hair's width of the gate.

Yet, still, the creature leaned into them.

The monstrosity broke free from the bounds with a vicious roar and stretched all of its limbs wide, calling the wind to him. Airwerk of incredible magnitude threw some of the girls into the trees beyond the clearing, their bones cracking against the trunks, and the Edicisi tumbled head over foot, slamming into the stone altar. Alik held onto a thick Batiwood root with bloodied fingers, her legs dangling behind before the wind finally died down.

The creature dropped his Airwerk, and in that moment of reprieve, Elaine blinked back from the edges of the opening, Rifting. She jabbed her sword deep into the creature's glistening foot, the pain shocking the Hayalet monstrosity backward, and he shrank down to the size of a man again. At that exact moment, the blonde woman swung a long, thick Batiwood branch into him.

The creature tipped, limbs flailing and hundreds of voices screaming, into the gate. Even the Eye turned away as every monster inside the gate converged at once, swallowing the creature that was once Hayalet whole.

Alik could no longer see the writhing bodies or the Eye without her Dua. Her heart thudded in her chest. Cheers erupted around her. She took several steadying breaths before scanning the space between the trees again with her Dua to confirm if the gate was still there. The cheering faded to the background as heavy dread cloaked her.

"The gate remains," she said, though no one seemed to hear her. The gnashing teeth drowned out any hope Alik had that this gateway to demons closed with Hayalet's death.

The joyous crowd around her seemed oblivious to the Eye watching her now. Someone hugged her, Shauna beaming and laughing, jostling Alik back to the happiness of the auras around her. She shook her head to clear her Dua but could still feel the menacing pupil tracking her from the space between the trees. Through the celebrating crowd, she caught Tenida's eyes.

The haunting feeling must have read plainly on her face because Tenida shouted, "We must close the gate!"

The cheers ceased as the bedraggled girls looked questioningly at the empty space between the trees. The Magarans pushed through the crowd, grabbing Elaine's frail arm and pulling her to Alik. Tenida shoved Alik forward with a gust of Airwerk so that she was mere inches from the gap in trees where the gate loomed.

Shauna cried out behind them, but Tenida held Alik in place even as she struggled to back away. One of the Magarans shoved Elaine down to her knees to Alik's right. Another Magaran scout stood behind them, bow at the ready, and wings flared out. The Edicsi, barely able to sit up, was dragged to the other side of Elaine so that the three of them now kneeled shoulder to shoulder before the gate.

The Magaran leader ignored Agnian and Ty's protests and took Tenida's place at Alik's back. Alik hissed at the sharp kiss of the Magaran's blade at her neck as the leader said, "There is no time to explain. Do exactly as we say. Hold hands."

Hundreds of questions ran through Alik's mind, but she could still feel the Eye watching her. She focused her Dua to see limbs reaching for her from within the gate, inches from her face. Alik reared back despite the grip on her hair and the knife drawing blood at her throat. "Let us go!"

The Magaran growled, "Hold still, or I will push you through myself. Now, hold. Hands."

Shaking, Alik linked hands with the Edicisi and Elaine. Alik pulled Elaine a few inches away from the gate, whispering for them to lean away. The Edicsi slumped against Elaine, eyelids drooping. Tenida screamed a curse as she kicked him, and he came to enough to sit up. Tenida frantically scanned the space between the trees before turning to Alik.

Alik focused her Dua on the gate and explained, "They're pushing. The film separating them from us is being pushed outward at their hands. The Eye is on you," Alik gestured towards Tenida without breaking her focus.

Blonde hair appeared in the corner of her eye, and Alik tore her focus away to watch the woman from the woods shove Tenida aside and dodge the Magarans. She dropped to her knees, tears streaking her soot-dusted face. She shrugged out of a Magaran's grasp as she cried, "Reed! Where are you hurt?"

The woman ran trembling hands over the Edicisi's bloody

face. She tried to rip her shirt, but he released Alik and grabbed the woman's hand to stop her. He kissed her palm and whispered something too low for Alik to hear before pulling her fully to him for a kiss. It was brief, passionate, and Alik felt a pang of jealousy and embarrassment at the intimacy of the moment.

Reed still held Elaine's hand in his left, though he now turned entirely to the crying woman. He cupped the side of her face, and Alik saw confusion and denial in her brows as the air rippled behind her.

Tenida and the Magarans screamed as the Edicisi shoved his lover through the line.

Alik searched all around them to see where the woman disappeared, confusion and astonishment trampling each other in her mind. Elaine wilted, her frail bones falling against Alik in exhaustion, and Alik understood.

He Rifted his lover somewhere.

Incredulity and rage replaced understanding.

He just Rifted his lover somewhere! That's what he did with his power? That's what he did with hers?

Alik knew before even the Magaran hissed, "You fool! You used her strength, and now we cannot close the gate!"

Tenida tugged the Magaran back and said, "Uci, we have to get out of here!"

To Alik, Tenida said, "Get your people out of the woods. I will come back for both of you."

Agnian was at Alik's side in an instant, scooping Elaine into his arms. Alik stuttered her questions to Tenida as she stood up. "Wait---wait, what? Who are you?"

Tenida ignored her and pulled the stone altar with an Airwerk into the air, her face straining at its weight. She shoved the monolith between them and the gate, tipping the massive altar on its side against the space between the trees.

The Magaran leader, Uci, spread her wings wide and grabbed Reed by the shoulders as her scout joined her. The Magarans shot into the air, dragging Reed with them through the trees before Alik could process an objection. Tenida put her arms around the neck of the remaining Magaran scout.

To Alik, she said, "Run! There is no time; they will break free! Get out of the woods!"

The winged Magaran cradled Tenida against his chest, and they too were gone before Alik could respond. Ty grabbed Alik's arm, pulling her away from the altar behind the fleeing girls.

"Move faster!" Mara shouted as she led the surviving girls back into the Batiwood and the path they took in from the valley.

Shauna waited for Alik where the altar once stood at the edge of the clearing, "Let's get--" she stopped speaking, mouth gaped open.

Alik's blood chilled as her best friend's eyes left hers for something over her shoulder. Thumps, like pulpy fruit hitting stone, came from behind the wedged altar.

Time slowed and spun, and Alik barely registered running with Ty and Shauna to escape the woods. She did not dare to turn around as they raced from the inhumane screams and heavy footsteps of writhing bodies running after them.

Too close. Too close!

Bone white Yurutecs appeared alongside her group and tried to cut them off the path leading out of the woods, their guttural calls screaming out all around them. Mara shouted orders from somewhere up ahead and shot Airwerks against the Yurutecs herding their fleeing group. Tears streamed from Alik as she willed her body to run faster, chest burning, and she prayed to each Goddess to get them out of the woods. The valley clearing was a pinprick in the distance, but the screams a hot breath on her neck.

The chanting filled her mind again, though discernable now. *We are coming. We are coming.* Elaine covered her ears in Agnian's arms ahead of Alik, as if she too could hear their mantra.

Their ragtag group broke through the edge of the Batiwood like birds thrust in the air. Warm pink smudged the bottom of the inky black sky as the sun rose. Yet, the relief washing over Alik came from the wave of armed Hordesmen and Duawielders barreling towards them across the valley, Queen Firtina at the lead.

Alik fell to her knees with the others. Wind battered her, and hundreds of Aygir hoofbeats drowned out all sounds as the Horde ran past to face what followed from the woods. Firtina's voice rang out above the rumbling, a clear, brutal war cry crushing past the thundering in her head. Alik's ears popped at the boom of power Firtina Iktidar thrust at the Batiwood.

She turned, fearing what would emerge. Sunlight glittered off her mother's gold and jade armor as her arms thrust in the air, aimed at the Batiwood. Firtina's arms shook with her Groundwerk as she hefted a wall of soil the size of ten Tiers stacked on top of each other and twenty Tiers wide. She dropped the massive wall between herself and the demons chasing them, and Alik waited for the limbs and teeth to crest the top. But the wall stood firm, the demons trapped behind it.

Firtina gritted her teeth, arms splayed open and still shaking. A crack etched across the ground. The land split apart, and Alik felt the shake in the ground reverberate up into her spine as the Horde backed away from the growing divide. Queen Firtina rose in the air, bellowing her rage, as she split the land apart into two. A deep ravine now separated Efendi from the wall holding back the demons of the Batiwood.

"To the Perimeter!" Firtina commanded as she dropped to the ground, her voice carrying across an Airwerk to all those that followed her. She heaved herself up onto her massive black Aygir and rode hard for Efendi's gates, bypassing Alik without a glance.

The Horde scooped up Alik and the others, and they ran the beasts without pause the entire way home. Alik did not dare look behind her until the Tiers of Efendi came into view. As she entered the gates of her kingdom, a thousand Duawielders stood at the ready along the edges of the Tiers, waiting for their Queen's commands.

REED

Reed flitted in and out of consciousness but came to at the smell of the salt-tinged air. Uci and another Magaran held each of his arms as they flew over a glittering sea streaked red with the rising sun. The Magarans dropped him and the woman, Tenida, with a thud onto a ship's deck far at sea. She spoke rapidly to the Magarans before they flew off in the direction of the mountains.

Tenida stalked away to the captain's quarters without a glance at Reed, who now sprawled out on his back on weathered wood planks warmed from the sun. *I have never been farther from Maddy than I am right now.*

Bone-tired, confused, and alone, he thought back to the shock on Monti's face when he pushed her through the Rift to his old yellow house in Texas. *There will be hell to pay for that call, but if I'm the Edicisi everyone claims to need, I need anyone I care about as far away from me and this curse as possible.*

The ship's crew shuffled around him, and he finally rolled to a stand, wincing at the aches and cuts ripping across his body. He walked to the captain's quarters to find Tenida standing in leather pants with daggers strapped in neat rows across her chest.

She looked at him with disgust as he asked, "Where are we going?"

"To a place where you can learn how to use your gift. To a place where we can prepare our next move in battle since you wasted our chance to end this war."

"And where would that be?"

She tossed a knife to a map pinned on the table between them. "To the sand palaces of Bakilar."

ALIK

Alik never once used her Dua to scan her mother. It felt too intimate, too invasive, and she was afraid of what she'd see most of the time. But she did the night they returned to Efendi.

Firtina sat in her study's chair, face unmoving, as Alik, Ty, Damari, Mara, and even Shauna gave their accounts of what led to the demons in the Batiwood. Wary still of the terrifying woman across from her, Alik did not mention The Reader. Yet she felt that Firtina heard the half-truths in her story.

Elaine leaned against Damari's side, barely able to keep her eyes open. Occasionally, Firtina watched Alik while the others spoke, and Alik's belly filled with sick dread each time they locked eyes.

Taavi remained silent in the corner of her study for the hour it took to explain what happened, eyes volleying between Alik and the Queen as the story progressed. Her friends described in vivid detail the horror Hayalet became, his insistence that he was Firtina's soulmate, and how he disappeared. They backtracked and told her of Hvard's involvement, though no one knew where he went in the chaos and how his men kidnapped the girls with cloaks under Hayalet's orders. They told her of the Magarans, Tenida's involvement, and how the Magarans and Tenida took the Edicisi with them. Alik still had a hard time reconciling the young, terrified man with the Edicisi's reputation as the most powerful Duawielder.

Firtina would eat him alive, Alik thought.

The Queen paced behind her polished desk. "Did the Magarans or Tenida mention a third person required to close the gate? They told you they needed the Edicisi and the Rifter, but was there anyone else they named?"

Alik stiffened, and Shauna straightened in the corner of her eye. Mara spoke the lie before anyone, "No, my Pillar. None that we heard."

Firtina clenched her teeth, her angular jawline pulsing as she said, "Everyone but you three out."

Shauna, Ty, and Mara stood to leave when she continued, "Leave the Rifter with the guardswoman and tell her to take her in my quarters. I have questions for her."

Alik's stomach dropped at the implication, but before she could object, Damari asked the question everyone soon will be discussing outside these walls.

"Who was Hayalet? What are those demons?"

Firtina watched him with unblinking eyes, allowing Alik to scan her without notice. Swirls of blue despair and icy silver rage pulsed even as her mother lied, "I have no idea."

Chills doused Alik at the lie, and she did not meet her mother's eyes as she asked, "What do we do now, my Pillar?"

"We?" Firtina asked, one perfect eyebrow cocked up.

Alik felt lightheaded. She longed for the comforts of her home after the nightmare in the Batiwood. To feel safe inside the Tier walls and to deal with the aftermath with Shauna. *Is she still banning me? I expected to be punished. To be watched, perhaps. Not this.*

Taavi walked behind Alik, placing a hand on her shoulder. "Surely you do not mean to exile Alik still? She tracked the Rifter you required. She led us all to the—the thing that stole our Daughters."

"And for that, I am not forcing your hand in marriage or shipping off your bastard brother to Bakilar. You're welcome."

Taavi stopped mid-word at Firtina's stare. She continued as if Alik was not in the room in between them. "She did not fight back. *I* saved her. *I* saved all of you. My mother would have killed me had I run from those demons as she did. No. I have no need for a useless Duawielder as my heir. And I have even less for one that is both insolent and disobedient. Alik, pack your things for Dvari. Perhaps the prince there will find some use for you even without my mother's name."

***

"Alik, wait," Taavi said as the doors to her mother's study shut behind them.

She did not want to face her brothers' concern just yet. "Taavi, Damari, you'll need to smuggle Elaine out. Send word to me in Dvari as soon as you safely can. And do not believe anything she says. Firtina knew Hayalet, and I know she helped him. I just can't prove why or how just yet."

"I'll work on it," Damari promised.

"No," Alik said. "She will watch you even more than before. Just get Elaine out. And I want you and Taavi out of Efendi at the first hint that Firtina and the Dua Ordu cannot kill the demons. I don't care what your responsibilities are; your first is to stay alive."

They hugged her, and she lingered in their familiar arms until she noticed Agnian waiting in the hallway behind them. *I can't wait any longer and be escorted out by my mother's guards, on my mother's ship, like a prisoner.*

She turned to him, "Does your offer still stand, Agnian?" Alik forced herself to look him in the eye, willing out any shame that blackened the edges of her mind. "To come with you to Dvari?"

He opened his mouth, shut it, and tried again. "I---"

Alik stamped the hint of tears down to nothing. She moved around him, heading to her quarters to pack. "Nevermind, I'll find passage elsewhere."

"No, Alik," Agnian said, tugging on her hand to stop. "Of course you will come with me, but we must sail immediately."

"That's not a problem," Alik said, relieved.

"There's something you have to know, though," he continued, glancing between her brothers on either side of Alik.

A door opened behind him, interrupting whatever he tried to say. Shauna strode out, carrying a stuffed bag across her back.

"What are you doing?" Alik asked.

"Coming with you. Obviously."

Alik covered her mouth, preparing for an ugly cry. The fear of moving to Dvari as a disgraced exile felt a little less heavy as she took in her friend's bags and confident face. *We'll figure this out together.*

Alike asked, "How did you know I was exiled?"

"Mara told me. And knowing what a bitch your mother is, I assumed the decree still stood."

"Besides," Shauna smiled, taking Alik's hand. "I think an island a couple of weeks away by sea sounds like the perfect distance from the Batiwood right about now, don't you think?"

Alik squeezed her hand, smiling for the first time since she found Shauna. "I don't know. Agnian, you aren't hiding any monsters in Dvari, are you?"

His weak smile faltered her own.

ELAINE

Elaine shuffled into the Queen's private quarters after food and a bath under the watchful eyes of the guardswoman. Queen Firtina was regal and terrifying, sauntering hips and cruel lips, but she smiled at Elaine as she led her to a small room splintered off from her own.

"This is where you will stay from now on. There will be others that will begin to look for you, but you are always safe with me."

Safe. Elaine shuddered at thoughts of the monstrosity she fought in the woods, of the gleam in the Queen's eyes, and at Kara's retreating form in the Silos. She didn't trust Mara's whisper that she'd get her out when Mara handed her over to the Queen's guardswoman. *Like a mutt passed on to be someone else's problem. Nothing about this world is safe, and no one is going to help me other than me.*

The Queen flicked open the door with an Airwerk as she said, "I underestimated your role, but I believe you are bound for a higher purpose. Rest. When your powers return, we'll begin your training."

The tick of a lock clicking into place echoed around the small room at the Queen's exit.

Elaine thought back to Kara walking away from her in the

Silos, her pleas hitting deaf ears. She imagined a family waiting for her across the sea in a place called Bakilar. She closed her eyes, determined to find her way to people that would love her.

Elaine was sure of few things in her life, but she knew what it felt like to be prey. To be weak. And she was tired of it.

As she closed her eyes, she told herself, *even the smallest creatures can become predators.*

MONTI

The beep was faint yet persistent. The familiar pulse towed Monti up from her subconscious. She glimpsed a white room lined with plastic wrap, the breathing tubes clunky in her nostrils. Two men in dark suits waited to her right, one stabbing keys on a laptop that straddled his legs and the other watching her.

The latter stood at her flickering eyes and gave her a millisecond to register where she was. "Agent Banks, glad to see you awake."

Monti pushed back the feel of Reed's desperate lips against hers, his plea, focusing instead on the task at hand.

She asked, "How long was I over there this time?"

ACKNOWLEDGEMENTS

To my readers, thank you so much for picking up this book. I would be eternally grateful if you would write an Amazon or Goodreads review to help me spread the word about this world and its characters. I can't wait to finish this trilogy, so for chapter sneak peaks, please check out my website and subscribe to the newsletter. **www.ccyorkbooks.com**

I've never been punched in the face, but I imagine that it might be more pleasurable than self-publishing your first book. Writing is the easy part. The rest takes a village, and my village was a mix of staunch ready-to-fight-for you friends, relatives, and kind-hearted strangers that made this possible.

To my first reader/editor/copywriter/critique partner, AKA the Alpha Reader, Amy Carden…thank you so much for diving headfirst into this story with me. Your feedback, suggestions, and line edits helped make this into a much stronger story from the get-go, but it was your enthusiasm that made me confident enough to move this to the next step.

To my Beta readers Lindsey Epperly, Katie Milliner, Katie Reid, Ashley Perry, Jamie Harris, Katie Rice, Micah Schutte, thank you so much for your feedback, questions, suggestions, and support. I was blind going into the beta round, floored by the responsiveness, and incredibly grateful for the time you gave these characters. Agnian thanks you as well for keeping him a much more integral part of the book.

To my Reedsy dream team, Arley Concaildi, Lena Yang, and Lorna Reid, thank you for taking painfully naïve questions, for helping me make this book professional and whipass, and for your advice on the Indie publishing side of this business.

To H.K Jacobs, thank you for the inspiration and for forging the path forward for us both. If anyone could be a pediatric emergency physician during a pandemic, a mother to two under 7, and get a binge-worthy romance read written and published in under 6 months, it was you. Thank you for the advice, the support, and for the distractingly fabulous read. Can't wait for more Alex Wilde!

To my parents, Lynn Stotz and Dan Stotz, thank you so much for all your support, for the last-minute babysitting so I could sneak off to anywhere without toddlers, and for your unwavering love.

Emmy, the very first time I felt like an author was maybe midway through my second draft of this book. You apparently announced to your Pre-K class that I was an author, and from then on I realized I could never move backwards in this journey. Batey, you kept me on an early 5am clock to get this written, and I'm appreciative for the forced time restraints because it kept me focused. You two are the most important people in our cadre of 4, and I am so proud to be a part of your lives. I love you both.

Danny, you were the only one who knew I was kicking this story around for years. I would have bagged this a long time ago had you not kept asking how it was going. I wouldn't have been able to dedicate the time to write this had it not been for your unwavering support. I wouldn't have enjoyed the end of the day had I not heard you coming in the door. I love you. You make this life worth more than a hundred lives.

***

To the writers knee deep in writing, publishing, or still simply imagining your story…do it.

This journey is different for everyone, but it's certainly one that requires a healthy dose of advice from strangers that have been where you are now. I wrote this book in a bit of a vacuum, assuming as soon as I finished the last "last" draft, I would be ready to give it to a top 5 publishing house and await the applause. It was a bit of a wake-up call to say the least, but thank God for the internet.

I highly recommend listening to the 88 Cups of Tea Podcast, particularly the interview with Molly O'Neill if you are on the early steps of querying to an agent. I am extremely grateful for having stumbled into the Atlanta Writer's Convention, and highly recommend participating. Kyra Nelson (aka Captain Query Hook) and the conference director, George Weinstein, are immensely helpful.

If you decide to self-publish, check out The Self-Publishing Show podcast and Six Figure Authors, and know that you are in good company.

If you are still in the middle of writing or early on in the story, check out The Writer's Toolbelt and the folks at StoryGrid, as well as Neil Gaiman's Masterclass series. And get on Twitter. Even as I write this in 2021 it feels a bit antiquated for social media, but the #writingcommunity is vibrant, supportive, and incredibly helpful. Drop me a line @ccyork_writes on Twitter or @ccyork.writes on Instagram and let me know what you're working on. The first like is much more meaningful than the 10,000th.

To Sarah J. Maas, thank you for writing stories that I always want to come back to, even after I have read them several times over. To Victoria Aveyard, thank you for being funny and open on your social media, and for making the author-life a bit more relatable. And finally, thank you Leigh Bardugo for showing us all what a badass looks like in this business.

WANT MORE

For a free novella that introduces one of the next characters in the second book of The Rifted Series, please sign up for my newsletter at **www.ccyorkbooks.com**

In the meantime, please enjoy this sneak peek of Stories from Sakalid!

*****

Kinsi Korsan held the cards loose in his right hand while his other palmed the dagger hidden under the rickety table. The two barrel-chested men looming to his right watched in silence as their captain idly ran her fingers over the edge of her leather corset in the seat directly across from him.

She rapped a coffin-shaped nail on the table for the dicethrower to toss the seven-sided dice once more. The gaunt man with sweat-slicked back hair rattled the die between them as she spoke

"I've always been the curious sort, working out details of how people came to be where they are--" she shifted so that the dried coral braided in her black hair pooled over the swell of her breasts.

Kinsi snorted. The likelihood of this Perisien pirate being curious beyond more than coin and favors was as slim as his chances of winning this hand of Bones. But he learned that letting others talk often gave him what he needed more than any of his own words could.

She continued, "--and who they are."

And there it is. Kinsi leaned back in his chair, his black tunic pulling across his chest as he folded his arms. The two bodyguards with her stiffened at the movement, but their captain never lifted her chalk-rimmed eyes from the cards in front of her.

Kinsi rapped for another toss of the die, waiting to see how the next few moments would play out.

When she spoke again, her voice toyed over her words. "Tell me stranger, how is it that a Prince of Dvari came to wallow down here in a dice pit?"

"I haven't been a Prince of Dvari for fifteen years now. And I like the ale."

The bodyguards chuckled. No one liked the ale in the Bones.

The dark wood floorboards creaked as the last remaining patron left through the curtained doorway leading to the bowels of Dvari. The bartender wiped down tables in the corner, pretending she was not listening to each word exchanged.

"Of course. But when the Efendian Queen beheaded your grandfather--"

"Watch it."

She tsked. Her accent, picked up among thieves from all over Sakalid, paused over every few words while the rest rushed in. "I'm merely stating facts, not trying to drudge up bad memories."

"Facts is it?" Kinsi leaned forward over the table, jaw tense as the captain continued.

"Facts. Like take Tika here," She said, nodding to the guard closest to Kinsi. "I found him dangling over the edge of a ship, pleading with his last crew to pull him back in. Fact is, you can't swim can you, Tika?"

The bodyguard with a sun-bleached tattoo over the right side of his face shook his head, "Nope."

"See, how is it a man that lives his life at sea can't swim? That's a story I wanted to hear. So, I fished him out. And the fact is, he doesn't like to get wet."

"Can't stand it," Tika affirmed.

She let her eyes rove over Kinsi, pausing once at his full lips. "So I'd like to know how someone as pretty as you tries his hands at a game he cannot win when there are other, more lucrative, and dare I say *more enjoyable*, ways to make some coin as a former Prince. Surely the Efendian vassal keeps you in nice things?"

The weight in Kinsi's pocket grew heavy, a physical reminder of how desperate he'd become.

"Do you intend to stall more or are you ready to make our bets?"

"Why the hurry? You've sailed this world a time or two. Surely you know a woman should be warmed up first before diving in."

The dicethrower's eyes volleyed between the pair before lingering on the striking woman smirking at Kinsi.

I'll have to kill him before this night is over, Kinsi thought. Part of him acknowledged how fucked up his life had become that he would mull over that fact without pause.

And perhaps, he thought, *this necklace could stay in my pocket instead of on the rat bones scattered on the table.*

Bartering his body for the things he needed most happened more than he'd care to admit, and if the whispers were correct, the item in this pirate's ship was worth every scrap of self-respect he still clutched.

Kinsi smiled, knowing the dimple his friends ridiculed him about would show. "Very well. What would you like to learn about me?"

All mirth fled from her eyes. "A good number of things, but we can start with why you're slumming down here and not in the court of that fat bitch. Tell me, does she still wear your mother's jewels?

It took a moment for the dicethrower to drop his stupid smile.

Whispers could be more lucrative than coin in Dvari, and *that bitch* paid well for the tongues of those damning whisperers.

Kinsi glanced at the man likely calculating this conversation's worth. "It's impolite to speak ill of a country's leader when you are standing on their sand."

She snorted, "We're a long way from sand, aren't we?"

The actual scrap of land Dvari claimed rested beneath the halls Kinsi once ran as a child. The rest of his country spilled several times over into the sea, built on wooden planks his grandfather pilfered from their once abundant fleet of ships. The planks stretched across their archipelago, making way for more Dvarians and lost souls stuck crossing the Turkaz Sea. That bandage now bound an overrun and starving population to this miserable scrap of land, and his grandfather's embarrassing err of judgment marred how Kinsi remembered his once-proud king.

He fisted his hand at his side. Even his bones willed him to take action. *I'll settle that debt soon.*

Kinsi said nothing as the bodyguards peeled away from their captain and approached the bar. The captain pulled a tiny tin from somewhere in her leathers and applied its purple salve to her lips with a finger littered with tattoos and rings.

She tossed a coin to the gawking man still sitting between them. "I think we can toss our own die now." She crooned over her shoulder as he slunk away, "But don't go far, yeah? I like an audience."

The captain turned back to Kinsi. The sultriness she flaunted for the last hour dissipated and a weariness settled over her statuesque frame like a heavy cloak in its wake.

"This corset makes my tits ache, and I could use a good night's sleep with someone that doesn't want to slit my throat so let's cut to it, yeah?"

He blew out a relieved breath. "Please."

"Oh, but I do like it when you say please. Perhaps we can do that again?"

"I thought you were done playing games?"

Her smile returned as she barked a deep, genuine laugh. "Hard habit to break I suppose. And you truly are pretty. Particularly when you look like you want to strangle something."

"Have we met before?"

"No, but that means little in a country like Dvari where whispers travel faster than the tides, yeah?"

Kinsi gestured to the dank walls and the broken glass around them. "And what whispers brought you to this beauty?"

"That a former prince is planning an uprising against the most powerful ruler this world has seen in centuries."

Kinsi barked his laugh now. "You make it sound as if I'm preparing for battle. I'm merely keeping my country afloat."

Lies.

The captain leaned back in her chair, arms folded across her chest, but didn't push. "I believe I have something that could be of use to you."

Kinsi fingered a coin along the edge of the table, spinning it on its side while he mulled over how the rest of the conversation could go. *Nothing is that easy. Particularly when you have nothing to give,* he thought. "I have no idea what you're talking about."

The captain pursed her lips and rapped her knuckles on the table in two quick successions. The first bodyguard blocked the curtained doorway just as the other dragged a knife across the bartender's throat.

Kinsi grabbed the dagger from beneath the table, but not before the captain spun away from him. She tossed her blade across the room and into the chest of the dicethrower cowering in the corner. The captain sat back down, picking up her discarded cards to fan herself without another spare glance to the corpses in the room.

Gesturing with her fan of garish cards, she said, "Sit, Prince. There are whispers across the tides about a change coming, and I prefer to be far out at sea when that happens."

STORIES FROM SAKALID

THE RIFTED SERIES
NOVELLA, VOL I

C.C. YORK

Made in the USA
Las Vegas, NV
21 June 2021

25171366R00184